THEIR LU

can only be satisfied ... unwary prey into their power, the power of death over life. With seductive spells that promise ecstasy however brief or immortality to those chosen few allowed to join their dark and deadly ranks, they lure their victims to an untimely doom. Now, at last, their secrets are revealed as eighteen intrepid tale-tellers brave the perils of the night to share such blood-draining stories as:

"A Vision of Darkness"—Confronted with an opportunity to learn the truth about life after death, will the great Socrates choose knowledge or darkness?

"Scent of Blood"—Can Hadrian and his legionnaires defeat an enemy who strikes in darkness, vanishes without a trace, and cannot be slain with the standard weapons of war ... ?

"The Ghost of St. Mark's"—World War II had taken a deadly toll on the small English town, but fifty years later there was still one soul left to be accounted for. . . .

THE TIME
OF THE VAMPIRES

HORROR ANTHOLOGIES
published by BP Books, Inc.:

The Time of The
VAMPIRES

EDITED BY

P.N. Elrod

&

Martin H. Greenberg

BP BOOKS, INC.
new york

www.ibooks.net

A Publication of BP Books, Inc.

Copyright © 1996 by P.N. Elrod
and Martin H. Greenberg

Complete acknowledgments can be found on the next page.

Reprinted by permission of DAW Books

Distributed by Simon & Schuster, Inc.
1230 Avenue of the Americas, New York, NY 10020

ibooks, inc.
24 West 25th Street
New York, NY 10010

The BP Books World Wide Web Site Address is:
http://www.ibooks.net

ISBN 0-7434-8733-8
First ibooks, inc. printing September 2004
10 9 8 7 6 5 4 3 2 1

Printed in the U.S.A.

ACKNOWLEDGMENTS

CONTENTS

INTRODUCTION

I'll keep this short since as a reader you're probably like me and usually skip this part of a book.

The stories are presented in chronological order from ancient times to the near present.

I'm very pleased with and proud of this collection and want to say thank you to the Tuesday Night Writer's group and the Fort Worth Writer's Group for their feedback and support; double ditto for my spouse Mark.

Okay, now you're on your own in all times and places dark and maybe not as dreadful as we've been led to believe.

P.N. "Pat" Elrod

A VISION OF DARKNESS
Lois Tilton

I think you know me, don't you?

It was during the Panathenaic Festival, almost thirty years ago, and I fell in behind a group of men leaving the poetry competition. One of them was saying that the singer was the best he'd heard in years, the best in the city, and another man argued no, that a rhapsode named Ion of Ephesus deserved the first prize. "When he sang the lament for dead Patroclos, he had me breaking out in tears."

Naturally, then, I took an interest in their conversation, so I was surprised when the stocky fellow with the snub nose and satyr's ears spoke up. "If it were up to me, we wouldn't have that kind of performance in public at all."

They were all indignant. "How can you say such a thing, Socrates? How could you have a sacred festival without music? Or recitations from the poets?"

"I certainly don't mean we should forbid all music, no. Just the mode that moves grown men to tears, as Melesias said. And maybe I'd forbid some passages from the poets— yes, even Homer! I don't think that citizens of a free city should be taught to lament at a hero's death, like women."

I drew closer to them, although they couldn't see me yet, as it was just dusk. So this was Socrates. I'd heard of him. They said he was a wise man.

He was saying, "We're at war, aren't we? When we send our hoplites and our fleet out to face the Spartans in battle, what do we want them to prefer: death or slavery?"

His companions were obviously used to supplying the answers to his questions. "Oh, death is better than slavery, of course," they all declared, the way brave men are supposed to say.

"Exactly. We know there are worse fates than death, but

11

how can we expect men to believe it when the tragedies show them great heroes lamenting over the dead? Or when they hear lines like: *His disembodied soul took flight to Hades' realm, bewailing his fate, cut off in his young manhood and strength.* Or when Achilles says: *Better if I were a slave laboring to till a rocky field, than to be king and ruler of the dead.* Or when the soul of Patroclos visits him, lamenting: *Grim death, my fate, my doom, has spread its hateful jaws to swallow me,* and then, *Like a fog the ghost vanished, drawn back beneath the earth, gibbering as it fled.*"

"But, Socrates, those passages are part of the highest glory of the poet's art!"

"Indeed they are, and a man would have to have a heart of stone not to be moved to tears when he hears those lines sung. But don't you see, the more powerful and effective they are, the more they can weaken the spirit of men we have to send out to face death in battle."

From their expressions, I could see that his friends weren't entirely convinced, although none of them offered to argue the point any further. And so the group broke up to return to their homes. But the poet's words had stirred me, no matter that I'd heard them so many times before, those particular lines, and it was almost as if I were being invoked by name. It was dark enough now, so I stepped out of the shadows and confronted this man who was supposed to be so wise: "Socrates? The sophist?"

He frowned a little and shook his head. "A sophist? One of those men who teaches politicians and demagogues the tricks of convincing a crowd that black is white and their enemies are guilty? Not I, stranger."

I apologized, "I'm sorry for intruding, but I've heard men speak of you here in Athens, and I couldn't help overhearing your conversation."

"And you're shocked, is that it? You think I'm impious to criticize the words of the poet?"

"Not exactly. But men say that you know the true nature of the gods, that you have visions. I want to ask if you are saying the poet was wrong when he wrote those lines? That death really isn't something all men should fear? Is this something you've seen? In a vision?"

Now his expression changed. "Sometimes ... a sign

comes to me, it's true. And I believe that if a man is good, nothing can really harm him—not in life or in death. Not if the soul is immortal and the gods are good."

I tried to choose my words carefully. "What if someone told you that the poet was right? That death is what all the songs say it is—a dark, gray place, with no joy in it, and men's souls are only shadows of what they were in life? Suppose someone had seen this—in a vision?"

He looked at me—for the first time, he looked hard at me, and what he saw must have made him hesitate. "What kind of vision?"

"Of dying, of death. Just like the poet described it. There's the pain, first, with the spear through your belly, and your enemy standing over you, mocking you because he's still alive and you're dying. Then your breath fails, and the darkness falls over you, and at that moment you know you'll never see the light of life again. It's all over, forever. Everything you were—a man, a warrior—is finished. Everything you ever loved—family, friends, everything that was good in your life—is gone. And in that moment you know you'd give anything, do anything just for one more day of life, but all you are is a shadow, and the only thing you can do is cry for what you've lost."

He was quick to say, "It sounds like you had a bad dream, not a true vision," but I could see that he was still looking at me with a frown, and there was a touch of doubt in his voice, even as he dismissed my words. I wondered how he might have reacted if I'd appeared to him earlier, just at dusk, but now that it was night I appeared as solid and real as any living man, though it had been my own death I was speaking of, my own death that the poet had described in such words as Socrates now wanted to forbid men to hear.

I pressed him. "What if it were true, though? What if a man you knew came to you as a ghost and told you all this? And you believed him. Would you still say there was no reason for a man to fear death?"

"If it were true, what you say, if a vision like that ever came to me, I think I'd still tell men not to fear dying. Because how can a city survive if it can't defend itself in war? How can it remain free if its men aren't taught that death is preferable to slavery?" He looked me straight in the eyes. "Did you ever serve in a war?"

"I did, yes."

"Then you should know how it is in battle, when you're hard-pressed by the enemy and you see the men on either side of you fall. How easy it would be to throw down your arms and drop down to your knees and give up the fight. And especially if at that moment the words of the poet come into your head, where Achilles says that he'd rather be a living slave than a dead hero—Achilles, who should be the first model of inspiration for our fighting men!"

(But he'd been a man, I thought sadly, remembering: a man with a man's fears, not a model hero. And he dreaded death as much as any other man, but he believed it was his fate to die, that he had no choice.)

"Then you'd rather have the poet's words forgotten?" I pressed Socrates.

"No, not forgotten. I think it would be better to make them part of a mystery that only the initiated would be allowed to hear—the men finished with their years of active combat. Not the young men and especially not the impressionable boys."

"So, to them, you'd lie. That seems strange, doesn't it, coming from a man with your reputation for seeking the truth." And because his words had so disturbed me, I did what I rarely do: I let my hand brush across his. Instantly, he snatched back his hand and stared at me with a horrified expression, for what he'd felt wasn't warm human flesh, it was cold, lifeless substance that only wore the form of a living man. But I give him credit. He was brave, he didn't run off into the night gibbering with terror.

"Well, now you know how I come to speak of death," I told him.

He turned his eyes away and refused to look at me again. And he said, "A wise man knows that his spirit only inhabits the body for a brief time, until its release at death. But if there were ever a man so impure in his life and thoughts, so uncaring of his immortal soul, that he could cling to the flesh even after all life had left it—he might become a creature that every man would dread becoming, rejected even by Hades. This is no good reason why any righteous man should fear dying."

Then he left me, careful not to brush against me as he passed.

But now I can tell him—tell you:

I never wished for this unnatural life in death, I never would have asked for other men to die as my funeral offering. It was Achilles' last gift to me, but he never knew what he was doing, nor what the consequence would be. He was in a rage of grief, not just at my death but knowing that his own would be next, and soon—the signs were everywhere. Why should other men be spared when he had to die?

But he honored me as only he could, with offerings and sacrifices at my funeral pyre. Those twelve Trojan captives—only boys—he cut their throats, one by one, invoking my name, spilling their blood on the ground where my body lay ready for the fire. All that blood! Human blood! The bodies of those boys burned with me, but their blood was for my taking!

Do you remember that passage where Odysseus invokes the shades of the dead, how they crowd around the blood of the sacrifice so he has to hold them off with his sword? How they weep and moan? I suppose you do, I suppose it's one of those parts you don't want men to hear. But even the poet can't completely describe what a cold, hollow thing it is to be a lifeless shade—the pain of the emptiness that can never be filled, not even by the gifts that the living make: the hot blood of a sacrifice spilled out on the ground. If you knew what it was like, you'd never have to wonder why the dead demand such offerings.

But the blood of those boys—human blood—it warmed me as the blood of a whole hekatomb of cattle hadn't been able to warm me, it filled the emptiness that I thought would never be filled again. While my body burned on the pyre, I lapped it up, nothing could have stopped me. There was Hektor's ghost hovering nearby, unburned, unburied, tormented by his thirst far more fiercely than I was. I didn't hate him any longer, if I ever had; his own death had paid for mine, but the blood was for me, not for him, and I drank it down, all that blood from twelve innocent boys, with not an instant of regret that it was spilled for my sake, for their lost lives.

And after it was gone there was more blood, every day, as much as I wanted and even more, men dying on the battlefield, men stabbing each other with spears and swords, spilling each other's blood—Trojans and Achaians both, it didn't matter to me. Never an end to it, especially when the city was sacked and blood flowed in the streets of Troy. And the more I drank, the more the hollow emptiness in me was filled, and I began to take on substance, the shape of the man I had been, until that night in Troy when for the first time as I walked past the gutted bodies lying in the streets, men saw me, just as if I were a living man.

I went to Neoptolemos, then, I stood in front of him in his tent and asked him: "Son of Achilles, sacker of cities, do you see me? Do you know me?"

And he did, although I'm not sure whether he thought I was a ghost or some god taking the form of a dead man to speak to him. But he knew my name, and then I told him, "If you truly honor your dead father, this is what you have to do: sacrifice one of the Trojan captives at his tomb. Cut his throat and let the blood spill onto the ground."

He believed me. Part of his share of the spoils of Troy was Polyxena, one of Priam's own daughters, and he cut her throat and spilled her blood on the ground where Achilles' bones were buried. To Neoptolemos his shade was invisible, his words were less than the blowing of the wind, but I saw my old companion appear from out of the earth, thin and faded and desperately eager for the blood. When he recognized me he moaned and wept dry tears for his lost life, but he had no substance, even after he drank, and in a while his form dissipated again.

I'm not sure why he never became as I am now. It may be that it had been too long since his death and he'd already passed too far into Hades' realm. If Hades exists. If he has a realm.

But he's still there, Achilles is. His shade is still bound to his tomb, faded by now almost to nothingness, so faint that even I can barely make out his form or hear his voice.

He doesn't remember me any more, though, even when I bring him a sacrifice and let the blood spill onto the ground. I still do this from time to time, though I have to travel back to Troy, back to a land where even strangers know who he was and offer sacrifice to his memory. I think maybe that one day he'll even forget his own name, and then he'll be gone forever, not a trace of him left. Or maybe not, as long as men still remember who he was.

I always will.

As for my own tomb, it was lost hundreds of years ago, and the only time my name is invoked is in the poet's songs. Can you wonder that I don't want them forgotten?

But I can seek out my own blood now, I don't have to wait in the grave for living men to come with offerings and invoke my name. Achilles' gift, though I wasn't able to return it to him. The Achaians sailed away from Troy and left only the bloodless dead behind—a city of dry bones. I went with them, went to find new wars where blood was being spilled. There are always wars.

In my day, men killed for plunder and called it glory. Now you kill for plunder, but you call it politics and expediency. It's still essentially the same, isn't it? It's still men with spears and swords, spilling out each other's lives. I know there's never a shortage of blood, and that's always what matters to me.

I remember that same summer after the festival, you Athenians executed a thousand men—the Mytilenaian hostages. The blood ran in the gutters like a flood, as if a holocaust were being offered. Oh, I know, you say you don't perform human sacrifice in these days, you think it's a barbaric practice now, but what better way to sanctify your cause than with an offering of human lives?

Of course it made no difference to me. Whether those men were innocent or not, their blood was just as red, just as warm. But I do wonder—how did you vote? To kill them or spare them? Or did it make no difference to you whether they lived or died? It's better to die than be a slave, or so you say. Was it for their own good, then, that they had to die?

But they weren't so wise, not like Socrates, to know that death was nothing to fear. Oh, yes, they did fear it. I could hear the cries from their souls when the executioner's sword took off their heads, as the poet says: bewailing their lost lives. And of course no one ever mourned them, no one sacrificed for them, not here in Athens, no one ever poured offerings at the pit where their bodies were thrown in and buried. It was pitiful to see their shades, dim and starving things.

But then, all men have to die, sooner or later, don't they? No one can escape it, just postpone it for a while. That's the kind of thing the philosophers say, isn't it? The wise men? But none of them knows what it's like to feel yourself torn away from the warmth of life, fading into the chill and the dark. None of them knows what he'd do if he could cling to life then, even something close to life. So I drank up the blood of those men with no misgivings, no regrets. They would have died regardless, would they not? And it was already spilled. I tell myself they would understand, that they would have done the same thing, if they were given the choice. Anything to escape the darkness of death.

Lately, I was gone from Athens for a while. Your war with the Spartans was finished, all your leaders finally executed, and it was time to move on. But then I heard that they were putting the famous Socrates on trial for his life. I had to know—now that you're facing death, do you still believe there's nothing to fear?

I was in time for the trial, I listened from the crowd, though it was daylight, so none of them knew I was standing among them. No one could have seen me if I'd cast a vote, even though I'm not a citizen and not entitled, under your laws. Should Socrates live or die? Do you want to know how I would have voted?

The charge was impiety, wasn't it? Tell me then, don't you believe in the gods, after all? Zeus and all that crowd on Olympos? And Hades? Do you believe in the ruler of the dead?

I admit: I've never seen the lord of the underworld, or his bride, or the judges of the dead. Or the river, the dog, the boatman—any of that. Only darkness. And the shade of every man I've spoken to, all of them say the same: all there is, is darkness, terrible darkness.

Is it because my soul was so impure, is that it? Did I

commit some heinous crime? Or was it just because I was a warrior in my life, not a philosopher, like you?

You can see me, I think, now that the sun is going down. You didn't wait to take the poison, so it won't be long. It's already working in you, isn't it? Your feet are already starting to go cold. Soon you won't be able to speak, and your heart will fail, and then ...

I'm going to be right here when it happens. When death tears your soul away and the darkness takes you. When you realize exactly what you've lost and that there's no way back. When you first start to weep and moan like the shades the poet describes.

What I couldn't do for Achilles, I'll do for you.

I bought a slave when I learned you were going to die tonight. He was a war captive originally, and I bought him from the mines, so he wouldn't have lasted much longer in any case. I've told him not to be afraid, that the wisest philosophers say death is nothing to fear and certainly better than slavery, but he doesn't believe me, he still keeps begging for his life.

When I cut his throat, when I sacrifice him at your grave, invoking your name, will you come for the blood? Will you lap it up and beg me for more? Will you choose what I have—this half-life—over the darkness of death? The warmth of human blood over the cold, hollow existence of a disembodied soul, fading to nothingness?

Yes, now you know me. The sun has set outside. Darkness is coming, and it's too late for any regrets.

Author's Note:

I was writing another story using the Iliad *and the Greek tragedies as background, and so naturally it was full of unburied bodies, ghosts, and funeral sacrifices—the usual neat stuff. So I thought of that passage from the* Odyssey, *where Odysseus uses blood to summon the shades of the dead, and I realized: Of course! They're all vampires!*

I was probably unfair to Socrates. I'm sure he would have voted against executing the Mytilenaian hostages. But he re-

ally did propose bowdlerizing Homer, or at least Plato has him doing it. And that would be unforgivable.

Lois Tilton has written four novels, including *Vampire Winter* and *Darkness on Ice,* both about vampires. This ought to be enough for any normal person, but she keep seeing vampires everywhere and also has stories about the undead in such publications as *Science Fiction Age, Amazing Stories, 2AM, Dragon, The Ultimate Witch,* and *100 Vicious Little Vampire Tales.*

SCENT OF BLOOD
by Susan Booth

According to the tales, the nearer you go to the edge of the world the colder it gets until there is nothing but snow and even the animals wear coats of ice, but here we were in the middle of Dacia and it was hot enough to fry an elephant's backside. Not that we had any elephants: Trajan was too canny for that. No, we had five legions, a host of *auxilia,* the Praetorian Guard, more siege engines than you've ever seen, and a supply train stretching all the way back to Rome.

This time, the Emperor was going to teach Decebalus a lesson that he wouldn't live long enough to forget, if the entire army didn't die of heatstroke first.

Even the night was hot, so much so that we had drawn lots to decide who should tend the fire. Our Primus Pilus had bribed the surveyors to pitch our tents as far away from the *Legio XIV Gemina* as we could get; there's no love lost between our legions, and even less between regulars and us *exploratores*. Every legion has its team of scouts and messengers, and I suppose mine are no worse than most, but that doesn't make them the most popular people in the army.

Rufus had come back from his scouting duties the long way, bearing half a sheep, hence the need for a private cooking fire. I was about to carve his spoils into bite-sized pieces when someone harumphed behind me.

"Ulp!" Menas said.

Turning, I was forced to concur. The tall man with the carefully curled hair and beard and a broad purple stripe on his immaculately draped toga was all too familiar.

Our Legate, Hadrian, the Emperor's nephew. Also rumored to be his heir. Lots of other rumors, too, about his private life, but a damn good soldier, for all that.

The cold gray-blue eyes saw altogether too much. "More got past the sentries than Rufus' loot," he said abruptly. "A native woman just made her way into the Emperor's tent, presumably in an attempt to kill him. Certainly she died before she could deny it.

"I am not going to ask how she got into the camp," the Legate went on. "I wouldn't like to estimate the number of women we have following the army. What the Emperor wants to know is how she got into his quarters. He has charged me with finding out. Which means, Decurio Alpinus, that you are charged with it, too."

"Yes, sir," I said. "But why us? Surely this is Praetorians' work."

"*They* were guarding the tent when she got inside and *they* were the ones who ran her through when the Emperor called for assistance, much to his annoyance: He had plans for questions. We don't even know what she wanted."

"One thing's for sure, she couldn't've been looking for the Emperor's favors." Everyone in the army knew that Trajan, like Hadrian himself, wasn't much interested in women. I didn't mention the unspoken undertow beneath the Legate's words: If the Praetorians had let the woman in, they had everything to gain by killing her before she talked. "Can we take a look at the body?"

"You can bring this squad of thugs to move it," Hadrian snapped. "Follow me."

The Emperor's tent wasn't that much different from any Legate's except that, instead of the usual legionary guard, there was a whole troop of sheepish-looking Praetorians lurking outside in the *via principalis* around their standards. Hadrian waved then aside. "In here. As you can see, she's one of the nativ–" He stopped dead, both verbally and physically. Crowding about him, we soon saw why. The place was empty of anything even vaguely dead, male or female.

"Where is it?" I asked, stupidly.

"It's gone," he said, in what I might have said was an equally stupid manner, if he hadn't been who he was. "It was here, lying on the carpet, with men standing guard. You can see where it was ..."

"Gone? Who in Hades would have taken it?" Menas' voice asked from behind me. "Rations aren't that low."

"That's a joke in very poor taste," Rufus sniggered.

"You get to be hard-boiled in this man's army—"

"Enough!" the Legate snapped, but he was smiling into his beard, poise fully recovered. He turned and stuck his head out of the tent. "You! Who authorized removal of the body?"

There was a chorus of protest that amounted to the traditional cry of, "It wasn't me, sir."

This did not please Hadrian, who was not inclined to believe them. As he was telling them so in no uncertain terms, the rest of us took a look around the tent.

Apparently, the body was supposed to have been here, in the part of the big tent that served as the Emperor's HQ, which explained the folding stools and tables and a rack containing rolls of maps and books, if not the woman's presence—or lack of it. A couple of wax writing tablets lay on one of the tables. I sneaked a quick look, but they contained nothing more than a list of forts that we already knew we were going to have to take, with notes on their defenses. Hades, I'd provided some of those myself.

"Decurio ..."

A curtain closed off the rear of the tent, where the Emperor had his sleeping quarters. Everyone was looking at it, but even these battle-hardened villains hadn't got the nerve to pull it aside.

With rank comes responsibility. Besides, I knew the Emperor wasn't there.

I peeked around it, and swore.

There wasn't just one body but half a dozen, and not a single one of them was female. All were in uniform—somewhat disheveled, but definitely army uniforms—and also definitely deceased. Judging by the wave-shapes in the carpets, they had been dragged here.

There was also something odd about the scene that I couldn't pin down now but which would no doubt surface in my mind at a suitably inappropriate moment.

"Rufus, get the Legate," I snapped and, moments later,

Hadrian appeared beside me, snarling a curse that would have done credit to the longest-serving Centurion in the Empire. He was still cursing as he marched outside to collar an unfortunate Praetorian and hustle him through into the inner sanctum. "Who?" he demanded.

The man swore even worse than he had, then reeled off a string of names. I suspected that these meant no more to Hadrian than they did to me.

Unexpectedly, one of them meant something to Rufus. "I know that one," he said suddenly. "The bastard stole that gold torc I—I mean, he was a member of the Praetorians, sir. An *Optio* called—"

"No more names, please," Hadrian said tiredly. "Even if he was a member of the Praetorian Guard, the question is, how did he and the rest of this garbage get in here?"

"They were the men you set to guard the woman's body, sir," the live Praetorian finally managed to explain.

Hadrian glared at him. "And who killed them, can you tell me that?"

Menas had been kneeling beside the bodies, whether to examine them or with a view to finding out if they had anything to loot I wasn't sure. He rose to his feet and stepped back abruptly. "Not to mention how they were killed."

It was then that I realized what had been bothering me: the blood, or the lack of it. I couldn't even smell it, only the leather of the tents and the wood smoke of the fires.

"Suffocated?" I suggested hopefully.

Menas shook his head, giving me a look of pure Greek scorn. "Look at them, Alpinus. Look at their faces and their lips. The only time I ever saw anything like that was when we found old Plotius Civilis in his bath after he'd lost that battle out on the Germanica borders."

"Well, I don't supposed *they* opened their veins and committed suicide," I protested.

"If they did, they did it conveniently into an amphora which someone carted away. Invisibly."

Rufus shivered. "Magicians," he said. "The Dacian priests, the smoke-walkers. You know they're magicians."

"I've never heard of someone who could magic blood out of anyone," Menas sniffed.

"Well, however they did it, someone got into this tent and killed the guard in order to retrieve the body," Hadrian said. "They can't be long gone. It should be easy enough to track them down."

No one got much sleep that night, at least not the *exploratores* and the cavalry *alae* who were dispatched to scour the surrounding countryside. With more than a thousand experienced soldiers searching for them, it was impossible for someone on foot—and there were no horses missing—to remain undiscovered.

Except that's exactly what happened.

"Magicians," Rufus said again. Often. Until I got tired of it and sent him out to obtain someone with more accurate information.

The prisoner Rufus and Pollio brought in for questioning was as nervous as anyone would be with that gruesome pair hanging over his shoulders. His Latin wouldn't've won him any accolades from a rhetoric master either, but he'd traded down at Viminacium and Salonea before the war and, together with what Dacian we'd picked up and some odd bits of Greek, we understood each other well enough.

Of course, he knew nothing about any attempt on Trajan's life and we weren't about to enlighten him; we told him we wanted to know why someone would kill a man and drain his blood, or we'd try to find out by practical experimentation. . . .

Even before we'd finished making the threat, our prisoner became exceptionally animated, his beard jumping up and down like a frog on a hearth as he apparently called on his gods in Dacian so thick it would have bogged us down until winter.

Pollio dug a knee into his kidneys. "Speak civilized Latin, excrement," he ordered, fingering the back of the man's neck in a thoughtful fashion.

That slowed him up a bit. "This . . . this . . . it happened? Truly?"

Pollio and Rufus looked at me for a lead. I looked at Hadrian, who had insisted on keeping an eye on us. He nodded.

I glowered and shoved my far from beautiful face near enough to bite. "Would we be wasting time talking to scum like you instead of killing them if it didn't?"

He pulled back as far as Pollio and Rufus would allow him. "Night," he announced portentously. "It happened in darkness."

It wasn't phrased as a question, but Menas answered him. "Yes."

The beard bobbed. "When the dead live again, they have great powers at night."

"Ghosts," Rufus said inevitably.

"No, no. The *dead*. Or rather, the *not*-dead. This is why we expose anyone who dies to the sunlight and the carrion birds; the powers of the not-dead fade with the sun and flesh cannot regenerate inside the birds' gizzards. Even the not-dead cannot be reborn from bones."

"I've never heard such nonsense!" Menas exclaimed.

"Perhaps it is not nonsense," the Legate said thoughtfully. "The great magicians of Persia also expose their dead in much the same way. It could be for the same reason."

"Maybe, but even if it appears these precautions work because there aren't any not-dead, how can we be sure that there ever were any of these not-dead in the first place?"

"A good point," Hadrian conceded, with a nod of approval. He glowered at the prisoner. "Can you answer it?"

"The not-dead exist! The kapnobatai tell us so!"

Menas rolled his eyes upward in disgust. "So we're back to the smoke-walkers."

In a way it made sense. The kapnobatai were not just magicians or priests, depending on your point of view: They were recruited from the local nobility, as the Druids had been, and Decebalus was not just the king, but chief among the smoke-walkers. "Well," I said, "assuming that our lady friend was sent by Decebalus, it might be worth further investigation in Sarmizegethusa."

Hadrian nodded. "We need to check its defenses, in any case. A job for you and your men, Alpinus."

So the passing of three nights saw me crouching on the mountainside amid the pines above Decebalus' capital, Sarmizegethusa. To the west loomed the stone walls of the biggest fort we'd yet seen in Dacia. It looked as if it was going to be a tough nut to crack. However, I was more concerned with the temple complex directly below.

Rufus had kept saying "Magicians" until Hadrian heard him, and our Legate was by no means as skeptical as some. So we had a *haruspices* with us. One Marcus Nornanus Crispus, a well-educated man who'd joined the army to escape his debts and then wangled his way into the nearest cushy post. He hadn't wanted to come with us and we hadn't wanted him, but Hadrian had said that if we encountered magic a priest would come closer to understanding what was going on than any of us, and there's no way you can argue with Hadrian and stay alive.

The nearer we got, the more uneasy we all became, and not just because the area around Sarmizegethusa had more forts than the Danuvius frontier, all crawling with soldiers. This was the heart of a land with an age-old reputation for magic, whose king ruled from a temple rather than a town.

A temple would be easier to get into, but we'd be much more likely to be noticed, so, in an attempt to blend in with our surroundings, we had donned native tunics, girdled and falling in long folds below our knees. We'd also abandoned our own swords and now carried *falas* and *sica,* long and short blades both curved wickedly. I didn't like them; it's damned difficult to use the point of a sword shaped like that, but straight swords would have made us conspicuous. So would our shaven chins, so carefully-glued horsehair now hung from them in imitation of Dacian beards.

I scratched myself thoughtfully—the native wildlife came with the tunics—as I peered down into the temple precinct. It was bigger than I'd expected. At its heart was a circular stone building, unlit and barely visible in the starlight, but there were also several large oblong temples with torchlight flickering between their columns.

The place reminded me too much of Gallia Lugdunensis, where I'd been stationed for a time, guarding various luminaries. Rufus would have had more ghosts than he could cope with there: I'd never visited a more haunted country and had been glad to be transferred to the Germanica frontier. I'd never been to Britannia, but from what I'd heard they had similar temples there, rings of stone and wood under the sky, places that even the Druids had held in greatest dread.

The Druids were gone now, though the stones still stood. Their Dacian equivalent waited for us below. We could smell smoke, and burning, and blood. Above us, the moon was full: Hecate's moon. Something fluttered against it—a bird perhaps, though they don't like the night. A bat, possibly.

"Quiet and inconspicuous now," I told my squad, more in hope than expectation, and eased my way down the slope. Behind me, I could hear Nornanus slipping on the stones; I only hoped Decebalus' guards were deaf.

The two guarding the entrance to the temple precinct certainly appeared to be. Assuming that they were not blind as well, and because we had no time to think of anything more original, we decided to use the old drunk trick.

So Rufus produced a flask of wine and he and Pollio reeled toward the gate, singing in what might have been Dacian, if you could have distinguished any words.

"Dacians don't drink wine, or anything stronger than water," Nornanus protested, in his usual self-important tones, though hushed in deference to our circumstances.

"Officially. Just watch and learn." I'd guessed the guards would show no suspicion at such immoral perfidy from their countrymen, and they didn't. They just moved in to clear the drunks away from the temple and to confiscate the flask, no doubt for their own use. While they were struggling with Pollio, Rufus suddenly sobered up and clamped one massive hand over the rearmost guard's mouth while the other slid a dagger into his heart. As the second guard started to turn at the small sound, Pollio looped a thin cord around his neck and pulled it tight. By the time the rest of us reached the entrance, the bodies had been interred in the darkness. Pollio and Menas took the guards' places at the entrance, while Nornanus, Rufus, and I walked in. Menas had a steadier head, but I'd decided that, as Rufus was so interested in the smoke-walkers, he might as well see them in their native haunts.

Ahead, we could see a fire flickering behind the colonnade of one of the temples. It seemed a good place to start.

*   *   *

Inside, we found ourselves amid a dimly lit forest of pillars. Like hunters, we dodged from column to column in air dense with aromatic smoke coming from the very center of the temple, where a fire burned in a huge, gilded brazier. Around it clustered a number of richly clad men, arguing ferociously in what was presumably Dacian. Another man robed in the finest imported silk sat on a golden chair. I drew a quick breath of surprise as I recognized him. Though I'd seen him only once before, I was sure that this was Decebalus himself.

There was only a single woman present. Darkly beautiful, pale and impassive, she was bound to a pillar by chains that shone red in the firelight. The men kept breaking off their conversation to cast quick, sideways looks full of scorn in her direction.

Rufus took cover behind one of the columns. I dragged Nornanus into the shelter of another, where I could keep him under control. The argument seemed to be reaching some sort of conclusion and someone might just decide to look around in time to see us moving.

Indeed, we had just gotten settled, though Nornanus seemed no more pleased to have me breathing in his ear than I was in having to inhale his cheap-scented oiliness, when a yellow-robed priest stepped forward and bowed to Decebalus, offering his curved dagger on the palms of his outstretched hands. It didn't look like a very effective weapon, being heavily carved and inlaid with slightly tarnished silver. The king seemed to hesitate, then nodded, making a small gesture toward the bound woman.

The priest straightened. Keeping his eyes lowered, he moved toward her. In a detached sort of way, I wondered why. For some reason, I no longer felt as if I were in any personal danger, but as confident and light-headed as if I'd had a cup or two of wine.

Why wouldn't any of them look directly at her? Was she some sort of royalty, a relative of Decebalus, or a priestess? Or was it simply forbidden to look at women in this place? Who could tell with these barbarians?

It was then I remembered why we had Nornanus along. "What are they doing?" I hissed in his ear, pressing him against the column because he showed a tendency to spread beyond it.

"How I am supposed to know?" he whispered back.

Through the smoke in the air and the mist in my head, I saw the yellow-robed priest reach the woman.

"You're the expert," I said. "So give us your expert opinion—" I stopped as, almost casually, Yellow-robe slashed the dagger across the woman's throat. She made no move, no sound, just sagged gently against the pillar. Another priest moved swiftly to catch her blood in a huge golden *krater* that shone with rubies. Even at that moment I could feel Rufus coveting it from the column next to mine. Maybe I should have brought Menas after all. . . .

"I think he just killed her," Nornanus said.

I kneed him in the small of the back.

"Sacrifice . . ." he added hurriedly. "Barbarians. The Emperor should know of it."

He was right at that. Human sacrifice provided a wonderful excuse to kill all the local priests. Not that we had any intention of leaving them alive after we'd killed Decebalus. Which I might yet have a chance to do here, tonight. There'd be a promotion, honors . . .

Soft drums behind us stopped my meandering thoughts.

A procession was approaching from the direction of the risen moon: vulture-masked priests surrounding an old man in chains. Presumably they had come from elsewhere in the temple complex, or Pollio and Menas had decided to let them through without challenge.

As the old man was led toward the brazier, I began to wonder if the chains were ceremonial rather than meant to restrain him, for he was ancient and white-bearded, his dough-colored skin hanging in folds almost as long as the beard flowing over his black-clad chest. He looked ordinary enough and cleaner than most Dacians, yet the priests drew away from him, dragging back their robes as if he had been wallowing with pigs.

The old man bowed to the king and spoke for a time, his voice so low that none of us could hear him. Yet something about that whisper made me shudder. I began to think less about the rewards for killing Decebalus and more about getting out of there with my skin intact.

Decebalus didn't look very happy either, as he sat fingering the silver medallion that lay on his chest, and I noticed he avoided the old man's eyes in the same way everyone had avoided the woman's. The king didn't look at him even when he knelt to swear what I supposed was some sort of oath of allegiance.

No one offered to help him up either, and it took him some time to rise. Once the maneuver had been accomplished, though, Yellow-robe offered him the *krater* containing the woman's blood. The old man grasped it in both hands and, without hesitation, raised it to his lips and drank.

Then the *krater* clanged on the flagstones. The old man collapsed as if he had been poisoned. Perhaps he had, for he writhed for a few moments, then lay still. I couldn't see if he was breathing.

Yellow-robe bent over him and removed the chains. Then, to my astonishment, the whole lot of them, including Decebalus, filed out to the continuing beat of the drums, leaving the old man lying beside the gilded brazier and the dead woman still bound to the pillar.

After what seemed like an age, I decided to leave cover to take a closer look. After all, what harm could a dead woman and an old man do to us? Yet, if it hadn't been for that half-drunken feeling, I doubt that I could have moved, let alone bullied Rufus and Nornanus into coming with me, for beneath the euphoria lay a fear greater than any I have ever felt facing hordes of suicidal barbarians during Domitian's Germanica campaigns.

On reaching the brazier, I located the most unburned log and extracted it, not without a singed finger or two, then used its light to take a closer look at the old man.

It was Nornanus who noticed it first. He grabbed my arm and yabbered with fright, pointing to the white hair spread over the stones ... and the new, dark stubble sprouting through it from the old man's scalp. It was growing even as we watched.

Shaking Nornanus's hand off my arm, I called on the gods to protect me, then reached down and jerked the old man's shoulder to turn him.

His skin was still pale, almost white, but it no longer covered the face of an old man. The rutted lines of great age were vanishing even as we watched, and his beard was as pied as his hair.

I stepped backward hurriedly. Behind me, something hissed. Expecting anything from snakes to the entire Dacian army, I spun round, my free hand reaching to my sword hilt.

The woman's eyes were open and she was looking straight at me. Nor could I see any mark on her slender neck. Her red, red mouth was open, though, in a snarl that showed the fangs of a wolf. Somehow, I knew that they had not been filed into that shape but were as natural to her as my own flat teeth were to me.

Yet I wanted her. Wanted, even, to feel those teeth in my throat. I forgot my sword, forgot my fear. Blind to my surroundings, I took a step toward her, awkward because of the agonizing pleasure of my need.

Rufus kicked me in the shins.

The pain did two things; it made me aware of what was happening, and it broke the death grip of her gaze. Instinct driving my hand, I thrust the firebrand at her face.

"Run!" Rufus yelled and I regret to say that we did just that, overtaking Nornanus before he left the temple, despite his head start.

Bats swirled about us like leaves blown by a storm. We knocked them away with our fists, not daring to let them slow us. Any moment now and the hunt would be up. I shouted to Pollio and Menas to join us. If we could make it out of the precinct, we could cut our way to our horses.

I could see Menas and Pollio now, only a few feet away. Both had their swords out in the double-handed Dacian grip as they ran to meet us.

"What's happening?" Menas asked. "Did you find—?" He broke off, shoving me behind him as a pack of dogs came howling out of the night at our heels, huge, shaggy, and red-eyed, and more than usually determined to attack.

We turned our backs against each other and Rufus, Nornanus, and I drew our swords. Maybe we weren't a Century, but we'd all trained in the ranks, even our priestly friend. We had no armor or shields to protect us, but the dogs' teeth were shorter than the spears and lances of human enemies.

"Steady, lads," I ordered, and knelt as the leading dog leaped, stabbing upward into its chest.

As I pushed it from my sword with a boot in its belly, I realized that it wasn't a dog at all.

Wolves?

Trained, maybe, I wondered, as Rufus battered at a huge black she-wolf with the gold *krater* I hadn't even noticed him appropriate. Nornanus was wailing as he tried to shake another off his arm. I beheaded it for him, and left him to work out how to pry the teeth loose.

Some of the wild animals trained for the Arena attack everything on sight but these wolves were more cautious. They knew all about weapons, too, drawing back out of reach of our swords, then sitting on their haunches, waiting either for us to attack or, more likely, for aid. For their masters.

I couldn't understand why they hadn't appeared. By rights, the place ought to be full of Dacian soldiers. Then it occurred to me that if I could see well enough to tell the difference between wolves and dogs, it must already be dawn and, indeed, the night was graying about us.

I breathed a prayer to Mars and another to Mithras. I don't hold with these newfangled eastern gods, but it couldn't hurt to call on soldiers' gods, of any kind.

The wolves still waited. There was no sound but our harsh breathing and their panting. Behind them, something moved in shadow, darker than the night. More wolves? Their missing masters? Something worse . . . My heart failed inside me.

Then the first shafts of sunlight glinted along the crescent edges of our swords, made daystars of the points, reflected constellations in the surrounding eyes. And the wolves retreated, turned tail and vanished into the smoke as if they had never been.

I redoubled those prayers, let me tell you. Nor did I wait around to see if they were effective. Picking up our wounded, we made a strategic withdrawal.

Rufus and Pollio spent the whole ride back squabbling over possession of the *krater*. I spent it trying to figure out how I was going to explain what had happened to Hadrian.

*   *   *

Surprisingly, he was philosophic about the retreat.

"We'll destroy the place soon enough," he said, when he had heard our story. He had shown no signs of disbelief, though I'm sure he suspected that much of what we had seen had been delusions caused by the smoke. To be honest, I was coming to that conclusion myself. "What awful magic these barbarians have discovered is no match for good Roman steel—and Gaulish cunning," he added, with a nod in my direction.

I started to protest that my family had been citizens for two hundred years, then thought better of it. Gaulish cunning was fine if it kept him sweet-natured.

As the moon waned, so did the horror of what we had seen—or had not seen. The army was proceeding slowly but inexorably toward Sarmizegethusa, leveling the forts and burning the villages as it went. The camp was full of loot, including prisoners held as a temporary amusement for the troops before being shipped off home by the slave traders following in our wake.

So it was odd that, while making my way back through the camp one late night, a particular group should catch my eye. It consisted of a number of youngish women and a few men. It was even odder that it should be one of the men who drew my attention.

A youth. A beauty, too, if you liked that sort of thing; slender, dark-haired, very light-skinned, with huge brown eyes.

Much to my mount's disgust, I made him pause in his rush to reach the horse-lines and his evening meal and asked the troops what they were doing. Their Centurion told me that Decebalus had just sent this lot to Trajan as a preliminary gift before opening peace talks. Though why, he added, he couldn't send them in daylight like any normal barbarian king he was damned if he could think. Probably to make trouble for poor Marius' Mules like him.

I knew that this time Trajan had no intention of talking peace. What's more, he wouldn't even get to see this beautiful lad if Hadrian caught sight of him first, which was more than likely as Trajan had saddled his nephew with the responsibility for all prisoners. Indeed, the Centurion confirmed that he wasn't going to risk troubling the Emperor before he'd spoken to Hadrian. I agreed that this was the best idea and wished him well rid of his prisoners, then dismissed the lot of them from my mind.

Well, I tried to dismiss them. For some reason, the youth's face haunted me. Which was puzzling as I certainly didn't want to sleep with him. (I like wenches, preferably with big tits.) Let Trajan or Hadrian have him.

So it certainly wasn't jealousy, and I'd spent too many years in the army to care much about the newly enslaved; they're generally lucky not to be dead. Nor did he remind me of any of my relatives and a good thing, too. I'd been trying to forget them for years. So maybe I'd seen the kid before. If so, I couldn't remember when, so why worry about it?

It was only after I had wrapped myself in my blanket and was drifting off to sleep that the two faces merged: the child, and the old man in the temple. The features were the same. His son . . . I hoped it was his son . . . grandson. Prayed.

Surely Hadrian had had the sense not to take the youth into his tent?

Surely the Praetorians had had the sense not to let the woman into Trajan's. Sense, it appeared, did not come into it.

Huh.

With a grunt of annoyance, I shrugged off the blanket and found my sandals. No one else moved.

I debated whether to wake some of the others and decided against it. They'd only argue. Besides, I'd rather make a fool of myself unobserved. Any other way is bad for discipline.

The legionary guards outside Hadrian's tent appeared to be asleep, but when I touched one on the shoulder, he fell limply to the ground. His face was as white as the half-moon above us.

Jupiter protect me! He had certainly not protected this man.

Nor would he protect me from Hadrian's wrath if I was

wrong. Being flogged to death was probably the mildest punishment I might expect.

I drew my dagger and moved on into the tent toward the light of the oil lamp.

Hadrian, I knew, liked to make it clear he was as good at roughing it as any legionary. So I was not surprised that there was no rich furniture: The Legate slept on the ground, as we did.

Which was where he lay, his eyes wide open, flushed and panting, the blanket lying over his hips not concealing his sexual arousal. Yet he was unmoving, staring straight into the eyes of the beautiful youth who knelt over him. The boy's lips were drawn back from teeth as fanged as the woman in the temple's had been as he bent toward the Legate's exposed throat.

I did the only thing I could. Yelling, "No!" I darted forward across the tent.

With a snake's hiss, the youth turned.

I thrust my dagger into his chest and stepped back.

He should have choked, fallen, bled to death on the floor of Hadrian's tent, and left me to explain my actions. What he did was to pull the knife from his chest and turn it toward me. There was no blood on the steel.

Not-dead.

It occurred to me that I hadn't a weapon and that no one else was conscious, perhaps no one else was alive.

Look at me.

I'd swear even now that the words were not spoken aloud.

His eyes were red coals, igniting sexual heat. Suddenly, I wanted this creature to take me as he had almost taken ...

Behind him, Hadrian groaned. For a moment, the hot gaze wavered. I tore my own away.

Hadrian had raised himself on one elbow. He was blinking, as if beginning to see. I had to get this ... thing ... away from him.

I kicked out at it, hardly knowing if I connected, whirled, and ran, out under the moon, which glinted gold on the eagle's outstretched wings and the thunderbolt beneath them.

Something—maybe it was that voice in my head—made me stop and turn. The youth was standing right behind me, smiling.

Look at me.

Not this time.

It was because I was trying to stare past the youth rather than into those burning eyes that I saw Hadrian stagger from the tent.

Look at me.

Instead I looked wildly to left and right for aid. Row after row of tents lay dark under the thin moon, like so many bodies waiting for burial.

You are mine.

If I did not act, it would be true. So, in my terror, I did something no one but the *signifier* should ever do; I snatched up the eagle standard from its place among its fellows and swung it at the youth.

It was desperation—the thing was never meant as a weapon—but he cried out as if it had burned him and fell to the ground. Reversing the standard, I drove the steel-tipped shaft like a javelin into his chest, so it stuck into the soft earth beneath him.

He writhed and screamed on the wooden pole, dark blood gushing from the wound. Even as we watched, he became insubstantial, his body turning to dust which was whirled away on the wind.

The *aquilia* standard stood erect in a patch of muddy ground.

Somewhere, a wolf was howling. Maybe it could also taste the blood in every breath it took. A good omen, in any event.

I stroked the bright gold of the eagle, caressing each scratch where the silver showed through the gilt.

"Honorable scars," Hadrian's voice said from behind me. "And well fought, Alpinus. You saved my life. I will not forget it. Now we must destroy those who created that ... thing."

We burned Sarmizegethusa. Our city of Ulpia Traiana stands on the ruins. Decebalus is dead by his own hand. Yet still I wonder, have we killed all the magicians, or do they keep their deadly knowledge in some secret place?

Our new Emperor wonders, too, or why else would he send spies to report every rumor of smoke-walkers still alive within the bounds of his newest province?

I pray to all those gods I don't believe in that there will be no word until long after we are both dead, for I fear that the not-dead will outlast even the Eternal City we serve. May the gods grant our luck to those who face them in that hopefully far off time. They'll need it.

Author's Note:

Susan Booth thinks that you are unlikely to be as interested in the lifestyle of a middle-aged British civil servant as in the fact that in 106 AD the Roman Emperor Trajan invaded Dacia (modern day Romania). In respect of the equipment, tactics, engineering, and logistics he used we have a wonderful record carved on the column he raised to commemorate his victory. Unfortunately, his written account of his travels into Transylvania, unlike that of Jonathan Harker, has not survived, so we remain unenlightened about the details of what and where and when things happened and whether or not he met any vampires. In the circumstances she has not hesitated to extract what suited her from matters subject to scholarly dispute, or to plug the gaps with imagination.

Trajan's and Hadrian's sexual preferences are well attested to in ancient texts. However, she has almost certainly libeled the kapnobatai, who probably did nothing worse than smoke pot!

Susan Booth was born in Yorkshire, England, in 1949, but is happy to be a Londoner by adoption. She has been reading and writing science fiction and fantasy since discovering "The Marmalade Cat Visits Venus" in the local library when she was six. Despite this early start, she was sidetracked into working for a living—at present for the British Civil Service—and has only recently started to write commercially.

THE GIFT
by *Teresa Patterson*

The Lady waited at twilight, still as a carven statue in the shadows of the mist-shrouded forest near Camlann. The light of the rising moon breached the shadows, setting her long pale gown aglow and gently illuminating the delicate planes of her face. Highlights, like fireflies, glimmered in her long dark hair, but her eyes were deep lightless pools as she studied the frenzied activity of the war camp on the hill just beyond the wood. The encroaching darkness proved no hardship for her keen vision, aided only a little by the torches and cook fires scattered throughout the camp.

One figure stood out from all the rest. She straightened slightly as she recognized the one she sought. Draped in a crimson mantle edged with elaborate golden knot-work, a tall, lean man strode briskly about the camp, pausing for a moment to stare out into the mists as if looking for something. She could see his smooth, dark, shoulder-length hair, only slightly streaked with silver, framing a strong well-chiseled face. His brow was adorned by a gleaming golden circlet worked in the form of a writhing dragon. He touched his mustache, now more silver than dark, as if in contemplation. She knew that mustache hid an old battle scar that marred the symmetry of his upper lip. The cloak, held on one shoulder by a single ornate dragon brooch, fluttered about him as he continued to work his way through the camp, his sure movements exuding a confident strength that was clear even at a distance.

The Lady watched him pause to give a word of encouragement here, a reassuring touch there, or sometimes just an approving look as he unconsciously worked his magic, weaving these men, Celts, Picts, and even the descendants of Romans, into a cohesive whole that would follow him into the Other World of Annwfn itself if he but led them.

She had seen his like only once before in all her years, in the land of her birth. *But this one may be greater,* she thought. *This one may rival the Dagda, warrior King of the Tuatha De' Danann.*

The camp's fires burned low as she waited, but she knew he would come. She knew he could feel her presence, as she could feel his. The years of separation had done nothing to dim the bond. It was only a matter of time. But time, so limitless for her, was precious to him.

She remembered her first sight of him, years past, only a moment ago for her. The Druid priest and seer Emrys had brought him to her, as he had brought many others, knowing that she liked the blood young and hot.

The Druid had his own power, different from hers, and quite mortal, but potent in its own way. He usually brought the young men to her by night. She would appear to them at the sacred grove or the holy lake. Sometimes they were sacrifices, given to her with great ceremony as others looked on, the price of the cycle of ongoing life. She drained these, then let the Druids take their heads to insure that they could not return to life. Their skulls were used as adornments and sacred relics.

More often, especially since the Romans had come, they were novices to be initiated into the mysteries, and she was their goddess. She gifted them with the ecstasy of forbidden desire and they gifted her with nourishment for body and heart. She drank of their strength, their youth, challenging their mettle, inspiring their courage, and leaving them with joy in their devotion and battle fury burning in their souls. They would return to their homes, exhausted, but full of the praises of the goddess. They would dream of her, fight for her, die with her name on their lips. Years before in the land of the Tuatha De' Danann they had named her *Morrigan,* the battle goddess. In those times she had haunted the battle fields at twilight, taking nourishment from the fallen. Draped all in black, she had often been called the Raven of Death.

But here in Albion, Druid priests such as Emrys had made such things unnecessary. So long as the Druids re-

mained, she would have sustenance from willing victims—
if she met their price. The Druids had no qualms about
bargaining with their gods. For Emrys that price had been
knowledge. He had hungered after the tidbits of ancient
lore long forgotten by mortal scholars, but burned into her
memory. She had given them to him, one tiny piece at
a time.

On that day, however, the Druid had asked a different
price—a gift, not for himself, but for the young man he
would bring. This one, Emrys said, understood the value
of the old ways of honor, and had been taught the rule of
law. He wanted a very specific gift for this boy, and spoke
an ancient name from a city lost long ago beneath the
water, the city where she had breathed her last. The gift
he named was the province of kings. Did he think to make
one of his novices into a king?

She had wondered why the old priest would seek a king
for a place that even Rome had discarded. The spirit of
this wild land could never be tamed by one man. Civilized
things like kingdoms and crowns were for other places,
other times. Still, she was intrigued and decided to comply
with his request.

Her changed nature, that which gave her life beyond
death, gave her the ability to travel beneath the stillness of
the water without need of breath or light. The tides pulled
at her, but they were nothing compared to that first terrified
awakening far under the thrashing waves.

She still remembered those moments—gaining her senses
to find herself somehow alive, trapped far beneath the
waves in the rubble of the dead city. She had desperately
clawed herself free of the masonry that imprisoned her,
frantic as instinct drove her to reach the surface for air she
no longer needed. She had surged above the water, only to
be driven back beneath its cool protection by the blistering
fury of a sun turned malevolent and deadly. Since that time
the lakes, rivers, and inlets had been a welcome shelter
despite the disorienting tug of the currents. Beneath their
murky darkness, she had found she could travel by day
even in the brightest glare without fear.

Locating the artifact, she carried it to the agreed meeting
place to watch and wait. Soon Emrys approached the rocky

outcropping and called for her, but she had eyes only for the raven-haired youth who stood with him. Young though he doubtless was, no more than sixteen summers, there was very little boyishness about him, not with that lean, hard body. His eyes were intensely bright, with the look of the hunting hawk in his gaze. He moved with the easy grace of a warrior born, yet stood with the stillness of one long accustomed to listening to the wind. He followed the Druid priest, deferring without subservience, as one even then accustomed to leadership.

Emrys reached out to take her burden, but she ignored the Druid. Rising slowly from the water, she advanced toward the young man, watching in satisfaction as his eyes widened in amazement at the sight she presented. She could feel her gown clinging to her lithe body, knowing that the water would make it all but transparent, feel the water cascading from off her in glittering sheets, the weight of her long hair as it swung to hang like a mantle about her shoulders. Even the slight pain of the cloud-dimmed sun was worth enduring for the small gasp of wonder that escaped from the young man's lips. It was a credit to his courage and self-control that he held his ground. Carefully she handed him the gift. She felt him shiver slightly as his warm hands brushed her fingers in the passing. He never took his gaze from her. He seemed to be trying to devour her with his eyes.

"It is named *Caledfwlch,* and has an ancient and honorable history. It came from a house of warrior kings. If you are worthy of it, it will serve you well. See that you do not dishonor it."

Only at her words did he lower his gaze to look at the gift, gleaming wetly in his grasp. He reverently ran his hand over its length.

"*Caledfwlch*" he whispered, then looked gravely into her eyes. "I will not fail your trust, Lady."

She smiled and nodded, then sank back into the cool balm of the lake.

The old Druid had been no fool. He had known she would recognize the boy's potential, had known she would hunger for him. With the Romans gone, chaos threatened all the land. Saxons invaded from the east, Picts pressed from the north, and the remaining Romans lived in uneasy balance with the native Combrogi. If Emrys' chosen warlord was to have a chance to survive, let alone unite anyone under a crown, he would have to have the help of the gods. The Druid priest knew well what she was, yet he also believed her to be a goddess. *Caledfwlch* was not the real gift he sought. The true gift was her protection.

That night she had come to the young warlord, touching his dreams like a caressing mist, intending only to taste of him while he slept and begin the binding. But he awakened, despite her care. He did not cry out to find an intruder in his home, or raise any alarm. He simply smiled and reached for her, welcoming her fearlessly into his embrace. She discovered he was more the man than his years suggested as he entwined his fist in her hair and pulled her down beside him on the sleeping-furs. His fierce passion matched her hunger and ignited an almost forgotten flame of desire within her. So many had come to her as helpless victims, worshipers, or supplicants, mere cattle to be fed upon. But this man embraced her as an equal, asking no quarter, and giving none.

When she left him sleeping in the first glow of dawn, his fiery blood burning within, it was she who was bound.

Over the years that followed, she had watched the boy grow into a man, in time becoming the warrior-king that Emrys had foretold. He defeated the Frisians at Glein, the Scots along the river Dubglas, the Picts at the River Bassus, and the Saxons at Caledon, Caerguidn, Caer Wisc, and Tryfrwyd. Always she was there, feasting on the blood of his enemies, taking by night in stealth what he could not win by day on the battlefield. At Badon Hill when he finally drove the Saxons from the land, breaking their military might once and for all, she had been there. The sky had been heavily overcast that day, bathing the land in an almost twilight dimness that allowed her to stand by his side, though heavily cloaked, using teeth and claws to destroy any enemy who avoided Caledfwlch's deadly bite. It was said later that the battle raven had guarded the king's back during his greatest victory. She had reveled in the glory of that fight despite the weakness that the light of day always brought. It was almost like being alive again. Such foolishness had its price, however. It had taken her a fortnight to recover from the burns she suffered that day.

That victory heralded a time of peace for the land. The king married a high-born woman of sun-gold hair, and retired to the stronghold at Camulodunum. The Lady did not begrudge her king a living wife, for what were the affairs of mortals to her? His heart could have been given to any number of women and it would not have mattered. His soul was hers. On nights when the moon was high and the song of passion danced in the wind, he still came to her.

One such night, it was the old Druid who called her. She entered the wooded glade to find him draped in rich blue robes, seated on the altar stone with his staff lying casually across one knee. She knew he was very old, far older than most mortals lived, but he was still quite strong and vital. His hair and beard had turned silver long ago, but his eyes held the bright intensity of youth.

"What do you wish, priest? I await another."

"I am the Myrddin, the adviser to the High King, not just a priest anymore." He stood and stalked toward her, challenging. "The king will not come to you tonight, I have seen to it."

A trill of fear ran through her. "Have you harmed him?"

"No. Just a potion to make him sleep deeply, beyond your reach. You must not see him more."

Fury quickly replaced the fear. "Do you presume to command me? You forget your place, Druid. You gave his life to me as the price for Caledfwlch and victory. You have no coin with which to buy him back. He has become quite precious to me."

Anger flashed in the Myrddin's eyes. He lifted his staff, and for a moment she thought he might attack. The wooden staff could bring her true death, if used correctly, where steel could not—and the Druid knew just where to strike. She balanced herself, prepared to kill him if necessary. Time hung suspended for several heartbeats, each of them coiled for battle. Eventually the old man relented and lowered his staff, dispersing the tension.

"I shall make it a humble request then, my Lady. He belongs to the land of Albion now. He has grown beyond both of us. For the sake of Albion, let him live out the measure of his days free of your influence. His care for you weakens him. He is inattentive to his wife and duty, and there are others that will use this weakness to shatter the realm."

"I am his strength."

"Only in wartime. We are at peace now. He needs a different kind of strength." Emrys returned to the altar stone and sat carefully upon it, using the staff for balance, as if the weight of all his years had suddenly come upon him. "I fear for his marriage. It is hard enough for Gwenhwyfar to share him with his people without having to share him with you as well. In her loneliness the Queen has begun to turn to another for comfort."

"What does that matter to me?"

"It will matter to him. And what affects him affects the realm entire. Medrawd lies in wait for the least sign that the brotherhood is failing. He and his ilk are scavengers and Albion is the prize they seek. Artur is only a temporary dalliance for one such as you. Let him be and find another."

She turned away as if considering, unwilling to let Emrys see the torment she felt. A strange disquieting pain nestled within her chest. It was a feeling she had not known since her breathing days, one she never thought to feel again. *Is it possible that I am in love with a mortal? How could I not know it? Why do I only realize it when I might have to give him up? And if true, how can I ever let him go?* Controlling her expression, she faced the Myrddin.

"If he really belongs to neither of us, then he is his own man. As such, he should have the right to choose. I will let him make a choice."

"You would have him choose to give up his life and join you in eternal darkness." It was not a question.

"I have said I will let him make a choice. That is as much as I am willing to grant."

The next night the lady traveled to the city of Camulodunum, the center of the High King's court. The king's hall was a remnant left by the Romans, a broad stone villa with tile floors and wide terraces instead of the clay and rushes of most of the other buildings. The keep was quiet, save for guards and two heavily cloaked travelers departing from the stable. She avoided them easily, ghosting through the sleeping villa to the king's chambers, guided by the feel of Artur's presence. Moving like mist in the shadows she entered the darkened room to find him seated by the window, still dressed in a fine day tunic and boots, staring out at the full moon. Caledfwlch rested lightly across his lap, gleaming wickedly in the moonlight. She glided across the room to stand behind him, stilling the impulse to reach out and stroke his shining raven hair.

"You risk much to come here." He did not turn away from the window.

"There is very little here that can harm me."

He nodded, as if to himself, still refusing to look at her. She could feel the tension in his body even without physical contact.

"The Myrddin told me what you really are—that you were once mortal. He told me that the Christians consider you to be damned."

That meddling fool, she fumed.

"I am what I am. I have never pretended to be other. It is men who have named me and given me titles. It is men who now claim damnation for me. I simply exist according to my nature. The old gods have long taught that life will continue after death. They have simply seen fit to give me my second life in this world rather than in the Summer Land, with a body no longer subject to the weaknesses of mortality." She moved between Artur and the window, forcing him to look at her. "And they have given me the ability to pass that gift on, to grant eternal life to those who are worthy." She reached out to stroke his face. "I would choose you."

He recoiled as if burned, knocking the stool over as he stood and backed away, holding the sword protectively between them. "So that I will be as you? Scavenging off the blood of others? Skulking in darkness and shadow?" His words lashed her like a whip. "I saw the burns you wore after Badon Hill, though you tried to hide them. The sun was but a pale shadow that day. What kind of creature cannot bear the sun? If you are not a demon, you must at least be from the Dark Sidhe. I understand now that those were not bites of passion you gave me when we lay together. You were feeding off me! I was no better than a fatted calf to you! And I dared to love you!"

Stunned by the vehemence in his tone as much as by his admission of love, she could only stare at him. Then, slowly, she sank to her knees before him. "If you truly believe me to be a demon, then treat me as you would a demon. Destroy me. I give you my life. Take my head and I will die the true death." She watched his grip tighten on Caledfwlch's hilt. "It is fitting for me to die by the blade that brought us together." She inclined her head forward, shaking her hair free of her neck for his stroke. Imagining she could feel Caledfwlch hovering above her, she waited, tensed for the blow.

"No." The great sword clattered to the tile floor and Artur stumbled back, falling onto his raised sleeping couch. "I cannot. No demon would sacrifice its life so easily. I do not know truly what you are, but you are not damned." There was a tightness in his eyes as he stared, not at her, but at the sword that had so nearly taken her head.

She rose to embrace him and was overjoyed to feel his powerful arms close desperately about her, crushing her to his chest.

"Then let me give you the gift. It is not a curse." she whispered, kissing his neck until he groaned. "I would have you by my side for all eternity."

"And what of my kingdom?" He gasped as she ran her tongue along the line of his jaw, thrilling to the taste of him, the pulse of his vein just under the skin. She felt him tremble at her touch on his body.

"You will be able to watch over it for all time, as I have watched over you." She gently pushed him onto his back, trailing kisses into the hollow of his neck as his hands coursed roughly over her body.

"You make it very difficult to refuse." He turned his head to allow her greater access to his throat. She felt the familiar ache as her teeth extended.

The chamber door burst open, flooding the room with the glare of lamplight. The Lady rolled free of the bed, instinctively baring her teeth and shielding her eyes. She could barely make out the Myrddin's cloaked form in the doorway. He was deliberately avoiding her eyes, focusing only on his king.

"What is the meaning . . . !"

"My Lord, the Queen is taken. Lugh Strong Arm is gone as well."

Artur bolted from the bed, pulling his rank about him like a well-used mantle. "Prepare the horses. Sound the alarm and I will meet all assembled in the Great Hall. This may be Medrawd's doing." The Druid left, and Artur scrambled about the room, gathering his sword and helm.

"Let her go."

He stopped, one hand on his scabbard, another on his cloak. Slowly he dropped both to look at her, dark suspicion in his eyes. "You knew about this?"

"No. But I do know that she went willingly."

"Why?"

"What does it matter?"

He stared hard at her, waiting. "Very well. Perhaps she wanted one man to love, not a kingdom. She could not have you without the titles and duties you bear. Do not begrudge her her happiness."

"She is my Queen and mate for this life. My duty is to her and the kingdom. I must go after her."

"And what of me? A moment ago you were willing to give up everything to join me."

"And this is my punishment for that moment of weakness." His eyes were tight with anguish. "Can you understand nothing of mortal duty? You helped place the crown on my head, but to be worthy of that crown, I must deny you. The responsibilities of that office do not end until my death. No matter how much my heart wishes to stay, I must go." He grabbed up his gear and stepped through the door, his face tight as he turned to look at her. "And I must never see you again."

"Why?" Her voice sounded amazingly calm despite the strange pain searing through her. She had not felt this much pain since the day of her death.

"Because I could not look upon you and find the strength to do this again. Please honor me in this, dear Lady." She could see tears streaking his face, his eyes were open and pleading. She could not deny him.

He rubbed his face with a brisk gesture and turned away to disappear down the corridor.

She watched from the window as he gathered his men and rode from the city, then she turned her back on Camulodunum, determined to force all thoughts of the city and its charismatic king from her mind.

Until tonight.

A twig snapped, pulling her attention back to the present. She followed the sound to see a cloaked figure enter the mist that spread about the wood like a moat. Her keen vision spotted the unmistakable dragon brooch and the glint of a metal circlet beneath the concealing hood. At last he was coming. She moved to light the fire she had prepared, knowing that his eyes would need the additional light, his body the warmth. Her hand trembled slightly as she lit it. Inwardly she cursed her weakness, including that weakness of the heart which had brought her here, to Camlann. Forcing herself to stillness, she waited.

"I had almost forgotten how beautiful you are."

He stepped into the clearing, reflected firelight sparkling in his eyes as he studied her. "You have not changed. Not since that day at the lake."

She saw that age and care had taken their toll on him, leaving creases around his eyes and shadows in the hollows of his face. New scars over old had etched garish patterns in the once firm skin of his arms. He limped slightly as he crossed the clearing to stand before her. The liquid grace of his youth had given way to a more dignified gait. But his eyes were still clear, his carriage regal.

"You have. Yet not so much that I cannot see the young warlord still within you."

"I had hoped you would forget."

"I could never forget you. Everything about your fragile mortality is engraved upon the remnants of my soul." She gently reached out to caress his cheek.

He closed his eyes at her icy touch, bringing his hand up to trap hers against his face as if to absorb the feel of it. "As you are etched into my dreams." He kissed her palm lightly, then pulled away to stare at the fire. "I admit I have tried to forget you. Tried to live my life as a king should, for duty and country. But ..." He shrugged. "They say no man touched by the fair folk can ever be free of them. I've seen the truth of it. I cannot hold a woman in my arms but that I compare her to the feel and smell and taste of you." He chuckled bitterly. "No born woman has a chance against that. Gwenhwyfar understood. Even when we lay together, you were always there, between us." He knelt down to stir the fire. She watched from a safe distance. "Did you know she took vows with the nuns of the Christian god rather than return to me?"

"Do you regret my patronage?"

"I am growing old. The touch of winter makes it easy to regret the choices of spring. And the battles seem to grow ever longer."

"Then let me give you another choice, and a chance to reclaim that spring." She stepped up to him, ignoring the acrid smoke of the fire, she gave him her hand and guided him to his feet. "Come with me now. You know what I offer."

"Is that why you are here? To ask me to abandon my men on the eve of battle?" He pulled his hand free of her gentle grasp. "Surely you know me well enough to know I cannot do what you ask." He stalked to the edge of the clearing to look out at the camp. "Medrawd has amassed a great army. He would see Camulodunum burnt to the ground. He wants Albion for himself, not for the good of her people." He gestured toward the sleeping camp as she came up beside him. "This is all that stands between Medrawd and the heart of Albion. I cannot let him destroy all that we have built. I took an oath to hold the well-being of the land over my own life years ago. I will not betray her now. She is the one thing that I love more than you."

"But she will fall, once you are gone. Is that not reason enough to take my offer?"

"But not tomorrow. She will not fall tomorrow so long as I am alive when the battle begins."

The Lady turned to walk back toward the fire, feeling strangely in need of warmth. There was no way to avoid telling him of the vision. She turned to face him, holding his gaze with hers. "I have seen your death. In a dream. If you fight tomorrow, you will be mortally wounded."

"I did not know that prophecy was one of your gifts."

"Nor did I. But it fits with a vision that the Myrddin once related to me. He said you would fall at Camlann."

"Emrys is gone."

"But that does not change his vision—or my dream."

"How do you know your dream is not just some wild imagining based on Emrys' words?"

"I know because my kind do not dream."

The king turned to stare out into the darkness, his expression distant and cold. He stood very still for a long moment; then, as if suddenly remembering he was not alone, he turned toward the Lady. "Then it would seem the gods have chosen. I will still fight tomorrow. I owe that much to those who follow me."

"And if the prophecy is true?"

He shrugged, smiling slightly. "Then I die. I am a warrior. Death is a constant companion. How can I expect others to live by a code if I am unwilling to die by it?"

"You know I could force you to come with me. I have that power."

"Of that I have no doubt. But you also have honor. You will not reduce me to the state of an unwilling slave."

Her voice dropped to a whisper. "No. I will not do that. Not to you." He turned to leave.

"But I will have what is mine." He looked at her in surprise. "Your life was given to me, by the Myrddin, in exchange for the great sword of the De' Danann." She drew herself up very straight. "I give you back your life, to spend as you wish. But I will have Caledfwlch returned to me. Tomorrow eve you must bring the sword to me at the Severn's edge."

"And if I am no longer able?"

"By your honor, of which you hold such store, I require you to live long enough to see it done." She fought to still the quaver in her voice.

He took her hands in his and brought them to his lips to kiss her wrists. She pulled them back, then took a dagger from her belt and slashed her right wrist. As thick blood welled in the cut, she offered it to the startled king.

"If you would kiss it, kiss it now, and drink of my love. I have taken of *you* many times. Tonight I wish you to taste of my life."

He hesitated. Staring at the deep wound that was beginning to heal before his eyes.

"Do not worry. Drinking of my blood like this will not affect your battle tomorrow."

"Will it help afterward?"

"I do not truly know. Perhaps."

Obediently he took her wrist in both hands and held it to his lips, kissing the flesh around the wound. Tentatively he began to suck on the wound. The Lady gasped, trembling from the ecstasy of this most intimate kiss. Tingling fire ran up her arm and through her body, awakening a deeper burning low in her belly. She closed her eyes to savor the feeling.

Too soon he stopped. She opened her eyes to see him studying her. A few drops of blood clung to his mouth and mustache. His eyes were fever bright. She could hear the blood pounding in his veins. Releasing her wrist, he took a deep breath as though to steady himself. She moved into his arms and gently kissed his lips, thrilling to the taste of her own blood on them. Suddenly he wrapped his arms tightly around her, tangling his fist in her hair as he crushed her against his hard body, returning her kiss with desperate fervor.

After a long moment he pulled back, breathing heavily. "I must go. The dawn comes soon." He pulled his cloak tightly about him, then slowly turned to walk through the trees at the edge of the clearing and into the dark mists beyond.

The Lady waited beneath the waters all the next day and into the night. She fought a hard-won battle with herself to avoid going to Camlann. She knew she could do nothing there. She must honor his choice.

It was almost morning before a rider galloped up to the shore, wearing a sword and carrying another. For a moment she dared to hope it was Artur, but as the warrior slid from his lathered mount to approach the water she recognized a much younger man. It was Peredur. One of Artur's own sworn liegemen. Her chest tightened painfully as she saw he was alone.

Peredur sobbed as he ran a hand lovingly over the rune-covered blade, then stepped into the edge of the lake. He studied the moonlit water as if looking for something. Apparently not finding it, he shrugged and threw the sword end over end out toward the deep water. Effortlessly the Lady lifted out of the lake to catch it by the hilt, letting the water streaming down her face and body take the place of her tears. She brandished the sword once, then advanced toward the waiting warrior.

"My Lady!" Peredur dropped to one knee, bowing his head before her.

"How fared the battle?" She was amazed at how cold and calm her voice sounded.

"Medrawd is slain, we have won the day." His voice held no joy, only grief.

"And what of your king?" She fought the dread building within her. "Why do you come in his place?"

"He is mortally wounded, my Lady."

A trill of forbidden hope fluttered within her breast.

"Where is he? Where does he lie?"

"They are taking him to the shrine on the isle of Annwfn."

The flutter of hope grew stronger. Annwfn was one of her strongholds. The mist-shrouded island held one of the great subterranean caverns where she made her home. The old Druid had known of it; he must have told Artur, knowing that he might not be around to help when his prophecy came true. Or perhaps there was more to the prophecy than he had spoken of. She disappeared into the lake, leaving the grieving man behind.

It was nearly midday when she emerged from the hidden caverns of Annwfn. Mist clung to the trees and cloaked the ground, giving the whole island an otherworldly glow. The sky had turned dark and brooding, as if it too mourned, but she could still feel the sun's merciless presence burning through to her bones as she left the shelter of the stone.

A small boat approached through the thick fog that surrounded the island. Hidden, she watched as the boat pulled up onto the shore. Three darkly cloaked women lifted a shrouded form from the bottom of the boat and bore it past the standing stones to the ancient shrine beyond, built deep into the hill. The Lady followed, silently, trying to still her impatience.

As the women set the bier upon the altar, the Lady could hold back no longer. She stepped out of the concealing mist at the shrine's entrance and approached the altar. Heedless of the women's gasps, she went straight to the shrouded body. Running her hands over it, she used her enhanced senses to search desperately for some vestige of life. There was something. A tiny spark of latent life pulsed deep within the body. *My blood has made a difference. Perhaps it is not too late.*

"He is dead." The tallest of the three spoke, golden hair spilling from her hood. "We have come to consecrate his body to the gods. Have you come to honor him as well?" Her voice cracked. The lady turned and was surprised to recognize Gwenhwyfar's tear-streaked face beneath the black drape. *So she had loved him after all!*

"No. He is not dead. He sleeps." She began to unwrap the shroud.

"How dare you touch him." One of the other women darted forward to push the Lady away from Artur. She grunted with surprise when her victim proved immovable. The Lady gently grasped her attacker's arms and pushed her away, then bent over Artur to continue to remove the bindings that covered his too pale face.

"Who are you to lay hands upon the High King?" the woman demanded again.

The Lady spun to face her, fury in her face. Pulling herself up to her full height, she trapped all three of them with her glare.

"I am called Morrigan!" She saw them gasp and fall back to huddle in the corner as they recognized the name of the De' Danann Goddess of Death and Rebirth. "I have come to take your king from the realm of death to give him eternal life. I would see Artur rise from his slumber to rule again. Would you aid me in this?" The trembling women nodded. Satisfied, the Lady took a gilded chalice from a hidden niche under the altar. Pulling a dagger from her belt she proffered both to the women. "Then give a token of your lifeblood into this chalice, that your gift may help him live again."

When they had finished, she added her own blood to the chalice, then sent them away. Returning to the still, cold figure on the altar, she gently lifted his head. *If only he had not been so proud, so stubborn.* Giving silent prayers to the Ancient Ones, she held the gleaming chalice to his pale lips and poured. If there was any chance of revival, it would have to be soon. The blood filled his mouth and trickled down his cheek. She waited, extending her senses to their limits as she watched his face, listening for any sound. She could feel the throb of the water on the shore, feel the progression of the sun overhead, sense the creatures in the moist earth of the shrine, but from the still form on the altar, nothing. She poured from the chalice again, willing him to drink, to breathe. Her fingers left deep groves in the edge of the altar stone as she watched and hoped.

Then, just as the veil of night descended, he swallowed.

Author's Note:

It is believed that the man Arthur may have lived and ruled Britain, known as the isle of Albion, in the time just after the Roman's abandoned their holdings there. Someone certainly kept the Saxons and Picts from destroying the ordered civilization that Rome had helped establish. Yet while there are remnants of historical genealogies that name him and his descendants, there is no established grave. Celtic belief of the time held that there was an afterlife that followed death.

The early Irish Celts believed that the Morrigan was one of the goddesses who took the dead to grant them eternal life. It is interesting to note that the Celts also often removed the heads from their enemies. Perhaps they did not want them returning once they gained the afterlife?

Teresa Patterson is the author of several other short stories on subjects that include medieval dragons and ancient Byzantium. She is also co-author, with Robert Jordan, of the *Wheel of Time Guide Book.*

OATHS
by Bradley H. Sinor

"So you were the one," Ryan DuLane said.

"Not entirely, but I suppose I did my share. It was more a matter of what had to be done at that moment than anything else," said Brother Ellis.

"Isn't that always the way, Brother?" DuLane hoped the distaste that he had for most religious types echoed in his voice.

Normally he would have barely even spoken to the monk, not to be deliberately uncivil but simply out of preference. Over the years DuLane had come to be highly selective about who he spent time with, and religious types were not high among his preferred company.

Tonight, however, he seemed to have little choice in the matter if he wanted company of any sort. The few other patrons of the Inn of the Crossed Scabbards had long since sought their beds, leaving DuLane and Brother Ellis alone in the large common room.

Located at the intersection of two growing trade routes, the Crossed Scabbards did a brisk business most of the year. But spring was not due for another four weeks at least, and six days of freezing rain had kept away all but the most hardy of travelers.

An hour's ride west of the inn, DuLane had come across the remains of a bandit ambush. Three ragged bodies, covered with blood and mud, lay where they had fallen. Nearby there had been two quickly made cairns and crude crosses, the last resting places of the monk's companions.

In spite of the roaring fire, the cold and dismal atmosphere that had settled over the countryside seemed to have penetrated even inside the tavern. They could hear the wind howling outside and the rolling crash of thunder.

"However I may have performed with my sword, the bandits took two of our number with them," said Ellis.

"But you did survive, Brother Ellis, much to your credit. From the looks of those three wretches, they would have been no easy task. Besides, I learned a long time ago, it is survival that matters."

"Even so, we did not come through unscathed. The one of our guards who lived required a dozen stitches to close up the wound in his leg. It will be several days at least before he is fit to ride. I wrenched my shoulder badly, and it pains me to move it if I am not careful."

The monk was a man in his midforties at the youngest, his tonsured hair streaked with gray that only added to the lean and wolflike appearance of his face. It was his eyes, though—they bothered DuLane the most. They were distant, not lost in contemplation of holiness but in something else.

"Still, you don't often associate a religious man with a sword," DuLane said lightly.

"Before God called me to the church, I found I had a small talent with the blade. It has been our Lord's will, as well as my superior's in the order, that I keep that talent sharp; in the service of God, rather than that of temporal princes," he said.

The monk was studying DuLane as much as DuLane had been studying the monk. As it would be, he told himself. The holy man would see only a man who had lived through too many battles, lost too many comrades and could barely remember what having a home and family were like.

"God needs many skills, Captain DuLane. Yes, your name was not unfamiliar to me," said Ellis.

"Indeed? To you personally, or to the Inquisition?"

Brother Ellis arched an eyebrow, the barest hint of a smile touching his face. "Both. I serve the church as God would have me, protecting it against heretics and those who would work against His holy will."

"And which am I?"

"As are all men, a little bit of both. You sell your sword at will, but you are good, very good, enough to have your pick of employment with any noble house in Europe. There have been incidents, it is true, but nothing to make the Holy Inquisition think you are a heretic . . . yet."

"I'm so very glad to hear that." DuLane ran his finger around the edge of his cup, collecting a few drops of wine, and then slowly licked them clean.

"You are traveling early in the season, Captain. It must be a matter of the gravest import," he said.

Trying to be diplomatic, are we? observed DuLane to himself. "Indeed. I must reach Sicily by the end of March or this whole journey, as inconvenient and painful as it has been, will have been for nothing."

"Then I wish you well." The monk wanted to know more; that much was obvious. It was a minor victory to leave him hanging, but one that pleased DuLane. If asked directly, perhaps DuLane would explain, but then again, perhaps not.

In his saddlebags was a letter he had received three weeks before. It was from Karl Lysroni in Palermo. DuLane had served with him in a half-dozen campaigns and with his father and grandfather before. He had watched the boy grow up. Now Karl was to be married and wanted DuLane to be his best man.

"Besides, who better deserving to stand with him?" he had laughed when he read the letter.

Brother Ellis leaned back in his chair.

Just then a young woman emerged from the kitchen. She balanced a tray with two bowls and a large pitcher on it, then set them in front of the two men.

DuLane had barely noticed her earlier, a few quick glimpses back into the kitchen as the door had swung open. This was the closest the two had been.

DuLane felt his stomach begin to churn. The face, the manner, he remembered them. Here in the south of France was the last place he would have expected to see her. And it had to be her; the figure, the movement, they were all the same. It was a memory as fresh as a spring breeze and oh, so very old at the same time.

"Ginnie?" he finally managed to say, turning the two syllables into three as he spoke.

"Sir?" She was no more than sixteen. Her dirty blonde

hair was tied in a single braid and then wrapped to hug her head. Her blouse and skirt were stained from the evening's work in the kitchen.

"Ginnie?" he asked again.

"No, my name is Emma."

A blanket of sadness fell across DuLane. It was the response that he would have expected, should have expected.

Yet for a brief moment, memories, odors. The feel of one hand on another. The sound of silk moving. They all flooded over him and were gone in a moment.

"You have been employed here long?" he said.

"Near three years, sir. Is there anything I can get for either of you?"

"No." DuLane waved her away. But his eyes followed her back out of sight.

"You know her?" asked Brother Ellis.

"No. She just resembled someone. Someone that I knew a very long time ago."

"If I were a musician, I would imagine that I could make a great deal of what just went on. I imagine it would make a fine ballad, of lost love, heroic deeds, and valor uncounted," laughed the monk.

Oh it has, DuLane reminded himself, *it has*.

DuLane stared at the door for a long time. After a while he had excused himself from the monk, pleading an exhaustion that he neither felt nor would have noticed. What enjoyment he had gleaned from baiting Brother Ellis had evaporated.

He went back into a shadowed corner in the upstairs hall and waited.

An hour passed. Brother Ellis made his way to a room, pausing just inside the door where the injured guard slept, before going on to another room farther down the hall.

Not a few minutes later she came.

Ginnie.

Guinevere.

NO! He reminded himself that she had said her name was Emma.

The light from the candle in her hand barely showed the

outline of her face. As she passed within only a few feet of his hiding place, he felt his stomach cringing.

The girl made her way to a door at the far end of the hall. The stair inside led to an attic bedroom. DuLane had discovered it shortly after his arrival.

He listened to her steps disappearing into the darkness. Ten minutes went by before DuLane could bring himself to even walk to the door. He paused there. The sound the ancient hinges made echoed loudly in his memory.

In between two breaths he shifted form and let himself slide between the ill-fitted boards and drift up the stairway. The wind outside of the attic room was enough to mask the sound from the wood taking the weight of his boots as he assumed solid form again.

A long time before, when he had discovered the ability, it had been painful. The pain had passed. Even now he did not know how he did what he did, only that he could. The first time he had shown Arthur, the king had stood slack-jawed as a peasant at a traveling carnival.

The room had no windows. That was no problem for DuLane. He had been born with good night vision; since the change that had only grown better and better.

There were few things in the room to mark it as anyone's home, but here and there he could see little touches. A small curtained alcove protected her few bits of clothing, a broken piece of mirror hung carefully in a niche on the wall, and a small wooden ring held a section of cloth from which needles protruded.

The girl lay beneath a blanket on a pile of straw in one corner of the room. Her face was buried in the dried grass for warmth. She stirred and shifted as DuLane stepped closer. A few syllables escaped her lips but were lost in the blanket.

DuLane knelt next to her bed. He could hear her breathing, matching it with his own. The soft flow of blood echoed like a cathedral chorus in his ears.

He had not fed for nearly a week, since leaving Bordeaux. The Hunger was something that was never completely gone from him. It was something he accepted, an annoyance that he had learned long since to control.

But as he knelt there, DuLane felt it begin to grow.

He knew he should not have needed to feed again for another few days, but the feeling was familiar, damnably so.

With the Hunger there were also memories.

Sunlight playing over yellow hair.

Laughter. Silk sliding across satin.

Water flowing.

The subtle movement of a smile that reached into the depths.

"Guinevere," he whispered.

Outside he could hear the wind rushing around the eaves of the tavern. In the distance thunder echoed across a leaden black sky.

Darkness.

Light being washed away in blood.

Pain.

Green eyes swept away in a flood of red.

"Ginnie," he said. His voice a hollow echo within the storm. Another voice echoed in his mind, the voice of the man who had been his best and truest friend.

"Swear by all that you hold sacred that you will stand for the right. That your sword will defend women, children, and all who cannot stand for themselves."

"This I do swear."

"Then stand forth and join us as our brother. Rise, Sir Lancelot."

Over the years he had answered to many names, worn many faces, and now it was DuLane who opened his eyes, staring at the girl.

It might be Ginnie's face, but it wasn't her.

She probably never heard of Guinevere, except as a sad ballad at harvest time. DuLane forced himself to stand, turning away from the girl's sleeping form. He could feel her blood, pulsing just below the skin, a sweet wine that could touch places in him nothing else had ever touched.

He remembered the oath he had sworn that long ago day in Camelot. On his knees before the throne, feeling the steel of Excalibur as it touched each of his shoulders in turn. The words burning into his very soul.

He had broken that vow many times over the years. As the centuries rolled by, he knew he would again.

Only not this time.

*   *   *

Emma came awake with a start. She had to struggle for every breath of stale icy air.

The feeling that she wasn't alone filled her.

For a long time she lay unmoving, waiting. But all she could be certain of was that there seemed to be a slight mist hanging in the still air. A mist that faded away.

The wind whipped through DuLane, cutting beneath his cape to his heavy fleece vest and jacket. If there was a warm spot on him, he didn't know where it was. At the moment he really didn't care.

DuLane bent forward as he slid through the barn's side door. Inside he could hear the sounds of the animals murmuring.

He cursed a small cat that brushed against his leg. The feline hissed, then vanished into the shadows. None of the horses or cattle took even the slightest notice of him.

The sound of the wind faded to a distant drone as Du-Lane walked among the animals. He selected a small shaggy pony. Stepping inside the stall, he touched the animal between the eyes. The strength of the pony echoed in its blood.

A few minutes later the Hunger had once more faded into the background. DuLane wished that the memories of Ginnie, Arthur, and all the others were so easily put away.

From the other side of the barn came a loud thump. DuLane reached for his sword. Only reached, as moments passed and he heard nothing but the sounds that should abound in the darkened barn.

He thought at first it was the cat he had seen earlier, but more than likely the animal had sought refuge in some corner well away from any intruder. No, the sound came from somewhere else.

The barn was divided into three sections. The largest was given over to the animals, the other two were for storage.

From one of them DuLane could hear singing. A hymn?

That there were plenty of empty rooms in the inn made it all the more curious. Through a crack in the wood he could just make out someone in the other part of the barn.

A monk sat, his feet resting on a nearby cask, in front

of a small brazier. Light from its little fire cast a network of shadows over the room. He appeared to be in his early twenties. He held his arms tight around himself for warmth, half singing, half whispering a new hymn, obviously in an effort to keep himself awake.

The older monk had mentioned a companion, Brother Francois. This had to be him. Perhaps he was serving some sort of penance.

Prudence no doubt dictated that DuLane should return to his own quarters, but this would certainly not be the first time he had followed the imprudent trail. Curiosity was a mighty irritant, and could be a deadly enemy at times.

Shifting to mist, he drifted into the room. For a few moments he hung in the air, then found his human form, standing just behind the monk. DuLane grabbed the man by the shoulders, his fingers grinding into hard taut muscle, as he pulled him up out of the chair in a single motion.

The two men's faces were only inches apart. DuLane reached out with his mind and seized the monk's will, freezing it before the man was even sure what had happened to him.

"You cannot move," he commanded. The young monk sat again, his lips hanging open, in the middle of a verse. "Now then, my friend, Brother Francois. I have a few questions."

Before he could say anything else DuLane realized that they were not alone. Hunched up in the far corner of the room was a man, bound hand and foot, clad in shabby rags, with a single thin blanket against the cold.

"So you're a guard, are you?" DuLane said, turning back to the monk. "This looks to be a truly dangerous fellow."

The prisoner appeared to be somewhere in his forties; his hair was matted and covered in blood and dirt. Grimy hands clutched the blanket close to his chest, fingers twitching convulsively, even in his sleep.

One eye began to open, slowly, unfocussed in the dark, but looking directly at DuLane. Gradually a look of awareness came across his face; his bound hands pulled the blanket even closer to his chest.

"Why have you come? Even God allowed the disciples to sleep in the garden." His voice was a cracked whisper.

A scar ran the length of his throat. No doubt a souvenir of some dark alley, thought DuLane.

"You certainly think highly of yourself. . . . The Lord's disciples are hefty company," said DuLane.

The man just stared at him, then pulled himself into a fetal position, the tremor now reaching through his entire body.

"Who are you?" DuLane said gently.

Nothing. DuLane repeated himself. He was reluctant to try to influence the man's mind; it seemed to be on the edge of becoming unhinged.

"If you don't know me, then it is best that I be forgotten. I only wish I had been. I don't even know me anymore."

There was something about the raspy voice that sounded like one DuLane had known. But that had been a long time ago.

"I'm not here to hurt you," DuLane said.

"Then you are a dream, a nightmare, given to torment me. If you're not here to hurt me, then help me." he said. "If nothing else, kill me."

DuLane found a waterskin hanging from the guard's chair. He squeezed a palmful of liquid into his hand. Lifting the prisoner's head, he offered a few drops to him.

"Help me," the man said again.

He went limp as he spoke. "Why do I let myself get into things like this?" DuLane asked.

Brother Franscious waited for DuLane's attention.

On occasion, DuLane had wondered if people he controlled this way were aware of what went on around them. However, he had never been willing to release them long enough to find out. Not that it mattered. A few words, a gentle push with his voice, and the entire encounter would become at best a fleeting memory.

"All right, monk, it's time that we talked," he said. "What do you know of this man?"

The young friar seemed to have trouble finding his voice. "He is a heretic. Arrested at the order of the Bishop of Marsalas, to be handed over to the Inquisition."

"What has he done?"

"I do not know. Brother Ellis ordered me to accompany him. He said only that we had to bring a prisoner back."

"I think you do know, Brother. Even monks have their gossips and I refuse to believe that the Inquisition does not have theirs."

"Yes . . . I overheard Brother Ellis telling someone that he is a member of a dissolved outlaw order of warrior monks. Brother Ellis thinks that he can lead us to some of their supporters here in France," he said.

An outlaw order of monks. Now this was intriguing, thought DuLane. "I've heard nothing of the Pope disallowing any of the martial orders."

"The papal bull was the *Vox in Excedo*."

DuLane arched an eyebrow at those words. He knew the name of that document all too well. The *Vox in Excedo* had been issued by Pope Clement V to formally dissolve the *Pauperes Commilitones Christi Templique Salomonis*, the Poor Fellow-Soldiers of Christ and the Temple of Solomon. The Knights Templar. That had been more than eightly years ago.

"Are you saying he's a Templar?"

"Yes." Even though they had been extinguished in France, chapters of the Templars had found homes in Portugal and Scotland. Mayhap this unwary fellow was a Templar.

"So who is he?"

"Penne. Oliver de Penne."

A chill went through DuLane. He looked over at the shivering figure on the floor. Oliver de Penne had been one of the prime instruments in the betrayal of the Templars more than eighty years before. He had traded his own life for those of thousands of members of the order.

"If that is who he really is, then he deserves everything that you can do to him, and more."

The engraving on the medallion was worn, but DuLane could still see the two figures, a pair of knights seated on a single horse. Around the edge were the Latin words *"Non nobis, domine, non nobis sed nomini tuo da gloriam."*

"Not to us, Lord, not to us, but to thy name give glory."

It had been in Jerusalem, in a place that some said was built on the remains of Solomon's Temple that DuLane, he had been called Karyl Ramirez then, had first heard those words.

There in the hot sands of the Holy Land, in a place given over by Baldwin II, King of Jerusalem, he'd sworn the vows that made him a Templar. The others who stood there that night had little known that one of their number had stood once in Camelot and now walked the world as an undying blood drinker.

DuLane turned the medallion over and over in his hands, remembering faces, voices, comrades all fallen into dust, just as the order had a hundred and fifty years after its founding. Not because there was no longer a need, but thanks to cruel betrayal and greed by King Phillip of France, the Pope and one of the Templars himself, a betrayer whose name, for DuLane and the surviving Templars, stood with that of Judas Iscariot—Oliver de Penne.

DuLane had barely escaped arrest himself that 13th of October in 1307. Only chance had allowed him to escape Paris. Countless others had been arrested, many tortured, and many of those sent to a fiery death at the stake.

Slowly he wrapped the medallion in what had once been a blood red piece of silk. Now the colors were faded with the passing of years, another memory struggling to hold on.

In the bottom of his saddlebags was a small compartment that could only be reached from the inside. The leather was stitched in such a way that unless someone knew exactly what to look for, they would most likely overlook it. He returned the medallion there.

He ran a practiced eye over the room, checking one more time for anything, any trace of himself he might have left behind. Nothing. The room was bare.

He thought once more of the man in the barn. It was not such a far-stretching miracle that Oliver de Penne might still be alive. Look at DuLane.

This was not the time, nor the place. If he was Oliver de Penne, then let the Inquisition have him; they would stretch out the pain far longer than DuLane might, though he was certain that none of them could enjoy it as much he would.

Swear by all that you hold sacred that you will stand for the right. That your sword will defend women, children, and all who cannot stand for themselves.

This I do swear.

Then stand forth and join us as our brother. Rise, Sir Lancelot.

For a long moment DuLane heard his own voice, the voice of Lancelot duLake and then Karyl Ramirez; the words had been different but the heart had been the same in each one.

If any in need ask for my help I shall give it.

Oliver de Penne's plea echoed in his ears. "Help me."

It was better to take himself away from here now.

DuLane had no sooner stepped into the hallway than he heard the creaking of hinges just behind him. Wrapping himself in shadows, he saw a single candle pass, held by the serving girl Emma. She moved slowly, careful to make as little noise as possible.

Once she was out of sight, DuLane found himself at a crossroads. He could leave, as had been his plan, but there was a gnawing inside him that made him want to look one more time at the face that he had loved and hated so many years ago.

He reminded himself she was not Guinivere. But that didn't matter.

The girl had gone straightaway to the kitchen. The small candle she had carried was shrouded behind several large boxes. He heard the sound of a metal dipper hitting against wood.

"Emma?" DuLane said.

The girl turned with a start, her face slack with fear as she searched the darkness for him.

"M–M–M'lord?"

"It seems we both couldn't sleep." He stepped close enough for her to see him.

"Can I get you something, m'lord?" The fear was beginning to evaporate from her. That was good, he thought.

"No . . . I couldn't sleep. I was considering leaving. I have a long road ahead of me."

"Leave? In this weather? It would be hard traveling."

He reached over to touch her cheek. The throb of blood in her veins had once more become like a thundering echo for DuLane. Only, the Hunger wasn't there. He had feasted too well in the barn. For now it was just a lonely echo. An echo of a love lost that would never be found again.

Ginnie! Ginnie! She had been the center that both he and Arthur had found themselves jointly moving around. It had been Morgana's curse that had wrapped the golden vision that was Guinivere in blood. She in turn had dragged Lancelot into the darkness, making him into a vampire as was she.

Together the two men that loved her had tracked Guinevere to a lonely castle in Scotland. There they had freed her from the curse in the only way either knew. DuLane could still remember the silent look of peace on her face after it was all over.

It had been Arthur who had denied Lancelot the same freedom, for reasons of vengeance and pain and love.

The girl pulled back slightly at DuLane's touch. No doubt other patrons had approached her, with fairly obvious intentions.

"Don't worry," he said. "I have no amorous plans for you, little Emma."

"You don't?" She sounded both puzzled and hurt, cocking her head slightly. It was just the same way that Guinevere had that first summer he had known her.

"No," he said gently.

"Oh. You loved her? And she hurt you? Now you don't know what to do?"

"That's right. Yes."

"And I remind you of her?" She smiled, with the faintest bit of seduction in her look.

DuLane suddenly realized that he had become something of a challenge for the village girl.

"You seem to be a wise young woman," he said.

"Me?" chuckled Emma. "I'm so stupid that the local priest couldn't even teach me my letters. Not that he should have been trying, anyway. I think he had other plans."

DuLane laughed. The sound of it seemed alien here in the darkness. "Even so, Emma, let me pose you a question," he said. "If you had once, a long time ago, sworn an oath, a mighty oath that bound your very heart and soul, would you stand by it? Especially if it involved doing something for someone that you hated with every fiber of your being?" It was Emma's turn to laugh. "Oaths, binding of heart and soul? You're talking in words that are too much for my head. I don't know if I can tell you the things that you want to hear. Just do what is right, I guess, is all I can say."

For a while the two of them just stood silently in the darkness. DuLane wasn't quite sure when the girl left. He remembered seeing her go, but the next thing he knew he was alone, listening to the wind and thunder echoing outside the door.

Midnight.

Brother Francois had taken to pacing about the room. He occasionally stopped and warmed his hands in front of the brazier, though his breath still hung in the air.

"Doesn't this man ever sleep?" DuLane muttered.

The suggestion that he had planted was simply for the monk to rest and forget DuLane's earlier visit. For Brother Franscious apparently that did not include the luxury of sleep.

The biggest problem was that the way he was walking he never completely turned his back on DuLane's spyhole. Shifting to mist would probably work, but it did take a second or two for him to materialize. DuLane admitted to himself that he had been lucky before. He had long since learned that luck was not something one relied on too frequently in any kind of a fight.

He was in the room in a matter of seconds, but before he could act, the outside door flew open, wind and rain rushing in with two people in its wake.

"Brother Ellis?" said the younger monk. "What are you doing here at this hour?"

The older man had a tight grip around the arm of Emma. She followed him, struggling with every step.

"Is there a problem?" Francois said.

Ellis looked grimly around the room, face wrinkled in disapproval, as he sniffed at the air. He yanked hard on Emma's arm, sending her to the floor at the two monks' feet. Rain mixed with tears ran off her face.

"We may have trouble tonight," Ellis said. "This 'little

lost lamb' was consorting with a man who was acting a bit too strange to suit me."

"You think he's a Templar, sent here to free de Penne?"

"I don't know what he is. I overheard part of a conversation these two had in the kitchen. It made me expect a visit from the man tonight, so I brought her, maybe as a bargaining point, maybe not. It never hurts to be prepared," Ellis said.

All the while de Penne lay on the floor. He hadn't stirred since the arrival of the older monk. DuLane observed that de Penne was either asleep, unconscious, or dead by now. The last would solve a number of problems.

Brother Ellis stood over him for several minutes. "You are a great deal of trouble, my friend. You will speak, have no doubt about that." DuLane found himself wondering if Ellis was addressing de Penne or him. "You can not escape God's justice. Like your grandfather, you will help us to exterminate this vile plague of the Temple."

Grandfather? Now that was interesting. It would explain de Penne's youthfulness, if a man in his midforties could be called youthful. It didn't really matter who he was; it had never really mattered. DuLane had simply forgotten that. He ran his hand over the Templar medallion that now hung around his neck.

Shifting his insubstantial self as close as possible to Brother Francois, DuLane took solid form once again.

This time his hand was knotted into a fist and hurling toward the monk. It connected on the man's chin, the impact staggering him. That was long enough for DuLane to grab his shoulders and slam Brother Francois hard against the barn wall.

He went down with a most satisfying thud.

Brother Ellis turned, rising as he moved; a sword that DuLane hadn't noticed leaped from the sheath hanging around the man's robes. Ellis was fast, far faster than DuLane might have expected, moving with a speed that he did not hesitate to use to his own advantage.

DuLane's own sword came free. As it did, he ducked to the side, feeling rather than seeing the blade pass within inches of his body. There was not a lot of area for maneuvering in this part of the barn.

Shadows mixed with what little light there was as metal clanked against metal, sparks leaping up into the darkness.

Whatever advantage DuLane gained, the priest countered quickly, as did DuLane on the priest. It seemed a contest of endurance. Then, as quickly as it had begun, something unexpected happened.

A cat, perhaps the same one that had confronted DuLane earlier, leaped out of the rafters, screeching, to strike against DuLane's face and chest. Claws dug into flesh, hissing filled the air. DuLane twisted and tried to push the animal away from him.

That was enough of an opening for the monk. His sword slid through leather, cloth, and fleece to drive itself hard into DuLane's flesh.

Pain. DuLane managed to shove the cat off as he went down to his knees, his sword falling from suddenly weak fingers. A curse in guttural French managed to escape his lips.

"I don't know who you are, Templar, bandit or hired assassin, and frankly I don't care," the monk said.

Ellis pulled his sword free. DuLane watched his own blood follow it, leaving a dark dab on his tunic vest and a trail of dots across his clothing and onto the floor. *At least he has the style not to rub things in and clean it with my own clothes,* DuLane observed.

The pain in his chest had already begun to fade. He knew that deep within him torn muscles, broken veins, and ripped cartilage had begun a tedious route to mending themselves.

"Aren't you going to give me Last Rites?" asked DuLane.

"I'm a monk, not a priest. Sometimes I think you heretics would have trouble telling your right hand from your left," said the monk.

"Then, brother, hear my confession while there is still time. Please," he said.

"Very well." Brother Ellis knelt beside DuLane. "Are you prepared to confess your sins, renounce your heresy, and free yourself in the sight of God?"

"I am."

"Then I will hear your confession, my son."

DuLane managed a faint smile. "Thank you, brother. My confession is . . . I don't like you."

His hand shot up and grabbed the monk's robe. DuLane's legs trembled under him as he struggled to his feet. Holding the other man at arm's length, DuLane felt the battle rage filling him now.

"I could prolong this," he said. "At another time I might have, but not now."

With that he slammed the monk hard against his knee. The crack of bones breaking filled the barn. From the cross beams above them came the satisfied sound of an owl's hoot.

Brother Ellis tried to say something, but blood filled his lips and then he went limp.

Through the whole scene Emma had stood quietly against the wall. Her face was a mask of confusion.

"What are you? A demon?" she asked.

"Just a man," DuLane answered. "A man who has had to do things that you might not understand, because he was a man and had pledged himself and his honor."

She stepped closer, looking at his chest. The dark patch of blood had grown bigger. "We've got to get a doctor to stitch that together or you'll die."

"I hardly think that is what I need."

Emma held her hand out to him. DuLane took it, his fingers gently wrapping around her wrist.

It was the sweetest wine that Lancelot had tasted in eight centuries.

Author's Note:

Depending on whether you were listening to their enemies or their supporters, the Knights Templar were either devil-worshiping heretics or good Christian warriors. It occurred to me that an immortal Lancelot, who was a religious man, might have sought them out. In their company, he could both serve his god and become the warrior he was born to be.

When the French king suppressed the Templars, the final

fate of ten Templars was reserved to the Pope. Nine of them were leaders of the order. The tenth, Oliver de Penne, was listed only as a member of the Templars. The fates of the other nine are well-documented, but de Penne's is unknown, along with why he was included on the list.

Bradley H. Sinor, who wrote "Oaths," has seen his work appear in the *Merovingen Nights* anthologies and other places. He lives in Oklahoma with his wife Sue and three strange cats.

THE BLOOD OF THE LAMB
by Lillian Stewart Carl

The creak of the cloister gate broke the morning hush. With a harsh cry and a flutter of wings a raven shot from the holly hedge beside the wall and disappeared into the sky.

Mother Catherine stepped outside the enclosure. Sunlight blazed from the surface of the snow, but there was no warmth in it. Her lips, still moist from the sacred wine, were touched by frost. The convent's store of wine might taste less of grape than of vinegar, but the symbolic blood of Christ was always sweet, and it wasn't the flavor of the wine that thinned her mouth into an anxious line. "Father," she murmured into the stillness, "I'm not strong enough to deal with what is coming. I'm frightened. Help me."

Warily she eyed the huddled roofs of Somersbury, the bare branches of the trees, the snow-clad hills so pale they blended seamlessly with the robin's egg blue of the sky. Below that brittle arch the world was as black and white as her habit and veil, except for the scattered berries of the holly bush, like drops of blood on the snow.

Nothing moved except a cart and horse laboring silently down the muddy track toward the town. Smoke smeared the shapes of the thatched roofs and blunted the edges of the castle keep. No flag flew from the topmost turret. Lord Waynflete and his family had not returned from keeping the Feast of the Nativity at court. What nobleman wouldn't take the opportunity of cultivating the king's favor?

Catherine could hardly ask Waynflete for help. He knew better than to oppose the will of His Majesty the King, Henry, the eighth of that name. If so noble a figure as Thomas More could be brought to the block at Henry's whim, if he could shed two wives as easily as a snake sheds its skin, what hope was there for a minor peer such as Waynflete?

And what hope for the nuns of St. Edwitha's? The vicar general's commissioners might not come today. They might not come tomorrow. But they would come, and they would destroy Catherine's world.

The cold drained the blood from her cheeks. Her flesh seemed as stiff and hard as a stone effigy's. She tried to imagine spring, and failed.

But her flesh and blood meant little. It was the work, domestic tasks, tilling the soil, tending the sick, that was important. The *Opus Dei*, the work of God, the daily round of praise, meant everything. Although the work would soon be snatched away from her, today she still had it to do.

Catherine turned toward the frost-rimed arch of the gate, then stopped. Loud in the crisp cold silence she heard a rustling and a moaning intake of breath.

She spun back around. There, something moved in the hawthorn thicket beside the road. An animal, a wolf or wildcat, its fear of humanity overcome by its hunger.... No, it was a man, kneeling among the whiplike branches. His head hung forward, his shaggy dark hair concealing his features. The back of his neck was exposed as though to the headsman's ax.

Catherine hurried to his side, her habit and veil billowing behind her. "Let me help you." She leaned over, grasping his shoulders. Her crucifix swung away from her breast and brushed against his hair.

Beneath her hands his shoulders were thin but wiry. He pulled away from her, only to collapse into the snow.

She took his body in her arms and helped him rise to his feet. He tilted his face toward the radiance of the sun, cried out as though in pain, and quailed.

"You're ill," said Catherine. "Come with me."

He didn't reply. He didn't move. Catherine waited, counting the ragged wreaths of his breath.

His cloak, though threadbare, was of fine wool trimmed with fur, and his shabby doublet was well-cut. His features were lean, the bones of cheek, nose, and chin sharply defined. His skin was whiter than any noblewoman's, as pale as the snow, so that his large dark eyes seemed like win-

dows into night. The only color in his face, the only soft-
ness, was the pink and supple curve of his lips.

He must be a lord's son who'd wasted his inheritance
gambling and drinking. But he didn't smell of strong drink.
About him hung a warmth, a tang of coppery sweetness,
even though his hand in hers was cold as the grave.

"Come with me," she repeated.

His lashes fluttered over his eyes in silent acquiescence.
Slowly they walked, linked, toward the gate of the convent.

Sister Emily, the infirmarian, laid the stranger on a narrow bed close to the fireplace at the end of the ward and
went to fetch a bowl of soup for him. The long room
seemed close, its many stinks thickening the chill air. The
feeble glow of the fire barely warmed the hearth where
Catherine stood. Their new patient was out of place among
the others, those crumbs of humanity who coughed and
hawked and peered rheumy-eyed at the approach of death.

"I'm Mother Catherine," she said softly. "Can you
speak?"

His ashen features twitched, but his eyes did not open.
"Yes, Reverend Mother. As well as can be expected."

"What's your name?"

"Stephen."

"How appropriate, then, that today is the Feast of St.
Stephen, the first holy martyr."

One corner of his mouth indented itself. "Indeed."

His voice was cultured, and his manners belied his circumstances. "How do you come to Somersbury?" she
asked.

"A horse and cart. Until the carter discovered me in his
straw and cast me out."

"That's not quite what I meant."

"My home is in the east," he said. His long, graceful
fingers made a vague gesture and then dropped to the
pallet.

"Surrey?" she asked. "Kent?"

His mouth was still indented. He knew, Catherine suspected, what she was really asking, and he chose not to
answer.

Sister Emily returned with the soup. Catherine took it

from her, knelt beside the bed, and cradled Stephen's head so that his mane of hair filled her hand. His eyes opened suddenly, gazing up at her. She felt as though she were being questioned closely even though he said nothing.

"Drink this."' She set the rim of the bowl against his lips. He slitted them, took one drop of the thin bean and herb soup, and turned his head away. "No. I am hungry. I need flesh. Fresh meat." And he added faintly, "If you please, Reverend Mother."

Catherine laid his head back down. "I do please," she said. "But my resources are limited this time of year. I'll ask in the kitchen."

His eyes shut. His lips curved in an unmistakable smile but stayed closed, reminding Catherine of the serene smiles of the saints in the statues behind the altar. But Stephen's smile was not serene but sad. How odd that he would smile at his own grief.

Catherine returned the bowl to Sister Emily and walked away down the room. Eyes turned toward her, hands reached for her. For them she had to pretend to have strength she didn't feel.

The most difficult part of being a nun was that she owned nothing herself, so that she had nothing to give. And everything to lose.

Father, help me to find courage.

The smoke of the incense shimmered ghostlike in the rays of sunlight. Outside the brilliant beams the recesses of the church were dark. The black and white habits of the nuns gathered in their choir stalls rustled invisibly. The only color in the church was the red glow of the altar lamp. Even the delicate colors of the painted glass windows were bleached white by the sun.

Stephen's flesh, Catherine thought, looked as though it had been bleached white by the sun. He had quailed from the glare of light. There was something in the angles of his face and the darkness of his eyes that was not of good English soil. . . . But she had more important things to worry about than this mysterious stranger.

Her lips shaped the Latin words of the plain-chant, her voice soaring and quieting in its turn. When she had been a young girl, the choir had been full. Now only twenty nuns remained, many of them older than she was. She wondered again why she, of all the nuns, had been elected Mother Superior last fall upon the death of aged Mother Agnes. Poor Mother Agnes had been stricken at the news of the despoliation of the shrine of St. Thomas of Canterbury, the most important shrine in England. Its gold and jewels had filled many more cartloads than the minor gems taken from the shrine of St. Edwitha, but they had all reached the same destination, the treasuries of King Henry in the Tower of London.

Edwitha's shrine was now nothing but a scarred patch of stone behind the altar. The—the looters, Catherine named them—had torn apart the gilded casket, destroyed the bones within, smashed the stone throne to bits and carried everything away. Why? Because the veneration of relics and the making of pilgrimages were undesirable superstitious practices.

Undesirable to whom? To the king, who wanted to separate the English church from Rome. To Thomas Cromwell, the vicar general. *Not to us.*

But such looting was only the first step. Catherine visualized Cromwell's commissioners returning to Somersbury as they had returned to Lewes, Titchfield, Jervaulx. In what they called "voluntary surrender," Catherine would be stripped of the keys and the deeds. The men would collect the precious metals, the altar furnishing, the vestments, and the window glass. They would tear out the choir stalls with their intricate carved canopies, burning them to melt the lead ripped from the church's roof. The stone carvings of the rood screen would be broken to bits—the pelican in its piety, like Christ feeding its young with its own blood—the lamb, the redeemer of sins—the dove, the Holy Ghost—the eagle of St. John and the lion of St. Mark and the exquisitely smiling lips of Our Lady. . . .

The looters would take all the beautiful things prepared for the service of God and turn them to the service of the king. They would sell the farmlands and the very stones of the buildings. The ancient foundation of St. Edwitha's would be left a crow-haunted ruin.

And for us? The nuns would be turned out, perhaps with

a tiny pension, perhaps not. They could no longer célebrate the *Opus Dei*. Losing their own enclosed community, losing their usefulness, there would be no place for them in the world.

Voluntary surrender? Catherine thought bitterly. *I can't.*

"Domine Deus, Agnus Dei, Filius Patris, qui tollis peccata mundi, miserere nobis," she sang. And she wondered, could the Lamb of God who took away the sins of the world ever remove this stain from England's brow. *"Miserere nobis."*

Have mercy on me.

The hour of None was nearing when Càtherine found a few moments to return to the infirmary. Sister Emily was at the near end of the ward, tending to a feverish child, and greeted her Mother Superior with a distracted, *"Benedicite."*

"Deo gratias," Catherine returned, and continued on toward the fireplace.

The fire had burned down to embers. In their crimson glow the stone walls flushed pink. But Stephen was as pale and drawn as he had been earlier. Catherine wondered whether he was as young as she'd first thought. A stone carving left out in the rain and wind will slowly smooth itself, but a human face becomes more and more furrowed. And yet, while the lines in Stephen's face were etched deep, his skin was stretched tautly over the skull beneath.

As she pulled up a stool and sat down beside him, his eyes fluttered open. "Good evening, Reverend Mother," he whispered.

She held up the bowl she'd fetched from the kitchen. "I have meat for you."

"Thank you." He struggled to sit upright, and with Catherine's help managed to prop himself against the wall. She handed him the bowl and the knife and sat back, her hands folded in her lap.

Stephen speared a morsel of mutton and placed it between his lips. A quick grimace betrayed his distaste. With difficulty he chewed and swallowed.

"It's not particularly fresh," Catherine ventured.

"No," he agreed. "And overcooked. I'm grateful, nonetheless." He forced down a few more bites.

I have duties elsewhere, Catherine told herself. But here, in spite of the failing fire, the odd breath of warmth caressed her cheeks. So she sat, and watched Stephen eat, until at last he handed her the knife and bowl and sank down again onto the bed.

"Have you ever been to Canterbury?" she asked.

"Yes. Many years ago."

"Then you saw the shrine of St. Thomas before it was despoiled."

"I was never in the cathedral, just in the town."

"To go to Canterbury, but not to the shrine!"

Stephen's dark eyes turned toward her. They were no longer dull, but shone like polished marble in the light of the embers. His voice was stronger, smooth as a fine silk vestment. "The King plans to take it all, doesn't he?"

"Yes. He began by combining the depopulated monasteries, so that their resources could be put to better use. Then his eye turned to the vast lands owned by the greater abbeys. In truth, some of the abbots have become almost secular noblemen, forgetting their vows of poverty, deserving of reform."

"And the smaller houses, such as this?"

"We stand accused of 'manifest sin, vicious, carnal, and abominable living.' Or so reads the Act of Suppression, which declares monastic life to be little more than a vain and superstitious round of 'dumb ceremonies.' We're told we can live a better Christian life outside the cloisters...." She closed her lips on her rebellious voice and looked down into her lap.

"Some monasteries have grown lax," Stephen said. "I'm told that the rule of chastity is broken more often than that of poverty."

"Not here. Never here. For the sins of a few, we all suffer."

"That is the way of the world, Reverend Mother."

She looked up again, meeting his lustrous dark gaze. "But Our Lord took the sins of the many upon Himself. With his love he redeemed us all."

Stephen shrugged. She couldn't tell whether he was accepting or rejecting her words. For a man in his pitiable state he was remarkably well-spoken. "You've traveled widely, then."

"Yes. Very widely. And you?"

"No. I was left here as a small child. I know nothing but the Rule of St. Benedict."

"Then you're fortunate," Stephen said, "to be given the opportunity to expand your knowledge."

"But I don't want ..." She stopped. *Your will be done, Father, not mine.*

"What do you want?"

She stared at him, wondering if he was mocking her. But no, his expression was quite sober, and his eyes compelled an answer. "To sing the office. To work. To serve God now and in the life eternal."

Stephen's eyes dropped to her crucifix. "Well then, Reverend Mother," he said quietly, "are you sure eternal life is such a worthwhile goal?"

A charred log collapsed into glowing charcoal. Sparks showered over the hearth and onto Catherine's skirts. Briskly she brushed them away. Her hands were warm. She couldn't remember the last time her hands had been warm. But she could linger here no longer. "Tomorrow, if you've regained some strength, you may attend mass in the church."

One of his black brows arched upward. "I doubt if I'll be that strong."

"Then I'll visit you here. Good night."

He nodded. If he'd been standing, he would have bowed, with the grace of a prince dismissing a courtier.

Smiling—he was a bold one—Catherine walked from the infirmary across the cloister. She was in her own stall before she remembered to glance over her shoulder. The day was ended, and the king's commissioners had not come.

The new morning was just as bright as the morning before. Today Catherine stepped out of the gate at an earlier hour, in that quiet interval between the offices of Terce and Prime and the saying of the conventual mass. Today the shadows of tree and wall lay long across the snow, feebly, like sins purified by holy light.

A raven sat on a hawthorn bough and watched Catherine

with black beady eyes. Ravens, she reminded herself, were the symbol of God's providence.

The road was empty, but as she turned back toward the gate, she saw two figures standing close together at the corner of the wall. The woman wore the white veil of a novice, the man the cloak and doublet of a townsman. Shaking her head, Catherine pushed open the gate and passed through. Some of the younger women might be pleased to be released from their vows. They would find husbands. Not so an old woman like Catherine, in her fortieth year. She would never know what it was to stand in close conversation with a man, his mušky breath warm on her face. She was irrevocably the bride of Christ, whether safe within or cast out of the cloister.

She walked across the garth, looking with loving eyes at the arcade of the cloister walk and the spire of the church lifted in praise toward the face of heaven. The convent was under seige just as surely as though an army camped outside. The townsman outside the gate, the stranger Stephen—they were soldiers of a wide and threatening world.

The red light burned before the altar, proclaiming the constant presence of the Holy Spirit. The glass windows were pale and bright. Catherine took her place and turned her eyes toward the convent chaplain, old Brother Roger, as he intoned the Introit and the mass began.

From the Kyrie to the Gloria to the Sanctus, the familiar words comforted her. *"Hic est enim calix sanguinis mei, qui pro vobis in remissionem peccatorum."* The words were majestic, despite Roger's cracked and quavering voice. *This is the chalice of my blood, which shall be shed for you unto the forgiveness of sins . . . .* The mystery of the mass thrilled her. God moved in mysterious ways. He would provide. Her role was to love, and to trust, and to obey.

"Ite, misse est," Roger concluded, and Catherine returned heartened to her work. It wasn't until almost the hour of Vespers that she entered the infirmary and found Stephen sitting on his bed. His pale face was upturned, his eyes fixed on a slit of evening sky held in the aperture of a lancet window. "Good evening, Reverend Mother."

"If you're feeling stronger, I thought you might like to pay your respects at the church."

He hesitated, lashes lowered, and then smiled that same closed, sad smile. "Very well then, if you'll go with me."

She took his arm, raising him from the bed, and supported him into the evening. The sky, the snow, the shadows were all blue. The cold air itself took on substance like deep water. The interior of the church seemed warm by comparison, the odors of incense and mildew playing elusively through the dimness.

Despite his weakness, Stephen shrugged away Catherine's guiding hand and found his way up the darkened aisle sure-footed as a cat. But he would go no farther than the rood-screen, no farther than the villagers went when they attended Sunday mass. When he looked cautiously up at the great carved crucifix, the altar light reflected twin red glints in his eyes.

Catherine's quiet voice barely stirred the hush. "How did you come to Somersbury, a man of gentle birth hiding in the back of a cart?"

"It's winter. The hunting is poor." His eyes fell to her face, their becrimsoned depths both amused and wary.

"You have no home, no family?"

"On my travels I've found fortunes and lost them again, but no, I have no home and no family."

He still wasn't answering what she asked. "Where do you come from?"

"The city of Zara. Do you know of it? It's on the Adriatic Sea."

Catherine had seen the name in one of the books in the convent library. "Yes. It belonged to Hungary, but fell to Venice in the fourth Crusade."

"It was sacked in the fourth Crusade. By men who wore the cross emblazoned upon their tunics. Who murdered and looted under the sign of Christ, even though we of Zara were good Christian folk."

"That was a great evil," Catherine agreed. "But it happened over three hundred years ago."

"Did it? I remember it well. I was only a child then, but I saw it all. I suffered it all."

The silence rushed in Catherine's ears. "You are mad," she said at last.

For the first time Stephen smiled openly, and she

glimpsed the teeth white between his lips. "No, I'm afraid I'm not at all mad."

She stepped away from him. A chill touched her face—odd, how warm it was close to him—but he was—wrong. . . . "You're no longer a good Christian?"

"No," he replied. "Not even a bad one. In my bitterness after the sacking of Zara I turned to—well, let's say I followed the Crusaders' example of avarice and cruelty. And so I was excommunicated."

Catherine gasped. She'd never met anyone who'd been excluded from communion with the church and cast into outer darkness. Again she felt a chill, this time of horror. "You seek forgiveness, don't you?"

"I am beyond forgiveness, Reverend Mother. I died excommunicate, you see. And for my sins I rose again—rather like Christ, although I daresay the irony escapes you. I'm doomed to walk the earth seeking eternity, hungry—thirsty—like all dumb creatures clinging to life, however wretched."

She stared at him. He was no longer smiling, but still there was humor, black humor, sketched in the shadowed lines of his face. His eyes challenged her not only to listen but to believe.

The poor afflicted soul. Catherine extended her hand toward him. "I shall pray for you. To the Lamb of God, Son of the Father, who takes away the sins of the world. Prayer is all I have to give."

"Is it, then?" Stephen took her hand in his cold clasp. His forefinger touched the beating pulse in her wrist and traced the blue line of the blood vessel a handsbreadth up her arm. It was as though a snowflake gently touched her flesh and didn't melt.

He leaned closer, eyes glittering red, so that once again Catherine's nostrils were filled with his coppery sweet scent. And then, with a short laugh, a sound that was a almost a cry, Stephen dropped her hand. He turned away from the altar light and the painted windows and faced the darkness. "I've known many women, Reverend Mother, but never one like you. Utterly guileless, your blue eyes like the innocent depths of the sky."

"I have blue eyes? I didn't know, I've never seen my own face. . . ."

Something stirred in the shadows behind the choir, a quick scrape and scamper. Stephen's head went up. With his lean features and his mane of black hair he looked like a lion scenting prey.

Silently he took one step, then another, then swooped into the darkness. A squeak, and he rose holding a rat fastidiously between thumb and forefinger. Its head dangled, neck broken. Stephen eyed it resignedly. "I came to England in the last century, in the retinue of Margaret of Anjou. Good pickings there were then, during the wars between York and Lancaster. But now the king is the greatest scavenger of all, and you and I, in our different ways, are reduced to dining on such poor scraps as this. If you'll excuse me. My thirst is great, but some indignities I choose to suffer in private."

His uncertain steps diminished down the aisle. With a gleam of indigo light the door opened and shut.

Catherine realized she was holding her breath. When she exhaled, her breath made a shimmering cloud in the still air. She'd never before met a mad man who sounded quite so sane. His soul, his center, was horribly empty, and yet his hollow shell was burnished with nobility. . . .

He had gone to eat the rat's raw flesh, to drink its blood. Catherine's stomach shuddered. Here was a soul in extremity. She groped her way to her choir stall, sank to her knees, and lifted her rosary. The beads fell through her fingers like pellets of sleet. Her words stumbled one over the other—*Ave Maria plena gratia*—full of grace, grace. . . . her thoughts steadied.

God's will had brought the stranger Stephen to St. Edwitha's. Why? So Catherine, in the throes of her own weakness, could pray for him? So she could help him to find forgiveness, despite all? But how?

Stephen had been driven mad by his sins. God told her to hate the sin, but to love the sinner. Whether Stephen were actually excommunicate Catherine couldn't say. If so, surely he would have an aura not of warmth, but of evil.

No matter how cold the flesh, she thought suddenly, the

blood is warm. And that was what he smelled of, the coppery sweet scent of blood.

She sat back in her stall and turned her eyes toward the altar. Faint in the crimson light she saw the sculpted pelican, the lamb, the lion. Tormented soul that he was, Stephen was still one of God's creatures. And God desired not the death of the sinner, but rather that he might turn from his wickedness and live.

She could not drive the unclean spirits from his mind any more than she could redeem the sins of the many. But she might be fortunate enough to redeem the sins of the one, so he could in time find his way back to God.

She knew what she had to give. All that she had to give. Herself.

It was the day of the feast of the Holy Innocents. The sun rose between the hours of Prime and Terce and flooded the world with cold radiance. Catherine moved through her daily round of offices and work, a round broken only by her now customary look outside the gate. The world was still there, more immediate than ever. Waynflete's flag drooped above the castle keep, the frozen air too still to lift it.

Between the hours of None and Vespers the sun set, drawing with it the sharp contrast of black with white, leaving the world a crisp and silent blue. By the hour of Compline the sky was dotted with stars brighter than any gem looted from St. Edwitha's shrine.

Catherine walked quietly among the snoring, groaning bodies in the infirmary, shading her candle with her hand. The fire was a pile of ashes. Stephen lay on his bed watching her approach, his eyes a slitted gleam. "How was your poor scrap of a meal yesterday?" she asked.

"Wretched," he replied.

"Even if I were reduced to dining upon a rat," Catherine told him, "through the grace of God, I would find it a splendid repast. Come with me. Come and eat at the table which God, in his mercy, has prepared for you."

Stephen's sharply shadowed expression wavered between bafflement and suspicion.

"Come." Catherine help him to his feet and led him toward the door.

The candlelight was a tiny halo bobbing through the darkness. Her veil and habit rustled gently. Behind her Stephen's steps were hesitant but light, the steps of a hunter. Once inside her own cell, separate from the others, she shut the door with an almost inaudible thump and set the candle down. It filled the room with a thin, fine light.

Stephen hung back, his shoulders against the door, and averted his eyes when Catherine lifted the cord of the crucifix over her head and veil and hung it on the wall. "You're mocking me," he said.

"No. Look here." From her sleeve she produced a small but sharp knife. Setting its point against her wrist she said, "My body belongs to Christ, but my blood I'll share with one in need."

"You're indulging in theological hairsplitting," Stephen told her, but he took a step closer.

"I'm no theologian. I'm the obedient servant of God, loving the sinner as He directed."

Stephen took the knife and turned it thoughtfully in his hand. "And what do you expect from me in return?"

"That you will live."

"That seems a poor bargain. But, beggar that I am, I won't refuse it." He set the knife down. "No knives. There is a better way."

Catherine, curious, let him lift first the black veil, then the white under-veil, and set them aside. Gently he removed the fillet from her brow, the cap from her head, and the wimple that framed her face and enclosed her throat. Those, too, he folded and set aside. He released the top button of her habit and opened the fabric.

The candlelight quivered in the corner of Catherine's eye and gilded Stephen's dark hair. She was trembling as though with a fever. When Stephen eased her down onto her narrow bed, she did not resist.

Reverently he knelt beside her, like a supplicant at the altar rail. He cradled her head in his left hand. "You have red hair beneath your veil," he murmured, "like blood beneath the skin." His words became a smile, his supple pink lips parting and turning up, extending beyond pleasure to joy.

His teeth, Catherine saw, glistened long and white. The longest were his eyeteeth. Sharp and moist, they seemed almost to extend over his lip. *How odd,* she thought, but he was no Englishman, he'd said so himself.

She took his right hand between hers, in the same gesture of homage the other nuns had made to her upon her election. His hand was cold, but his breath on her throat was honeyed hot. For a long moment his lips against her flesh were also cold, ice-cold, but then they warmed, drawing her blood to the surface of her skin. The damp touch of his tongue and the delicate double prick of his teeth sent a strange and wonderful thrill through her body.

Whether this manner of eating was typical of the Hungarians she didn't know. There was so much she didn't know, so much she'd feared. This submission, then, was her atonement for her doubt and fear.

With the small contented sounds of a child at the breast, Stephen drank. Catherine stared toward the beams of the ceiling. The beams sprouted branches and grew leaves and beyond them opened the sun-drenched sky. She seemed to be borne upward, lifted over the walls of St. Edwitha's, and carried away beyond the familiar fields and hills of Somersbury. The earth shed its mantle of white, turning richer shades of brown, green, gold, and red than the finest vestment Catherine had ever embroidered. The sea lapped at the shore, and in its green-blue depths strange creatures cavorted, just as in the blue depths of the sky the birds flew. Catherine, weightless, spun in unity with all of creation. Creation itself—life, love, and joy—lay between her hands, her warm hands. Her entire body blushed with warmth, at one with the world she'd so dreaded and at one with the eternity she desired.

Her center was not and never would be empty. The altar light could extinguished, but not the Holy Spirit. No one, not the King nor any of his commissioners, could take away Catherine's faith. Could take away her love of God, and her obedience to His will.

With a shudder and a sigh Stephen withdrew. He took his hand from hers and wiped his lips with his fingertips, leaving a faint smear of carmine in their corners. His face was flushed. His eyes were so large and dark Catherine saw what must have been her own face reflected in them.

"I ..." Stephen began, and swallowed, and with a smile went on, huskily, "I have known for too long that vanity and vice were the ways of the world. But you, Catherine, in this narrow cell have shown me a new and wider world."

The room was so still Catherine heard her heart—or perhaps Stephen's heart—beating faintly in her ears. The air was filled with sweetness, as though all the herbs and flowers of the earth concentrated their nectars in her senses. *Glory,* she thought. *Glory be to God in the highest.*

The door opened and shut. Stephen was gone. Stephen, not a soldier of the outer world but its emissary. The poor mad soul of the world, which could be redeemed with love.

Catherine lay, her hands clasped on her breast, her eyes gazing not at the ceiling but beyond, into the face of mystery, until the bell rang for the office of Matins.

Quietly she rose, and quelled a brief shakiness in her limbs. Even as she broke the ice atop her water basin, she felt enveloped in warmth. She dabbed cool water on the two tiny wounds in her neck, and covered them neatly with the white cloth of the wimple. Surely she glowed in the dark as she found her way to the church, tongues of flame lapping her chin and illuminating her face.

Kneeling in her stall, she set her hands together and gave thanks for the grace of God, which passed all understanding.

Christopher, Lord Waynflete, was a hearty, bearded man. His presence filled the vast stone hall with its vaulted ceiling like some secular shadow of the Holy Spirit. He seated Catherine in an armchair and Sisters Agatha and Emily on low stools. He ordered servants to bring cups of warm spiced wine. Fire leaped on his great hearth, but the warmth flowing in Catherine's veins came not from her flesh but from the strength and courage in her heart.

"I think I know," said Waynflete, "just what you want of me."

"Do you, my lord?" Catherine returned. "Then tell me, please."

"When the day comes—and it will come soon—you want me to buy your farmlands and fishponds, so that the workers may find continued employment."

Catherine bowed slightly and sipped her wine. Its rich flavor seared her lips and tongue and glided silkily into her stomach. She wondered if that was a feeble echo of what Stephen had sensed. Had tasted.

"You want me," Waynflete continued, "to buy the church, to use as the parish church of Somersbury."

"Saving the choir stalls and the rood-screen, since their beauty is pleasing to the sight of God."

Waynflete grinned. The lacings on his doublet glinted gold in the firelight. "You know then, what is pleasing to the sight of God?"

"Yes," said Catherine.

He leaned back in his chair. "What else then, Reverend Mother, can I do for you and for God?"

"Not for me, my lord. Never for me." Catherine drank again. "I would like to purchase from you a cottage in the village, something small and poor, with a plot of land for a garden. Where I may live with those of my sisters who choose to keep the Rule. There's nothing in the Act of Suppression about people choosing to live and pray together, is there?"

"No, there isn't," said Waynflete. "But you said 'purchase,' Reverend Mother?"

"Yes. My sisters and I will teach your children to read and write. We'll teach your serving women the secrets of fine embroidery. We'll teach your physician the use of herbs and simples."

"How can I refuse such a bargain?" asked Waynflete, throwing his massive hands up in the air and tilting his head in a laugh.

"May the blessing of St. Thomas of Canterbury, whose feast day this is, be upon you." Catherine rose from the chair. "Now, if you'll excuse me ..."

"By his martyrdom, St. Thomas of Canterbury won his argument with *his* King Henry," Waynflete said. "But you won't win yours, Reverend Mother."

"Neither winning nor losing, my lord, is the issue. Thank you for your kindness." Followed by the other two nuns,

Catherine walked from the Hall, down the spiral stairs to the gate, and into the light of day.

An icy wind scoured the street, sending gusts of smoke swirling across the black-timbered and whitewashed fronts of the houses. Clouds scudded overhead, rendering the sky the same silvery gray as the earth. The groom Waynflete had sent to harness his wife's carriage looked pale and frostbitten. Sisters Emily and Agatha clasped their cloaks more tightly around them.

Catherine turned her face toward heaven. Waynflete was a good man. It was possible to be secular and good. It was possible to take the cloister into the world. "Thank you," she said to the groom, "but we'll walk back to St. Edwitha's. The carriage is too grand for such humble servants of God."

She led the way through the town and out the other side, returning the greetings of the few folk to be abroad on such a cold day. The snow crunched underfoot. Snowflakes danced down the wind, obscuring the shapes of wall and steeple atop their hill.

Catherine imagined the spring, daffodils nodding on the slopes of the meadow, boughs of cherry heavy with pink blossoms, lambs calling to their mothers. Doves would coo in the thatch of a cottage just as surely as in the eaves of a church. The bloodless cheek of nature would flush with warmth, *gloria in excelsis Deo.*

The curtain of snow blew away. Stephen came striding down the road, his dark hair rippling in the wind. He was a most unlikely answer to her prayer, Catherine thought, but then, who was she to question God's providence?

Stephen stopped when he saw the three nuns. Bowing more gracefully than Waynflete had, he said with a smile, "Thank you, Reverend Mother."

"You're welcome," said Catherine. "Peace be with you."

His smile was still sad, but his cheeks were rosy. He pulled the hood of his cloak close around his face, plunging it into shadow. With a flash of his dark eyes he was gone, leaping over the ditch and bounding through a snowy field like a newborn lamb rejoicing in its own strength. Catherine watched him until he was out of sight beyond the town. Perhaps he would find another worldly fortune. Perhaps he would in time find forgiveness. Some day when he, too, had learned the virtue of surrender.

"Mother," said Sister Emily, quietly.

Catherine turned. Another flurry of snowflakes shrouded the stone walls of the convent, then parted. Horsemen were dismounting outside the gate, well-dressed horsemen attended by men with tools and ox-drawn carts.

Some indignities might be suffered in public, but could be suffered nobly for all that. Catherine folded her hands and bent her head to the wind, so that her veil billowed like wings behind her. "We have guests. Let us show them hospitality."

She walked on, her firm tread leaving footprints in the snow.

Author's Note:

I don't know where I got the idea for "The Blood of the Lamb," in which Henry VIII meets St. Teresa of Avila meets Bela Lugosi, except to say that an episode of "Robin of Sherwood" started it off. It was the episode with the Kurosawa-style horsemen at the beginning, where Rula Lenska raises Satan in the basement of a convent....

The historical background of the story is true, right down to the quotes from King Henry's directives. The Crusaders did sack Zara. The sequence of feast days at the end of December are as named. And St. Teresa was having similar—if different—mystical experiences in Spain within a few years of the English Dissolution.

Isn't it good when a plot comes together?

I've never done a vampire story before. I've published several science fiction and fantasy short stories, four fantasy novels in a style I've named "gonzo mythology," and three contemporary novels which are part mystery, part romance, and part ghost story ladled over a historical background. I'm now doing a series of mysteries starring a psychic detective who works the murky byways of the art and antiquities trade. I've also begun a series of romantic suspense novels;

the first is the wicked tale of an eighteenth century Scottish soldier and the twentieth century scholar he seduces—or who seduces him, as the case may be.

Lillian Stewart Carl is married, has two adult sons, and lives in Texas.

THE DEVIL'S MARK
by P.N. Elrod

"She's a witch! Burn her!"

"What if she's *not* a witch?"

"Burn her anyway, it's cold!"

"Mr. Bainbridge! If you please!"

Belatedly realizing that his enthusiasm and dark humor were out of place—for the moment—Bainbridge got firm control of himself an presented his audience with a chagrined smile and a respectful bow. "Your pardon, gentle sirs, but when one is doing the Good Work, one may easily be carried away by the nobility of the task."

The audience—that is to say the men who made up the leadership of the town of Little Evesham-on-the-Wash—made forgiving noises. Lucky for him, that. There was a proper way of going about these things, but Bainbridge had allowed his mind to be distracted by his pending reward, and he'd gotten ahead of himself. The time would come for the people to indulge themselves in a good bit of fire and riot, but one had to build them up to it first, get them used to the idea.

Their mayor—or whatever he was in this rustic hellhole—Mr. Percy, cleared his throat. "Indeed, Mr. Bainbridge, but my question still stands: What if the female you have accused is *not* a witch?"

"Why then, she will suffer no harm, but," his gaze swept over the lot of them in such a manner as to indicate *he* understood his responsibilities perfectly well, "I know that once you are made acquainted with the evidence, you will not hesitate to deliver her to the cleansing flames and thus rid your beleaguered village of the devil's vile influence."

Little Evesham-on-the-Wash was no more beleaguered than any other place had been in the last few years since

King Charles and Parliament had gotten down to serious fighting. But each little hamlet Bainbridge had swept through when he began the lucrative work of witch-finding always thought its troubles to be unique to itself. He had but to ask if some oaf suffered mysterious fits or if farms were plagued by sickly livestock to start it all; there was always something wrong somewhere that he could seize upon as evidence of devilish doings. It had been an excellent day for him when he began to emulate the glorious work of the great Witch-Finder General, Matthew Hopkins.

The men conferred briefly, their voices low, but Bainbridge knew what they'd be thinking and discussing. Upon his arrival in town that winter's afternoon he'd made sure to get a few timid souls at the local tavern worked up about the dangers of witchcraft, and within hours they'd carried their worries straight to their leaders. Now those learned men in charge of a fearful flock would be afraid themselves. If they forbade Bainbridge's witch-finding, might that be taken to mean they were in fellowship with the devil as well? If, on the other hand, they hired him to dig out the evil, they'd only be short some trifling pounds from the town treasury and no harm done except to the witches, and what were a few old men and women more or less to them?

Bainbridge accurately read the reply in their faces when they turned back to him. Percy looked worried, almost morose, but some of the others had a gleam of expectation in their eyes. Certainly the news of all the witch hunts taking place in nearby towns had aroused their curiosity. Now it seemed they'd have the chance to see one at first hand. Soon would come the real work for him: the sorting of gossip as hidden jealousies surfaced, as old grievances were recalled, then the searching of houses, discovery, the triumph of good as the flames burned away the evil. Every town was bursting with such opportunities, and it was a dull man who could not turn them to his own profit. Bainbridge fully intended to give them their money's worth.

"Very well," said Percy with an air of resignation. "Have the accused brought before us."

Two strong young men standing by the council chamber's door obliged him. As they returned almost immediately

with their charge, the others seated judgelike at the long
table leaned forward with interest.

" " 'Swounds!" one of them muttered.

The soft exclamation was justified. No aged crone for
tonight's event—the sweet-faced young girl that stood before them had the figure of a temptress, with or without
the help of stays. For the present she was without, being
clad only in a plain chemise of very thin and revealing
weave. Her cap was gone as well, exposing an abundant
crown of dark hair that tumbled all over her shoulders and
down her back. The flesh of her partly bared arms and a
fair length of leg was a pleasing white and unblemished.

"Why, it's Gweneth Skye," said another man.

Bainbridge knew her name. He knew all about her, or
as much as he could pick up from the tavern gossips. The
spinster Skye made her way in the world tending sheep like
most of the others living here, but she lived *alone* in her
modest loft. Alone, except for a few cats. Bainbridge *loved*
cats, especially when combined with a solitary female. Usually the women he picked out for accusation were old, but
this one's youth and beauty would work in his favor just
as well, if not better. There was always a contingent of
respectable harpies—goodwives, that is to say—in any town
ready to think the worst of any well-favored, unattached,
and therefore threatening female. They'd nag their husbands into lighting the first fire. Once that milestone was
reached, the real frolic would begin.

Gweneth rubbed her arms as though cold and glanced at
the row of men gaping at her.

"See, but she's a bold and shameless wench," said Bainbridge, planting his favorite and most fruitful seed. "Given
the chance she'd gladly seduce any one of you goodly souls
to the service of her dark master, if she hasn't been doing
so already in the town." Oh, but that always gave them
something to think about. Once he'd introduced the idea
of her lustfully preying on their weak physical natures, the
men would have her tied to the stake quick as spit before
their wives could think to suspect them.

"It has yet to be proven that she is in league with the
devil, sir," Percy reminded him.

"Then I will tarry no longer." Bainbridge turned full

upon the girl, thrusting his face at her. "What is your name?" he roared.

She regarded him with calm eyes, showing not the slightest hint of alarm. "Gweneth Skye," she answered in a clear, church-cool voice. "What's yours?"

Bainbridge blinked. She should have at least flinched at such a vocal assault. "I am," he announced loudly so any villagers with ears pressed to the chamber door could hear without strain, "the Witch-Pricker Bainbridge."

She favored him with a bored smile. "Meaning you run about the countryside pricking witches when the fancy takes you? What do you do with all the brats that come of it?"

He rounded on the mayor and his men in time to see their sniggering reaction. That was bad. If he lost control of things at this early point, he never would see his twenty shillings per head fee.

"Are you very *good* at pricking, Mr. Bainbridge?" she inquired innocently.

"Honest sirs," he said keeping his gaze steadily on his restive audience to better regain his hold of them, "You have just heard for yourselves that this female not only has a lewd mind, lacks the natural womanly virtue of modesty, but she also holds absolutely no respect for authority."

Gweneth Skye gave an audible yawn.

"She's ever been modest enough, sir," said one of them, Cameron by name. "As you've taken away her clothes, it makes modesty near impossible."

"Ah, but there is a good reason for that, sir. The most infallible way to prove anyone is in the service of the devil is to find the mark of his filthy claw upon their body, so it was necessary to make the woman ready for just such a search. Since I have much experience at this, I will conduct my query here and now—with your permission, of course."

"With our permission, eh? How do *you* feel about it, Gweneth?"

That was unexpected. Bainbridge hadn't thought she'd have a friend here. Perhaps later, when the time was ripe for it, he could bring an accusation against this Cameron and remove his sympathetic influence. He was a handsome, well-set young bravo, though, and men like that always had friends. It would be a nimble trick, but just possible to play if Bainbridge worked things right. Once the panic had firm hold of them, the hunt took on a life and course of its own. When that happened, he'd leave this place with full pockets and another tale of success to add to his growing reputation.

"I suppose so," Gweneth replied with an indifferent shrug. "I've nothing to hide."

More laughter. Percy cast a sour glance at the others to quell it, then nodded. "Very well, permission is granted."

Bainbridge swung upon Gweneth and reached toward her, but she was too quick for him. Her chemise was off her shoulders and in a crumpled ring at her feet fast as lightning, inspiring a collective gasp from the men and a snarl of baffled annoyance from Bainbridge.

"So there, witch-pricker," she said feet apart and hands on her bare hips. "Are you content now?"

Guffaws and hooting now, but Bainbridge wasn't worried; he'd found what he needed. This smirking wench was headed straight for the flames. First she'd be given the opportunity to name others in her coven, and once that was out of the way then perhaps a jolly barrel roll to finish her off. Yes, pound a few knives between the staves so the sharp points are on the inside, shove her in, hammer the lid shut, then roll her merry-o down a nice, long hill, to burn barrel and all at the bottom. That was *fine* sport, never failed but to rouse up the young fellows of a town, to make them want more of the same. . . .

Percy cleared his throat. "Mr. Bainbridge? Does the girl bear the devil's mark?"

"She does, sir."

"Indeed? Are you ready to prove that to the rest of us?"

From his doublet, Bainbridge drew out a small, elongated box. "In a trice, sir, in a very small trice." He opened the box and plucked from it a slender silver object. "As everyone knows, witches cannot abide the touch of silver. Some even squeal at the very sight of it."

Gweneth gave no sign she was one of that number.

"But it is also well known that the part of the body branded with the devil's mark is wholly without feeling and may be deeply pierced without the witch giving the least cry of pain or bleeding so much as a single drop of blood."

Those gentlemen not still distracted by Gweneth's ample charms managed to nod sagely at this bit of information.

"You will see that when I pierce the devil's mark on the wench with this silver pin that she will neither give outcry nor will she bleed, providing unquestionable proof of her guilt."

"Let us see the mark first."

Gweneth, disdaining Bainbridge's touch, stepped forward and pointed out a small red patch on her left forearm. "If this is what all the bother is about, then have a close look, sirs. It's no devil's sign, but merely a strawberry blemish I've had since birth. 'Tis likely you've seen such before on others if not on your own selves."

"Do not try to deceive us with your foul master's lies!" cried Bainbridge, clamping one huge hand hard around her arm. Startled, she struggled a moment, then held still, glaring defiance at him. His fingers pinched tightly on her flesh, hard enough to cut off all blood and all feeling. After a moment, when he judged her limb to be suitably numbed, he gently eased the silver pin into the spot.

Gweneth very unexpectedly said, "Ow!" and tore herself away. She gave Bainbridge a slap so resounding that it knocked his hat off, then pulled the pin from her arm and threw it on the floor. "You clod-pate bastard!" she snarled, trying to staunch the blood flow.

"It would seem," said Percy, raising his voice to be heard over the robust amusement of his fellows, "that she is not a witch after all, sir."

Bainbridge hadn't quite recovered from the blow—his ears were still ringing—but he wasn't about to give up yet. "She *is* a witch, and puts on a false show to trick you. 'Twas the silver pin that—"

"The false show I believe, sir, is what you are doing. You come into our town, get everyone all frothed up—which is very bad for the liver—about witch-hunting, repeatedly insist you won't take money until you smell out a witch, but as soon as may be, you do manage to accuse someone: an obviously innocent woman."

"Not innocent, I say! But mayhap *you* are bewitched by her, sir. She is a comely wench, after all."

Percy made no reaction to this accusation. Odd. Usually when Bainbridge called *that* one out, the respectable element would go either huffy or fearful, vigorously deny everything, and hurry the proceedings along their normal path, meaning Bainbridge could get on with the business, take his earnings, and leave.

"Oh, bumfay and nonsense," said Cameron impatiently. "Come on, Percy, we'll have to do something about him. Can't hang about all night with this."

"I suppose not," Percy said with a sigh. "Well, Mr. Bainbridge, we of Little Evesham-on-the-Wash do judge that the accused, Gweneth Skye, is not a witch and may go free. Your services are no longer welcome here; you may leave as soon as you will."

Bainbridge saw his fee slipping away faster than an oiled snake. "But you cannot make such a judgement!"

"Why not? It's our town."

"Aye, but there're others who'll not be so easy to deny the presence of the devil in their midst. Word will get out of your laxness in seeking out and punishing heresy—"

"Perhaps it would be best for you to just—"

"If I have to go to the Witch-Finder General himself, I shall. There *is* evil in this place, and if you're not going to purge it, then he will!"

"There's no reasoning with his sort, Percy, and you know it," said Cameron. "Things have gone too far already."

Percy, rather mournful of countenance, looked at the others. "Are the rest of you in agreement?"

They all nodded, including, surprisingly, Gweneth. She'd not bothered to pull her chemise back on, but for all her base nakedness she didn't look or act in the leastwise vulnerable or shamed.

"One last chance to forget about all this and go on your way, Mr. Bainbridge," said Percy, in a tone of appeal.

"Oh, aye, but I'll be going straight to the Witch-Finder Gen—"

"Yes, yes. Well, you can't say I didn't try." He looked up to the men acting as guards by the door. "Call in the others."

Bainbridge suddenly found himself close surrounded by several of the townspeople. Closest of all, to his shock, was Gweneth, who regarded him with a strange hot gleam in her remarkable eyes.

"I'll go first if you please, Mr. Percy," she said.

"Seeing what he did to your arm, it's only fair."

Bainbridge's world went all soft as her gaze locked onto his. He heard her clear melodious voice speaking right into his mind, telling him all kinds of interesting things, strange things, imparting a feeling of absolute contentment and safety such as he'd never known in all his hard life. She opened the top of his doublet, undid the ties of the shirt beneath, pushed back the small collar. It was wanton, utterly improper, and in front of all these people terribly embarrassing, but he held still for her, so lost in her words of comfort that the presence of the others did not matter at all.

Then her sweet face went out of view as she leaned close. He felt a profound leap of pleasure in his privy parts as her mouth fastened on his throat. The people behind him held him fast, but he wasn't about to move, not even when her long corner teeth began to grind away at his flesh. He groaned with delight as she broke his skin and started to suck.

" 'Ow is 'e, Gwen?" someone inquired a few moments later.

"Tolerable," she replied, lifting away. The whites of her eyes were gone, flushed blood-red now. "Likes his ale too well for me. Someone else want a turn?"

"Ale, eh? No, thank you, my girl. Used to love the stuff, but now ..."

"I'll have a try," said Cameron, coming forward.

Gweneth stepped aside for him. To his shame, Bainbridge again offered no struggle as that handsome young man now suckled at the wound she'd made. It was shameful to him because the bliss that seized him was just the same, just as intense, so much so that he soon altogether forgot himself and gave over to the joyance again, moaning.

One by one the others gathered around him had their turn until Bainbridge could no longer stand by himself, and with all kind consideration from his hosts, he was gently carried to the council table and stretched upon it. The room tilted—no, *he* was tilted. Two of them had lifted the end of the table by his feet. A feeble rush of blood went to his head.

"That's better," said Percy, after he'd finished taking his own drink. He did not appear to be quite so morose as before. Blinking hard, Bainbridge could just see them all looking down at him like toothy, red-eyed angels at the Last Judgment and finally began to understand the true nature of his mistake.

"If this goes on much longer it's going to get noticed," Percy remarked to Cameron. "*We're* going to get noticed."

"Then perhaps we should do something about this Witch-Finder General person. He's the one behind all the mischief."

"I agree with you, and I know we could. The question is *should* we?" Percy shook his head. "The last thing we want is to draw any sort of attention to ourselves."

"It might be worth the risk. If he's made to retire from the field, then perhaps all this nonsense will stop, and things will settle down again."

"I wouldn't care to wager on that. You know how people are once they start killing." There was an object in Percy's hands now. It was a sturdy length of wood, charred and fashioned into a sharp point at one end. He idly turned it over and over, his mind obviously on other things. When he noticed Bainbridge staring at it, he whisked it from sight with an apologetic smile. "Best if we let things happen as they should in the rest of the world and just pay mind to our own matters."

"You're usually right about that, but," Cameron gestured at Bainbridge, who was finding it hard to keep his eyes open, "this poor clot's our third one this year. I think we should make an exception about the Witch-Finder General. He stirs people up and in the wrong way."

"Agreed, but we'll have to be very careful about it if we do anything. Danger of discovery and all that, you know."

"I know." Cameron licked a stray blood drop from his very red lips. "But mind you, danger of discovery aside, they are *such* a tasty lot!"

Author's Note:

Matthew Hopkins of England, the Witch-Finder General, as he liked to call himself, was directly responsible for the torture and deaths of hundreds of men and women in the years 1644-1646. He had many imitators who brought suffering and death to thousands more. There is a story he was finally discovered to be a witch himself when forced to submit to his own swimming test and floated before finally drowning. However, one of his associates recorded that he died untroubled of conscience in his bed in the summer of 1647 "after a long sickness of Consumption." (Sic) Most scholars of folklore understand that the disease of consumption (tuberculosis) was often seen in past eras as evidence of a vampire preying upon the sufferer.

P.N. Elrod is the author of eleven books featuring vampires as the main characters, including *The Vampire Files* detective series and the eighteenth-century adventures of Jonathan Barrett. She is hard at work on her next line of toothy titles.

BLOODTHIRSTY TYRANTS
by Catt Kingsgrave-Ernstein

She writhed beneath him, hair flung wild in her passion, her nails digging into the chill flesh of his shoulders. She cried something he couldn't understand, craning back and up to meet him—a bow drawn taut, the winged victory in living flesh—in living ecstacy. Blood pounded in his ears to give him warning; it would not be long. The white of her throat beckoned him as the carnal thunder stalked nearer ... he wanted it.

She thrashed again, her raven curls dashing across the linens, and he struck; lightning crashed through him the instant he felt her flesh between his jaws.

Then she shrieked—a thin and distant sound until she wrapped both hands in his hair and yanked. He released his mouthful with a yelp of his own, then collapsed into the bed as she scrambled out from under him. Another breeze from the sunlit window shivered across his back with the distant, bitter smell of black smoke and sulfur.

Naked at her vanity, Julia was weeping.

"Oh, Dolfo, you promised! You promised you wouldn't anymore!"

Rudolph Schaussburgh sighed and rolled over to look. "Oh, it does no harm, my Sparrow—"

"No harm?" She rounded in her chair and pulled her hair aside. Already the flesh of her shoulder was crimson but for the white mark of his teeth, and purpling next to that. A couple more seconds, he supposed, and he might have broken through that fine skin of hers to the sweetness he imagined underneath. Wouldn't that have been something?

"You know, my Sparrow, you might find you liked it if

you fought back. *I* wouldn't weep over a bite now and then."

She sniffed. "I am not going to bite you, beastly Hun savage! I am a Contessa, not a bitch!"

Rudolph considered the raw places on his shoulders and thought of a cat instead.

Lucky for him, it seemed the young mistress Verrazano missed the half smile that crossed her paramour's face. She was preoccupied with her mirror. "I will have to wear my cousin's ugly English dresses with the high collars to hide this mark!"

Rudolph yawned. "A tragedy indeed, to cover that bosom."

"—And if my father sees this mark he will throw me out into the street! He will sell me to a nunnery in Sicily!" She looked back to him, her dark eyes lit with tears. "And he will beat you until your back is bleeding, and you will never lose *those* marks!"

Well, perhaps there is trouble, he thought, rolling out of her bed and reaching for his shirt. "Come now, my pretty Sparrow, there will be no beatings," he soothed. "Your father is away with the Archduke. You will have no mark when he sees you next." Rudolph lay a hand on her shoulder—the one he hadn't bitten—and smiled down at her.

Julia sniffed and glared. "You think that I am stupid! You think that I do not hear the cannons, or see the fires in the *Innere Stadt*?" She pushed his hand away and stood, a blush of anger in her cheeks and breasts. "I know that Bonaparte's army has come here! I know it!"

He shrugged and picked up his pants. "Then your father will have better things to think about." He heard her sharp intake of breath, the way it hissed through the clench of her teeth. He thought of a cat again and smiled, careful that she did not see.

"Dog." She spat, "Your brother is in the army, too—Whatever army Austria may have left with the French so close to Vienna! Do you not even care that he may be dead—he, and my father, and the Archduke as well?! Dog! Dog-pig!"

He buttoned his trousers and straightened. "The word you want is *schweinhund*, my Sparrow, meaning pig-dog.

And it only works on Germans." He reached for his boots and claimed her vanity chair to pull them on.

"Pig-dog, dog-pig, *pezzo di madre*, you are still a beast and I will have my brother beat you!"

To his delight, she was approaching a high temper, and being Italian, her tempers were something to see. He expected breakage any moment.

"Oh, Julia, why disturb the man? Mph. I am sure the ladies of the *Graben* district have far more to interest him than I. Push on the sole, would you, my dear?"

"Push it yourself! He would kill you if I wanted him to! Anatole fought with the nephew of the Duke of Hambourgh and killed *him*!"

"Mph-hm. Of course he did, Sparrow, no need to shout it. Everyone knows how Hambourgh's nephew drank—how could Anatole help but win? There." He examined his booted foot from one angle, then another, all the while watching the nude beauty from the corner of his eye. Her fists hooked, then closed, then opened again.

"You call my brother a coward?" Her voice was low, and he smiled at the sound of it.

"Of course not, my love." He beamed at her, reaching for his waistcoat. "It takes great courage to fight a man so drunk he cannot walk—especially when that man is also three times your weight. Anatole could have been crushed if Jakob had fallen on him. Tsk—Tsk. I should not have had the courage for it."

That did it. First came the bedclothes, too bulky to fly well, then her shoes, and a vase. *Smash!* Rudolph crowed inwardly as porcelain met Julia's vanity mirror with devastating results. Glass flew everywhere and he ducked away, laughing as he grabbed the rest of his clothes.

He flailed his coat like a duelist, like a matador, deflecting the makeshift missiles as fast as Julia threw them, enjoying the adventure as she cursed him in Italian.

She stopped for breath—or perhaps to find more ammunition—and he contrived to look meek. "Was it something I said, Sparrow?"

"Get *out* of my house!" She pointed at the door. "Get out or I will have Guisseppe beat you with the carriage whip!"

"Guisseppe? The *butler*?" He grinned and headed in that direction. "A moment ago, I was to be beaten by your father, then your brother. If it is only the butler, then I know you are not truly cross with me."

She snatched up a brush from the shard-littered vanity and flung it with another volley of Italian, but Rudolph was on the other side of the door when it hit.

He poked his head into Julia's room once more, meeting her feral eyes with a grin. "*Auf wiedersehen*, my Sparrow. I will come again on Thursday." Then he ducked back out just as she hefted an expensive-looking perfume bottle.

Rudolph was halfway down the stairs and still chuckling when Julia di Verrazano's throaty voice shook the rafters.

"GUISSEPPE!!"

He wondered if she would remember to put clothes on before the butler arrived.

Still laughing inwardly, the youngest son of Victor Schaussburgh saw himself out into the velvet gold of a fine Viennese evening. Rudolph indulged in a moment's self-appreciation, pausing on the doorstep to stretch and smell the cleansing breeze that rushed down the *Landstrasse*. The early evening was chill with the breath of the steppes, even in May.

Dog, his Italian mistress had called him—and not for the first time. Well, it was a fitting image, and it troubled him none to admit it. Even the crest of his father's banner (a relic from when the Schaussburghs had held land as well as titles) had a black hunting hound displayed on it in tattered thread. To Rudolph it had looked more like an alley cur than a courser, but after his brother had beaten him for saying so once, he was careful never to let his opinion show again.

Rudolph shrugged on his coat and started down the street. Personally the image of the alley dog appealed to him; the survivor to whom pride and honor meant nothing more than whether the prize was worth the fight. The one who could make a meal of the noble lapdogs with no reserve—not even notice that they were his own kind. Remorseless.

He often thought that he should like to be truly remorseless, but he had too much a mind for the preservation of his skin—brawling did not suit him. Actually, it was more that broken bones did not suit him, since (as his elder brother had found out early) Rudolph wasn't very good at fighting.

Just not big enough, I suppose. He grimaced inwardly, noticing too late that the turn of thought had destroyed his good mood. *Look here, though—Theo is even at this moment being marched here and there in the face of those French cannons. Look where all his fine fighting has gotten him! I hope he does not even see the man who kills him, and there for all his fine honor and manliness!* Rudolph always reasoned that if he had to put up with a bad mood, it helped to be spiteful while he was at it.

However, all such higher feelings gave way the instant he heard the gate behind him crash open. Rudolph didn't even turn—he had a fair idea that Guisseppe would be there, whip in hand. He lit out for the nearest corner and put it between himself and that supposed whip. Shouts from behind as he ran down the alley made him grimace; that loud baritone could be none other than Anatole, whom he'd *thought* out of the house. Damn! They *were* following, too!

He turned another corner, ducking between a sagging eave and a broken wagon. Evading the butler was one thing—he was too old to run far. But Anatole . . . While it was all very well to tease Julia when they were alone, her brother's sword could do him considerably more damage than a lobbed shoe!

Rudolph made two more turns, each one to a street a little dirtier than the one he'd left. Moments later, he heard a crash (presumably the wagon) and several men cursing. He grinned and slowed a little, but snaked three more turns between himself and the commotion for prudence sake, before he stopped running.

By which time, unaccustomed as he was to such upright exercise, Rudolph had hardly the breath to laugh as he would have liked. There again was proof of the wages of brute force—it hadn't impressed the wagon much. Then again, recalling the crash, it seemed likely that they had made quite an impression on it after all.

The sky was fire above, but in the huddle of buildings,

it was getting too dark to clearly see the street. He stopped. The laughter was too much—it made his head swim. Good thing for him there was a wall for his shoulder; he had a feeling neither his coat nor his breeches would survive the muck his boots were mired in. Falling over was simply *not* an option.

It was fully dark by the time his breath had returned . . . time enough for Rudolph to examine his surroundings and find them totally alien. He hadn't a clue where he was, and there didn't seem to be anyone setting lamps outdoors to light the streets. Or torches even. A tickle of apprehension began at the base of Rudolph's neck, and he greeted it sternly. *No, it is just an alley—like any other to a street dog like you. You are as at home here as in Comte Verrazano's parlor, stealing luncheon.*

Still, he would have preferred it if there had been more light . . . or if he'd brought a sword with him.

Being lost, it didn't take him long to realize that he was being watched. Dressed as he was in this crumbling slum, it was only natural; But it soon became obvious that he was being followed as well.

Swallowing, he dropped a hand to his purse, amazed at how heavy it felt when it had been so light when he'd left home this morning. Still, he closed his fingers tightly around it as a pair of broad, dark figures separated from the shadows to block his way.

Anatole! was his first panicked thought, then the smell reached him—sour sweat and onions, and something bitter and burned. A glance behind showed that way blocked as well, by three more men each with a brace of pistols.

Throat suddenly rasping dry, Rudolph pulled the purse loose from his belt and held it out. "Here, it is all I have."

His answer was a chorus of ugly laughter. Grinning, the smaller of the two mountains in front stepped forward to take the bag, grinning. "No it isn't, *Mein Herr*. Not by far."

The look of the man sent a chill through Rudolph's spine before the meaning of his words even registered: One eye sunken back without even the grace of a patch to hide it, scar writhing above and beneath. His hair was almost as disgusting as his clothes and both better than his teeth. Here was a man of decided class—low.

No it isn't, Mein Herr. Not by far? The words returned and Rudolph felt his blood go cold. But they wouldn't kill him—they couldn't kill him, vicious, evil thugs though they were. He would just explain, surely they would see. . . . "You, you have my money—" he began, tone higher than his usual tenor.

"Your coat is fine brocade, *Mein Herr*," came a voice behind him, "I see a month's rent for more than one family in each of those buttons."

"Silver is valuable here, *Mein Herr*—*we* use it for money, not buckles for boots." Another sneered.

They meant to steal his clothes?! Rudolph imagined explaining the loss to his mother, with the servants all snickering at the door . . . and then he would have to tell Victor. The shame . . . he couldn't. *They* couldn't, they simply couldn't!

"N-now see here, what will I wear?"

"You'll wear what any soldier wears, my lad." A new voice came from behind, accent more refined, though a trifle out of fashion in its style. The men there stepped aside to let the speaker through. He was a tall man, old by the color of his hair, but wearing about him an officer's heavily stitched and braided coat along with the air of a cold and merciless master. "You'll wear your shirt and breeches, and you'll not care any more than your enemy does."

"B-but *I* am not a soldier." Rudolph could not keep the nervous laugh from his voice.

"That you're not, *Fraulein*." The one-eyed man nudged him hard in the ribs. The others laughed until the old man called them to order.

"Hans, Deitrich, stop at once—there is no time. We still need three more for the last of the guns. Go, and be quick, or the French will have us, and that damned Corsican will sleep in Schönbrunn Palace tonight!"

The two thugs glanced at each other, then bowed. "Yes, Admiral,"

The roar of an explosion, so close it rattled dust from the tottering eaves above, drowned out their words. Rudolph yelped and covered his head, not certain he hadn't been shot.

"Go! Go at once!" the admiral was shouting. "The French must be moving again and they won't be long in returning that fire! And you, sir, off with that coat or I'll have these men help you with it!"

Rudolph tried to duck away, but one of the three remaining men circled to cut off his only escape. "B-but *Herr* Admiral, I am Victor Schaussburgh's son, my brother is with the Archduke's army—"

"Well you're with my army now." The old man scowled, his eyes smoldering. "And you are out of uniform. Take off that coat."

One of the men grabbed Rudolph's shoulder, grip heavier than Theo's had ever been. "But, *Mein Herr*, you don't understand—" he wailed, ready to beg if necessary.

The admiral snarled, his teeth a flash of wolfish white as he snatched one of his follower's pistols. "No, *you* do not understand! Allow me to explain!"

Rudolph froze, breath seized tight in his throat as the barrel centered inches from his eye. A small and distant part of his mind giggled hysterically even as his best coat tore away under his captor's ungentle ministrations. *It is bigger than my head, that gun! How can he hold it so high?*

The admiral glared, eyes bright, almost glowing in the dark as another explosion shook the night. "The French have come to Vienna, over top of all the Archduke's brave and noble army. So if Vienna is not to fall, then I must fight for it, even if I must beat an army out of the cowardly and the poor that are left here in his absence!"

Rudolph swallowed carefully and took a breath. "I—I am not a coward . . . s-sir. But I cannot fight. Well. I know a strong man who can, though; he is Anatole di Verrazano, and—"

The admiral gave him a look of unbridled disgust, then turned and strode away, shouting to the three men that still surrounded Rudolph. "Bring him. If he's too much a fool for anything else, we can always put him on the ram rods."

"Aye, *Mein Herr*!" the one behind him called, grabbing Rudolph's shoulder and hauling him forward. "Well then, Shlopsburgh's son, I am Colonel Brunden, these are Sergeants Werstadt and Dobling of the admiral's third cannon crew. Do you want a name, or shall we just call you Rod Boy?"

"No, I *don't* want a name, you ass! I want you to let me go!" Now that the admiral's dark figure was out of sight, thoughts of his ill treatment—not to mention his coat— were returning. Rudolph was in no mood for chumminess, especially with these ruffians.

With a loud guffaw, the so-called colonel landed a slap between his shoulders that nearly sent Rudolph sprawling into the filthy streets. "So! Rod Boy it is, then!"

One of the sergeants, Werstadt, he thought, laughed and shoved Rudolph forward again as they all broke into a jog. "Rich bastard. I'll enjoy this, Otto, and no mistake! Rod Boy— Hah! Twig Boy's closer to the truth!"

"My name is Rudolph!" He protested between jolting steps, though none of the three seemed to care.

"Aye, Rod Boy. As he said," Werstadt crowed.

They rounded a corner, and at last there was light—a lot of it, right in front of them. Rudolph stopped, blinking to get his bearings.

It was a bonfire, casting orange blazes up the height of the wall. The city wall. It was littered with rickety looking winches, ladders, tangles of rope, and dancing with shadows. The mysterious admiral had disappeared without trace.

Another explosion roared from the top of the wall as Rudolph stared. A shower of sparks lit up a cannon as it rolled back against the abutment. Dark forms swarmed over it immediately.

Rudolph thought seriously about running and looked around for possible routes of escape.

"Too late for that now, Rod Boy." The colonel shouted, grabbing a fistful of his shirt and dragging him toward one of the ladders. "It's to the buckets with you, and mind you don't think of slipping away. This is the admiral's army, and we shoot deserters here!" He twisted Rudolph's collar a bit tighter, all but lifting him onto the ladder. "I'll be watching you, Rod Boy. Now climb!"

"Worm the bore!" The colonel bellowed as soon as the gun lumbered to a stop. "Move it, Rod Boy!"

Rudolph moved, guessing which of the wretched tools he was supposed to jam down the cannon's muzzle next. *Oh, yes, the one with the hooks on it. Imagine it's that awful sergeant's belly, and* twist!

· "Wet sponge!" Rudolph did not so much hear the colonel's shout as remember that he *would* be shouting about now. The report of the old gun had stolen his hearing with the first of its volleys, and the other three of its fellows were no more merciful; each crew fired in time for a few seconds' silence before its neighbor spoke up. The rhythm had altered but little in his evening of hell.

Rudolph pulled out the worm and dropped it with the smoldering remains of the powder bag. Then he slopped the sponge rod out of its bucket and down the smoke-filled barrel, too tired even to choke on the cloud of sulfurous steam that erupted.

In the three hours he had spent under durance vile, he had gone from wishing he could slip away, through wishing the so-called officers around him would die memorably and soon, to wishing that he himself might bring this about. Not long after that, he was wishing he were anywhere else in the world; dead even began to seem like an improvement.

However, as his wishes seemed to be having no effect on the situation around him, Rudolph finally resigned himself to wishing for simpler things; a glass of water, for instance, or a chance to sit down and cry for an hour or two. Or a foot rub. Gretchen gave such amazing foot rubs. . . .

"Dry sponge!" This was his cue to rest a moment. He shoved home the padded rod, pulled it back out, then stepped out of the way, leaning on the wall as the other two men moved to load the powder and ball.

Even in full dark and through a screen of smoke and dust, it was not hard to see the French lines 500 yards away, with muzzle flashes lighting the entirety. They were just field guns, the Viennese told each other, no match in range for the admiral's ship guns. Napoleon could only move when Vienna stopped firing.

Rudolph privately thought it odd, in that case, that the *Innere Stadt* had been so mysteriously demolished over the past day or two. Still, he had to admit, the French artillery seemed never quite to reach the walls or the gunners thereon. He also had to admit that he preferred it that way.

"Ram home the charge!" The colonel was shouting again.

Rudolph groaned and turned to find the tool just as one of the other cannons went off. Out of sequence. *Far* out of sequence.

Every eye turned to that gun. Rudolph was just quick enough to see what remained of that crew's ram-rodder fly off the wall in a sticky-looking flourish that made him glad it was too dark to see colors. The rest of the crew stayed where they had fallen, staring in shock at the betraying cannon. The match-man of the next crew down began retching, and Rudolph looked away.

Forgot the wet sponge ... caught an ember in the charge and boom ...: match-man's fault. For all the assignment of blame might be true, it was not the match-man who had paid for the blunder. Rudolph looked down at the ram rod in his own hands. They seemed to be shaking. *Should have done the wet sponge anyway. Fool probably deserved to die.* Somehow his habitual spite wasn't fortifying him as it usually did. Rudolph was just turning around to suggest that they all go home when he found the colonel's pistol in his face.

"I said ram home that charge!" Rudolph read the command from his lips and ducked back to the front of his own crew's gun. The pistol tracked him as he raised his ram rod to the bore and stopped.

Had *he* wet sponged the bore? He couldn't remember. Rudolph bit his lip and tried to see past the charge, looking for any kind of spark. It occurred to him then that he had his face inches from the muzzle of a cannon and he stumbled away, dropping the rod.

Sergeant Dobling grabbed him before he'd gone two steps and cuffed his ear. That distant part of Rudolph's mind was almost disappointed that it didn't ring.

"Ram the charge, worm-shit!" The man screamed, spittle flying. He shoved Rudolph back to the front of the gun, where he almost tripped on the rod. Bending to pick it up, his gaze fell on the next crew over, where the loader was hefting a lopsided ball into the mouth of his gun.

This image tickled in the back of Rudolph's mind, though it was not as alarming as the colonel's pistol was. Or come to that, as alarming as the thought of the missile his ram rod would become if there were any live fire in the gun when he drove it home. Holding it with his fingers upward, Rudolph stood to one side and fumbled the rod into the gun.

There. He thought, yanking the rod out and stepping back, *Not as tight as before, but it's only going to come back out anyway, so no one will care!*

Luckily, no one did care enough to make him do it again. "Roll it up!" The colonel bellowed, and Rudolph reached for his rope to haul the gun up to its firing port. That was when the meaning of his tickle manifested with a roar.

The next cannon down exploded into a rain of flying ash and metal, razoring through everything flesh, stone or wood around it. One chunk shattered the axle of the rickety ox-cart that their own gun was mounted on, and *it* began to go down—toward Rudolph.

Screaming, he hurled himself backward out of that iron shadow, fetching up against the abutment as the wagon splintered and dropped the loaded cannon onto the old city wall. It rolled as if preordained, into the match-man's torch. Which was still in the match-man's hand. Which was not, however, on the match-man.

Rudolph began to giggle as the night exploded once more around him.

Well then, she told herself, *I am satisfied.* The wine, un-drunk in her glass, had chilled from her handling it. Not quite appropriate for a street man's cheap and sour red, but a trick she enjoyed anyway.

Chloris mimed a sip when the soldier who had bought her the wine leered at her. He was little more than a thug in a uniform who probably thought that he was buying a bedmate for the price of the wine, but that was the rub; he was buying, not trying to rape. That fact, and an evening full of encounters and observations just like it, served to convince her that things would be safe enough.

When Chloris had first realized that the conquering

French had come to Vienna, she had been ready to flee.
However unpleasant the prospect of such a move, it was
nothing to the thought of being caught in another sacked
and burning city: Rome had been bad enough.

The soldier turned away to babble something in French
to one of his passing comrades, and Chloris poured her too
cold wine into his cup. Nights of watching had changed
her mind.

She had measured their progress—careful and measured.
She had crept to their camps under cover of the guns that
senile old fool had hoisted up to the South wall, watched
them from the shadows there. Last night she had come to
the decision that the French, though still barbarians, were
not quite as battle maddened as the Picts had been.

Though still unsure, Chloris resolved upon a less drastic
plan. Immediately upon her awakening, she had set about
the task of watching the invaders as they took command
of the Habsburg's royal city—assessing them, their mood
and their conduct. Here speaking to one, there following
another. Officer and commoner and camp follower, she
watched them all.

Now most of her fears were put at ease, if not to rest;
The French did not seem likely to pillage and burn the city.
They were stealing provisions, and overflowing every inn
in the city, but it would be safe enough to stay.

The soldier beside her squeezed her breast by way of an
arm over her shoulders again, and this time, rather than
shrug it away, Chloris turned to stare at him. Then she let
the Darkness bloom in her eyes—clouding her sight with
the radiance of his soul-fire. His heart beat three times
bright, hers none at all. She smiled at his terror, and leaned
close to his ear as he sat, blinded still by the shadows she
carried in her eyes.

"You may forget, Frenchman, if you like. Or you may
follow me outside. . . . If you are not afraid of the dark."

He did not follow, and she smiled to herself as she left
the inn's light and embraced the night outside. *He has forgotten. Good. I thought he was wiser than he looked.* Chloris
turned and walked away—there was another inn she meant
to check, and one or two of her scholar friends with whom
she had promised to share her conclusion of the night. The

rattle of hooves sounded several streets away as she walked, a sound like fear in the night; but not, thank the Dark Goddess, like panic.

Rudolph's first realization upon awakening was that he was being dragged by his hands, and that it hurt. A lot. He groaned and tried to shake his head, the effect of which was even more painful.

From somewhere above him came a gasp. The dragging stopped, and Rudolph opened one eye to glare upside down at the old man who had hold of his arms. Who promptly shrieked and dropped him.

"Mein Gott!" The man shouted, stumbling away as Rudolph rolled to his side and groped at his battered skull, "The dead men awaken! Armageddon is upon us!" Then he ran away into the darkness before Rudolph could summon the breath to shout at him to be silent.

Darkness. Stars, though that could have been residuum of having his head dropped onto a brick. Pain—that was unmistakable, and cold, too ... but there was something else.

All in all, Rudolph was certain that the old man had been wrong: He hurt far too much to be dead. And he was cold too—the dead weren't supposed to mind the cold.

Rudolph began to consider getting up. That was when he noticed that his boots were gone. Sitting, he stared around himself in outrage. Not only his boots, but his waistcoat, his belt and even his stockings had been appropriated. There was nothing left in the street but rubble, brick, and scorched wood.

And a mule cart full of dead bodies. Rudolph considered throwing himself back to the ground in a flourish of misery, but thought better of it considering the state of that ground—or more precisely, the rocky litter upon it. He settled for folding his arms on his knees and then burying his head there.

As if it weren't enough that the soldier/brigands had taken all his money and his coat also, now the parasites had stripped him of everything else of value that he'd had and left him for dead in the street. Even the buttons from his sleeve-cuffs were gone, he noticed with a groan.

So now he hurt everywhere, including his bare feet, which would only get more abuse if he got up and tried to walk without his boots. *Perhaps I should just wait here to die.* he thought miserably, then shook himself.

Come on, Rudolph, use your head. There's a mule right over there. You won't have to walk home if you just go and get it.

That effort, however, proved to be fruitless in the extreme. The mule had as little liking for Rudolph as he did for it. The beast had only to lay back its ears and snap its yellow teeth at him once to convince him that it would be no suitable mount for the son of Victor Schaussburgh, however desperate. Besides, he couldn't make heads or tails of its harness.

Careful to avoid kicking range, Rudolph went around to give the dead-cart a cursory inspection—not close enough to actually *see* anything nasty, but just in case there might be someone in there with a pair of boots that he wouldn't be needing anymore.

The first couple of feet he came to were as bare as his own, the next after that hardly a foot at all anymore. Rudolph took a few moments to wipe his hands on another corpse's shirt before continuing his search. He touched a few more clammy feet before his hand fell suddenly on a length of thick, heavily embroidered wool toward the back of the cart.

He moved to get a better look, and lo: There, alone in the back of the cart, almost in state ... was the admiral's fine officer's coat—still wrapped around the admiral's purpling officer's corpse. Come to that, his boots were still on him, too. There was a part of Rudolph that was angry that these expensive clothes had been passed over when his own had been stolen, but that quickly gave way to simple joy at his luck.

It took a lot of work and jostling to get that coat off, for the corpse was stiff and uncooperative in its corpselike way. The mule had begun to complain and fidget by the time he had wrestled the thing off.

The boots he had to leave, however; the corpse's feet had swollen to the point that not even a week of tugging could have gotten them loose. Though it did make sense,

Rudolph had to admit as he jumped back down off the cart, that even the scavengers of Vienna had respected the dead officer's belongings. With Bonaparte so close to the city, the military of any sort, whether applicable or not, was bound to get the utmost respect. Even if they *were* dead and beginning to stink.

Well, Herr Admiral, I respect you, too. He dusted the braided lapels as the mule cart lumbered away. *At very least, I respect your coat.* With that thought, Rudolph turned and began mincing his way home.

Actually, it was closer to the truth to say that he just began walking away from where he had been, since he still had no idea where he had gotten to. Being dazed, cold, hungry—God he was hungry—and generally miserable, he soon resorted to the one trick that had never yet failed him, even on the drunkest spree. He closed his eyes and began singing tavern songs without any particular regard to pitch, key, or the hour of night. The Great Maestro would have shuddered to hear, perhaps, but everyone knew *Herr* Beethoven was deaf, so it did not particularly matter.

Besides, paying attention to the song meant that he didn't have to pay attention to other things; things like his snarling stomach, or exactly what he had just put his foot into, and whether it would ever wash off. And how ungodly silent it was—as if he were the only soul out in the night.

It would have unnerved him had he been paying attention, but, he told himself firmly, he was not; so he didn't notice. Eventually, as the streets got cleaner, wider, and more even, he began to sneak glances through his eyelashes, hoping to recognize his surroundings.

The few people he did see in those glimpses were hunched, hurrying and faceless, as though in terror of the darkness. He had never seen the streets of Vienna so grey and empty at any hour. At least if he had, he hadn't been sober.

A sudden, chill wind stole his breath away, even through his borrowed coat, and left behind it the distinct reek of burning. The smell, and the nagging dread it brought with it grew with each step he took.

Finally, Rudolph could no longer deny that he knew where he was and where the smell was coming from; for before his very eyes a crowd of servants were looting the burned-out ruins of what had been the Schaussburgh family home. Rudolph's first impulse was horror, followed by outrage and righteous indignation. Even by the flickering torchlight he recognized these people; they were *his* servants! How *dare* they be digging through the wreck of his home?

He strode forward, intent upon seizing the nearest of them and giving him what for until the man bent close to his lantern. The light played over bunched muscle and rough hands—stableman's hands, and a face that (now that he thought about it) he had called stupid on more than a few occasions.

Perhaps another man would be a better choice. Maybe his father was there in the wreck? But no; after several minutes squinting from behind the rose hedge, Rudolph had to admit that neither his father, nor the butler, nor any other kindly soul was there.

He turned to regard the stable, its roof shingles still reflecting damply in the moonlight. *Burned,* he thought, staring. *A stable is all I've got left. Father and Mother... if not dead, then where?* Then suddenly, the realization struck him: Of course his father wouldn't be out digging through the wreckage—he was Lord of the Manor! He'd have set the servants to it, and he'd be somewhere comfortable. He'd be in the stable.

It still took him several minutes to get up the nerve to cross the courtyard. But finally, he hunched his shoulders, stuck his hands into his pockets, and just went. He belonged there, after all. It would all be his, assuming Theo got himself killed in the war.

Rudolph was just reaching for the rough wood handle when a shout from the house froze his pounding heart for an instant.

"Hoy! Luck's here, fellows!" A youth—one of the kitchen boys, Rudolph thought—brandished something black and lumpy in the lamplight. "Think I found the Missus' silver service here!"

"Aye?" Came the reply, though he couldn't see the speaker, "Well, I'm pretty sure she and his highness are cooking in the coals over here. Want me to tell her when I dig her out?"

The laughter that followed was as ugly as the joke, but all Rudolph could muster was a profound sense of disappointment; Theo would inherit everything after all. He opened the door and went into the stable with all the dignity he could muster.

Once inside, however, he allowed himself to sink miserably down against a rather soggy stack of hay.

What a wholly revolting development this was—nothing left to his name but his brother's barn. He couldn't sleep in a barn, for God's sake! The smell alone would probably kill him if he stayed there too long, let alone whatever rats and such might be hiding there. And his stomach was twisting into knots. Which was not too unreasonable considering that once he thought about it, the last he'd eaten had been a light luncheon at the Verrazano manor the previous morning. Somehow he doubted that Julia or her brother would welcome him just yet.

Gretchen, however . . . The idea shot like lightning, straight to his stomach. She had an inn and was the best cook in the whole of Vienna—and she loved him. She would take him in—take care of him, he was sure of it. And that fat lump of a husband of hers would probably never even notice he was there.

He scrambled to his feet and went to find a horse. They were his until Theo showed up to claim them after all, so he could take them if he cared to. It took him some time, however, once he found an animal that didn't seem to mind his being near it, to figure out how the bridle went on. He almost gave up on getting the bit into the horse's mouth until it took pity on him and opened its jaws.

After that, Rudolph simply felt too weak to try and figure out how to manage the saddle. He didn't know where they were kept anyway. It took some doing, and more than a few dirty looks from the horse, but eventually he managed to clamber onto the creature's back. Then he unlatched the door to its stall—a feat of no little bravery and skill, he decided after regaining his balance—and rode out into the chilly night. A couple of the servants called after him, but he ignored them and urged the horse on faster. They were

nothing to him now; his beautiful Gretchen awaited him—
he had only to go to her and all would be well.

Bewitching as such thoughts were, he quickly found them
giving way to thoughts of his own discomfort. He had no
idea that riding without a saddle would prove so difficult.
Or so *painful*! He could have sworn that the horse was
jouncing that way on purpose just to hear him groan. If his
feet hadn't already hurt worse, he'd have seriously considered abandoning the creature and walking the rest of the
way.

But just in time, the right street presented itself and Rudolph nearly cried with relief as he dragged the horse to a
stop outside *Der Orangerie*. He dropped the reins on the
animal's neck and looked up at the vista of his salvation,
only to see it crowded with men. Jammed into the common
room and the street tables, jostling each other on the terraces, and leaning out the windows of the upper level to
stare as dense silence spread like a cancer through the
building.

They were all staring at him. And they were all wearing
French uniforms. *The French will have us and that damned
Corsican will sleep in Schönbrunn Palace tonight!* The admiral's words echoed once more in his mind as he felt his
blood go cold. Vienna was occupied—occupied by the people he had been shooting a cannon at the night before.

But how could they know? A wily corner of his mind
whispered, *Act like you belong and they will say nothing. It
isn't as if they saw your face, is it?* Rudolph swallowed,
smiled at one of the Frenchmen and raised a hand to wave.
Then he looked at the braided cuff of his stolen coat—his
stolen *officer's* coat, looked back at the glowering soldiers,
swallowed again. Then wheeled his horse and kicked it as
hard as he could.

The beast squealed and bolted, leaving behind a chorus
of shouts and scrambling pursuit. Clinging to the horse's
heaving shoulder, Rudolph chanced a quick look behind at
the inn, boiling like a stirred anthill. He could almost have
laughed—until they began shooting at him. With a curse
he kicked the horse harder just as a thunderbolt slammed
into his shoulder from behind, flattening him against its
neck.

Numb and wheezing, he clung to the beast, watching the dark street speed past his face while the fine wool of the treacherous coat darkened to black in the intermittent moonlight. The horse ran on, answering whatever urge of self-preservation that horses answered to, and more or less ignoring him. That would be because he'd dropped the reins, he supposed.

Rudolph tried to lift his head and see if he could catch them again, but the movement shocked agony through his neck and shoulder like none he had ever known. Dropping his head again made no difference; the demon pain, once wakened, had no intention of loosing him. The horse swerved suddenly, and it was too much for his failing grip. Rudolph tumbled to the street, not even able to groan as oblivion overtook him.

A late mist swirled around Chloris' feet. She was tired and hungry, but in this case she did not begrudge the time she might have been eating, or the early bedtime either. Peace of mind concerning the continuance of her life was a valid predecessor to consideration on matters of comfort. Still, she *had* stayed out quite late.

Already the sky was beginning to grow paler than she liked. She could see the silhouette of the *Stefansdom*'s Gothic towers and silly little Renaissance cupola against the gray heavens. They would soon be fired with rose and gold, picking flame from the high places of the city. Or so she remembered, and the paintings of late seemed to agree that dawn was pretty much now as it was before.

Respects unto you, Lady Aurora, but I must decline your entertainment. She smiled to herself, turning onto the road that would lead her home. *The Lady Hecate has filled my calendar of engagements for quite some time to come.* As if in affirmation, the smoky, biting wind died down, then leaped up again the instant she left the crossroad.

Chloris paused, groping her riot of black curls under her hood again, and beating her cloak back down. By which time the rogue breeze had run away, its message unuttered. The whole of which made Chloris uneasy—in its own way, more so than the invading French had.

The gift of her living had come from that dark Goddess,

and even through all the passing years and kings and gods and churches, Chloris had never forgotten that gift. Learned men might call Hecate's a dead cult, but Chloris' continued existence was proof enough for her that the goddess was undying. As such, when odd things happened in Hecate' favored places, she did not often miss their meaning.

She considered returning to the crossroad, but a glance at the sky changed her mind. It might have been nothing, but scrying to find out could mean a search of hours. She bit her lip, looked up again, then shook her head. The Goddess knew where to find her if the message was really important, and they both knew that it had better *not* be out here in the light of dawn.

She breathed a sigh of relief when the dome of the *Karlskirche* came into view, a pearl and sea-mist confection of imagination against the silvering sky. Old Poseidon might have been pleased with it . . . from this far off anyway. Close up, the church revealed its architect's ignorance regarding the definition of "classical."

Stately Greek Ionic columns supported a Turkish dome whose smooth lines were littered with Italian baroque doodlings, and flanked by Roman bas-relief triumphal pillars with eagles on the tops! Even now the presumption made her laugh. *Hmpf. Neo-classical indeed! As soon mate a cow to a goat because they both have horns.* Still, of all the safe places Vienna had to offer her, it amused her best to take her refuge in this mishmash of a church. She had all her life been of a religious caste, and to her, the building seemed a fitting metaphor to the faith itself; the irony suited her.

They are not so unlike the Romans as Luther would have liked to believe. Again she laughed, remembering the fat German's rage at her arguments when they had drunk together in *Hoher Markt* so long ago.

A smell invaded her thoughts as she neared the church, scattering them like so much ash. It was subtle under the reek of the burned and blasted *Innere Stadt*, but it was there. Chloris caught sight of the stain almost at once, even through the carpet of mist. Dark against the footworn marble steps, it pooled on the third, then dragged inward to the church door. Blood.

Her middle twisting, Chloris knelt and dipped a finger into the syrupy puddle. Then she brought it to her lips and tasted. It was cold, but still connected—still alive. Her pale brow furrowed as she mused, finger still in her mouth. The mark of blood on the steps of this place was the last thing she needed; all irony aside, the *Karlskirche* was safe. It would not remain so if people began dying there.

Taking a corner of her cloak, she swabbed up the pool, and the dampest of the smudges. Then, eyeing the sky distrustfully all the while, she returned to the street and picked up two handfuls of black mud to hide the rest of the stains. The task took forever—or at least it seemed that way with the light going pearly around her, but at last, the entrance looked more like the passage of careless road menders than of a wounded meal. . . .

Man. She corrected herself, wiping her hands on her ruined cloak, *Not meal, Man. I truly should have fed tonight.* There was still, however, the wounded man to find and remove—hopefully before the light grew too hateful.

It was a distinct relief to slip through the massive oaken doors into the church's welcoming dark. The darkness was sacred to Hecate, sacred to herself. Chloris had not left it since even before the Goddess' dark gifts had been granted her—some pair of thousand years, as she guessed. She had no idea what would happen to her if she did stray into the daylight, but her instinctive, dreaming mind suggested it would be painful, and she saw no reason to doubt.

Pushing the street door closed, she dropped the bar, thanking Hecate again for the young priest who habitually forgot to check the door in the night. *"You breathe in darkness, Thrice Mother. I drink your breath and live of it."* The prayer came easily to her lips, being the only remnant of her first language that she had occasion to speak any more. Even in these days of supposed enlightenment the tongue of Athens dumbfounded the scholars and churchmen—for them the world was limited to the dregs of the Roman's tongue—less if they had taken Luther too seriously and renounced even Latin.

The sound of a whimper stopped her prayer short. Chloris grew still—an owl in wain, listening for the mouse to move again. When it did, she stooped, and had the rag-

ged youth swept up in her arms before he could squeak
again and alert the stirring priests.

He lay limp against her breast as she ran for the safety
of her underground chambers; if not for the maddening
reek of his blood and warmth of his skin against hers,
Chloris might have thought him dead and wasted. Carrying
him made it less than easy to wrestle aside the huge beer
cask and then push back the stones that guarded her sanctuary, but Chloris did not think of setting the youth down.
The scent of his blood had reached the predator in her,
and *that* creature did not mean to risk losing its prize.

Only inside her cavern did she lay him aside, though
reluctantly, to replace the barrels and stones that camou-
flaged the place.

Then she turned, scenting breath in the darkness and
trembling. It was tempting, so tempting to consider this
ragged boy a gift from her Dark Mother, but Chloris had
not survived the wreck of four civilizations by being careless. Whoever he was, there would be someone who cared
for him, or at least would notice that he was gone.

So while the beast within her snarled its impatience and
frustration, Chloris slipped to the youth's side and examined him carefully. What she saw pleased her in part, and
made her worry in other ways. His coat had to be stolen—
he was too young for the rank of those braids, and besides,
it fit him poorly—so he could be a thief, common and un-
missed should he disappear.

But his hands, though torn and dirty now, had no calluses
and were slim and rather delicate beneath the grime—not
the hands of a street dweller. And, too, once she pulled
the heavy coat aside, his ruined shirt was expensive linen,
and embroidered at the shredded collar.

The rich blood scent assaulted her again as the movement of the fabric pulled open his wound and started it
bleeding afresh. With a low moan, she twitched away the
rags of linen and lowered her face to the bullet wound in
his left shoulder. *Just to smell . . .* she promised herself
sternly, *And see if he is dying anyway . . . No more than
that. . . .*

The scent brought vague ghosts swirling through the dark
of her closed eyes—thin shreds of his life that the taste of

his blood would bring into brilliant focus. But the shades bore no taint of mortality—the wound he bore now would not kill him without the aid of an infection or some other added shock.

A shock like me, perhaps. She let out the breath in a chuckle, then jerked stiff as he put his arms around her and moaned.

"Julia . . ."

Chloris smiled to the darkness, knowing he could not see as she could. "Yes, beloved. What happened to you?"

"Damn . . . French. I knew you weren't angry . . ."

"Of course not." His hand strayed up to her hair, wrapped itself in the curls there as she whispered. "But I am concerned. Is anyone looking for you?"

His wheeze turned into laughter, then choking. Chloris trembled as the blood surged out, then put her hand over the wound to block it. "Ow . . ." The boy whined, then he shook his head. "They were too slow . . . too stupid. I got away. Kiss me, my Sparrow."

"Almost" got away, my lad. She smirked silently. Then aloud, "But what about your parents? Your friends? Are they not looking?"

He whimpered and writhed under her, trying to clasp her body to his. "No, no one but you. No one but you. They're dead . . . Gretchen, sleeping with the French army . . . slut. . . . I knew you were not angry . . ." His petting became more personal and he whimpered again. "Please, Julia . . ."

Thrice mother! Chloris thought as his hand went to her breasts, *If Hecate breathes in me, then surely Aphrodite breathes in this child—how could anyone want to rut with such a wound?* He nuzzled against her neck and shoulder, and she fought the urge to laugh.

Well, why not? It is obvious that he is alone, after all, and people always disappear and die strangely in war. She wrapped her hand around to the back of his neck. *I shall take him, then give his body to the Danube tomorrow night—*

Then the probing of her prey's lips against her shoulder and neck turned suddenly into teeth, and a grip of his jaws that shot pain throughout her. Chloris gasped, seized the boy's neck to pry him away as he thrust his groin against her—her flesh tore under his blunt teeth as he came loose.

The little beast was babbling apologies even as she dropped him against the stones and backed away. "Sparrow I'm sorry I'll never again I meant no harm I promise—"

Chloris ignored him, touching her neck with bloody fingers that had pressed closed *his* wound. The tear on her neck was a small one, and she could already feel the skin beginning to knit—not much damage at all, but the hungry beast inside her was enraged.

"Come back, please, Julia, I swear it was an accident, I never meant to hurt you, I can't find you, where, please forgive—"

"Oh, be silent, Dog!" Chloris snarled, yanking him off the floor with a shake, as she might a whining cur.

"Sorry . . ." He trailed off, dangling limp from her fist.

She glared at him for a moment, distrusting the pitiful thing in the extreme. But her healing flesh demanded payment: his blood. She lowered him to rest against her and wrapped one arm around his waist to keep him there.

"Just *do not* do that again!" she growled, forcibly tilting his head to the side. She licked at the shoulder a moment, her body sighing in every pore at the taste, then she settled her jaws over the muscle and—

And he did it again! The little wretch of a motherless Hun bastard bit her again, in the same place, and even harder this time! Chloris roared as she tore him away, throwing him against the wall. He hit with a thud, then fell boneless onto the alter, tipping it over in a clatter. He was laughing—a near silent wheeze as he lay sprawled in the wreck of her shrine.

"Be silent!" she screamed at him, pressing her hand against her neck.

His bloodstained lips formed a grin as he rolled his eyes in the darkness. "I know . . . you are not angry . . ."

She dove at him then, covering that smeared mouth (with *her* blood—smeared with *her* blood!) and tearing into his throat. Gone was the priestess—here was only the predator enraged. She gulped the blood down, not tasting it much. Chloris worked her jaws savagely to keep it flowing, hoping that it hurt him. A lot. She did not notice the new smell until the blood trickled to a stop and she felt his heart seize up against its cage of bone. Then the warmth against her leg betrayed his total depravity; he had spent his seed with his life, and now he lay with a silly grin as his eyes glazed over in Hecate's sacred darkness.

With a snarl, Chloris smacked his head aside and stood to straighten her gown. It, like her cloak, was ruined; blood-stained, mud-stained, and ... possibly worse. She grimaced and tore the garment off, throwing it over her erstwhile victim.

Rudolph Schaussburgh. The shade of his memory sang to her as she paced in her tiny shrine. Like prancing Dionysian maskers, they sang her stories of the life she had consumed. Chloris could not decide if it was more of a tragedy or a farce.

The one thing she could settle upon was that this little prat would be missed by no one—likely the whole world would be pleased to know that he was dead. Or it would if it had the memories in its head that she now did; coward, braggart, bully and weakling—he was far better off dead.

But is he dead? Really dead? A darker voice than the singing memories intruded, chilling her to her core. Trembling, Chloris sent her mind back, ranging through two thousand years, to the midnight of her own gifting—trying to remember the rite, what had happened that night. Always before, it had been shrouded—a mystery of the Goddess, and so she had not probed it. Hecate's secrets were always well guarded, and her priestesses knew that it was best to leave them lie.

But now a taste from that night stung her tongue, and the pain in her healing neck was not unlike what the past whispered to her. She had tasted men's blood for the first time that night, and a ... a wolf? A giant? A Goddess? Had tasted hers, leading her through Hades, and back out again. There was a cold feeling in the pit of Chloris' stomach as she looked at Rudolph and his bloodstained mouth again.

"DAMN!" she exploded finally. "He cannot be gifted! The Goddess would never accept a worm like him—He *cannot!*" But the words sounded hollow even to her. "I will

leave him in the sun, rotting in the sun. That will anger the gift and it will leave him." .

Chloris seized the hope like a lifeline and dove immediately to pull away the stones at the temple's entrance. But there she stopped. Even through the barrels, even in the brewery cellar, she could see the light of dawn in the church above, hear the priests talking one to another. She was too late.

The ancient priestess sat down on the stone floor and for the first time in centuries, considered crying. "*Auf weidersehn*, my Sparrow." Rudolph's shade giggled, "I will come again on Thursday."

"Never," she snarled to the dispossessed memory, getting back to her feet. "I will tear your body to pieces if I must, but you are not *stealing* the Goddess' dark gift! Not here, and not from me!" She dragged the cooling body through the gaping stones and jammed it between one of the heavier casks and the solid East wall.

"There," she told it as she brushed the dust from her knees, "With luck, the rats will find you. And if the Fates say not . . ." she reached back into the crevice and snapped first one leg, then the other—twisting both for good measure. "Then that will hold you still until I can dispose of you."

The corpse answered nothing but its smile. With a final curse, Chloris covered the head with her gown and turned back to her home.

"And after all," she soothed herself as she dragged the great stones back into place, "he could not hide long even if he did escape. *He* would not even know not to wander out into the sun, or not to eat salt—perhaps he would kill himself." Chloris gave the stones a final shove, wedging them tight, then chewed for a moment at the ragged edge of her fingernail, considering all she had ever known of godly perversity.

Then in the darkness, she laughed—to herself, and her Goddess. "And of course if he does not, who will notice one *more* bloodthirsty tyrant? Bonaparte *is* in Vienna after all!" She laughed again, shook her head, and knelt to repair Hecate's alter. And all around her, the sacred darkness breathed—its worship reborn at last, in the first new acolyte in two thousand years.

Author's Note:

I suppose if I had to cite one source of inspiration for this story, it would be the movie Immortal Beloved, *and one little trivial fact that it revealed: Ludwig van Beethoven wrote his 5th symphony in honor of Napoleon Bonaparte, then scratched his name out when the French started shelling Vienna. That little symptom of betrayal of hope was what tickled the setting and time into place—and desperation did the rest.*

I'd never written a vampire story before this, and frankly hadn't seriously considered it—I figured it'd all been done, right? Imagine my stress when I suddenly needed to find a way that it hadn't *been done! So what happens when you take the* last *person in the world who should be granted eternal life and you make him a vampire? I don't know, let's find out, shall we?*

Catt Kingsgrave-Ernstein's talents extend beyond writing into many other creative areas. She is an accomplished artist, musician, award-winning costumer, and sings in the Neo-Celtic Group, *Ravens*. She says of herself, "I do everything that is artistic that makes no money." It is to be hoped this story is very much the exception to that rule.

WHAT MANNER OF MAN
by Tanya Huff

Shortly after three o'clock in the morning, Henry Fitzroy rose from the card table, brushed a bit of ash from the sleeve of his superbly fitting coat and inclined his head toward his few remaining companions. "If you'll excuse me, gentlemen, I believe I'll call it a night."

"Well, I won't excuse you." Sir William Wyndham, glared up at Fitzroy from under heavy lids. "You've won eleven hundred pounds off me tonight, damn your eyes, and I want a chance to win it back."

His gaze flickering down to the cluster of empty bottles by Wyndham's elbow, Henry shook his head. "I don't think so, Sir William, not tonight."

"You don't think so?" Wyndham half rose in his chair, dark brows drawn into a deep vee over an aristocratic arc of nose. His elbow rocked one of the bottles. It began to fall.

Moving with a speed that made it clear he had not personally been indulging over the course of the evening's play, Henry caught the bottle just before it hit the floor. "Brandy," he chided softly, setting it back on the table, "is no excuse for bad manners."

Wyndham stared at him for a moment, confusion replacing the anger on his face, instinct warning him of a danger reason couldn't see. "Your pardon," he said at last. "Perhaps another night." He watched as the other man bowed and left, then muttered, "Insolent puppy."

"Who is?" asked another of the players, dragging his attention away from the brandy.

"Fitzroy." Raising his glass to his mouth, his hand surprisingly steady considering how much he'd already drunk,

Wyndham tossed back the contents. "He speaks to me like that again and he can name his seconds."

"Well, *I* wouldn't fight him."

"No one's asking you to."

"He's just the sort of quiet chap who's the very devil when pushed too far. I've seen that look in his eyes, I tell you—the very devil when pushed too far."

"Shut up." Opening a fresh deck, Wyndham sullenly pushed Henry Fitzroy from his thoughts and set about trying to make good his losses.

His curly-brimmed beaver set at a fashionably rakish angle on his head, Henry stood on the steps of his club and stared out at London. Its limits had expanded since the last time he'd made it his principal residence, curved courts of elegant townhouses had risen where he remembered fields, but, all in all, it hadn't changed much. There was still something about London—a feel, an atmosphere—shared by no other city in the world.

· One guinea-gold brow rose as he shot an ironic glance upward at the haze that hung over the buildings, the smoke from a thousand chimney pots that blocked the light of all but the brightest stars. Atmosphere was, perhaps, a less than appropriate choice of words.

"Shall I get you a hackney or a chair, Mr. Fitzroy?"

"Thank you, no." He smiled at the porter, his expression calculated to charm, and heard the elderly man's heart begin to beat a little faster. The Hunger rose in response, but he firmly pushed it back. It would be the worst of bad *ton* to feed so close to home. It would also be dangerous but, in the England of the Prince Regent, safety came second to social approval. "I believe I'll walk."

"If you're sure, sir. There's some bad'uns around after dark."

"I'm sure." Henry's smile broadened. "I doubt I'll be bothered."

The porter watched as the young man made his way down the stairs and along St. James Street. He'd watched a lot of gentlemen during the years he'd worked the clubs—first at Boodles, then at Brook's, and finally here at

White's—and Mr. Henry Fitzroy had the unmistakable mark of Quality. For all he was so polite and soft-spoken, something about him spoke strongly of power. It would, the porter decided, take a desperate man, or a stupid one, to put Mr. Fitzroy in any danger. *Of course, London has no shortage of either desperate or stupid men.*

"Take care, sir," he murmured as he turned to go inside.

Henry quelled the urge to lift a hand in acknowledgment of the porter's concern, judging that he'd moved beyond the range of mortal hearing. As the night air held a decided chill, he shoved his hands deep in the pockets of his many-caped greatcoat, even though it would have to get a great deal colder before he'd feel it. A successful masquerade demanded attention to small details.

Humming under his breath, he strode down Brook Street to Grosvenor Square, marveling at the new technological wonder of the gaslights. The long lines of little brightish dots created almost as many shadows as they banished, but they were still a big improvement over a servant carrying a lantern on a stick. That he had no actual need of the light, Henry considered unimportant in view of the achievement.

Turning toward his chambers in Albany, he heard the unmistakable sounds of a fight. He paused, head cocked, sifting through the lives involved. Three men beating a fourth.

"Not at all sporting," he murmured, moving forward so quickly that, had anyone been watching, it would have seemed he simply disappeared.

"Be sure that he's dead." The man who spoke held a narrow sword in one hand and the cane it had come out of in the other. The man on the ground groaned and the steel point moved around. "Never mind, I'll take care of it myself."

Wearing an expression of extreme disapproval, Henry stepped out of the shadows, grabbed the swordsman by the back of his coat, and threw him down the alley. When the other two whirled to face him, he drew his lips back off his teeth and said, in a tone of polite, but inarguable menace, "Run."

Prey recognized predator. They ran.

He knelt by the wounded man, noted how the heartbeat faltered, looked down, and saw a face he knew. Captain Charles Evans of the Horse Guards, the nephew of the current Earl of Whitby. Not one of his few friends—friends were chosen with a care honed by centuries of survival—but Henry couldn't allow him to die alone in some dark alley like a stray dog.

A sudden noise drew his attention around to the man with the sword-cane. Up on his knees, his eyes unfocused, he groped around for his weapon. Henry snarled. The man froze, whimpered once, then, face twisted with fear, scrambled to his feet, and joined his companions in flight.

The sword had punched a hole high in the captain's left shoulder, not immediately fatal, but bleeding to death was a distinct possibility.

"Fitz . . . roy?"

"So you're awake, are you?" Taking the other man's chin in a gentle grip, Henry stared down into pain-filled eyes. "I think it might be best if you trusted me and slept," he said quietly.

The captain's lashes fluttered, then settled down to rest against his cheeks like fringed shadows.

Satisfied that he was unobserved, Henry pulled aside the bloodstained jacket—like most military men, Captain Evans favored Scott—and bent his head over the wound.

"You cut it close. Sun's almost up."

Henry pushed past the small, irritated form of his servant. "Don't fuss, Varney, I've plenty of time."

"Plenty of time is it?" Closing and bolting the door, the little man hurried down the short hall in Henry's shadow. "I was worried sick, I was, and all you can say is don't fuss?"

Sighing, Henry shrugged out of his greatcoat—a muttering Varney caught it before it hit the floor—and stepped into his sitting room. There was a fire lit in the grate, heavy curtains over the window that opened onto a tiny balcony, and a thick oak slab of a door replacing the folding doors that had originally led to the bedchamber. The furniture was heavy and dark, as close as Henry could come to the furniture of his youth. It had been purchased in a fit of nostalgia and was now mostly ignored.

"You've blood on your cravat!"

"It's not mine," Henry told him mildly.

Varney snorted. "Didn't expect it was, but you're usually neater than that. Probably won't come out. Blood stains, you know."

"I know."

"Mayhap if I soak it . . ." The little man quivered with barely concealed impatience.

Henry laughed and unwound the offending cloth, dropping it over the offered hand. After thirty years of unique service, certain liberties were unavoidable. "I won eleven hundred pounds from Lord Wyndham tonight."

"You and everyone else. He's badly dipped. Barely a feather to fly with so I hear. Rumor has it, he's getting a bit desperate."

"And I returned a wounded Charlie Evans to the bosom of his family."

"Nice bosom, so I hear."

"Don't be crude, Varney." Henry sat down and lifted one foot after the other to have the tight Hessians pulled gently off. "I think I may have prevented him from being killed."

"Robbery?"

"I don't know."

"How many did you kill?"

"No one. I merely frightened them away."

Setting the gleaming boots to one side, Varney stared at his master with frank disapproval. "You merely frightened them away?"

"I did consider ripping their throats out, but as it wasn't actually necessary, it wouldn't have been . . ." He paused and smiled. ". . . polite."

"Polite!? You risked exposure so as you can be polite?"

The smile broadened. "I am a creature of my time."

"You're a creature of the night! You know what'll come of this? Questions, that's what. And we don't need questions!"

"I have complete faith in your ability to handle whatever might arise."

Recognizing the tone, the little man deflated. "Aye and well you might," he muttered darkly. "Let's get that jacket off you before I've got to carry you in to your bed like a sack of meal."

"I *can* do it myself," Henry remarked as he stood and turned to have his coat carefully peeled from his shoulders.

"Oh, aye, and leave it lying on the floor no doubt." Folding the coat in half, Varney draped it over one skinny arm. "I'd never get the wrinkles out. You'd go about looking like you dressed out of a ragbag if it wasn't for me. Have you eaten?" He looked suddenly hopeful.

One hand on the bedchamber door, Henry paused. "Yes," he said softly.

The thin shoulders sagged. "Then what're you standing about for?"

A few moments later, the door bolted, the heavy shutter over the narrow window secured, Henry Fitzroy, vampire, bastard son of Henry the VIII, once duke of Richmond and Somerset, Earl of Nottingham, and Lord President of the Council of the North, slid into the day's oblivion.

"My apologies, Mrs. Evans, for not coming by sooner, but I was out when your husband's message arrived." Henry laid his hat and gloves on the small table in the hall and allowed the waiting footman to take his coat. "I trust he's in better health than he was when I saw him last night?"

"A great deal better, thank you." Although there were purple shadows under her eyes and her cheeks were more than fashionably pale, Lenore Evans' smile lit up her face. "The doctor says he lost a lot of blood, but he'll recover. If it hadn't been for you . . ."

As her voice trailed off, Henry bowed slightly. "I was happy to help." Perhaps he *had* taken a dangerous chance. Perhaps he should have wiped all memory of his presence from the captain's mind and left him on his own doorstep like an oversized infant. Having become involved, he couldn't very well ignore the message an obviously disapproving Varney had handed him at sunset with a muttered, *I told you so.*

It appeared that there were indeed going to be questions.

Following Mrs. Evans up the stairs, he allowed himself to be ushered into a well-appointed bedchamber and left alone with the man in the bed.

Propped up against his pillows, recently shaved but looking wan and tired, Charles Evans nodded a greeting. "Fitzroy. I'm glad you've come."

Henry inclined his own head in return, thankful that the bloodscent had been covered by the entirely unappetizing smell of basilicum powder. "You're looking remarkably well, all things considered."

"I've you to thank for that."

"I really did very little."

"True enough, you *only* saved my life." The captain's grin was infectious and Henry found himself returning it in spite of an intention to remain aloof. "Mind you, Dr. Harris did say he'd never seen such a clean wound." One hand rose to touch the bandages under his nightshirt. "He said I was healing faster than any man he'd ever examined."

As his saliva had been responsible for that accelerated healing, Henry remained silent. It had seemed foolish to resist temptation when there'd been so much blood going to waste.

"Anyway . . ." The grin disappeared and the expressive face grew serious. "I owe you my life and I'm very grateful you came along, but that's not why I asked you to visit. I can't get out of this damned bed and I have to trust someone." Shadowed eyes lifted to Henry's face. "Something tells me that I can trust you."

"You barely know me," Henry murmured, inwardly cursing his choice of words the night before. He'd told Evans to trust him and now it seemed he was to play the role of confidant. He could remove the trust as easily as he'd placed it, but something in the man's face made him hesitate. Whatever bothered him involved life and death—Henry had seen the latter too often to mistake it now. Sighing, he added, "I can't promise anything, but I'll listen."

"Please." Gesturing at a chair, the captain waited until his guest had seated himself, then waited a little longer, apparently searching for a way to begin. After a few moments, he lifted his chin. "You know I work at the Home Office?"

"I had heard as much, yes." In the last few years, gossip had become the preferred entertainment of *all* classes, and Varney was a devoted participant.

"Well, for the last little while—just since the start of the Season, in fact—things have been going missing."

"Things?"

"Papers. Unimportant ones for the most part, until now." His mouth twisted up into a humorless grin. "I can't tell you exactly what the latest missing document contained— in spite of everything we'd still rather it wasn't common knowledge—but I can tell you that if it gets into the wrong hands, into French hands, a lot of British soldiers are going to die."

"Last night you were following the thief?"

"No. The man we think is his contact. A French spy named Yves Bouchard."

Henry shook his head, intrigued in spite of himself. "The man who stabbed you last night was no Frenchman. I heard him speak, and he was as English as you or I. English, and though I hesitate to use the term, a gentleman."

"That's Bouchard. He's the only son of an old emigre family. They left France during the revolution—Yves was a mere infant at the time, and now he dreams of restoring the family fortunes under Napoleon."

"One would have thought he'd be more interested in defeating Napoleon and restoring the rightful king."

Evans shrugged, winced, and said, "Apparently not. Anyway, Bouchard's too smart to stay around after what happened last night. I kept him from getting his hands on the document; now we have to keep it from leaving England by another means."

"We?" Henry asked, surprised into ill-mannered incredulity. "You and I?"

"Mostly you. The trouble is, we don't know who actually took the document although we've narrowed it down to three men who are known to be in Bouchard's confidence and who have access to the Guard's offices."

"One moment, please." Henry raised an exquisitely manicured hand. "You want me to find your spy for you?"

"Yes."

"Why?"

"Because I can't be certain of anyone else in my office and because I trust you."

Realizing he had only himself to blame, Henry sighed. "And I suppose you can't bring the three in for questioning because two of them are innocent?"

Evans' pained expression had nothing to do with his wound. "Only consider the scandal. I will if I must, but as this is Wednesday and the information must be in France by Friday evening or it won't get to Napoleon in time for it to be of any use, one of those three will betray himself in the next two days."

"So the document must be recovered with no public outcry?"

"Exactly."

"I would have thought, the Bow Street Runners . . ."

"No. The Runners may be fine for chasing down highwaymen and murderers, but my three suspects move in the best circles; only a man of their own class could get near them without arousing suspicion." He lifted a piece of paper off the table beside the bed and held it out to Henry, who stared at it for a long moment.

Lord Ruthven, Mr. Maxwell Aubrey, and Sir William Wyndham. Frowning, Henry looked up to meet Captain Evans' weary gaze. "You're sure about this?"

"I am. Send word when you're sure, I'll do the rest."

The exhaustion shading the other man's voice reminded Henry of his injury. Placing the paper back beside the bed, he stood. "This is certainly not what I expected."

"But you'll do it?"

He could refuse, could make the captain forget that this conversation had ever happened, but he had been a prince of England and, regardless of what he had become, he could not stand back and allow her to be betrayed. Hiding a smile at the thought of what Varney would have to say about such melodrama, he nodded. "Yes, I'll do it."

The sound of feminine voices rising up from the entryway caused Henry to pause for a moment on the landing.

". . . so sorry to arrive so late, Mrs. Evans, but we were passing on our way to dinner before Almack's and my uncle insisted we stop and see how the captain was doing."

Carmilla Amworth. There could be no mistaking the faint country accent not entirely removed by hours of lessons intended to erase it. She had enough fortune to be considered an heiress and that, combined with a dark-haired, pale-skinned, waiflike beauty, brought no shortage of admirers. Unfortunately, she also had disturbing tendency to giggle when she felt herself out of her depth.

"My uncle," she continued, "finds it difficult to get out of the carriage and so sent me in his place."

"I quite understand." The smile in the answering voice suggested a shared amusement. "Please tell your uncle that the captain is resting comfortably and thank him for his consideration."

A brief exchange of pleasantries later, Miss Amworth returned to her uncle's carriage and Henry descended the rest of the stairs.

Lenore Evans turned and leaped backward, one hand to her heart, her mouth open. She would have fallen had Henry not caught her wrist and kept her on her feet.

He could feel her pulse racing beneath the thin sheath of heated skin. The Hunger rose, and he hurriedly broke the contact. Self-indulgence, besides being vulgar, was a sure road to the stake.

"Heavens, you startled me." Cheeks flushed, she increased the distance between them. "I didn't hear you come down."

"My apologies. I heard Miss Amworth and didn't wish to break in on a private moment."

"Her uncle works with Charles and wanted to know how he was, but her uncle is *also* a dear friend of His Royal Highness and is, shall we say, less than able to climb in and out of carriages. Is Charles . . . ?"

"I left him sleeping."

"Good." Her right hand wrapped around the place where Henry had held her. She swallowed, then, as though reminded of her duties by the action, stammered, "Can I get you a glass of wine?"

"Thank you, no. I must be going."

"Good. That is, I mean . . ." Her flush deepened. "You must think I'm a complete idiot. It's just that with Charles injured . . ."

"I fully understand." He smiled, careful not to show teeth.

Lenore Evans closed the door behind her husband's guest and tried to calm the pounding of her heart. Something about Henry Fitzroy spoke to a part of her she'd thought belonged to Charles alone. Her response might have come out of gratitude for the saving of her husband's life, but she didn't think so. He was a handsome young man, and she found the soft curves of his mouth a fascinating contrast to the gentle strength in his grip.

Shaking her head in self-reproach, she lifted her skirts with damp hands and started up the stairs. "I'm beginning to think," she sighed, "that Aunt Georgette was right. Novels are a bad influence on a young woman."

What she needed now was a few hours alone with her husband but, as his wound made that impossible, she'd supposed she'd have to divert her thoughts with a book of sermons instead.

Almack's Assembly Rooms were the exclusive temple of the Beau Monde, and vouchers to the weekly ball on Wednesday were among the most sought-after items in London. What matter that the assembly rooms were plain, the dance floor inferior, the anterooms unadorned, and the refreshments unappetizing—this was the seventh heaven of the fashionable world, and to be excluded from Almack's was to be excluded from the upper levels of society.

Henry, having discovered that a fashionable young man could live unremarked from dark to dawn, had effortlessly risen to the top.

After checking with the porter that all three of Captain Evans' potential spies were indeed in attendance, Henry left hat, coat, and gloves and made his way up into the assembly rooms. Avoiding the gaze of Princess Esterhazy, who he considered to be rude and overbearing, he crossed the room and made his bow to the Countess Lieven.

"I hear you were quite busy last night, Mr. Fitzroy."

A little astonished by how quickly the information had made its way to such august ears, he murmured he had only done what any man would have.

"Indeed. Any *man*. Still, I should have thought the less of you had you expected a fuss to be made." Tapping her closed fan against her other hand, she favored him with a long, level look. "I have always believed there was more to you than you showed the world."

Fully aware that the Countess deserved her reputation as the cleverest woman in London, Henry allowed a little of his mask to slip.

She smiled, satisfied for the moment with being right and not overly concerned with what she had been right about. "Appearances, my dear Mr. Fitzroy, are everything. And now, I believe they are beginning a country dance. Let me introduce you to a young lady in need of a partner."

Unable to think of a reason why she shouldn't, Henry bowed again. A few moments later, as he moved gracefully through the pattern of the dance, he wondered if he should pay the Countess a visit some night, had not made a decision by the time the dance ended, and put it off indefinitely as he escorted the young woman in his care back to her waiting mama.

Well aware that he looked, at best, in his early twenties, Henry could only be thankful that a well-crafted reputation as a man who trusted to the cards for the finer things in life took him off the Marriage Mart. No matchmaking mama would allow her daughter to become shackled to someone with such narrow prospects. As he had no interest in giggling young damsels just out of the schoolroom, he could only be thankful. The older women he spent time with were much more ... appetizing.

Trying not to stare, one of the young damsels so summarily dismissed in Henry's thoughts, leaned toward a second and whispered, "I wonder what Mr. Fitzroy is smiling about."

The second glanced up, blushed rosily, and ducked her head. "He looks *hungry*."

The first, a little wiser in the ways of the world than her friend, sighed and laid silent odds that the curve of Mr. Henry Fitzroy's full lips had nothing to do with bread and butter.

* * *

Hearing a familiar voice, Henry searched through the moving couples and spotted Sir William Wyndham dancing with Carmilla Amworth. Hardly surprising if he'd lost as much money lately as Varney suggested. While Henry wouldn't have believed the fragile, country-bred heiress to his taste—it was a well-known secret that he kept a yacht off Dover for the express purpose of entertaining the women of easy virtue he preferred—upon reflection he supposed Sir William would consider her inheritance sufficiently alluring. And a much safer way of recovering his fortune than selling state secrets to France.

With one of Captain Evans' suspects accounted for, Henry began to search for the other two, moving quietly and unobtrusively from room to room. As dancing was the object of the club and no high stakes were allowed, the card rooms contained only dowagers and those gentlemen willing to play whist for pennies. Although he found neither of the men he looked for, he did find Carmilla Amworth's uncle, Lord Beardsley. One of the Prince Regent's cronies, he was a stout and somewhat foolish middle-aged gentleman who smelled strongly of scent and creaked alarmingly when he moved. Considering the bulwark of his stays, Henry was hardly surprised that he'd been less than able to get out of the carriage to ask after Captain Evans.

". . . cupped and felt much better," Lord Beardsley was saying as Henry entered the room. "His Royal Highness swears by cupping, you know. Must've had gallons taken out over the years."

Henry winced, glanced around, and left. As much as he deplored the waste involved in frequent cupping, he had no desire to avail himself of the Prince Regent's blood—which he strongly suspected would be better than ninety percent Madeira.

When he returned to the main assembly room, he found Aubrey on the dance floor and Lord Ruthven brooding in a corner. Sir William had disappeared, but he supposed a two-for-one trade couldn't be considered bad odds and wondered just how he was expected to watch all three men at once. Obviously, he'd have to be more than a mere passive observer. The situation seemed to make it necessary he tackle Ruthven first.

Dressed in funereal black, the peer swept the room with a somber gaze. He gave no indication that he'd noticed Henry's approach and replied to his greeting with a curt nod.

"I'm surprised to see you here, Lord Ruthven." Henry locked eyes with the lord and allowed enough power to ensure a reply. "It is well known you do not dance."

"I am here to meet someone."

"Who, if I may be so bold as to ask? I've recently come from the card rooms and may have seen him."

A muscle jumped under the sallow skin of Ruthven's cheek. To Henry's surprise, he looked away, sighed deeply, and said, "It is of no account as he is not yet here."

Impressed by the man's willpower—if unimpressed by his theatrical melancholy—Henry bowed and moved away. The man's sullen disposition and cold, corpse-gray eyes, isolated him from the society his wealth and title gave him access to. Could he be taking revenge against those who shunned him by selling secrets to the French? Perhaps. This was not the time, nor the place, for forcing an answer.

Treading a careful path around a cluster of turbaned dowagers—more dangerous amass than a crowd of angry peasants with torches and pitchforks—Henry made his way to the side of a young man he knew from White's and asked for an introduction to Mr. Maxwell Aubrey.

"Good lord, Henry, whatever for?"

Henry smiled disarmingly. "I hear he's a damnably bad card player."

"He is, but if you think to pluck him, you're a year too late or two years too early. He doesn't come into his capital until he's twenty-five and after the chicken incident, his trustees keep a tight hold of the purse strings."

"Chicken incident?"

"That's right, it happened before you came to London. You see, Aubrey fell in with this fellow named Bouchard."

"Yves Bouchard?"

"That's right. Anyway, Bouchard had Aubrey wrapped around his little finger. Dared him to cluck like a chicken in the middle of the dance floor. I thought Mrs. Drummond-Burrell was going to have spasms. Neither Bouchard nor Aubrey were given vouchers for the rest of the Season."

"And this Season?"

He nodded at Aubrey who was leading his partner off the dance floor. "This Season, all is forgiven."

"And Bouchard?" Henry asked.

"Bouchard, too. Although he doesn't seem to be here tonight."

So Aubrey was wrapped around Bouchard's little finger. *Wrapped tightly enough to spy for the French?* Henry wondered.

The return of a familiar voice diverted his attention. He turned to see Sir William once again playing court to Carmilla. When she giggled and looked away, it only seemed to inspire Sir William the more. Henry moved closer until he could hear her protests. She sounded both flattered and frightened.

Now that's a combination impossible to resist, Henry thought watching Wyndham respond. With a predator's fluid grace, he deftly inserted himself between them. "I believe this dance is mine." When Carmilla giggled but made no objection, there was nothing Wyndham could do but quietly seethe.

Once on the floor, Henry smiled down into cornflower blue eyes. "I hope you'll forgive me for interfering, Miss Amworth, but Sir William's attentions seemed to be bothering you."

She dropped her gaze to the vicinity of his waistcoat. "Not bothering, but a bit overwhelming. I'm glad of the chance to gather my thoughts."

"I feel I should warn you that he has a sad reputation."

"He *is* a very accomplished flirt."

"He is a confirmed rake, Miss Amworth."

"Do you think he is more than merely flirting, then?" Her voice held a hint of hope.

Immortality, Henry mused, *would not provide time enough to understand women.* Granted, Sir William had been blessed with darkly sardonic good looks and an athletic build, but he was also—the possibility of his being a spy aside—an arrogant, self-serving libertine. Some women were drawn to that kind of danger; he had not thought Carmilla Amworth to be one of them. His gaze dropped to the pulse beating at an ivory temple, and he wondered just how much danger she dared to experience.

Obviously aware that she should be at least attempting conversation, she took a deep breath and blurted, "I hear you saved Captain Evans last night."

Had everyone heard about it? Varney would not be pleased. "It was nothing."

"My maid says that he was set upon by robbers and you saved his life."

"Servants' gossip."

A dimple appeared beside a generous mouth. "Servants usually know."

Considering his own servant, Henry had to admit the truth of that.

"Were they robbers?"

"I didn't know you were so bloodthirsty, Miss Amworth." When she merely giggled and shook her head, he apologized and added, "I don't know what they were. They ran off as I approached."

"Surely Captain Evans knew."

"If he did, he didn't tell me."

"It must have been so exciting." Her voice grew stronger, and her chin rose, exposing the soft flesh of her throat. "There are times I long to just throw aside all this so-called polite society."

I should have fed before I came. After a brief struggle with his reaction, Henry steered the conversation to safer grounds. It wasn't difficult as Carmilla, apparently embarrassed by her brief show of passion, answered only yes and no for the rest of the dance.

As he escorted her off the floor, Wyndham moved possessively toward her. While trying to decide just how far he should extend his protection, Henry saw Aubrey and Ruthven leave the room together. He heard the younger man say "Bouchard" and lost the rest of their conversation in the surrounding noise.

Good lord, are they both involved?

"My dance this time, I believe, Fitzroy." Shooting Henry an obvious warning, Sir William captured Carmilla's hand and began to lead her away. She seemed fascinated by him and he, for his part, clearly intended to have her.

Fully aware that the only way to save the naive young heiress was to claim her himself, Henry reluctantly went after Aubrey and Ruthven.

By the time he reached King Street, the two men were distant shadows, almost hidden by the night. Breathing deeply in an effort to clear his head of the warm, meaty odor of the assembly rooms, Henry followed, his pace calculated to close the distance between them without drawing attention to himself. An experienced hunter knew better than to spook his prey.

He could hear Aubrey talking of a recent race meeting, could hear Ruthven's monosyllabic replies, and heard nothing at all that would link them to the missing document or to Yves Bouchard. Hardly surprising. Only fools would speak of betraying their country so publicly.

When they went into Aubrey's lodgings near Portman Square, Henry wrapped himself in the darkness and climbed to the small balcony off the sitting room. He felt a bit foolish, skulking about like a common house-breaker. Captain Evans' desire to avoid a scandal, while admirable, was becoming irritating.

"Here it is."

"Are you sure?" Ruthven's heart pounded as though he'd been running. It all but drowned out the sound of paper rustling.

"Why would Bouchard lie to me?"

Why, indeed? A door opened, and closed, and Henry was on the street waiting for Ruthven when he emerged from the building. He was about to step forward when a carriage rumbled past, reminding him that, in spite of the advanced hour, the street was far from empty.

Following close on Ruthven's heels—and noting that wherever the dour peer was heading it wasn't toward home—Henry waited until he passed the mouth of a dark and deserted mews, then made his move. With one hand around Ruthven's throat and the other holding him against a rough stone wall, his lips drew back off his teeth in involuntary anticipation of the other man's terror.

To his astonishment, Ruthven merely declared with

gloomy emphasis. "Come, Death, strike. Do not keep me waiting any longer."

His own features masked by the night, Henry frowned. Mouth slightly open to better taste the air, he breathed in an acrid odor he recognized. "You're drunk!" Releasing his grip, he stepped back.

"Although it is none of your business, I am always drunk." Under his customary scowl, Ruthven's dull gray eyes flicked from side to side, searching the shadows.

That explained a great deal about Ruthven's near legendary melancholy, and perhaps it explained something else as well. "Is that why you're spying for France?"

"The only thing I do for France is drink their liquor." The peer drew himself up to his full height. "And Death or not, I resent your implication."

His protest held the ring of truth. "Then what do you want with Yves Bouchard?"

"He said he could get me . . ." All at once he stopped and stared despondently into the night. "That also is none of your business."

Beginning to grow irritated, Henry snarled.

Ruthven pressed himself back against the wall. "I ordered a cask of brandy from him. Don't ask me how he smuggles it through the blockade because I don't know. He was to meet me tonight at Almack's, but he never came."

"What did Maxwell Aubrey give you?"

"Bouchard's address." As the wine once again overcame his fear—imitation willpower, Henry realized—Ruthven's scowl deepened. "I don't believe you *are* Death. You're nothing but a common-cutpurse." His tone dripped disdain. "I shall call for the Watch."

"Go right ahead." Henry's hand darted forward, patted Ruthven's vest, and returned clutching Bouchard's address. Slipping the piece of paper into an inner pocket, he stepped back and merged with the night.

Varney would probably insist that Ruthven should die, but Henry suspected that nothing he said would be believed. Besides, if he told everyone he'd met Death in an alley, he wouldn't be far wrong.

As expected, Bouchard was not in his rooms.

And neither, upon returning to Portman Square, was

Maxwell Aubrey. Snarling softly to himself, Henry listened to a distant watchman announce it was a fine night. At just past two, it was certainly early enough for Aubrey to have gone to one of his clubs, or to a gaming hall, or to a brothel. Unfortunately, all Henry knew of him was that he was an easily-influenced young man. Brow furrowed, he'd half decided to head back toward St. James Street when he heard the crash of breaking branches coming from the park the square enclosed.

Curious, he walked over to the wrought-iron fence and peered up into an immense old oak. Believing himself familiar with every nuance of the night, he was astonished to see Aubrey perched precariously on a swaying limb, arms wrapped tightly around another, face nearly as white as his crumpled cravat.

"What the devil are you doing up there?" Henry demanded, beginning to feel that Captain Evans had sent him on a fool's mission. The night was rapidly taking on all the aspects of high farce.

Wide-eyed gaze searching the darkness for the source of the voice, Aubrey flashed a nervous smile in all directions. "Seeber dared me to spend a night in one of these trees," he explained ingenuously. Then he frowned. "You're not the Watch are you?"

"No, I'm not the Watch."

"Good. That is, I imagine it would be hard to explain this to the Watch."

"I imagine it would be," Henry repeated dryly.

"You see, it's not as easy as it looks like it would be." He shifted position slightly and squeezed his eyes closed as the branch he sat on bobbed and swayed.

The man was an idiot and obviously not capable of being a French spy. Bouchard would have to be a *greater* idiot to trust so pliable a tool.

"I don't suppose you could help me down."

Henry considered it. "No," he said at last and walked away.

He found Sir William Wyndham, the last name on the list, and therefore the traitor by default, at White's playing deep basset. Carefully guarding his expression after Viscount Hanely had met him in a dimly lit hall and leaped away in terror—Henry declined all invitations to play. Much like a cat at a mousehole, he watched and waited for Sir William to leave.

Unfortunately, Sir William was winning.

At five, lips drawn back off his teeth, Henry left the club. He could feel the approaching dawn and had to feed before the day claimed him. He had intended to feed upon Sir William, leaving him weak and easy prey for the captain's men—but Sir William obviously had no intention of leaving the table while his luck held.

The porter who handed Mr. Fitzroy his greatcoat and hat averted his gaze and spent the next hour successfully convincing himself that he hadn't seen what he knew he had.

Walking quickly through the dregs of the night, Henry returned to Albany but, rather than enter his own chambers, he continued to where he could gain access to the suite on the second floor. Entering silently through the large window, he crossed to the bed and stared down at its sleeping occupant.

George Gordon, the sixth Lord Byron, celebrated author of *Childe Harold's Pilgrimage*, was indeed a handsome young man. Henry had never seen him as having the ethereal and poignant beauty described by Caroline Lamb, but then, he realized, Caroline Lamb had never seen the poet with his hair in paper curlers.

His bad mood swept away by the rising Hunger, Henry sat down on the edge of the bed and softly called Byron's name, drawing him up but not entirely out of sleep.

The wide mouth curved into an anticipatory smile, murmuring, "Incubus." without quite waking.

"I don't like you going to see that poet," Varney muttered, carefully setting the buckled shoes to one side. "You're going to end up in trouble there, see if you don't."

"He thinks I'm a dream." Henry ran both hands back through his hair and grinned, remembering the curlers. So much for Byron's claim that the chestnut ringlets were natural. "What could possibly happen?"

"You could end up in one of his stories, that's what."

Unable to read, Varney regarded books with a superstitious awe that bordered on fear. "The secret'd be out and some fine day it'd be the stake sure as I'm standing here." The little man drew himself up to his full height and fixed Henry with an indignant glare. "I told you before and I'll tell you again, you got yourself so mixed up in this society thing you're forgetting what you are! You got to stop taking so many chances." His eyes glittered. "Try and remember, most folks don't look kindly on the bloodsucking undead."

"I'll try and remember." Glancing up at his servant over steepled fingers, Henry added, "I've something for you to do today. I need Sir William Wyndham watched. If he's visited by someone named Yves Bouchard, go immediately to Captain Evans; he'll know what to do. If he tries to leave London, stop him."

Brows that crossed above Varney's nose in a continuous line, lifted. "How stopped?"

"Stopped. Anything else, I want to be told at sunset."

"So, what did this bloke do that he's to be stopped?" Varney raised his hand lest Henry get the wrong idea. "Not that I won't stop him, mind, in spite of how I feel about you suddenly taking it into your head to track down evil doers. You know me, give me an order and I'll follow it."

"Which is why I found you almost dead in a swamp outside Plassey while the rest of your regiment was *inside* Plassey?"

"Not the same thing at all," the ex-soldier told him, pointedly waiting for the answer to his question.

"He sold out Wellington's army to the French."

Varney grunted. "Stopping's too good for him."

"Sir William Wyndham got a message this afternoon. Don't know what was in it, but he's going to be taking a trip to the coast tonight."

"Damn him!" Henry dragged his shirt over his head. "He's taking the information to Napoleon *himself*!"

Varney shrugged and brushed invisible dust off a green-striped waistcoat. "I don't know about that, but if his coachman's to be trusted, he's heading for the coast right enough, as soon as the moon lights the road."

*   *   *

Henry stood on the steps of Sir William's townhouse, considered his next move and decided the rising moon left him no time to be subtle.

The butler who answered the imperious summons of the polished brass knocker opened his mouth to deny this inopportune visitor entry, but closed it again without making a sound.

"Take me to Sir William," Henry commanded.

Training held, but only just. "Very good, sir. If you would follow me." The butler's hand trembled slightly, but his carefully modulated voice gave no indication that he had just been shown his own mortality. "Sir William is in the library, sir. Through this door here. Shall I announce you?"

With one hand on the indicated door, Henry shook his head. "That won't be necessary. In fact, you should forget I was ever here."

Lost in the surprising dark depths of the visitor's pale eyes, the butler shuddered. "Thank you, sir. I will."

Three sets of branched candelabra lit the library, more than enough for Henry to see that the room held two large leather chairs, a number of hunting trophies, and very few books.

Sir William, dressed for travel in breeches and top boots, stood leaning on the mantlepiece reading a single sheet of paper. He turned when he heard the door open and scowled when he saw who it was. "Fitzroy! What the devil are you doing here? I told Babcock I was not to be . . ."

Then his voice trailed off as he got a better look at Henry's face. There were a number of men in London he considered to be dangerous, but until this moment, he would not have included Henry Fitzroy among them. Forcing his voice past the growing panic he stammered, "W-what?"

"You dare to ask when you're holding *that*!" A pale hand shot forward to point at the paper in Wyndham's hand.

"This?" Confusion momentarily eclipsed the fear. "What has this to do with you?"

Henry charged across the room, grabbed a double handful of cloth, and slammed the traitor against the wall. "It has everything to do with me!"

"I didn't know! I swear to God I didn't know!" Hanging

limp in Henry's grasp, Sir William made no struggle to escape. Every instinct screamed "RUN!" but a last vestige of reason realized he wouldn't get far. "If I'd known you were interested in her . . ."

"Who?"

"Carmilla Amworth."

Sir William crashed to his knees as Henry released him and stepped back. "So that's how you were going to hide it," he growled. "A seduction on your fabled yacht. Was a French boat to meet you in the channel?"

"A French boat?"

"Or were you planning on finding sanctuary with Napoleon? And what of Miss Amworth, compromised both by your lechery and your treason?"

"Treason?"

"Forcing her to marry you would gain you her fortune, but tossing her overboard would remove the only witness." Lips drawn back off his teeth, Henry buried his hand in Sir William's hair and forced his head back. Cravat and collar were thrown to the floor, exposing the muscular column of throat. "I don't know how you convinced her to accompany you, but it doesn't really matter now."

With the last of his strength, Sir William shoved the crumpled piece of paper in Henry's face, his life saved by the faint scent of a familiar perfume clinging to it.

Henry managed to turn aside only because he'd fed at dawn. His left hand clutching the note, his right still holding Sir William's hair, he straightened.

"*. . . I can no longer deny you but it must be tonight for reasons I cannot disclose at this time.*" It was signed, C. Amworth.

Frowning, he looked down into Sir William's face. If Carmilla had insisted that they leave for the yacht tonight there could be only one answer. "Did Yves Bouchard suggest you seduce Miss Amworth?"

"I do not seduce young woman on the suggestion of acquaintances," Sir William replied as haughtily as possible under the circumstances. "However," he added hurriedly as the hazel eyes locked onto his began to darken, "Bouchard may have mentioned she was not only rich but ripe for the plucking."

So, there was the Bouchard connection. Caught between the two men, Carmilla Amworth was being used by both. By Bouchard to gain access to Wyndham's yacht and therefore France. By Wyndham to gain access to her fortune. And that seemed to be all that Sir William was guilty of. Still frowning, Henry stepped back. "Well, if you didn't steal the document," he growled, "who did?"

"I did." As he turned, Carmilla pointed a small but eminently serviceable pistol at him. "I've been waiting in Sir William's carriage these last few moments and when no one emerged, I let myself in. Stay right where you are, Mr. Fitzroy," she advised, no longer looking either fragile or waiflike. "I am held to be a very good shot." Her calm gaze took in the positions of the two men and she suddenly smiled, dimples appearing in both cheeks. "Were you fighting for my honor?"

Lips pressed into a thin line, Henry bowed his head. "Until I discovered you had none."

The smile disappeared. "I was raised a republican, Mr. Fitzroy, and I find the thought of that fat fool returning to the throne of France to be ultimately distasteful. In time . . ." Her eyes blazed. ". . . I'll help England be rid of her own fat fool."

"You think the English will rise and overthrow the royal family?"

"I know they will."

"If they didn't rise when m . . ." About to say, *my father,* he hastily corrected himself. ". . . when King Henry burned Catholic and Protestant indiscriminately in the street, what makes you think they'll rise now?"

Her delicate chin lifted. "The old ways are finished. It's long past time for things to change."

"And does your uncle believe as you do?"

"My uncle knows nothing. His little niece would come visiting him at his office and little bits of paper would leave with her." The scornful laugh had as much resemblance to the previous giggles as night to day. "I'd love to stand around talking politics with you, but I haven't the time." Her lavender kid glove tightened around the butt of one of Manton's finest. "There'll be a French boat meeting Sir William's yacht very early tomorrow morning, and I have information I must deliver."

"You used me!" Scowling, Sir William got slowly to his feet. "I don't appreciate being used." He took a step forward, but Henry stopped him with a raised hand.

"You're forgetting the pistol."

"The pistol?" Wyndham snorted. "No woman would have the fortitude to kill a man in cold blood."

Remembering how both his half-sisters had held the throne, Henry shook his head. "You'd be surprised. However," he fixed Carmilla with an inquiring stare, "we seem to be at a standstill as you certainly can't shoot both of us."

"True. But I'm sure both of you *gentlemen . . .*" The emphasis was less than complimentary. ". . . will cooperate lest I shoot the other."

"I'm afraid you're going to shoot no one." Suddenly behind her, Henry closed one hand around her wrist and the other around the barrel of the gun. He had moved between one heartbeat and the next; impossible to see, impossible to stop.

"What are you?" Carmilla whispered, her eyes painfully wide in a face blanched of color.

His smile showed teeth. "A patriot." He'd been within a moment of killing Sir William, ripping out his throat and feasting on his life. His anger had been kicked sideways by Miss Amworth's entrance and he supposed he should thank her for preventing an unredeemable faux pas. "Sir William, if you could have your footman go to the house of Captain Charles Evans on Charges Street, I think he'll be pleased to know we've caught his traitor."

". . . so they come and took the lady away, but that still doesn't explain where you've been 'til nearly sunup."

"I was with Sir William. We had unfinished business."

Varney snorted, his disapproval plain. "Oh. It was like that, was it?"

Henry smiled as he remembered the feel of Sir William's hair in his hand and the heat rising off his kneeling body.

Well aware of what the smile meant, Varney snorted again. "And did Sir William ask what you were?"

"Sir William would never be so impolite. He thinks we fought over Camilla, discovered she was a traitor, drank ourselves nearly senseless, and parted the best of friends."

Feeling the sun poised on the horizon, Henry stepped into his bedchamber and turned to close the door on the day. "Besides, Sir William doesn't *want* to know what I am."

"Got some news for you." Varney worked up a lather on the shaving soap. "Something happened today."

Resplendent in a brocade dressing gown, Henry leaned back in his chair and reached for the razor. "I imagine that something happens every day."

"Well *today*, that Carmilla Amworth slipped her chain and run off."

"She escaped from custody?"

"That's what I said. Seems they underestimated her, her being a lady and all. Still, she's missed her boat, so even if she gets to France, she'll be too late. You figure that's where she's heading?"

"I wouldn't dare to hazard a guess." Henry frowned and wiped the remaining lather off his face. "Is everyone talking about it?"

"That she was a French spy? Not likely, they're all too busy talking about how she snuck out of Lady Glebe's party and into Sir William's carriage." He clucked his tongue. "The upper classes have got dirty minds, that's what I say."

"Are you including me in that analysis?"

Varney snorted. "Ask your poet. All I say about you is that you've got to take more care. So you saved Wellington's Army. Good for you. Now ..." he held out a pair of biscuit-colored pantaloons. "... do you think you could act a little more suitable to your condition?"

"I don't recall ever behaving *unsuitably*."

"Oh, aye, dressing up so fine and dancing and going to the theater and sitting about playing cards at clubs for *gentlemen*." His emphasis sounded remarkably like that of Carmilla Amworth.

"Perhaps you'd rather I wore grave clothes and we lived in a mausoleum?"

"No, but ..."

"A drafty castle somewhere in the mountains of eastern Europe?"

Varney sputtered incoherently.

Henry sighed and deftly tied his cravat. "Then let's hear no more about me forgetting who and what I am. I'm very sorry if you wanted someone a little more darkly tragic. A brooding, mythic persona who only emerges to slake his thirst on the fair throats of helpless virgins ..."

"Here now! None of that!"

"But I'm afraid you're stuck with me." Holding out his arms, he let Varney help him into his jacket. "And I am almost late for an appointment at White's. I promised Sir William a chance to win back his eleven hundred pounds."

His sensibilities obviously crushed, Varney ground his teeth.

"Now, what's the matter?"

The little man shook his head. "It just doesn't seem right that you, with all you could be, should be worried about being late for a card game."

His expression stern, Henry took hold of Varney's chin, and held the servant's gaze with his. "I think *you* forget who I am." His fingertips dimpled stubbled flesh. "I am a Lord of Darkness, a Creature of the Night, an Undead Fiend with Unnatural Appetites, indeed a *Vampyre*; but all of that ..." His voice grew deeper and Varney began to tremble. "... is no excuse for bad manners."

Author's Note:

The real Henry Fitzroy, Duke of Richmond, bastard son of Henry VIII, died at seventeen on July 22nd, 1536, of what modern medicine thinks was probably tuberculousis. Modern medicine, however, has no explanation for why the Duke of Norfolk was instructed to smuggle the body out of St. James's Palace and bury it secretly.

All things considered, who's to say he stayed buried.

Those who would like to see more of Henry Fitzroy, can find him in *Blood Price, Blood Trail, Blood Lines, and Blood Pact* (available from DAW Books, distributed by Penguin).

A MATTER OF TASTE
by Nick Pollotta·

"Hoot nay, one-two-tha-ree!" screamed the furious crowd of Scottish villagers, and the crude battering ram surged forward once more. With the sound of splintering wood the huge doors blocking the entrance to the abandoned coal mine crashed apart, splinters exploding into the night air like bold Celtic toothpicks heading toward the moon.

"For God and King!" bellowed a red-faced dollymop, brandishing an executioner's ax.

Shouting in victory, the mob of Highlanders dropped the old, weathered caber and started to charge in through the ruined barrier, the local constable and grimy navies waving their wooden stakes and blunderbusses. In the lead of the angry throng was a lean whippet of man sporting a soft-brimmed hat, swallowtail coat, tight breeches, and fine Hoby boots. Dapper gentleman's clothes from Weston in London. He looked a toff, but tucked firmly into his black leather belt was a short ebony baton crested with the imperial seal of England. And grasped in his big callused hands were a brace of ornate Collier pistols, the long tapering .72 barrels of the new style breechloaders gleaming like polished justice in the rosy dimness of predawn. Cocking both the curved hammers, the Bow Street Runner double-checked to make sure the copper percussion caps were firmly in place. Now was no time for a deadly misfire. As a duly empowered agent of the crown, it was his task to see that the inhuman beast who had plagued this peaceful Scottish valley for so long must never be allowed to kill man, woman, child, or even somebody from Ireland, ever again! And the heavy cold iron balls in his primed guns would hopefully do the bleeding monster up a treat, good and proper.

But the brave British posse stopped dead in their tracks as the flickering light of the torches clearly illuminated the interior. It was like a scene from hell, or the infamous American city of New York.

The ceiling of the mining tunnel was completely covered with fat chattering bats, thousands of the noisy beasts flapping their leathery wings, foam dripping from their cruel mouths. And the hard stone ground was solid with a living carpet of snarling rats. Millions of beady eyes stared at the humans, and the villagers could feel the tangible cloud of their living hate. And hunger. Even the one barrister in the crowd felt faint.

Suddenly a cold wind blew from deep within the old coal shaft, carrying with it a smell of newly turned earth, death, and mint leaves. As always before, that was when the torches sputtered out. But now, bits of hot oakum were used to ignite dozens of whale oil bullseye lanterns, the glass flumes protecting the delicate flames within, and brilliant white cones of light brightly illuminated the rocky passage.

The beams bobbed about in frantic search and soon converged on the source of the wind. At the rear of the mine, a dimly seen figure smirked at them and stuck out its long forked tongue. Standing brazen at the rear of the mine entrance, protected by the slavering army of night hunters, was a humanoid creature dressed in a double-breasted Duke Street coat, ruffled shirt, Beau Brummel breeches, roll top boots, and wrapped in a long flowing Spitfields silk cape. Very nice, indeed. However, his skin was deathly pale, his eyes glowing red and his teeth a dentist's nightmare.

"So, you silly, kilt-wearing fools actually did manage to find me," hissed the vampire, exposing every inch of his long white fangs. "Amazing. Bloody incredible."

Incensed, the tartan-clad Scots cursed in anger and started forward, but the bats and rats hissed in unison, stopping the invasion faster than it had begun. With the entire population of the remote village outnumbered thousands to one, even the alcoholic mayor and the more-than-slightly-insane junkyard dog wondered if it was time to try diplomacy. Immediately, the secret band of Freemasons in the group started writing a petition.

"It's a rum deal, my culleys," sneered the inhuman beast in a really bad Rookery accent. "Enter, and my servants will tear you to shreds! Oh, some may live to combat me, but will there be enough?" A truly devilish eyebrow raised in contempt and, self-consciously, he tucked the medical marvel of the recently invented Pierre Fuachard toothbrush deeper into a vest pocket. His personal hygiene was none of their damn business.

"I'm ready for battle!" it panted breathlessly. *"Are you?"*

In reply, the bow Street Runner fired both of his Colliers, the iron balls smacking the vampire directly in the chest. This triggered a barrage of blunderbusses, four-barreled "duck foot" fowlers, horse pistols, and muzzle-loading rifles from the attending crowd, whose strident discharge filled the mine with thunder and flame and boiling clouds of acrid black powder smoke. Wasting no time in a reload, the Runner dropped his Colliers, and pulled two squat .66 Newarks from the voluminous pockets of his great coat and fired again. Then dropped those and drew from his boots a matched pair of double-barreled Manton conversions. Deadly little barkers, without a doubt.

Another volley sounded from the blunderbusses and muskets. The assorted fusillade of rounds wildly ricocheted off the black wall and blasted the expensive clothing of the vampire to pieces.

Contemptuously, the beast brushed some imaginary lint off a riddled lapel, took a bit of snuff from his gold Nathaniel Mills box, sneezed, and smiled toothily at them.

"Ow," he chuckled.

The angry crowd made some more angry crowd noises, but much less sure of themselves this time. His flowing white beard abristle in fury, a determined piper doffed his tam o'shanter and started playing the bagpipes at full volume, but even that vicious attack seemed to have no debilitating effect on the man-demon. Deciding this was the appropriate moment to act, the barrister promptly took a huge swig of pure quill laudanum and fainted dead away. The priest began a lengthy exorcism.

Unexpectedly a flurry of wooden arrows twanged across the mine shaft—impacting everywhere except into the half-naked body of the muscular monster. At the rear of the mob, a doddering old groundskeeper glared hostilely at his impressed gang of apprentice archers. Britons who couldn't fire a long bow? What was the empire coming to? In return, the clerks, cooks, and coopers looked incredibly embarrassed. Well, at least they hadn't shot themselves in the hand again.

Inside the mine shaft, the laughing vampire twirled the remains of a bedraggled Spitfields cape about himself and was gone from sight.

"Good-bye, fools!" cackled the darkness, the words echoing strangely. "Within minutes I will be safely hidden within the endless natural catacombs beneath this mudhole of a city. A thousand men in a thousand years could never find me again!"

An elderly dairy farmer gave a juicy raspberry and the village tout shouted out a virulent oath that made even the blustering navies blanch at its raw vulgarity. Hot haggis, that was a good'un!

"And I will return to tap the claret," continued a whispery voice fading at every moment, the dire words invoking ghastly images of rivers of human blood. "Next year, on this very day, I shall come back to reap my revenge. For I will use the secret second sleep of a vampire. During the coming seasons I will rest, arising for but a single day one year from now. Three hundred and sixty-five times stronger than I am now!"

Fading rapidly, the words repeated in snarling fury. "Three hundred and sixty-five times *stronger*! How will you stop me then, you dirt-eating peasants? Seal the mine with iron boiler plate, and I shall break free through the granite with my bare hands. Run, and I shall track you each down across the whole world!"

The bats and rats screamed in victory and the pale Highlanders began retreating into the forest. Across the whole world? Even as unimaginably far away as Edinburgh? Bloody hell! Maybe this hunt hadn't been such a swell idea after all.

Reloading as fast as possible, even the valiant Bow Street

Runner seemed a bit daunted. 'Struth, what would Sir Henry Fielding, the heroic founder of the Runners, do in this rum job? Read the beast the Riot Act? Call in the Dragoons? Offer a stash of blunt as a bribe? Get royally pissed on dog-nose's at a dollyshop? Suddenly, the imperial baton in his belt seemed to weigh a thousand stone and hindered his every step.

"I win," whispered the cold wind in the rustling trees as the villagers and the sullen Runner shuffled along the king's road winding through the heather carpeted forest. Just then, the sun crested the western mountains, the golden glorious dawn only horribly counterpointing the humans listless retreat to their lonely vulnerable homes.

"See you real soon ... aha-ha-ha-ha-ha ..." evilly murmured the disappearing shadows.

But with those words the London lawman slowed and, ever so slightly, give a sly smile like a 200 point man at Eton facing a sticky wicket. No, that was incorrect. The vampire wouldn't be seeing them soon, would he? The West End fop had truly missed the mark with that remark. Thoughtfully, the thief-catcher fingered the loudly ticking Breguer watch in the pocket of his waistcoat. Time was on their—his—side. And he had a full solar year in which to act. A fact which gave the Bow Street Runner a bleeding dangerous idea that immensely appealed to his personal sense of justice.

Only ... would the chancy scheme work?

Three hundred and sixty-four days later, the people of the isolated Scottish town were busy erecting colorful booths, gay banners, and a huge canvas circus tent. Fresh fragrant flowers adorned every house, every barn and inn, while great iron cooking vats bubbled merrily away in the campsites, filling the air with right pungent fumes of meaty stews and fancy French souffles and zesty sauces. Squealing mudlarks happily dug in the ground seeking dropped coins, while rouged whores lifted their skirts for patrons behind every bush, and scarred pugilists pounded each other in drunken stupor. Lounging in false casualness, all six of the attending Bow Street Runners, including the right honorable Sir Henry Fielding himself, did nothing to stop any of it, even though prize fighting had been illegal since 1750. They merely sipped their blackjacks of hot gin and nutmeg, kept a close eye on their gold watches and ready hands on their loaded Collier and Manton pistols. Soon now, very soon.

During the daylight hours dozens, hundreds, then literally thousands of people from London, Paris, Italy, Germany, and even distant America, had responded to the imperial invitation and swarmed into the tiny highland village, adding to and augmenting the tantalizing cloud of cooking aromas with their own culinary contributions. By twilight, a boisterous party was in full swing with four different bands playing, scores of dancers twirling, and a hundred whole oxen roasting in huge pits full of crackling logs, the juicy meat spewing endless volumes of tangy smoke toward the distant twinkling stars. The staggering array of beef had been personally donated to the endeavor by good Queen Caroline and Prince William themselves. King George IV, having temporarily gone potty again, currently believed he was an Etruscan vase full of live mice.

The feasting and festivities went on far into the night. The only disruption to the happy revelry occurred at exactly midnight when the dance music was momentarily interrupted by a small explosion from the direction of the old abandoned coal mine in the foothills, closely followed by a loud squeak of inhuman horror. Seconds later, a barely noticed handful of dry ash blew across the joyous folk celebrating the first international Royal Garlic Festival.

Author's Note:

Established in 1749, during their short span of existence, there were never more than six Bow Street Runners total to protect all of suburban London, a city with over one million inhabitants. More than mere law enforcement personnel, they each carried a baton bearing the Great Seal of England, which gave them authority to go anywhere, question or arrest anybody with immunity and even to command the military.

All of the Runners, with the sole exception of their

founder, Sir Henry Fielding, were former master criminals themselves, caught and given the choice of death or becoming a Runner and capturing other criminals. From this came the expression "set a thief to catch a thief." In 1829 they were replaced by Robert (bobbies) Peel's (peelers) organization of uniformed police officers whose jackets sported giant copper buttons used to easily identify each other at night. The unique decoration quickly giving them, and eventually all police, the permanent nickname of "coppers."

And while exceptionally efficient, the stalwart constables of present-day Scotland Yard have never quite managed to generate the excitement or romance of the incredible Bow Street Runners.

Nick Pollotta is a former stand-up comic from New York with twelve (and counting) SF/Humor novels on the stands, including the international hit *Bureau 13*. His SF/Humor short stories have appeared in dozens of anthologies and magazines over the past five years. A bachelor, he currently resides in Columbus, Ohio.

VOICE FROM THE VOID
by Margaret L. Carter

As the speaker stood on the tigerskin hearth rug droning on about hypnotism and reincarnation, Claude D'Arnot contemplated the gaslight's gleam on the man's bald head and gold-rimmed spectacles. "Recently I recovered the buried memories of a gifted subject who had served as a priestess in the temple of Dagon on the island-continent of Mu before its cataclysmic destruction...."

Claude, bored with the speech, let his eyes wander to the fur rug, complete with tail, paws, and head. His sympathies lay with the tiger, a solitary predator vastly outnumbered by both its natural prey and the human interlopers.

He shifted his attention to his own quarry, the medium Violet, who sat beside him on the divan. Flushing beneath his scrutiny, the young woman met his eyes for a second, then looked back at the speaker. Claude sensed Violet's skepticism—no wonder, considering her own role in the group—as well as her lack of interest in the lecture. *She's disturbed about something.* She radiated unease, reinforcing the message Claude read in her depressed skin temperature, erratic pulse, and shadowed aura.

Could this be the opening I've waited for? He'd watched her for weeks, his desire mounting, but he'd held back. He wanted more from her than a casual supper engagement. *Why? What makes this one different from any other human female?*

The medium's friend Harriet Harmon, seated on Claude's left, showed greater enthusiasm for the saga of ancient Mu, as did the other dozen or so people grouped around the drawing room. Miss Harmon leaned over to whisper in Claude's ear, "Isn't this fascinating?"

"Indeed," he murmured, waving away a maid who hovered nearby offering a refill of his sherry. *Fascinating drivel.* Among the countless people he'd mesmerized during his lifetime, not one had dropped a hint of a previous existence. But he had joined the Esoteric Order of Leviathan for entertainment, not its intellectual resources. Women enthralled with the supernatural could easily be seduced into "ritual blood-sharing," so long as he clouded their minds to obscure the one-sided nature of the "sharing."

Claude had dabbled in several such cults, including that unsavory young fellow Crowley's circle, and the Leviathan devotees peddled the most imaginative brand of nonsense he'd encountered. As far as he could untangle the threads of their doctrine, they taught that when the Elder Gods broke through from the void beyond the stars to lay waste the Earth, their faithful servants, as sole survivors, would be transformed into powerful inhuman creatures and rule the world. Those who had died before the glorious conquest would enjoy reincarnation in similarly monstrous guise. *Why not? Sounds more exciting than a cloud-paved heaven with perpetual harp music.* All the religions practiced by ephemerals struck Claude, who wavered between deism and frank agnosticism, as equally silly anyway.

A patter of applause interrupted his thoughts. The High Archon of the Order took the speaker's place in front of the hearth. "Thank you, Professor Rinaldo, for that most enlightening presentation. That concludes the public portion of this week's convocation." He chanted a benediction in what he claimed to be ancient Sumerian. For all Claude knew, it might be; it resembled no language he'd ever heard.

The Archon, a bony middle-aged man, clean-shaven except for a bushy mustache that matched his tufted eyebrows, wore an aquamarine robe and a bronze pectoral set with semiprecious stones. A bronze circlet of similar design adorned his high forehead and abundant iron-gray hair. Though he made cryptic claims to an aristocratic bloodline, the Archon was actually a former stage magician named Matthew McFadden. Claude had satisfied his curiosity on this and other points—for instance, the medium's identity as McFadden's orphaned niece, Violet Cade—the first night they'd met, afterwards making the cult leader forget the conversation. Not that Claude disapproved of the spiritualist; as a former actor and something of a trickster himself, he could appreciate a clever charlatan.

While the maid cleared away the sherry decanters and trays of sweet biscuits, the butler ushered the guests to the front hall. Claude, along with Professor Rinaldo and Miss Harmon, had the privilege of staying for the medium's private performance, the weekly seance. During that first interview with McFadden, he'd implanted an impression of himself as a scholar of the occult who deserved a place in the Order's inner circle.

Standing up, Violet said to Claude, "Will you be joining us as usual, Mr. D'Arnot?" He heard an atypical strain in her voice. *Yes, something's bothering her tonight.* Clad in a loose, white robe, with her chestnut hair unbound, showing golden highlights in the lamp's glow, she looked ethereally delicate. Claude knew the appearance belied the facts: she managed McFadden's correspondence and financial affairs as well as any hired secretary could have. Despite her cheerful cooperation in her uncle's spiritualist schemes, in other matters she retained her innocence. Claude suspected she had no idea of the erotic symbolism of the bronze ankh pendant she wore.

Her fleeting blush, evoked by his intent gaze, stirred his appetite. He had to restrain himself from touching her by a stern reminder that he had no socially acceptable excuse for doing so. "You know I wouldn't miss it." He said more quietly, "Miss Cade, you seem troubled. Can I help?"

Violet's aura darkened, her smile fading. "There's no need." She cast a nervous glance toward her uncle, making his farewells to the uninitiated. "There's nothing wrong."

Without directly challenging the lie, Claude whispered, "Please keep in mind, if I can offer you any assistance, simply ask."

McFadden walked over to her. "Come along, Violet, it's past time to begin the sitting."

Violet flinched, though her uncle spoke softly. "Yes, I suppose so."

I've never seen her reluctant to participate before, Claude thought. *And what has the man done to her?* His own indignation at the idea of her being hurt surprised him. *Feeling possessive about the girl already? Not a good sign.*

McFadden headed for his study, where the "sittings" took place. Rinaldo, the hypnotist, followed, with Miss Harmon close behind. She said over her shoulder to Violet, "I can't wait—this is going to be so exciting."

The medium still hung back, gazing unhappily at her friend. *So that's part of it. It's Miss Harmon's first time, and Violet has scruples about tricking her.* Claude wondered why he didn't find Harriet Harmon irresistible; traits such as her intelligence and eccentricity usually appealed to him. She made a living as a journalist, scandalous enough in itself. She wore her own version of the Bloomer costume, a long tunic over billowy trousers, which most other suffragettes had abandoned. She openly advocated free love and quoted from the poetry of Baudelaire and Swinburne. Having attended one meeting of the Esoteric Order of Leviathan to write them up for the Society for Psychical Research, she'd lingered as, if not a convert, at least a sympathizer.

Yet Claude found himself fantasizing, instead, about Violet. He'd even begun dreaming about her. Since his kind seldom dreamed, certainly not with the sensuous clarity of the visions that had recently haunted his days, he couldn't deny how strongly the girl obsessed him. *I have to get her out of my system.* Or would this obsession yield to a night or two of dalliance? *What is it about her?* Maybe his fascination grew from the preoccupied frown with which she often stared at him, as if she saw something hidden from others. *Dangerous, if so. I ought to run the other way.*

When the group entered McFadden's study, a plump white Persian cat with mismatched eyes, one golden and one blue, leaped down from the desk and twined around Claude's ankles. Once he had overcome her instinctive animal aversion to him, the cat, Ishtar, had become his devoted friend. He bent to stroke her while McFadden directed the others to the circular table in the center of the room. The only illumination came from a pair of tapers on the desk; according to the Archon, too much light disrupted the "astral vibrations." *With an obvious ploy like that, how does he manage to gull so many victims? And people think of our kind as rapacious!*

Besides the candles, the desk held a mummified cat, still in its tea-brown wrappings, and a green statuette about a foot high. The sculpture represented a crouching, taloned, bat-winged, tentacled figure with a vaguely human visage. The table reserved for the "sitting" bore a silver chalice, with a silver-bladed dagger lying diagonally beside it, representing the feminine and masculine polarities, though of course McFadden would not be so indelicate as to make the symbolism explicit. The occultist nodded impatiently to Claude. "Mr. D'Arnot, perhaps you'll join us so we may begin."

"Certainly. I beg your pardon." Ishtar jumped up to her usual vantage point, the top of a bookcase. Claude took his seat between Violet and Miss Harmon.

"Please join hands," McFadden commanded in his sonorous stage voice, "and remember, whatever you see or hear, do not break the circle. Discarnate entities are both sensitive and capricious. Now, we require silence for the medium's concentration. You can aid Violet's entry into trance by breathing deeply and projecting tranquillity to her."

When Claude's fingers closed around Violet's slender wrist, his fingertips on the pulse point, he gave little thought to discarnate entities. The thoroughly incarnate woman at his right side held his attention, even to the exclusion of the equally healthy female on his left. The tiny hairs in his palm bristled at Violet's touch. Again he noticed that her skin was cooler than normal, and she stiffened as the others obediently relaxed into the deep-breathing exercises the leader modeled in gusty sighs. *Why this apprehension? Just because of her friend's presence? She usually treats the whole process as an entertaining charade.*

After a couple of minutes of silence, aside from the sitters' breathing, like the rush of surf on sand to Claude's sensitive ears, McFadden judged the moment ripe for a message from the "other side." Three sharp raps crackled through the air. Claude saw Rinaldo start and almost snatch his hand from McFadden's. "Good God, what was—"

"Silence!" the leader hissed. A louder rap punctuated the command.

Claude knew the origin of the noises; after the first seance he'd attended, he'd hypnotically induced McFadden to explain the tricks. The Archon wore no implements under his clothes and therefore had nothing to fear from a skeptic's search. Instead, McFadden produced the sounds by cracking his toe joints, a skill, Claude understood, possessed by many spiritualists.

"Is anyone present?" McFadden intoned.

Another minute or two of silence ensued. Claude sensed McFadden's annoyance. Violet wasn't following the script. Her fingers convulsively tightened on his. He gave her a reassuring squeeze in return.

"Is anyone here? Please reveal yourself to us. We are all sympathetic and open to your presence." A longer succession of taps.

At last Violet emitted a low moan. Her blue eyes widened in an entranced gaze that made her look almost childlike. *McFadden chose well; how could anyone suspect such an innocent maiden of fraud?* Her head rolled languidly from side to side, with parted lips and a feverish blush. Claude didn't know whether the pink tint arose naturally from her exertions or whether she was one of those rare ephemerals with some control over involuntary body functions. Either way, he enjoyed the effect.

"Yes, speak to us," McFadden said. "Do not be afraid. Span the gulf between this world and the next, and appear before us."

More raps. Another moan from the medium. A glowing vapor began to coalesce above the center of the table. Both Rinaldo and Miss Harmon gasped aloud. Claude had to admit he'd been impressed, too, when he'd first seen the phosphorescent cloud. McFadden produced it by stepping on a trigger underneath the Oriental carpet, activating a device inside the table. For the "ectoplasm" he had to rely on mechanical aids, risking discovery, but so far no observer had insisted on peeling up the carpet or dismantling the furniture. McFadden did have in his favor the conspicuous absence of the cabinet most physical mediums used; his seance room looked like a respectable gentleman's study.

"Who is there? Do you have a message for one of our number?"

Violet gave a hollow groan. *Why isn't she delivering the message, whatever that may be?*

"Speak, we await you," said McFadden. Even the other ephemerals, Claude reflected, should sense his impatience.

"Rinaldo," Violet sighed. The hypnotist jerked his head up. "Your work—" She exhaled a long breath, as if drawing the words from a deep well. "Sophia is here. She is watching over your work."

"Sophia! Oh, my God!"

"Who is she?" said McFadden in a soft, solicitous voice.

"My daughter—died twelve years ago—fifteen years old."

McFadden had known that, of course. Like any confidence man, the occultist had his sources. He passed on the relevant information to Violet and coached her in its use.

The Archon said, "Please be quiet, Professor, lest you disrupt the ether."

"Sophia is well—happy—" Violet murmured. *That's what the paying customers want to hear,* Claude thought. Not that the Archon would be so crass to ask for money, but grateful mourners never failed to make donations to the Order. If they didn't do so spontaneously, the "spirits" dropped hints. Claude couldn't fathom this fad for believing that, while waiting to reincarnate, the dead hovered at the beck and call of "sensitives" like astral parlormaids. *Well, maybe they do; what do I know about the post-mortem destiny of ephemerals?*

Violet continued, "Your work brings great comfort to many. But take care with your gifts, lest you unleash powers beyond your ken."

Good advice for anyone dabbling in mesmerism, but judging from McFadden's frown, not what he'd instructed her to say.

She finished with, "Sophia watches over you and waits to rejoin you in the next incarnation. Be of good cheer." She slumped in her chair, miming exhaustion from the strain of the otherworldly powers surging through her.

The phosphorescent mist thickened, coalescing over the table like steam from a teakettle until each face was shrouded in an eerie, bluish-green veil. More cracklings and poppings sounded. "Someone else is here," said McFadden. "Speak, we are listening!"

Violet gave a loud groan. Claude felt her hand quivering with tension.

"Yes, Violet, open yourself to the higher plane. Let the spirits emerge from the void beyond this world and deliver their message through you."

"Harriet Harmon," she breathed.

"Yes? You have a communication for Miss Harmon?"

That lady leaned forward, trying to peer around Claude at Violet without breaking their handclasp.

"Your father—"

Claude felt Miss Harmon go rigid. Her father, he knew, had died four years previously. "Is he there?" she whispered.

Instead of answering, Violet threw her head back and writhed in her chair, as if fighting an invasion from beyond. The undulations of her slender body in the soft robe impressed Claude as blatantly erotic. *Does she know that? Probably not; she's too upset about her friend.*

"Do not resist the power," said McFadden. "Let the departed one speak through your mouth."

The medium let out a wail and collapsed, facedown. Claude knew she wasn't unconscious, but Rinaldo and Miss Harmon accepted the "faint" as real. Scowling in unconcealed disgust, McFadden stood up. "Some hostile elemental is doubtless blocking the vibrations." He turned up the gaslight. "I apologize, Miss Harmon, for leaving you in suspense, but the spirits cannot be coerced."

"Never mind, it's Violet I'm concerned about." She propped up the medium, patting her face. "Someone ring for smelling salts."

Violet's eyes fluttered open. "No, that's all right. I'm fine now. I only need to rest." Between them, Claude and Miss Harmon helped her to her feet. *Effective performance,* Claude thought, *and if I were being threatened with a whiff of ammonia, I'd have a miraculous recovery, too.*

"Violet should be fully recuperated by tomorrow night," said McFadden with a pointed stare at his niece. "Miss Harmon, if you'll return then, we can hold a private sitting for you alone. Perhaps the spirits will become more amenable." The anger simmering behind his solemn facade made Claude's nerves itch.

"I'd be very grateful." She patted her friend's shoulder. "Are you quite certain—?"

"I'm perfectly well. You go home now." Violet cast a look of silent appeal at Claude. He responded with a minute nod, wishing he could answer more openly.

McFadden rang for the butler to show the guests out. Claude, bringing up the rear, cornered the butler in the foyer and said, "I left at the same time as the others. You may as well lock up for the night." With an unwary subject, imprinting a false memory took no more effort than that. As soon as the servant's back was turned, Claude's presence forgotten, Claude invoked a psychic shield that shrouded him from human sight. Although a mirror or a kodak print would show his image, and animals could sense his presence, to human eyes he was virtually invisible.

He had no trouble finding McFadden and Violet. The man's angry shouts echoed through the house. With the cat, Ishtar, padding at his heels, Claude followed the noise to a closed door. When he eased it open, Ishtar slipped in ahead of him. Violet, sitting on a divan in a stuffy parlor redolent of stale cigars, blinked at the sight of the door moving "by itself." Apparently deciding, though, that the cat had caused the phenomenon, she returned her gaze to her uncle. McFadden loomed over her, his back to the entrance.

"What's got into you, ye gormless chit?" A Scottish burr, usually disguised by his stage mannerisms, roughened his voice. "Why did ye not say the lines I gave you?"

"I won't do that to Harriet." Though her voice shook, she folded her arms and glared up at him.

"I'm the master of this house! It's not your place to say what ye will and will not do!" He made an effort to rein his anger, though his aura still smoldered a dull red. "Come, lass, ye had no such quibbles all the other times."

"Harriet is my friend. I won't trick her out of money she can't spare or wring her heart with 'messages' from her dead father."

"Don't tell me what ye won't do! I've fed, clothed, and

sheltered you these fifteen years; I have a right to some gratitude."

Violet sprang to her feet. "Gratitude doesn't go that far! I think I've repaid you more than—"

McFadden grabbed her shoulders and shook her. "Hold your peace while I'm speaking to you!"

She gave a choked gasp. On a table behind her, a tall vase vibrated momentarily, then toppled to the floor.

What was that? Claude wondered. *The cat? I don't see—*

He was distracted by a surge of fear from McFadden, accompanied by a hoarse shout: "Damn you, ye'll do as ye're told!" McFadden slapped Violet across the mouth.

Enough! Claude seized him and spun him around. Violet emitted a soft cry as Claude's psychic veil dissolved, rendering him visible. Only the fear in her eyes stopped him from hitting McFadden. *And a good thing, too; I would probably break his neck.*

"Listen to me, you worthless—" He couldn't think of an epithet that wouldn't shock Violet even worse. His eyes impaled McFadden's. "You will not strike your niece again. You will treat her with courtesy at all times. Now go to bed, and forget you saw me." He shoved the occultist toward the door. McFadden hustled into the corridor.

When the sound of the man's footsteps faded up the stairs, Claude turned toward Violet, perched on the edge of the divan. She trembled, and the normal rosy glow of her aura was dimmed. He sat beside her and took her hand before she could shrink from him. "Please don't be afraid, *ma petite.*" He succumbed to the temptation to kiss her fingertips. "Everything is perfectly all right."

She stared at him intently. "I'm not afraid now. But I never saw you come in." That puzzled frown reappeared.

What does she see when she looks at me that way? "Don't worry about that." He stood up, still holding her hand. "Walk with me in the garden. I want to talk to you."

When she hesitated, he encouraged her with a gentle psychic caress, light as the brush of a feather. She nodded.

They met no servants on their way, emerging into the garden through the French doors of a back sitting room. The house, a Queen Anne style mansion bookended by red brick chimneys and liberally studded with gables, lay on the outskirts of London. It enjoyed the convenience of closeness to the city while avoiding the noise, the stink of garbage and horse droppings, and the sooty reek of the ubiquitous yellow fog. Instead, white roses festooning a nearby trellis perfumed the summer night air.

On the graveled path, Claude offered Violet his arm. Her body heat warmed him like a roaring fire in midwinter. He longed to draw her into an embrace, but in her agitated condition, he would have to override her will, an act he wanted to avoid. *I don't want her as prey; I want her for a pet.*

The thought stunned him. *So that is what's the matter with me!* He was bored with entranced victims; he craved a donor who could accept him with a clear mind, fully aware of his nature and his needs—as much as he chose to reveal. With unwitting prey, he didn't dare resort to a given donor more than once or twice. He obtained most of his modest but necessary doses of human blood (a supplement to the staple diet drained from horses, rats, and stray dogs) from music hall dancers and ladies of the evening. *With Violet, it could be different.* And in her case, he wanted to offer something in return for the vital fluid and psychic energy he feasted upon.

Something besides pleasure. That aspect went without saying. He sensed desire in the rise of her skin temperature, heard it in the quickening of her breath and heartbeat, even if propriety wouldn't allow her to recognize her own passion. The previous century, the time of Claude's youth, had taken a more sensible attitude toward the mating dance; a human male of that era would have guffawed at the notion that women felt no sexual impulses.

Well, before he could consider seducing Violet, he had to settle this problem with her uncle. "Miss Cade—may I call you Violet? After tonight, we needn't stand on formality, need we?"

"I suppose not—Claude." She swayed closer to him, her fingers tightening on his sleeve. For a second he felt light-headed.

Not now, he chastised himself. "Tell me about that argument with your uncle."

"Harriet has a small annual income, inherited from her

father, enough to live on. That's why she can afford to write for the few newspapers that'll use her work—she doesn't earn enough to support herself. Not yet, anyway."

"And McFadden wants to get his hooks into that money, of course." They reached a stream rippling at the bottom of the garden. Claude guided Violet to a marble bench under a willow tree. "Forgive me for sounding like him, but why were you willing to play similar tricks on his other guests?"

"True, it wasn't honest," she said, "but it always seemed like a game to me. They're all rich people, or at least prosperous, I tell them what they want to hear, and Uncle Matthew never takes more than they can afford to lose—just a drop in the bucket, in most cases. He really isn't greedy."

Claude couldn't repress a derisive laugh.

"Really," she said, "he could have robbed them blind—some fake spiritualists do. I keep his books, so I know he isn't taking half the advantage he could."

"But it's different with Miss Harmon."

"I'm having second thoughts about the others, too. Poor Professor Rinaldo—" Violet shook her head. "But especially Harriet. I quarreled with Uncle Matthew about that earlier. Harriet's my friend; I can't lie to her, not when she joined the Order in good faith, out of scientific curiosity. And she *can't* afford to throw money away on Uncle Matthew's cult; she needs it all to live on. What little she can spare, she donates to suffragist societies."

Claude cupped her right hand in both of his. "Why don't you simply leave your uncle? Is it money?"

She sighed. "You must think me awfully mercenary."

"Not at all. Please continue."

"That's exactly what Harriet thinks I should do, and she doesn't even know that as a medium, I'm a fraud. She's invited me to move into her flat, but I can't live off her. I have no money of my own, not yet anyway. Uncle Matthew has control of my inheritance until I turn thirty, and I'm only twenty-six now." When Claude made no comment, she said,"Oh, it's easy enough to say I should earn my own living, but what skills do I have?"

"Granted," he said, "respectable employment agencies probably have few positions open for mediums."

She laughed at that, and her aura brightened. "I suppose

I could become a governess or factory girl. Both of those choices sound awfully grim. Harriet suggested I write a book about my experiences with spiritualism. She doesn't know it would have to be an exposure of fraud, and I don't want to do that to Uncle Matthew, whatever his flaws."

Claude swallowed the impatient retort that sprang to mind. "Surely you don't agree with his self-serving argument that you 'owe' him."

"He did take me in when my parents died of scarlet fever," she said. "It couldn't have been easy for him, dealing with a girl of eleven. He *has* fed, sheltered, and clothed me all these years."

"Yes, compensated by free access to your trust fund!"

"Remember, I keep his accounts," she said. "I'm not completely naive; I would have noticed if he'd skimmed off an excessive amount. And even though he's harsh sometimes, he's never really hurt me."

"Oh, barring the occasional slap?" At her blank look, Claude decided not to pursue the issue. Ephemerals routinely "disciplined" their young in ways "lower" animals wouldn't dream of. "Forgive me for asking, but has he ever—" *What's the currently acceptable euphemism?* "Does he—interfere with you?"

"Oh, no!" Her astonished tone and hot blush convinced Claude of her sincerity. "Uncle Matthew was very patient with me when I first came to live with him. He didn't have this house then; he bought it a few years ago, when he started to make money. He lived in a small cottage then, so it must have been even harder on him."

"Why? I can't imagine you as a difficult child." Sensing her reluctance to answer that, he gave her another mental nudge.

She drew a deep breath. "Things—objects—flew through the air. It only started after I moved in with him." She gave Claude an appealing glance. "I hope you don't think I'm lying or mad."

So that explains the falling vase. "Certainly not. I've heard of such phenomena."

"At that time, I hadn't. I was frightened out of my wits. I thought the cottage was haunted. So did the housekeeper—she gave notice after the first week." Violet giggled. "It wasn't funny then. Next, I thought *I* was haunted. Uncle Matthew helped me get over my fears. Until he coaxed me out of it, I was sure I was possessed by a devil. Sometimes I still wonder." A shiver coursed through her. "That was what gave him the idea of training me as a medium. He was terribly disappointed that I couldn't make it happen on command. Then, after a couple of years, the whole thing stopped."

"Fascinating," said Claude. *She doesn't realize the power still lies locked inside her mind.* When he paused to reflect on the details, he had to choke down a snarl. "That bloody—pardon me, your uncle—used you in his confidence games when you were a mere child?"

Violet shrugged. "I was twelve when we started. It was better than slaving away like Jane Eyre. And as I said, I've always thought of it as a game. I was good at it. It helps that I can see—something—a halo of colored light around living things. Uncle Matthew calls it the etheric body."

Claude nodded. *She can actually see the aura?*

"I can use that to pick up people's feelings and adjust my spirit messages to fit."

"Indeed?" Excitement tingled up Claude's spine, along with a whisper of danger that he ignored. "I've never met anyone who can perceive—etheric bodies." *No one human, that is.*

She gazed intently at him, though she couldn't have discerned details in the moonlight. "You do believe me, don't you?"

"Of course."

"I'm so glad. I don't dare talk about it, not to ordinary people outside spiritualist circles. They'd think I was out of my mind."

"I know you aren't." He put his arm around her shoulders, and she leaned against him instead of drawing away. The flutter of her pulse made his throat go dry.

"I shouldn't be surprised that you'd understand. The first time we met, I noticed how different your—halo—is."

"In what way?" *So that's why she keeps staring at me.*

"It's unique. I've never seen another one like it—streaked with velvet black and a sort of iridescent blue-violet."

"Interesting observation." *Is it safe to have her noticing that? Confound it, I don't care!* Now he knew why she enticed him. She sensed his difference, as few human females could. "And poetically phrased. Perhaps you *should* write a book."

"I already told you—"

"That you don't want to expose your uncle—though your reasoning still eludes me. But you don't have to. Join the Society for Psychical Research and use your background to expose other charlatans. Write novels based on your outre experiences. Live with your friend Miss Harmon and become a celebrated author."

She laughed at that but quickly sobered. "It sounds wonderful—once I get past the ordeal of explaining to Harriet that I'm a fake—but Uncle Matthew wouldn't let me go without a fight. It's not only the money; I know his secrets. And you've distracted me from the main problem. What about that seance he's planning for tomorrow night?"

"Leave that to me. I've acted onstage, and I have some skill in mesmerism." Both claims were true, though far from the whole truth. "You just make up with your uncle and convince him you've had a change of heart about tomorrow's performance. Then go into your trance act, put on a dramatic display of writhing and chanting—rather like the Delphic Oracle—and trust me for the rest. No matter how strange it may appear."

"What are you going to do?"

"It would be complicated to explain, and I prefer your reaction to be spontaneous." In fact, he wanted to leave matters vague in case she reacted so negatively that he had to erase her memory. "McFadden will know the—phenomena—I'll create aren't part of his own bag of tricks, and he won't realize I'm there. After the peculiar things that happened in your girlhood, he shouldn't be hard to convince that you have unplumbed occult depths. I plan to frighten him so thoroughly he'll give you whatever you demand and leave you alone afterward."

She shook her head. "It sounds quite incredible to me. But I do trust you—Claude."

Stroking her hair, he tilted her face toward him and lightly kissed her parted lips. She drew in a startled breath that, along with the fragrance of her skin. almost wrecked his fragile self-restraint. *Tomorrow night, damn it! This time I'll earn my reward before I take it.* If he planned to treat her as a pet rather than a victim, he ought to practice adhering to human ethical standards. *How else can I be honest with her? Or as honest as the situation permits, anyway.*

The next evening, Claude rode a hansom cab to McFadden's and ordered the driver to wait at a bend in the road just out of sight of the house. As soon as Claude was sure the cabby could no longer see him, he shrouded himself. Invisible to human eyes, he lurked near the front door until Harriet Harmon arrived, then glided inside with her.

Moments later he was ensconced in the study, leaning against the bookcase, the psychic veil still intact. Ishtar, of course, knew of his presence. She rubbed against his trousers and meowed up at him with an insistence that would convince any susceptible observer of a ghostly presence. Petting her, he hushed her with a silent command. With an insulted flick of her plumed tail, she jumped onto her customary shelf.

McFadden escorted Violet and Harriet to their places at the circular table. "The astral energies are perfectly balanced tonight," he said. "I feel it. Don't you agree, Violet?"

Noting the occultist's imperious glower at Violet, Claude had to remind himself that ripping the man's head off would spoil the plan.

"Yes, I'm certain of it." She surveyed the study, obviously wondering how Claude could appear out of the woodwork in a room ostentatiously devoid of hiding places. He wished he could somehow reassure her.

"Then let us begin." The three of them joined hands and commenced the breathing exercises that supposedly cleared the channels for energies from the void beyond the earthly plane.

Claude waited for the spirit rappings with which McFadden always began the performance. They duly occurred within three or four minutes. *Isn't he getting a trifle too predictable? Without Violet's talent, he'll wear out his repertoire in short order. He knows how much he needs her; that must be why he's controlling her so harshly.*

"Is someone attempting to break through from the other

side?" McFadden intoned. "Come forward and speak through the vessel prepared for you."

Violet emitted a keening cry. On cue, McFadden's foot pressed the button concealed under the carpet. Claude noticed the minute tension in the man's body and watched for his next reaction. When the phosphorescent cloud didn't appear, McFadden scowled at Violet, who lolled in her chair with eyes half closed, moaning. In the moment or two before the others had entered, Claude had gouged a tiny hole in the rug and disconnected the device. McFadden, of course, thought Violet had sabotaged him, but he couldn't give away his own trick by accusing her in front of Harriet. Smoothing over his expression, he continued, "Emerge from the void and speak to us! What message do you bear this night?"

Shrieking as if in agony, Violet went rigid, then shook all over like a woman in a *grand mal* seizure. McFadden fixed her with a dubious stare, obviously not quite sure her paroxysm wasn't genuine.

Well done, thought Claude. *Better not drag this out any further.* He projected a silent signal to the cat. Ishtar executed a flying leap from the bookshelf to the center of the table, knocking over the empty chalice. Face-to-face with McFadden, she screamed as if plunged into boiling water.

McFadden sprang to his feet, overturning his chair. Ishtar stopped yowling and vented a drawn-out hiss. Claude charged toward the occultist, simultaneously replacing his psychic shield with a new illusion, based on the green statuette on the desk, that he'd spent the last few minutes visualizing. At the instant he materialized from nowhere, he cloaked himself in an image of vast, dark wings, hawklike talons, blazing eyes, fangs, and a shadowy suggestion of tentacles. At least, that was what he aimed for, and McFadden's terror confirmed the success of the ploy.

McFadden raised his hands before his face and gibbered. Claude dug his nails into the man's shoulders and roared, "Puny mortal, do not meddle in affairs beyond your ken! Forbear to call up what you cannot put down!" The words reverberated around the small room like echoes in a cavern.

McFadden replied with a wordless cry of panic. Claude heard screams from the two women but couldn't break his illusion to console them. "Cease this blasphemy, lest worse befall you!"

He decided he'd better vanish before McFadden, with his own experience in similar deception, recovered enough to think rationally. To Claude's surprise, though, the occultist lunged for the table and snatched up the dagger. "Fiend! Begone to Hell! *Retro me, Sathanas!*" He stabbed wildly into the spectral, flame-eyed, bat-winged monster he saw before him.

Dark Powers, he believes that nonsense about silver! Silver or not, it didn't matter; with all his energy focused on the illusion, his external form in flux, Claude was almost as vulnerable to the weapon as an ordinary man. When the blade drove into his shoulder, pain slammed through him. As the attacker pulled it free, Claude felt as if a shaft of ice pierced him to the heart.

Behind him, Violet cried, "No!" On the desk, the green carving of the winged, tentacled idol rose into the air. It sailed across the room, gaining speed with every inch, and collided with McFadden's skull.

He collapsed facedown across the table. Claude, his vision clearing as he dropped the illusion and struggled to bring the pain under control, slumped into the nearest vacant chair. The sound of hurrying footsteps penetrated his awareness.

He gestured weakly to Violet. "Servants—don't let them in."

To her credit, Violet collected herself enough to open the door a crack at the butler's knock. His worried voice mumbled an inquiry. "There's nothing wrong," she told him in a surprisingly steady tone. "I'm sorry for the disturbance. It's only one of Uncle Matthew's experiments. You may retire."

Harriet, standing beside the table, cast frantic glances at McFadden and Claude. *Can't let her start asking questions. Bloody hell, I'm too tired for this.* And in a few minutes, when the shock wore off, thirst would ravage him. Well, he could use that; the need enhanced his mesmeric power. "Harriet," he whispered.

She looked straight at him. He captured her gaze and spoke more firmly. "Violet is right. This was only an experiment, a trick. No harm has been done. Go home at once, and forget the details of what just happened. It's nothing to be concerned about. Nothing but stage magic. You understand?"

Harriet nodded. "I'll go home now." She turned to Violet with a bewildered frown. "Violet?"

"I'm perfectly well. I'll call on you as soon as I can."

With another hesitant nod, Harriet groped for the door like a sleepwalker and disappeared down the hall. Fortunately she drove her own pony chaise, even at night (another unladylike habit), so she would have no difficulty in getting home.

Violet shut the door and turned on Claude. "I didn't ask you to kill him!"

"He isn't dead, only stunned. And I did *not* do that."

"Then what—"

"We'd better discuss it elsewhere." He'd managed to suppress most of the pain but couldn't concentrate well enough to eliminate all of it. As for self-healing, he could do no more than stop the bleeding. He needed a quiet, safe refuge—and nourishment. "I strongly suggest we get out before he wakes up."

"How—"

"I have a cab waiting. Come home with me. Yes, unchaperoned—at this point, does that really worry you? As soon as I'm sure you'll be all right, I'll send you to Miss Harmon's."

"Very well." After lighting the gas, she bent over her uncle and felt for the pulse at his wrist. "You're right, he's alive. Are you certain it's safe to leave him like this?"

"He'll recover." Although McFadden's scalp oozed blood—the scent made Claude's jaws ache—his aura showed that he'd suffered no permanent damage.

When Claude stood up and reached for Violet's hand, she focused on him for the first time. "You're wounded, too! He stabbed you!"

"It's nothing. It's already stopped bleeding." Violet had no way of knowing how serious the wound would have been for an ordinary man. He forestalled further conversation by grasping her arm and guiding her out of the study, closing the door behind them.

The night air energized him enough to make the walk to the waiting hansom less of an ordeal than he'd feared. After giving directions to the driver, Claude settled into the seat with an audible sigh. He didn't mind displaying his exhaustion to Violet now.

"You *are* hurt. We'll have to get a doctor."

"Absolutely not." He gazed at her, knowing she would see a glint of crimson in his eyes. After what he'd already shown her, that would scarcely drive her into hysterics. "It was worth it, *ma petite*. Your uncle will be well and truly convinced that you can 'call spirits from the vasty deep.' After that message from the void, he wouldn't dare deny you anything you ask."

Violet gathered her wits and managed a smile. "What shall I ask?"

"Strike while the iron is hot, before he has time to rationalize the experience. Tomorrow morning, send for your personal effects, and order him to contact his solicitor about transferring your funds into your control."

"You think he'll listen?"

"If he doesn't," said Claude with a feral grin, "I'll have a talk with him. But he will. You saw him go after me with that knife, silver for demons. He *believed*."

She stared hard at him. In the dim interior of the cab, she could only be examining his aura. "That statuette—if you didn't make it fly at him, then who—"

"That's obvious. You did. Just as you made that vase break earlier."

"No! I told you, I've never been able to—"

"Do it voluntarily? Perhaps not, but you did it under the stress of strong emotion. And now that you know you haven't lost the power, you may be able to train yourself to duplicate the feat." *No wonder she attracts me. Ephemerals with psychic talents of their own make the best donors.*

"For what?" she said. "I'm retiring as a medium, remember?"

"Research for those novels you plan to write."

She lightly touched his hand. The motion of the hansom made her sway against him. His head reeled at the tantalizing sensation of her warm skin, the blood throbbing in her fingertips. "Should I research you for my novels, too, Claude?"

"What do you mean?" *How much can she infer on her own? And how much do I dare let her comprehend?*

"Don't insult my intelligence! I've known all along that you were—different—because of those odd colors in your etheric body. I just never suspected how different! What I saw in there *wasn't* simple hypnotism, and it certainly wasn't stage magic. What kind of man are you?" She gulped. "Are you even human?"

His need made him reckless. *Oh, the Devil take it, if this turns out badly, I can revise her memory later.* "Let me show you." Putting an arm around her shoulders, he lifted her hand to his lips. He flicked his tongue in butterfly caresses over the palm down to the wrist. Violet's quiver of response had nothing to do with fear. Tilting his head, he used the razor-edge of his incisors to open a tiny incision— he had no fangs like the monsters in those absurd penny-dreadfuls. While he lapped the trickle of blood, she leaned into his embrace, her breath rapid and shallow.

Claude forced himself to stop long before he'd had enough. He allowed her to see him slowly lick the droplets from his lips. Applying pressure to the cut, he said, "I'll take no more without your free consent."

She gaped at him for a minute before collecting her wits to speak. "Are you a—one of those—creatures—in Mr. Stoker's latest novel?"

Good Lord, how long is that tripe going to haunt us? With any luck, that idiotic book will fade into the oblivion it deserves before the year's out. Well, at least she isn't screaming in terror. "Mr. Stoker's novel is a pack of bloody half-truths and damned lies!" He winced at the pain his incautious outburst reawakened. "Forgive my language. We feel very strongly about the way we've been libeled."

"Then it isn't true about—I won't become like you?"

"*Ma petite*, I am neither a walking corpse nor contagious. I'm as much a part of the natural world as you are." He decided to withhold further specifics until they'd become intimate.

She held up her hand near the window, trying to examine the minute wound in the moonlight. "This certainly isn't much like the book. Don't you need—have you had enough?" She blushed obviously recalling her own arousal.

"I've expended energy, not lost a large amount of blood, so what I need is quality, not fluid volume. However, your intuition is correct; that wasn't enough." He brushed his fingers gently over the bodice of her ceremonial robe, feeling her nipples tighten under the thin fabric. Her breath caught, but she didn't object. Virginal as she was, she would need little more than that caress and his mouth at her throat to bring her to fulfillment.

She offered her right wrist again. "Go ahead, then. I'm not afraid."

"Yes, you are, a bit; anyone would be. But you needn't be. It gets much better." He kissed her hand without grazing the cut.

"I'm not sure how I feel about serving as—well—food."

"Oh, no, my dear, if it were only that, I wouldn't even let you be aware of what I'm doing. You would enjoy it in a trance and forget immediately. You aren't a victim; you are my natural complement."

Her brow creased in puzzlement.

"That psychic talent of yours," he reminded her.

"I still doubt I could levitate objects on purpose."

"Why don't you try?"

"Now?"

"Certainly. I want to settle all your doubts before we—share—again." He removed his signet ring and laid it on her lap. "Go ahead."

She stared at the ring for over a minute. "It's no use, I haven't the slightest idea how to begin."

"Let me help." He cupped her chin, turned her head toward him, and gazed into her eyes. "Relax, let your inner strength flow freely. All the power you need lies within you."

When he released her, she shifted her eyes to the ring, and it floated two feet into the air as smoothly as if raised by an invisible wire. She gasped in delighted astonishment, and the object fell to the floor of the carriage. Picking it up, she said, "Are you sure you didn't do that yourself?"

"I'm not capable of it. You have my word."

She gave him a vigorous hug. "And all these years I was

afraid—thinking I'd been possessed by some evil force that might attack me again—and it was under my control all the time!"

Her vital heat made his teeth tingle in anticipation. *Not in a cab, damn it!* "Ease off—my self-control isn't what it should be at the moment." He untwined her arms from his neck and moved a few inches away from her. "We'll arrive at my townhouse in a minute or two." *And not a moment too soon!* "Then, if you're willing—"

Her aura scintillated in harmony with her smile. "To 'share'? That sounds like a most intriguing way to start my new life."

Authors Note:

This story takes place in summer, 1897—as readers of this volume doubtless know, the year Bram Stoker's Dracula *was published (specifically, in May). Dabbling in the occult was in vogue at this period, and spiritualism was taken seriously by many educated people (including Sir Arthur Conan Doyle). In 1858 an industrial chemist, Baron Karl von Reichenbach, claimed to have discovered that radiations emanating from magnets, crystals, and living things could be seen by "sensitives." The Society for Psychical Research was founded in 1882. Aleister Crowley (1875-1947), a notorious Satanist who sometimes claimed to be the Beast of Revelation, already had a dubious reputation when an undergraduate at Cambridge. Crowley, Doyle, and the poet W. B. Yeats, among other celebrities, were rumored to belong to the Order of the Golden Dawn, an occult society that loosely inspired the one in this story.*

Margaret L. Carter, a recognized expert on vampire fiction, has published six books on supernatural literature, most recently *The Vampire in Literature: A Critical Bibliography* (1989). To list her articles and short stories would lengthen this note by a couple of pages. Claude, in "Voice from the Void," will appear as a secondary character in a vampire novel, *Dark Changeling,* to be published by Transylvania Press.

IN MEMORY OF
by Nancy Kilpatrick

If memory serves, yellow marigolds and blue narcissus clotted the flower beds of my father's estate in Clontarf that August. The gardener had outdone himself, and it was as though at every turn, life itself permeated the grounds—short-lived life. But 1875 was the spring of my years. Barely seventeen and dreamy, the way Irish girls were then, my future stretched before me like an endless bare canvas, awaiting whichever colors and brush strokes I deigned to paint upon it. Had I but known the outcome of that fateful afternoon, surely I would have fled to the bluffs and hurled my young body over the cliffs and onto the jagged rocks below.

The lawn party my parents hosted was not as large as some, but the *crème de la crème* were in attendance. I recall gazing from the terrace, across the clipped lawn, at the finely attired men in their frockcoats, and the women in soft silks hidden beneath frilly parasols to ward off the sun's rays. Suddenly, for some unknown reason, I gazed upward. A flock of ravens swarmed overhead, so thick that they shrouded the sun's rays, darkening the sky temporarily, sucking up all the light from it. The sight sent a chill down my spine, as if this were a terrible omen of some sort. Just as quickly, that gloomy manifestation evaporated, like a nightmare on awakening, leaving behind only a wisp, a remnant. Immediately the sky brightened.

"May I present my daughter." My father's voice startled me, and I turned. "Florence, this is Mr. Oscar Wilde. Mr. Wilde is a writer, in his first year at Oxford."

"How very nice to meet you." The words caught in my throat, and I extended my gloved hand.

His face was almost an anachronism. Long, large-featured,

flesh pale yet ruddy, with emotion-laden eyes and a peculiar twist at the corners of his full lips. The exact nature of the crooked line between those lips was, for some time, a mystery to me. And what I felt then to be a grimace, I have now come to understand to be something entirely more sinister.

Mr. Wilde took my hand in his and kissed it, in the continental fashion. "Lieutenant-Colonel Balcombe, your daughter is both remarkably beautiful and, I can see already, utterly charming in a way which will shatter many hearts, all of which, no doubt, will be exceedingly eager to be broken."

I, of course, blushed at such a forthright yet backhanded compliment from this man so startlingly overdressed in a lilac-colored shirt with a large ascot clinging to his throat. If truth be known, more than anyone else, he resembled George IV, which made me smile secretly—what the French would have called *joli-laid*. His countenance was singularly mild yet his expression ardent. He spoke rapidly, in a low voice, and enunciated distinctly, like a man accustomed to being listened to. Yet beyond all that, his eyes arrested me. I'd never seen such wild intensity, juxtaposed with fragile sensitivity. To this day, try as I might, I simply cannot recall their color, which makes no sense, considering how strongly they held me. What I do recall is that they seemed to capture my very essence, as surely as if my dear soul were a butterfly, suddenly enslaved in a net. A delicate creature destined to be pinned to a board.

My father was called to greet another arriving friend, leaving me to the mercy of this peculiarly enticing stranger.

"There is nothing like youth," he said, in a theatrical manner, gesturing lavishly, speaking loudly, attracting the attention of those standing nearby, yet holding my eye as if it were me alone to whom he spoke. "Youth has a kingdom waiting for it. To win back my youth . . . there is nothing I wouldn't do. . . ."

I, of course, laughed at such melodrama. "Surely you know nothing of wanting your youth back. My guess, from your appearance, is that you are all of two and twenty."

"From appearances, your guess is nearly correct, less the two. Youth is not merely a chronological order of years, but more a state of mind. The life that makes the soul mars the body."

"How strange you are!" I blurted, then felt my face flame. After all, I hardly knew this man, and had not the familiarity with which to taunt him. But he took it in good humor.

"More peculiar than you at present can know. However, Florence, may I call you Florrie?"

"Well, yes, if you like—"

"I do like! Florrie, you must permit me to escort you to church this coming Sunday for the afternoon service."

Flustered, flattered, I could only stumble over my words. "Well . . . of course. I would be delighted to have you attend our simple country chapel—"

"Excellent! The day is too bright, not the proper setting for a man to offer attention to a woman."

"And church is?"

"One's virtues either shine or dim when the virtuous speak."

With that he kissed my hand again and was gone.

I recall standing, looking down at my hand, which felt as if burning ice had dropped onto it. Then I looked up. My eyes scanned the crowd of my parents' friends. Oscar Wilde had disappeared.

"Tell me about your work, Mr. Wilde." We walked, his hand cupping my elbow, guiding me through the tall, rock-strewn grass down the hill toward the rectory, and the chapel beyond, my parents not far ahead of us. I admit that this contact proved thrilling to my girlish body. My affections had already begun swaying in his direction, which, of course, both of us knew.

"My name is Oscar Fingal O'Flahertie Wills Wilde, but you may call me Oscar."

So formal a response made me laugh.

This caused him to glance down at me and frown slightly. "Is that mockery I hear?"

"Mockery, no. Amusement, Oscar. You are so serious. How do you get on in society?"

"I suppose society is wonderfully delightful. To be in it

is merely a bore. But to be out of it simply a tragedy. But you were inquiring as to my work."

"Unfortunately, I have not had the chance to read you as yet, although I'm certain you must be a fine poet and will go on to be an excellent writer of prose."

"You are either foolish or perceptive, but, of course, I favor the latter. And what do you know of poetry?"

"I know that it is a taste of God's passion."

"Poets know how useful passion is. Nowadays a broken heart will run to many editions."

"You speak of broken hearts on such a beautiful summer's day? Have you survived one?"

"A poet can survive everything but a misprint."

"You're not very forthcoming, are you, Oscar?"

He stopped walking and turned toward me. I felt my heart flutter. The air seemed to encase the two of us.

"Florrie, all art is quite useless. Before you stands a shallow man, make no mistake about that. One in need of a muse who will inspire him beyond mere banality. More, nourish him."

Words escaped me. I knew not what to answer, or if an answer was at all required. I only knew that we seemed to stand there for an eternity. And as we stood together, locked in an embrace, his eyes drew me until I felt myself dimming, willingly. I knew in those moments I would offer up to him whatever he needed, whatever he wanted.

"Miss Balcombe. It is so nice to see you. And may I enquire, who is your friend?"

The voice of Reverend Sean Manchester broke the moment. Suddenly it was as though I'd been under a spell. I felt stunned, aware that I'd not heard the birds or felt the intense heat for some time. But rather than perceiving the good Reverend's voice as a lifeline, cast toward a drowning swimmer, I felt it an intrusion. With some effort, I forced myself back to the surface of the waters known as reality.

"Reverend Manchester, may I introduce Mr. Oscar Wilde. You will have heard of him, no doubt. He is an aspiring poet, who has already had work published."

"Indeed. I have heard much."

"And I'm certain you shall hear more in future. There

is only one thing in the world worse than being talked about," Oscar said, "and that is not being talked about."

The two men shook hands, but perfunctorily. I was dismayed at this adversarial climate between them. I knew it could not be me, for after all, Reverend Manchester was an older gentleman, married a number of years, with several nearly grown children. I could not have known at the time the entirety of this wedge, but I soon had an inkling of its nature.

"You are a young man and already famous throughout the British Isles."

"Don't you mean *infamous*?"

"Infamy implies sin."

"There is no sin except stupidity."

"If you believe not in sin, I presume then that you also give no credence to conscience."

"Conscience and cowardice are really the same things."

"Then, sir, in your opinion, why do men go astray?"

"Simply, temptation. The only way to get rid of a temptation is to give in to it, it seems to me."

"Oscar!" I felt compelled to interject a note of sanity, for things had got out of hand. Even a poet should respect a man of the cloth. "Surely you believe in salvation! You were raised a Christian, were you not?"

At this, he turned to me again. A small, crooked smile played over those lips, and his eyes again compelled me to focus on him exclusively. That same potent pull threatened to overwhelm me, although his words kept me from sinking. "Florrie, dearest, we are all in the gutter, but some of us are looking at the stars."

"Heaven might be a better destination," Reverend Manchester said, "although there is an alternative."

"And that, I presume, is hell. Well, Reverend, I have visited that place and not, I suspect, for the last time. I have found it wanting."

Reverend Manchester said nothing more, but the look in his eyes spoke volumes. The church bells were tolling madly, the service about to begin. "I must attend to my parishioners," he said perfunctorily, and, almost as an afterthought, "It is good we have met, Mr. Wilde."

"Yes. A man cannot be too careful in the choice of his enemies."

Reverend Manchester looked startled by this blatant statement. But in my eyes, Oscar had merely said what was evident—the two men did not see eye to eye, although I should have thought "enemy" too strong a word.

Reverend Manchester excused himself. Oscar turned to me. Before I had the chance to collect my thoughts, he grasped my shoulders and quickly pressed his lips to mine. I was shocked. Embarrassed. Titilated. I scanned the small group of parishioners; none had seen this outrageous act, including my parents, thank God!

When I looked again at Oscar, all of this evident on my face, no doubt, something strange occurred. The contrast between us struck me. His face had become ruddy, while I felt light-headed and pale. He seemed sure of himself, whilst I, on the other hand, had been knocked entirely off balance. As I stared at him, time became irrelevant. The importance of my life seemed to diminish in my mind. The call of my soul's high longings became faint to my ears. A peculiar image came to me: I was composed of tiny particles which normally adhere together as a solid but were now being separated by some invisible dark force. And then, there was only Oscar.

"I must be off, Florrie," he said.

"What? You're not attending the service?" I heard my voice as if from a distance. Who is asking this question? I wondered. And who pretends to care for the answer?

"I have other plans. Permit me, though, to call on you this week."

It wasn't exactly a question, but more of a statement he made. And before I could respond, he turned and was gone.

I know that Reverend Manchester's sermon focused on the devil, finding him here and there, and being on guard, but I could only concentrate on snatches of what was said. You see, I was already in love. At least, I called it love then, but I have since learned to identify it as indenture. Bits of my soul were siphoned from me that day, and what would occur afterward would make a normal woman grieve for a lifetime. But already I had ceased to be normal and even my gender became inconsequential to me. And I was incapable of grief.

Oscar visited my home twice a week for two weeks. After that, he became a permanent fixture in our parlor. Nightly, mother, or my auntie, chaperoned, as was the custom then. Neither approved of him—Oscar was not an ordinary man. I was only too eager to assure them that he was, in fact, a genius, destined for great things. They would have none of it.

"You can't be serious!" Auntie chided me. "What kind of a husband do you think a man wearing a purple great-coat would make!"

"Style," I informed her, "is not a paramount concern, although his dress is avant garde, in my opinion."

"Your opinion," Mother said, "hardly matters here. You're but seventeen years of age. Need I remind you that your father and I make your decisions as long as you reside under our roof? This is not a match made in heaven."

"But it is not made in that other place either, Mother. Were you never young once? Did your heart not rule you when Father was near?"

"My head superseded my heart, or at least the heads of your maternal grandparents. Fortunately, their clearer minds prevailed. You are seeing entirely too much of Mr. Wilde."

"You're young, child," Auntie declared. "There are other suitors, more worthy."

In the way of youth, I created a scene, as they say, and left them both standing there speechless. But it was as though I watched my antics, disconnected. Then, of course, I interpreted my reaction to being overly intimidated at vexing my elders with my disrespectful behavior.

Time has proven Auntie's words both right and wrong—incorrect in the context of her meaning, but correct in a broader meaning, for I have been loved by at least one other man, much to his detriment.

Mother remained adamant, but Father, however, admired Oscar, and could see that his name would be remembered through the ages. Although, being my father, and concerned with my interests, he was not particularly comfortable with Oscar's financial situation. Unhappily, our family fortunes had taken a turn for the worse—I was dowerless and, in Mother's words, must count on a "strong pecuniary match." Oscar, you see, was a spendthrift. His inheritances and endowments were few and far between, and his wants exceeded his resources throughout his life. He spent much too freely, on both himself and his friends. And on me. At Christmas of that year, Oscar presented me with a token of his affections.

Inside the exquisite sculpted shell box of ivory I found a tiny cross. I held it up by the chain and the illumination from the gas lamp seemed to make the gold sparkle. I became mesmerized by that sparkle, and only Oscar's voice returned me to the room.

"Wear this in memory of me," he said, as though he were dying.

On one side was an inscription, uniting our names. My eyes must have shown what was in my heart.

"Florrie," he said ardently, grasping both my hands, falling to one knee before me, in the presence of Auntie, who instantly paused in her needlework.

"I am too happy to speak," I told him. "You must speak for both of us."

I expected a proposal of marriage, although I knew that while he was still a student, marriage was forbidden him. I would have been satisfied with a profession of undying love. But Oscar, in his theatrical manner, while Auntie gazed on, said something entirely unexpected.

"The worst of having a romance of any kind is that it leaves one so ... unromantic. You have, of course, won my heart."

And that was that.

Father and Mother, though, on hearing of this incident, took it seriously, although there had been no commitment elicited. They proceeded to check more deeply into Oscar's fiscal, and also personal affairs. Unsavory rumors were alluded to, but my parents refused to provide to me the details.

"Then they are only rumors," I said stubbornly, "whatever their nature. I believe it is un-christianlike to lower oneself to pay credence to mere hearsay."

Mother looked angry. "Now you're beginning to speak as rudely as he."

Father merely raised an eyebrow.

I took a deep breath. "I intend to marry Oscar Wilde!"

"Nonsense!" Mother laughed.

"And has he proposed?" Father wanted to know. "Because he has not as yet spoken with me."

"I know he will," I assured them, although I did not feel completely certain of this. I felt in my heart that Oscar loved me—for he said he did, or so I thought—and what I felt with him erased that horrible feeling of disconnection which became stronger and stronger each day. But the actual words which lead to a vow went missing.

My persistence forced my parents' hand.

"Then you will wish to know, Miss," Mother said in her crispest voice, "that your intended has been seen in Dublin."

"Well, of course. He was in Dublin just last month, which you know as well as I do."

"How impertinent you have become! What I know, which you are about to discover, is that Oscar Wilde was spotted dangling on his knee a woman known as Fidelia."

"Scandalous lies!"

"And further, Mrs. Edith Kingsford of Brighton has offered to intercede on his behalf with the mother of her niece Eva in arranging a match."

I'm certain that the look on my face betrayed my heart. Disassociated though I was, a feeling of being crushed overcame me. That after one year together, Oscar saw fit to toy with my affections seemed impossible, and yet . . .

Without apology or excuse, I raced from the room. I could not bear to hear more. I tried to deny to myself what my parents told me, and yet when I went over details, little incidents rose from memory. Despite his attentions toward me, I was not blind. Oscar flirted outrageously with every young woman in his sphere. And, since I was facing fact, I had also to acknowledge to myself that he paid equal attention to young men.

When next he visited over the holidays, I was cool to him. His inquiries as to my emotional state brought evasion on my part. "I shan't argue with you," I assured him.

"It is only the intellectually lost who ever argue," he declared.

"Must you always speak as if these are lines from your writings?"

"But they are, Florrie. What can life provide but the raw materials for art."

"I should think that life might be a bit more serious to you."

"Life is too serious already. Too normal. Don't you find it so?"

"And what's wrong with normal? God. Family. Work. Those are what life is all about."

He paused at that. "Fate has a way of intervening in what otherwise would be normal."

I looked at him seriously. "Oscar, I refuse to engage in a battle of witty repartee with you. You have broken my heart."

I waited, but his reply at first was silence. His eyes seemed to sparkle yet were, at the same time, embedded with impotent sorrow, the latter catching me off guard.

Auntie was, of course, in the parlor with us, although the hour was late and she must have been exhausted—when I glanced across the room, she was dozing by the window.

Oscar, it seems, had observed this also. We sat side by side on the loveseat before the fire. He moved closer and his arms encircled me. I cannot express the apprehension laced with arousal that filled my being. The silence in the room felt like a vise, holding me tightly in its grip, as tightly as Oscar's arms held me. Heat blazed through my body, as if I'd fallen into the fireplace; incineration threatened.

I recall noticing his lips as they came toward mine, twisted into a shape I can only describe as portraying cynicism. I felt both horrified and kindled, but I could not turn away. As his mouth found mine, I experienced a peculiar sensation, as if the breath from my body were being sucked from me. I know I began to panic, arms attempting to flail, legs kicking, noises coming from me. And then I watched helpless as blackness rushed toward me. In a moment of some hellish truth, I recognized that the universe itself was simply empty, Godless, friendless, a place so hollow that love had no reason to exist. And then, I remembered nothing more until I stood at the door, saying farewell to Oscar.

"So, this is good-bye," he said cheerfully, as though it were a happy occasion. I struggled to feel something, and yet I felt numb.

"Have a good trip back to England," I managed. "And be well. You will always be in my heart." The last was not something I felt, but something that came to me, like words on a piece of paper, as though they had no connection to either myself or the situation.

"Ah, but Florrie, you have no heart," Oscar laughed. "At least, not anymore." His voice was cold. And while the emotional impact escaped me, my dear body felt the attack and shuddered. In that moment, I recognized my fate. My essence had been taken from me and I would forever be vacant.

I did not hear from Oscar for two years. My parents had finally found a match for me of which they approved. He was an Irishman, of good breeding, a civil servant with ambitions to be a writer. Oscar, in his theatrical manner, sent a letter on hearing of my engagement. He declared that he was leaving Ireland, "probably for good," so that we might never have need to set eyes on one another again. He demanded that I return the golden cross, since, he stated, I could never wear it again. He would keep it in memory of our time together, "the sweetest of all my youth," he said. I could not help but picture that cynical twist to his lips as I read without passion this melodramatic epistle. I kept the cross.

The man I married was a giant, handsome enough, an athlete, an avid storyteller, but was never the good provider Mother had hoped for. In that way he was like Oscar. And in one other. His literary aspirations drove him to write for both the theater, and for print. Since I'd always entertained the notion of acting, once he discovered this, he endeavoured to win me over; I enjoyed a short career on the stage and made my theatrical debut in a play written by my husband. On opening night, I received an anonymous crown of flowers, death-white lilies—I knew they had been sent by Oscar. That was just his style.

I need not reiterate my own marital history. Because my husband obtained a modicum of fame in his lifetime, all of the "facts" of our life together are a matter of record. The birth of our son Noel. The various tragedies of my husband's professional life, and a scattering of successes. His illnesses, one of which led to his death. The fact that he left me exactly £4,723. Suffice it to say that outwardly our lives appeared normal, at least for those who travel in theatrical and literary circles. But a part of me went missing, and my husband was keenly aware of this lack. And he knew the source. I told him. It consumed his spirit as surely as my own had been swallowed.

As to Oscar Wilde, over the years I watched him ingest the souls of others—the poor woman he eventually married, Constance Lloyd, and Lord Alfred Douglas, the man with whom he had a lifetime affair, but two of the many whose lives were altered irrevocably. Indeed, Oscar portrayed himself accurately enough in *The Picture of Dorian Gray*. You have likely read the accounts of his life. As always, he sums himself up best: "I was made for destruction. My cradle was rocked by the Fates." Had I but the fortitude, I might have felt some compassion for his trials and tribulations. And in the end, when Robert Ross wrote that macabre account of Oscar's death, describing how "blood and other fluids erupted from every orifice of his body," I could view the words with but a scientific interest. Oscar had left me incapable of compassion. Nay, incapable of all feeling.

Try as he might, my loving husband could not overcome the damage caused by Oscar Wilde. And although I failed as a wife, still, in at least one regard I inspired my husband; his greatest work will live on, of that I am convinced, even as the works of Oscar Wilde seem to cling to life from beyond the grave. I have sworn to myself that I will preserve my husband's memory and protect his works to the end of my life—it is the very least I can do.

My husband was more than an insightful man, he was intuitive. If you have not as yet, perhaps you will eventually hear of him and the dark novel which depicts, in metaphor, the agony of the hollow existence of the woman whom he held dear, whose very soul had been absorbed for the refreshment of a psychic vampire.

A Personal Reminiscence,
by Florence Balcombe Stoker
Widow of Irish Writer Bram Stoker
May 1937

Author's Note:

I have always adored the writings of Oscar Wilde, and when I discovered who Wilde very nearly married, a natural connection occurred for me—I've wanted to write this story for a long time and am extremely grateful to P.N. Elrod for giving me the opportunity to manifest the idea. All my life I've been enamored with the British, because I love understatement, so that helped form the story as well. The "facts" of "In Memory Of" are all true. The interpretation of those facts is all mine.

Nancy Kilpatrick has published about 70 short stories, won the 1992 Arthur Ellis Award for best crime story, and has twice been a finalist for a Bram Stoker Award and an Aurora Award. Her novels include *Near Death,* and *Child of the Night* and under her pseudonym Amarantha Knight, four books in *The Darker Passions* series: *Dracula; Dr. Jekyll and Mr. Hyde; Frankenstein; The Fall of the House of Usher.* Also under her pen name she has edited the erotic horror anthologies *Love Bites; Flesh Fantastic; Sex Macabre* and *Seductive Spectres.* She has a limited edition collection out, *Sex and the Single Vampire,* and two more on the way, one being a collection of her vampire stories from Transylvania Press, Inc. She has written a series of comic books for VampErotic based on the stories in *Sex and the Single Vampire.*

DEATH MASK
by Rebecca Ann Brothers

Prologue

London, England—1910

"Yes, that's exactly right. Sign it now," he was told, and Simon Beaumont took the paper back and put his name to it, as commanded, then proffered it once more. "Perfect. We'll place it—here, do you think? Yes, that should do nicely." The letter, tucked into an envelope, was propped on the mantel in plain sight.

"Now, shall we get on with it? No reason for delay, is there?"

Simon could certainly think of none, and made no protests as a pistol was placed before him. Running his fingers along it, Simon savored its texture of cold metal and ivory, closing his fingers around the grip.

"Come now, let's have done with it."

Yes. Yes, best to get it over with, no sense prolonging things. Simon raised the pistol, pressed the barrel to his temple—and closing his eyes, squeezed the trigger.

All the evidence certainly pointed to Simon Beaumont taking his own life, so far as Jonah Atkins could discern. And why not? If Beaumont had been passing secrets, if—as his letter claimed—it had preyed upon his conscience, then the gentleman's way out was a perfectly reasonable and natural response. Were the widow not so young and lovely, would anyone's suspicions ever have been roused that there might be more to the story?

There it was, though: Corinna Beaumont, neé Maxwell, was a golden-haired beauty, thirty years her husband's junior, and that appeared reason enough to suppose she had at least been her husband's accomplice. What might she be at most? Jonah wondered. Deliberate seducer, paid agent of some interested other party? Yes, there might be something in that; and if Beaumont had made no mention of it in his letters—well, perhaps he'd been too much the gentleman to implicate a lady. Or, more likely, he had not cared to be posthumously known for a fool, whatever acts of treason he might confess.

So why not detain the lady for questioning? Jonah had asked, to be told it was hoped she would lead them to bigger game. It seemed a private inquiry agent, operating very hush-hush, had looked into the matter, and while unable to retrieve the Bryce-Paddington Plans, had speculated to the Admiralty that there was some mastermind behind it all.

Jonah supposed there could be some merit in the idea. Or it might be so much folderol. Who was to say the widow intended anything more sinister than a holiday upon the Continent, seeking solace from her grief? Meaning he was about to embark upon the wildest of goose chases.

His not to question why, however, and he tucked his notes away in his bag and went to catch a hansom for Victoria Station.

As the dining car filled up, Paris was left far behind as the Orient Express bore them into the heart of ever-turbulent Europe, and Jonah Atkins watched for those few individuals he had marked as noteworthy. Basil Zaharoff, for instance, thick-set and bearded, his presence meaning little in and of itself, as he virtually lived upon this train. But if the Bryce-Paddington Plans were here, Zaharoff would know—or know who might be interested. What, for example, was he discussing so intently with the very distinguished gentleman there? Tall and slim, wearing white tie and tails as though born to them, his name was Terence Lambert, and he came with an impeccable pedigree that rang a little false to Jonah.

Or perhaps he simply resented Lambert's effortless elegance, whilst he sat there feeling distinctly lumpish, suspecting his tie was askew, that his white shirt front would not be immaculate at evening's end, and that he really should have gotten a haircut before leaving.

He was made especially aware of the disparity between himself and Lambert because of Mrs. Beaumont. Not that she had behaved as anything but a very properly bereaved widow, paying the minimum of polite attention to any man other than her brother and traveling companion, David Maxwell. This was only the second time Jonah had seen her, in fact. The first encounter occurred in the hotel lobby the night before, exchanging names, marveling at the coincidence that they would be on the same train. Much too quickly, Maxwell had appeared to take her away, but those few minutes had done their work. Jonah meant to do his duty, but the part of him not owned by His Majesty's government would be cheering her on to emerge free of taint. That, in such an event, she would promptly vanish from his life mattered not at all. Or so he would insist with the stiffest of upper lips.

As her brother gravitated to Lambert and Zaharoff, however, the lady looked about for a moment, smiled as she spotted him, and approached without hesitation. Jonah barely had time to put down his newspaper and rise to his feet, before she was there: resplendent in mourning, her only jewelry jet beads and a mourning brooch made from a lock of her late husband's hair. With her blue eyes and glorious hair, she scarcely needed adornment—although those features were somewhat obscured by her hat and veil. Not one of the more elaborate models, he noted, frowning slightly as he remarked something else. Hadn't Beaumont's hair been a mousy gray? Who, then, had owned the lock of rich auburn now pinned to Mrs. Beaumont's bosom?

"Mr. Atkins?"

He blinked, aware of staring overlong, and accepted her gloved hand, offering an awkward shake, not trusting himself to a more debonair brush of his lips. Lambert would no doubt execute such a gesture with utter aplomb—yet another reason to hate him. "Mrs. Beaumont. Good evening. I trust you are enjoying your journey?"

"Yes, thank you. A touch of headache, I fear, but that is already past."

"I hope you will be troubled by nothing more serious."

"Thank you. And are you finding time for pleasure as well as work?" she asked, and Jonah had to think of what story he'd told her. Something in the academic line, wasn't it? As though accustomed to gentlemen suffering memory lapses in her presence, the lady prompted, "Your biography of Shelley . . . ?"

Oh, Lord. Is *that* what he'd told her? He detested Shelley's work. Had Shelley even gone to Vienna or Venice? At least Byron had gone to Greece. Inspiration striking, he said, "Did I say Shelley?"

"I believe you did, yes."

"I must have been overcome by your beauty," he said, in a clumsy attempt at gallantry, and promptly desired to go smash his head against a wall. Where Lambert would surely produce some witty bon mot, all Jonah could come up with was, "I meant Byron."

"How interesting," was her very polite reply. Then, "Women's shoes are so impractical, Mr. Atkins. One quickly wearies of standing."

He blinked owlishly at her, for a moment not fully comprehending that she wished him to ask her to sit down. "Ah, yes. Yes, of course. I do beg your pardon. Please, Mrs. Beaumont, will you join me?"

With another bewitching smile, she accepted, and when she was seated across from him, lifting her veil, she said, "My father disapproved of Byron's poetry—celebrations of depravity, he called them—so of course I read all that I could, with that unique pleasure of possessing the forbidden. He nearly had a fit when he discovered the works of Sir Richard Burton in my room."

"There could be nothing scandalous in accounts of exploration."

Her eyes sparkled with mischief. "Those were not the volumes in question, Mr. Atkins."

"Oh, yes, I see."

"Yes, one couldn't help but see such . . . interesting illustrations," she said, her merry eyes never leaving his face. "Do you disapprove, Mr. Atkins?"

"I would not presume to judge, Mrs. Beaumont."

"Are you scandalized?"

"Enlightened, I think." Doing a rapid reevaluation he

found he liked her all the more for her boldness. "May I say, Mrs. Beaumont, that you are not at all like the ladies I am used to meeting?"

"I daresay not, Mr. Atkins, I daresay not." Her smile showed she took it for a compliment.

Time he remembered what he was here for, however, Jonah thought, and asked, "Did your husband approve of your taste in literature?"

"Simon? Yes, he was most accommodating."

What breathing man would be otherwise? "Forgive me, I know you are but recently widowed—"

"Thank you. I knew my time with Simon would be short, but it was still a shock."

"I'm sure. Especially as he—" Catching himself in time, Jonah suddenly became very intent upon the intricacies of unfolding his napkin. The average British citizen, of which he was meant to be one, knew only that Simon Beaumont had died suddenly, not that he had taken his own life, nor that he was suspected of selling secrets to foreign governments.

A frown marring her features, she prompted, "Especially as he . . . ?"

"As he appeared in the best of health."

"It's true Simon was in fine fettle. But how do you know this, Mr. Atkins? Were you acquainted with my husband?"

"An acquaintance of an acquaintance, as it were," was his stunningly brilliant reply. What was it about her that reduced him to such doltish behavior? She was hardly the first beautiful woman he had encountered. Nor, viewed with strict objectivity, was she likely *the* most beautiful. Why then did her proximity banish his good sense?

"I see," she said, accepting his answer, though a thoughtful frown remained. "Tell me, do you believe Dr. Polidori did model his monster after Lord Byron?"

"Dr. Polidori's monster?" Jonah repeated, struggling to adjust to her abrupt change of subject.

"Lord Ruthven, *The Vampyre.*"

Oh, that. "That seems to have been the case, yes, from what I've gathered."

"Odd choice though, don't you think, making him a vampire?"

"Fanciful, certainly."

"You have no belief in vampires, then?"

"None." He had read Polidori's nonsense, of course, and if forced under torture might admit to finding an erotic appeal in certain passages from Stoker's novel. As any adolescent might. He had no time for such things now.

"If there is no substance to the legend, though, why does it persist, and occur in every corner of the globe?"

"Does it?"

"Oh, yes," she assured him. "In some fashion or another."

"And did you learn that from Sir Richard Burton?" Jonah asked, thinking this a very odd turn of conversation.

"Not him, no. I—"

"Corinna," David Maxwell took her arm, helping her to her feet. "I'm sure Mister—?"

"Atkins."

"Mr. Atkins is fascinated with your curious ideas, but no doubt he's anxious for his supper. Good evening, sir," said Maxwell, and hustled his sister off without a word of protest from her.

Jonah decided he didn't like the brother either.

No doubt the meal eventually set before him was an exquisite gourmet creation, but for all Jonah noticed it could have been sawdust. His attention was fixed on Mrs. Beaumont and her brother, not liking any of what he observed. While Maxwell consumed generous quantities of wine, he appeared to be hectoring his sister with equal fervor. After only a few bites of her food, Mrs. Beaumont pushed her plate away, looking ill, a hand pressed to her head as though it pained her.

Hard to believe those two were related really; Maxwell was as fair as she, but with a pinched and ferrety look to him. Unaware, or uncaring, of his sister's discomfort, he continued his harangue, voice never raised quite loud enough to be overheard.

Propriety forbade Jonah interfering, but he was quite prepared to damn propriety when the lady rose, throwing her napkin on the table and stumbling from the dining car in tears. Starting forward, not sure if he meant to go after

Mrs. Beaumont or give the brother a good thrashing, he was halted by a hand on his shoulder.

"I shouldn't, old son," advised a voice that awkwardly paired its British idiom with a ludicrously foreign accent, and Jonah looked around at Basil Zaharoff. "Family disputes, always very messy."

And he was meant to be operating with impartial discretion; he shouldn't need to be reminded of that.

"Mrs. Beaumont *is* the sort of woman who inspires gallantry, however, is she not?" Zaharoff added.

"She is—except in her brother, it seems." Maxwell was still at the table, finishing his meal with no sign of concern. The urge to wring the fellow's scrawny neck returned, but Jonah quelled it, sitting down and accepting a cigar from Zaharoff, inviting the other man to join him.

"Yes," Zaharoff exhaled smoke, took another savoring puff, "a woman such as Mrs. Beaumont might inspire a man to extraordinary action. Like Helen, do you think?"

"I doubt a thousand ships would be launched for the sake of a lovely face today."

"No? Well, perhaps not. Marvelous idea, though, that horse."

Jonah puffed his cigar and considered Zaharoff. "It would certainly be advantageous to infiltrate enemy territory, without fear of detection."

"Would it not? What nation would not welcome such an advantage?"

"Particularly if it came with a unique feature."

"Indeed. I have some little interest in these submarines, for example," Zaharoff said in a casually confidential tone, "and am always hearing of new, astounding developments. But then we live in an age of wonders, do we not, where our world alters daily. Who can know what to believe?"

Indeed. Jonah trusted he wore his most bland expression, well aware of Zaharoff's scrutiny, getting the sense the arms dealer was fishing for information. To confirm what he already knew? Or merely exercising curiosity? Hard to tell just yet, and Zaharoff seemed unwilling to commit himself any further.

Putting out his cigar, Zaharoff rose, finished his drink,

nodded. "I bid you good night, Mr. Atkins," he said, and departed.

Well, it hadn't been an entirely wasted evening, but it was drawing to a close, with Maxwell and Lambert departing, the former rather unsteady on his feet. It might be worth looking into that relationship, to see precisely what the gentlemen had in common. David Maxwell had not been mentioned in the information Jonah had received dealing with Lambert, but they gave the appearance of being very chummy just now.

In another day they would be in Vienna. Jonah suspected a few things would begin to come clear by then.

The first scream brought Jonah fully awake, dragging his pistol out from under his pillow and reaching for his dressing gown. By the second he was out in the corridor, clutching the gun in a pocket as he made his way to another compartment, pushing through the other passengers coming out to see what was going on. An attendant was there, hardly more than a boy, mouth open for another scream that came out a hoarse whimper as he collapsed to the floor, crossing himself and muttering fervent prayers.

After one glance into the compartment, Jonah couldn't say he blamed him.

David Maxwell was sprawled there, eyes wide and staring, his collar ripped open, his white shirt front splashed with blood. Dropping to his knees, Jonah leaned in for a closer look, frowning at the marks on Maxwell's neck. He had assumed the man's throat must have been slashed, but what he discerned in the dim light, amid the gore, were two small punctures, very close together. Very like a bite.

Identity swiftly changed from biographer of radical poets to private inquiry agent and—after a confidential interview with the conductor—Jonah took charge of the situation: ordering his fellow passengers back to their beds, asking that a doctor be found, and that a place be prepared to keep the body until they reached Vienna. In due course the doctor, a M. Chrétien, appeared, rumpled and cross from leaving his bed, humor not improved by the attendant's ongoing hysterics. Telling another attendant to take the boy away and give him the sedative Chrétien produced, the doctor then turned his attention to the body, confirming Maxwell's death, from extreme loss of blood. Then puzzling over that, turning to Jonah to demand, "But where *is* the blood, monsieur?"

Jonah couldn't tell him, not yet anyway. He could see that was not a satisfactory response, but the doctor departed in due course, and once he'd instructed the remaining staff to let no one else into the compartment, Jonah took only what time was necessary to pop back to his own and quickly dress, leaving proper grooming for a later time. He meant to make the most of these hours before other authorities would step in, and paused just long enough to ask if Mrs. Beaumont had been informed, belatedly thinking it strange she hadn't appeared before now. Told that she was sleeping soundly, Jonah decided the news could wait a few hours more; obnoxious as her brother may have been last night, his death coming so soon on her husband's suicide was bound to hit hard.

Even as he closed the door of the compartment and hauled out the first piece of luggage for inspection, however, a cynical voice in his head reminded him the lady was a prime suspect in her husband's death. Might she have had a hand in Maxwell's? She had been angry last night. Angry enough to kill, and in such a savage manner? Jonah could imagine Mrs. Beaumont killing in a fit of passion, shooting a man. But to stab someone, her brother, in the throat—no, his imagination faltered at that.

Which could turn out to be a fatal mistake, he sternly told himself, blanking his mind of the beguiling Mrs. Beaumont and focusing on the task at hand.

It was not immediately rewarding, only turning up the perfectly ordinary items that would be found among the personal articles of any man. Maxwell's cologne was rather appalling, but that was hardly a motive for murder. It wasn't until Jonah opened a large trunk that things began to get interesting, beginning with a revelation of the victim's lurid taste in literature. Had Maxwell been carting about a secret stash of pornography, that would have been something a man could understand; but such a quantity of rubbish about vampires, both novels and supposedly learned treatises, boggled the mind. Really, a grown man wasting his time on such things, and no doubt polluting his sister's mind with it as well—a fellow would have to be daft.

Then Jonah opened a Gladstone bag and felt his back hairs rise at the contents. "Good God . . ." Bulbs of garlic rested in one compartment, along side phials labeled HOLY WATER, and a large wooden cross; in the other compartment lay a heavy mallet and a half dozen shafts of wood, sharpened to a point at one end.

Rocking back on his heels, he thought back to those wounds in Maxwell's neck. Had his murderer known of this obsession, and somehow created those wounds to mimmick a vampire's bite, as some kind of irony? He didn't much fancy that idea though, as it singled out Mrs. Beaumont yet again.

Closing the bag and replacing it in the trunk, he knelt again, his knee pressing into something hard. Looking about, he found a silver crucifix and chain. Very beautiful—but the links were broken, as if the chain had been torn from someone's neck. Had Maxwell worn this, and had his murderer wrenched it from him? Testing its strength, Jonah saw that he could snap it easily, but could Mrs. Beaumont? It was hardly enough to exonerate her, but every little bit helped.

And while all very interesting, none of this put him any nearer finding the Bryce-Paddington Plans. Meditatively chewing a ragged thumbnail, he considered the question: Allowing that Maxwell, not his sister, was the thief—on his own, or in league with Simon Beaumont—where would he keep the papers? They hadn't been on his person, Jonah had checked; they weren't thrust between the pages of any of those books; the only other items were articles of clothing. As he lifted a pair of boots, a few ragged bits of paper were revealed. Digging deeper, he found more fragments, a couple of whole pages—and not a thing more. His first fear of its being all that remained of the plans was quickly soothed. They appeared to be the remnants of a diary. Had the rest of it been tossed out the window, only these few tatters missed in the dark? It looked very like it, as Jonah searched the room top to bottom and found nothing more.

Carefully placing the fragments in his notecase, he locked

the door behind him, then went along the corridor to Mrs. Beaumont's compartment, knowing he could put it off no longer. No response came to his discreet knock, nor to a more peremptory rap, and after a moment's hesitation he tried the door, finding it gave easily. That was entirely too trusting of the lady, and suddenly anticipating the worst he turned up the lamp, his heart resuming its normal cadence as he found her still in peaceful slumber. Crossing to her side, paying no more attention than was necessary to noting the way her golden hair was spread upon the pillow, nor the white shoulder bared to his gaze, he touched her arm, shook her gently. She barely stirred, made only a wordless moan, resisting his efforts to awaken her. The cause of her deep sleep was not hard to determine: A half-empty bottle of laudanum sat on her night stand. Taken for her headache, he assumed, knowing it was ridiculous to fret that she may have taken too much, but favoring her with a troubled gaze all the same, before leaving her side, asking the conductor to lock the door now—and inform him as soon as Mrs. Beaumont awakened.

In the corridor, his fellow passengers beginning to stir, he thought a moment, then went along to Lambert's compartment, rapping sharply on the door. No response there either, but this time he was barred entry. Interesting. But perhaps Mr. Lambert had had a busy night. He'd have to make inquiries into that. Surely something had been seen or heard; whatever struggle led to Maxwell's death could not have happened in total silence.

For the moment, however, breakfast would not come amiss, and he took himself off for the dining car.

Jonah was struggling with his tie once more that evening, when a soft knock came at his door. Crossing to it, hoping it was the conductor with news of Mrs. Beaumont at last, he quickly opened the door to discover the lady herself. "Mrs. Beaumont—"

"What has happened to my brother?" she demanded, barging inside and closing the door after her. "They told me there has been an accident, and that you would explain everything." When he hesitated, she came closer, imploring, "Please, tell me."

"I am sorry, Mrs. Beaumont, but your brother . . . is dead." He tried to say the words as gently as possible, watching for signs of faintness or hysteria.

Displaying neither, she asked, "And was his death a natural one?"

"No, it was not."

"Murder?"

Why didn't she suspect another suicide? he thought. "It looks that way, yes."

"Tell me how."

"I don't think—"

"Or show me his body. I *will* know how he died, Mr. Atkins."

He didn't doubt her persistence, but wondered what it was she expected to hear. "Very well. He was stabbed, in the throat."

Her eyes narrowed. "You're certain it was a knife wound?"

"I'm not sure what instrument made those wounds—"

Pouncing on that, she pursued it. "More than one? Do tell me how they appeared."

"Mrs. Beaumont—"

"Mr. Atkins," she seized his hands, "I do appreciate your concern, but you need not regard me as too delicate for the truth, however ugly. Were there two puncture wounds, close together?"

He sighed. "There were."

"And how much blood did you find?"

"I fear a great quan ... quantity." Except there really had not been that much, had there? "No, Mrs. Beaumont, I know what you're thinking, but it cannot be."

"Can it not? Oh, I do envy you your certainty, Mr. Atkins," she said, releasing his hands to pace restlessly. "*Why* did you not come to me when it happened?"

"I did try to wake you," several times through the day in fact, and Lambert, too. The conductor had caught him in the act of trying to pick the lock to Lambert's compartment and had not been terribly understanding of the urgency of the matter. M. Lambert had done nothing, so far as the conductor knew, to warrant being disturbed in this fashion. M. Atkins would be informed when M. Lambert and Madame Beaumont appeared; until then, M. Atkins had best watch himself. Zaharoff had brought some influence to bear, but Jonah's position was still a precarious one. "The laudanum you had taken—"

Again she interrupted him. "Yes, yes. It does take me that way sometimes." Her pacing took her to the dresser, pausing to peer at her reflection, then turn her back to it. "It may not be too late, though, if David's equipment has not been disturbed."

"You don't mean his vampire hunter's kit?" he demanded, skepticism sharp in his voice.

Censuring him with a look, she said, "I do mean that, Mr. Atkins. You've found it, then?"

"I have."

"Then we still have a chance."

Not sure he wanted to know, Jonah asked, "A chance for what?"

"To stop him before he kills again." Coming near once more, she said, "Mr. Atkins, I realize this sounds mad to you, but you must believe me. You must," she grasped his hands again. "I have nowhere else to turn now. First Simon, now David ... Mr. Atkins, if you desert me, what am I to do?"

The reaction she had so valiantly held at bay—ever since her husband's death?—threatened to overwhelm her now, and Jonah acted instinctively, clasping her hands in turn, drawing her close. "Mrs. Beaumont ... Corinna," he inhaled the scent of her hair, "please, trust me. I will do everything in my power to help you."

"But you don't know what you're dealing with." Her face turned up to his. "Jonah," his name on her lips wove a greater intimacy, "if you don't understand what you're hunting, the true nature of Lam—"

He interrupted her this time, with a kiss. A soft and fleeting touch of his lips to hers, startling to both of them as they moved back, staring into each other's eyes, only to kiss again with increasing ardor; Corinna's hands tangling in his dark curls as his hands caressed her back. Jonah's lips left hers, to graze her cheek, an ear, nuzzle at her throat.

Combing her fingers through his hair, she held him there a moment, then carefully pushed away. "This isn't right."

He caught her hand, tried to pull her back into his arms. "Isn't it?"

"It can't be. I'm sorry. Please, let me go."

"Corinna—"

"Jonah, please."

He released her hand.

She backed to the door, her eyes never leaving his face. "Good-bye," she whispered, and was gone.

The atmosphere in the dining car was considerably subdued, now word had gotten around of Maxwell's death, accompanied by many interesting rumors. Not even the wildest speculation Jonah overheard came near to Mrs. Beaumont's theory. Very few actual details had slipped out, thankfully; the popular idea seemed to be that Maxwell had been killed by some mad slasher, with liberal splashing of blood. It was gratifying to know his instructions had been followed, with even the doctor keeping mum—though he did draw Jonah aside to ask if the mystery of the blood was yet solved—for the time being willing to accept that Jonah's claim of being just as mystified was the truth.

Jonah doubted Chrétien would be any happier to know a vampire was suspected.

Only too aware of the casually curious looks turned his way, it wasn't hard to deduce that his true status had been revealed, however. Not necessarily a bad thing, as it gave him some little freedom to make inquiries without polite pretense, and without showing his real intent. And as there was no time like the present to begin, Jonah went over to Lambert's table, pleased the man had finally deigned to appear.

"May I join you?"

Startled, Lambert looked around, quickly recovered, and invited Jonah to sit down as though they were the best of old friends. "I say, that was shocking news about Maxwell, wasn't it?"

Jonah agreed that it had been. "Had you known him long?"

"I hardly knew him at all."

"No? You appeared to have some acquaintance with him last night."

Lambert elegantly shrugged it off. "Only in the way one forms an association with fellow travelers."

"Then it was only by the merest chance that you left together?"

"Quite."

Considering his next question, Jonah took the time for a careful perusal of Terence Lambert. Assuming, just for a wildly improbable moment, that there were such beings as vampires, how might they appear? Jonah considered, calling up images from Stoker's novel. Lambert's hair and eyes were quite dark, yet his skin was pale as a maiden's; there was a redness to his lips, though, that seemed a bit unnatural. His hands were well-kept, no unusual hairiness or long and dirty nails. His chest rose and fell at regular intervals, as a man's should do. He displayed no unnaturally long and sharp teeth, and if he were capable of exerting mesmeric powers, there were no indications of that as yet either. Lambert appeared annoyed and a bit fidgety under Jonah's long scrutiny, but that was scarcely to be reckoned peculiar under the circumstances.

Set against that, what was there to support Corinna's accusation? For this was surely who she meant to name, in warning that he did not understand the true nature of Lam— Lambert? Who else could she mean? Who else possessed the initials "TL" that turned up in those few tattered fragments from Maxwell's diary? "TL suspects," Maxwell had written; and ". . . am being pressed by TL; must protect . . ."; and ". . . suspects. Must finish with TL on this journey." Was it only jottings about the theft and sale of the Bryce-Paddington Plans, or was something far darker afoot?

"You're not eating, Lambert," Jonah said, observing the untouched food set before the gentleman, growing cold.

"I find I have no appetite."

"No? Pity about that. Perhaps some wine would restore you?" Jonah made to signal the waiter, but was forestalled.

"Thank you, no."

Jonah smiled. "I beg your pardon—you don't drink wine, do you?"

Lambert's eyes locked on his—sparked with irritation, nothing more. "Wine does not agree with me, Atkins—nor your foul tobacco, so please refrain from lighting that cigarette."

He hadn't really wanted to smoke so much as he wanted to catch Lambert's reflection in the gleaming silver finish of his cigarette case. Accomplishing that, however, he was at a loss to know what to make of it. Why *shouldn't* a vampire cast a reflection? Why should any of those beliefs of superstitious folklore have any true application?

Still, for the sake of thoroughness, he made one last foray, taking out a handkerchief and unfolding it on the table, revealing the silver chain and crucifix. "Have you seen this before?"

Lambert glanced at it, then quickly away, wincing. "No."

"Are you sure? Have a closer look." Jonah thrust the cross in his face—snarling, Lambert knocked it out of his hand, sending it flying across the carriage.

"I do not wish to look at it. I do not recognize it," Lambert said in a low and dangerous voice, eyes hot with a barely leashed anger. "I do not know what you're playing at, Atkins, and see no reason to indulge you."

"Be assured, Lambert, that I will give you a reason—and very little choice, when the time comes."

"We shall see, shall we not?" Lambert rose to his feet. "Good night."

Jonah watched him, knowing he'd made scant progress, only put Lambert on his guard, and drastically limited the time left to recover the papers before they reached Vienna, where they and Lambert would surely vanish.

Eyes narrowed and frowning, he watched as Lambert's departure was halted—by Mrs. Beaumont, looking very merry, taking Lambert's arm and leading him to a table. It could not be called an assignation, yet Jonah reacted as though it were, not at all reassured by the cool look she threw him, as though sensing his displeased stare.

"Very beautiful, is it not?" said Zaharoff, distracting him.

"What?"

Zaharoff opened his hand and showed the crucifix.

"Oh, yes." Jonah picked it up, trying to focus on it instead of the couple across the car. Why had Lambert reacted so strongly to this bit of metal? If that *was* what had provoked him. "Tell me, what impression do you have of Lambert?"

Considering the question, Zaharoff offered another cigar. "He is a difficult man to assess. He seems to hover about, on the fringes of some incident, never *seeming* to do anything, but when he moves on something has altered or changed hands." Flicking ash, Zaharoff shrugged slightly. "Of course, one could say that of many people, even myself."

"But do you keep Lambert's habitually nocturnal habits?" Jonah said, recalling some small item in his notes on Lambert, how the man was never seen about during daylight hours.

"Perhaps he is insomniac."

"Perhaps." Or perhaps Lambert had no choice but to sleep concealed during the hours of daylight, Jonah thought—and was annoyed at the thought.

Putting out his cigar, he got to his feet. "Please excuse me, there are matters I must attend to." Now, while Lambert was otherwise engaged.

He hesitated a moment, though, looking at the crucifix, then picked it up and dropped it back in his pocket, along with his gun, and with a last look at Lambert and Mrs. Beaumont, went out.

Lambert's compartment was locked once again, but Jonah didn't let that stop him this time. Inside, he turned up the lamps and set to work.

He'd barely opened the wardrobe when a scream rent the air. Gun in hand, Jonah bolted into the corridor, prepared for anything—except the sight of Mrs. Beaumont stumbling along the corridor, hair and clothes in disarray, hand pressed to her throat where blood trickled down her bosom. Clinging to the wall, she slid down in a crumpled heap, eyes wide with fear, not seeing Jonah, only the horror that clouded her vision.

A horror clad in evening clothes, not so elegant and debonair now as he came tearing along, blood staining his shirt front . . . his chin . . . his lips.

Halting, Lambert wore a dazed expression as he turned about, seeking escape but finding his way barred at every point by other passengers, train staff—and Jonah, pistol aimed unerringly at his heart.

Seeing, but not comprehending, Jonah began, "Corinna—"

"Now do you believe me?" Her voice was hoarse and weak, but still carried accusation.

Not taking his eyes from Lambert, he demanded, "Say it, Corinna. Tell me what he did."

"He attacked me—and tried to drink my blood."

Jonah stood still, letting that impossibility take root, not missing the stunned look on Lambert's face, nor his snarled, "You lying bitch!" When Lambert would have bolted, Jonah swung the gun, clipping Lambert with it, and that gentleman hit the floor with a thoroughly satisfying *thunk*.

Telling the attendants to take Lambert to his compartment and guard him, telling the onlookers to go about their business, Jonah swept Corinna up in his arms and carried her to his own compartment, settling her on the bed. "Zaharoff," where had he come from? "find the doctor, Chrétien—"

"No," Corinna protested. "I will be all right."

"You're bleeding."

"I will be all right, Jonah. Only let me rest a while."

"At least let me bathe your throat." He hated to see the blood, those wounds.

With a faint smile, she acquiesced. "You may attend me."

"Thank you," he replied with an answering smile. "Zaharoff ..." He sighed, and decided to go all the way out on this unsturdy limb. "Would you go along to Mr. Lambert and watch him, and tell me what he does?" He looked at Zaharoff to see that he was comprehended.

"Very well. I bid you good night, Mrs. Beaumont." And with a rather deftly executed bow, Zaharoff left.

"Who *is* he?" Corinna asked, lying back.

"An ally—for the moment." Should Lambert reveal too much and Zaharoff actually get his hands on the plans, however, that state of affairs could rapidly shift. Jonah's patriotic fervor was not so great that he truly believed the fate of the world rested in England's hands, let alone in assuring the Bryce-Paddington Plans remained in the possession of His Majesty's government. Sooner or later, all the great powers would have the same capabilities, and it seemed inevitable to him that one day these war machines would be used. If his retrieval of these plans could forestall that conflagration a few years more, though, he reckoned it a worthwhile endeavor.

Thus he told Corinna, "I fear I cannot stay long," as he bathed her throat in warm, soapy water, gently patted it dry, then dressed the wounds with supplies from his medical bag.

Noting that and other objects, she asked, "Do all literary biographers travel so fully equipped for dire events?"

"This one does. There, how does that feel?"

She touched the bandage at her throat. "Better, thank you."

"You're welcome. Now," he sat back, looking at her sternly, "what did you think you were doing with Lambert?"

With the good grace to look somewhat chagrined, she said, "I believed I could safely distract him while you searched for evidence."

Jonah quirked an eyebrow. "How did you know I intended that?"

"I saw you testing him, for signs of vampirism, but suspected it would require a good deal more to convince you on that regard." She quirked an eyebrow back at him. "*Are* you convinced?"

"That Lambert is dangerous, yes."

"No more than that? Even after this?" Corinna indicated her throat.

"He may suffer some form of dementia—"

"Or he may be a vampire."

"We'll know come dawn, won't we?"

"Rather drastically, yes."

"Should he *not* spontaneously combust?"

She smiled. "Then, Mr. Atkins, you will have been consorting with a madwoman."

"A most charmingly agreeable madwoman." Taking her hand, he added, "About what happened earlier—"

"I was distraught and behaved badly."

"You are the one owed an apology. I should not have taken such liberties."

"Even such charmingly agreeable liberties?" she countered, twining her fingers with his. "I doubt I should resist another such liberty," she added, and was as good as her word as Jonah leaned down, seeking her lips.

Parting to draw breath, he pressed another kiss on her, then drew back with reluctance. "I must go."

"I understand."

"You will be safe here."

"I know. Go."

He went—though perhaps with less enthusiasm than was right and proper.

Priorities readjusted by the time he reached Lambert's compartment, Jonah took stock. One attendant stood outside, the other hovered uncertainly inside, near the window; Zaharoff lounged comfortably in a chair, while Lambert sat on the edge of the bed. He'd washed the blood from his face and tried to achieve his accustomed nonchalance, but the mask had slipped too far askew. Something savage lurked in the eyes, particularly when they rested upon Jonah.

"Has he said anything?"

"Nothing a gentleman should repeat. He does frequently gaze upon this valise," Zaharoff indicated a piece of luggage at his feet, "and grows agitated if someone touches it."

"Have you touched it?"

Zaharoff blandly met his eyes. "Only to ascertain his distress. You have my word."

Jonah thought that might actually be worth something. Picking up the valise, he said, "You've no objection, Lambert, to my opening this?"

"Would it matter if I did?"

"Not in the least," Jonah pleasantly assured him, and opened the case. There were numerous documents inside, all innocuous. He searched through them carefully all the same, his sense of triumph beginning to dim as the Bryce-Paddington Plans were not revealed. Casting a suspicious look at Zaharoff, who maintained an appearance of cherubic innocence, he was about to toss the case aside and search that gentleman, when he caught a look on Lambert's face, an expression of feline-smug satisfaction.

He'd missed something, Jonah realized, but what? The case *was* empty—or perhaps not, he thought again, running his hands over it, inside and out, and finding the lining a bit loose, he gave a tug and it tore away completely, a sheaf of papers fluttering out.

"Why, Lambert, whatever can these be?"

"I'll see you in hell," was Lambert's quietly furious response to Jonah's mockery.

"I think not. I think," Jonah gathered up the papers—grabbing some back from Zaharoff—and putting them in the valise which he placed under his chair, "that we shall sit here these few hours until we reach Vienna. You've no objection, Lambert, to seeing the sun come up?"

The other man made no verbal reply, but something in his eyes, something haunted, sent a chill up Jonah's spine.

Conversation was impossible, and Jonah found himself glancing at his watch as frequently as Lambert looked out the window at an ever-lightening sky. The man's agitation was palpable, yet Jonah still could not credit the source, that Lambert feared the sun's first rays would burn him to ashes.

Tension getting the better of him, Jonah stood to ease his cramping muscles, toying with the crucifix, idly knotting the ends together, annoyed that both Zaharoff and the attendant had nodded off sometime ago. Pacing over to the window, he could just make out some of the passing scenery—the vast bulk of mountain, the dense darkness of forest, still grey and indistinct—and judged they were yet some distance from Vienna.

Dropping the chain back in his pocket, unable to stifle a yawn, he perceived movement behind him and whirled—too late—to find Lambert on his feet, a gun plucked from some hiding place, aimed squarely at him.

"Very unprofessional, not searching for weapons, old boy."

Not to mention downright imbecilic.

"Now then," Lambert smiled, "*I* choose how *you* die. Quickly," the gun pointed at Jonah's heart, "or slowly," the barrel dipped lower, and the smile turned vicious. "Slowly, I think," and his finger tightened on the trigger.

At the same moment a knock came at the door and Corinna called, "Jonah, is everything all right?"

That brief instant's distraction, as Lambert looked away, was all Jonah needed—and likely all he'd get. He charged, the gun went off, but its aim had altered, the bullet grazing his shoulder. Still shock enough to slow him, for Lambert to escape—dragging Corinna along with him. Pushing Zaharoff and the attendants away, Jonah sprinted after them, dodging more shots as they fled down the corridor, unable to fire back for fear of hitting Corinna.

Then they were out in the cold, rushing air, Lambert trying to force a struggling Corinna to clamber up a ladder—hitting her, hard, when she balked, and slinging her over his shoulder as he scrambled up, kicking out at Jonah, catching him on the wounded shoulder, just barely missing his head. Gaining the top of the carriage, Lambert shoved Corinna out of the way and turned to aim one more savage kick at Jonah as he came up. Prepared this time, Jonah latched onto the other man's ankle, using him as an anchor to haul himself on up and over, twisting and rolling as Lambert lunged at him. Grappling, the two men got to their feet, struggling for the greater leverage—Lambert was suddenly attacked from another front as Corinna recovered, came at him, kicking, clawing, laying into him with a very unladylike fury. Hitting a bump, the train jolted, all three went sprawling, Lambert rolling toward the edge, going over—Corinna crying out as he grabbed her ankle and dragged her along with him. Lunging after them, Jonah snagged her arm, muscles straining to hold onto both of them, reaching around with his free hand to try and pry Lambert's fingers loose, and might as well have tried uncoiling a boa constrictor.

"Give it up, man!" Jonah urged.

Fangs bared, Lambert only snapped at Jonah like a maddened dog.

Yanking his hand back, trying to get a better grip on Corinna, Jonah reached for his gun—his fingers catching the crucifix instead. Bringing it forth, the first rays of sunlight glinting off its silver, he smashed it into Lambert's face, looping the chain around his neck. At once the flesh smoked and sizzled, Lambert howling in pain and anger— but not relinquishing his hold on Corinna, who kicked and squirmed against him.

"Corinna, no, hold still," Jonah told her, holding onto her with both hands now—gasping as Lambert sank his teeth into Jonah's arm, but not letting go. Not until Lambert wrenched Corinna from him as the train jolted again, and she and Lambert fell together, hitting the ground, tumbling over and over down a ravine.

"Corinna!" He would have launched himself after her, but Zaharoff caught him from behind and held him immobile.

"It's too late, old son. She's gone."

No, no ... "CORINNAAA ... !"

But the train only hurtled onward into the morning light.

Feeling no particular urgency for hearth and home, Jonah turned up his coat collar as he left the Foreign Office and turned along Downing St. and Whitehall, the fog not putting him off a walk along the Embankment. The atmosphere suited his mood actually, had done for some weeks now. What was it, seven—no, nearer eight months since Corinna Beaumont's disappearance, and for all the frenetic pace life had set of late, there had scarce been a day he had not thought of her.

He remembered reaching Vienna and being frustrated by delays. Able, at last, to entrust the plans to the care of a senior agent, Jonah had returned to the area where Corinna and Lambert had fallen from the train—to find not a trace of her, not a scrap of cloth nor strand of hair. He'd called at every nearby house, asking: Had they seen an English lady? Had they heard of such a lady, perhaps with injuries? No one had, and Jonah was called back before he could search farther afield, convinced she lay injured and lost somewhere, or wandered amnesiac. That she was most likely dead, her body concealed somewhere in that dark forest, that he would not think of even now.

The fate of Terence Lambert remained a mystery also, but only because Jonah balked at reporting all he'd found, not sure he believed it himself. After all, what *had* he found? Only the gun Lambert had waved about, a few scraps torn from his clothes, and nothing more.

Except for a pile of what had looked very like ash.

He'd seen cremated human remains, knew the human body was not reduced to only fine ash, bits of bone would remain. But that was a mere mortal body, he'd thought time and again, and might not a vampire's flesh and bone be exceptionally vulnerable to the cleansing rays of the sun?

He'd waited weeks, now months, for Lambert to be spotted in some corner of the globe, but no such report appeared. No claim was made upon his substantial estate. In fact, not a single distant relative had come forward, an occurrence virtually unheard of, and that had prompted further investigation, which only yielded more mystery. Prior to a certain date, some twenty years back, there was no Terence Lambert. He was not descended of blue-blooded aristocrats; he had not attended Eton, nor graduated Oxford. The only Terence Lambert they discovered was a name on a London gravestone, born and died in 1751.

His colleagues were content with prosaic explanations of false identities, but Jonah could not share their conviction. Nor their continued belief that Corinna had been mixed up in it all, Lambert's mistress. If they were together, he'd told his superiors, that should make them far easier to locate, but that had been glibly dismissed. "Plain as anything, Atkins: they murdered the husband and brother and ran off together. You got the plans back, that's all that matters."

How could he give it up, though, when he knew that wasn't how it had been? When he sometimes could have sworn he sensed her presence?

If only she were nearby, he thought, his wanderings bringing him to Waterloo Bridge, where he paused to gaze at the fog-shrouded river. Perhaps it was only some sadistic twist of Fate's knife that turned him—who had so often scoffed at the foolishness of lovesick friends—into such a maundering romantic, pining away over a woman he hardly knew.

It hadn't made him more appreciative of Shelley, though, he reflected with a wry smile.

Thinking to hail a cab, he raised his arm as a hansom

approached, horse's hooves clip-clopping loudly in the foggy night, about to climb in when he realized it was already occupied. "I beg your pardon, ma'am, I—" he began and then stopped, staring.

"I believe you could catch pneumonia going about open-mouthed in such weather, Mr. Atkins. Do get in with me."

"Corinna . . . ?" He touched her hand and found it solid flesh enough. "You're alive."

"So it would appear," she agreed with a smile.

"But, I— Where have you been? What happened? Why—"

"Shh." She placed two gloved fingers against his lips. "Time enough for questions, but not now."

No, not now, with her there in his arms, quite willing to be kissed. "Where shall we go?" he asked after a pleasing interlude of reacquaintance.

"I believe you have lodgings nearby."

Not near enough, he thought, and wasted no time in giving the driver the address.

Their journey continued in an agreeable silence and growing urgency, making them eager to reach his rooms and lock the door behind them. Corinna spared not a glance at his decor, making it clear which room she'd come to see.

Some while later, Jonah leaned up on an elbow, watching her, bringing her hand to his lips. "Shall I be required to make a respectable woman of you now?"

"I think that could be beyond your powers," Corinna said, voice gone wistful as she sat up. "There are so many things you don't know about me."

"I know you didn't steal the plans or kill your husband."

"And David?"

"I think whoever killed him had a good reason."

Reaching for his dressing gown, she pulled it on, rolling up the sleeves, and sat facing him at the end of the bed, golden hair tumbling. "David Maxwell was not my brother. He blackmailed me into marrying Simon. It would be untrue to say I loved Simon, but I was fond of him, and tried to protect him."

"Protect him from what?"

"David and Terence. A very unlikely partnership, as you may imagine."

"What kind of partnership?"

Her look was doubtful, as if surprised she had to explain. "This kind of partnership," she said, gesturing at the bed and themselves. "Didn't you know?"

"There was nothing in their personal effects to indicate they were—" he balked at calling them lovers.

"No, there wouldn't be. Terence *was* discreet."

"Hold it—what about the crucifix Maxwell wore? If he and Lambert slept together—"

"I assume David always removed it beforehand."

Yes, he guessed that made sense. "So it was Maxwell who stole the plans, at Lambert's urging?"

"Yes. David was only looking for thrills when he met Terence, but was soon a willing accomplice to Terence's activities. They were going to grow rich from blackmail and espionage, and Terence had promised to bring David across soon."

"Then does that mean David's," this was insane, "back from the dead?"

"As a vampire?" She shook her head. "No. Terence was playing games, teasing him with immortality, but he'd never exchanged blood with David."

"And your husband—why did he take his life?"

"To spare me."

"To spare you what?"

"Revelation."

Of what? he wanted to asked, but couldn't quite, not yet. "So you killed Maxwell out of revenge."

"I did. And Terence."

"Lam—? How?"

"I . . . deceived him, a little, that last night. Suggested we would run off together. It wasn't very hard, and it was what he'd always wanted."

"Wait a minute. You said he and Maxwell—"

"Terence's tastes were . . . diverse. That's how he became a vampire, after all."

Shaking his head, trying to make sense of this tangle, Jonah said, "But he attacked you—"

"No, he didn't. I made those wounds, then smeared the blood on him, and put on a convincing act."

Very convincing. "You could have told me the truth, Corinna," he said.

"Could I? What I did tell you, you refused to believe. And I wanted him to die. I came to his compartment that morning hoping to witness the start at least, to see in his eyes that he knew what was coming." She pushed her hair back, tugged at the dressing gown as it slipped off a shoulder. Smile gone sad and rueful, she finished, "Changes things, doesn't it?"

"I don't know. I don't understand *why*. Corinna," he leaned towards her, grasping her hands, "tell me why."

"Because they killed my husband."

"You said you were only fond of Simon."

"Yes, it was for his sake, too—"

"Too? His sake, and another's? Corinna," he gripped her arms now, suddenly recalling that mourning brooch of auburn hair, "what secret did Maxwell hold over you?"

She met his eyes, searching and wary. "Jonah, don't you know? Haven't you guessed?"

"No," he whispered, longing to turn back from this path.

Pushing his hands away, she turned her head for a moment, and when she turned back her eyes had a brighter glow; when she parted her lips . . . "*Now* do you believe me?" And pushing him flat, pressed her mouth to his throat, piercing his skin with her long white fangs.

Disbelieving her strength, he moved to push her off, but she only held him down more firmly, and his struggles soon ceased as he felt her drawing his blood. Alarm gave way to the first stirring of arousal, and willing, now, to surrender completely, he felt a twinge of disappointment as she drew back, licking a few stray drops of his blood from her lips. With a forced attempt at wit, she said, "A pleasing vintage," with the air of a connoisseur. "Atkins '85?"

" '79," he corrected, feeling dazed.

"It's aging nicely," she teased, then her expression faltered, and she looked at him with an expression of one awaiting condemnation.

Cautiously sitting up again, Jonah said, "You're a vampire."

"Umm."

"How?"

"I had a lover. He took my blood, gave me some of his. One day I went out riding. A storm came up, lightning struck, the horse reared and threw me; I landed badly—and broke my neck. My lover found me and took me away. Three nights later I awoke."

"A vampire?"

"Yes. My family thought we'd run away, and disowned me. I didn't care, not with Anthony at my side. And then we met Terence, though that wasn't what he called himself then, and in time he brought David ... and they killed my darling Tony." Voice cold and hard, contrasting with the single tear rolling down her face, she made it explicit. "They drove a stake through his heart, and cut off his head, and left him in the sun to burn.

"I have hated but two people in my life, I have killed but two—*I* think with good reason," she declared and gave him a look that dared him to deny it.

"This Tony, he's the husband you spoke of, not Simon Beaumont?"

"Yes. Simon was a dear, sweet man who made no demands and asked no questions, and was too vulnerable to those monsters. I wanted justice for him as well." She paused, tracing a finger along his cheek. "I've *loved* but twice. First Tony, now ..."

"But that morning on the train," Jonah went on, not ready to face that implication, "why weren't *you* destroyed?"

Her look turned rueful again. "I nearly was." Groping under the pillows, she withdrew a small sachet. "This contains earth from my home in Cornwall—where I was born in 1799." She couldn't restrain a giggle at his jaw-dropped expression. "I did mislead you a little. It wasn't my father who disapproved my taste in literature, it was Tony. He always retained a Puritan streak, I fear.

"Well, vampires must keep some of their native earth near them, particularly when resting. That last morning, I *had* to leave your bed for mine, because that's where this," she hefted the sachet, "was hidden. But vindictiveness got the better of me and I stopped to see how you were faring with Terence—and events transpired unexpectedly." She gave him a severe look. "Had you simply shot him, much could have been avoided."

"I was afraid of hitting you."

"It wouldn't have hurt me."

"I had no way of knowing that," he replied. "Besides, it wouldn't have hurt him either."

"Noooo ... Not fatally, at least."

Vindictive wasn't the half of it, he thought. And thinking of something else, he said, "But I saw you eat and drink."

"Did you? Are you sure?"

"The laudanum?"

"Camouflage," she said, and gave him a cheeky smile. "Better to be thought a drug addict than a vampire, my dear."

"Yes, well, you have an answer for everything," he said, unable to restrain a grumbling tone. "Wait a minute—Maxwell's diary, the fragments torn from it. What about that?"

"Yes, that was a bit tricky, I'll admit, leaving you with a few bits to indict Terence and not implicate myself."

"And, of course, with both of them dead, there *is* only your word for any of this."

"Yes, it is convenient for me, isn't it?" Rising from the bed, she rummaged among the pile of discarded clothing, coming up with her reticule and extracting a leather-bound book. Handing it to him, she said, "It's all in there, Terence's vampirism, his relationship with David. They even took photographs of what they did to Tony."

Yes, they had. After only a brief glance, Jonah closed the book and set it aside, drawing her back into his arms. "I am sorry," he murmured, pressing a kiss to her forehead, holding her quietly for a time. Then, "You didn't mean to fall, then?"

"I had no intention of leaving you," she assured him.

"But it's been eight months, and not a word."

"Jonah, for a time I literally crawled into a hole and nearly died, I was so badly burned, and without my earth it was difficult to rest and heal. At last I was able to reach a very old friend of Tony's who helped me. I was always afraid to get in touch with you—until tonight. I've been watching you for weeks, trying to get my courage up, and tonight you looked so forlorn, there in the fog ..." She framed his face, looking at him intently. "Do you hate me? Do I disgust you?"

"Neither," he said, and marveled that it was so. "I *should* want to put a stake through your heart, I suppose."

"In that case, I *should* probably drain every drop of blood from your body."

Hazel eyes met blue, both sets sparkling.

"Is there a third alternative, Mrs. Beaumont?"

"A third—and a fourth, Mr. Atkins. We can go on like this—"

"And when I grow old?"

"—or I can do to you as Tony did to me," she whispered and drew back, letting the dressing gown fall from her shoulders. Drawing a sharp nail over her flesh, she broke the skin, and Jonah watched wide-eyed as a thin line of blood welled out and slowly dripped down her bosom.

Immortality, with her at his side, he thought, looking into her face. Then, closing his eyes, he leaned forward, put his lips to the blood, and drank.

EPILOGUE

Ypres, Belgium—1918

"... Here's another one, cold as stone. Looks like he were an officer—yeh, Captain Atkins. He's left a widow somewhere, too. Well, give us a hand with him ... There ye go, Captain Atkins, rest you easy now. Well, come on, there's more to gather ..."

As the vehicle jolted along, bearing the dead from the battlefield, one of the bodies stirred, limbs jerking convulsively, eyes snapping wide and taking in the grim surroundings, nostrils flaring at the stench of death ... of blood.

For a few moments Jonah rejected the truth of the situation, but its reality slowly sank in, as he put his hand to his chest where he'd felt the bullets rip into him. Now he felt torn cloth and dried blood. Reaching inside, however, there was no corresponding wound. Nor heartbeat. The packet of native earth Corinna had insisted he carry was still present.

Running his tongue along his teeth, he found canines grown longer and sharper, stimulated by the scent of blood. Well, *this* was going to be interesting.

Author's Note:

At the turn of the century, many passengers boarded the Orient Express with secrets to sell, or hide. Spies such as Robert Baden Powell and Mata Hari, or the arms dealer, Basil Zaharoff, who virtually lived upon the train as he supplied the great powers with submarines. Traveling through the heart of Europe, they passed through lands rife with intrigue and unrest, and still under the shadow of far more ancient beliefs. It was an age of modern wonders—where the vampire still walked.

Rebecca Ann Brothers has published many stories in various small press anthologies over the years and has at last been persuaded to share her talents with a larger audience. It is to be hoped that she will make a frequent habit of it.

FAITH LIKE WINE
by Roxanne Longstreet

She was young yet, but I knew what she would become—
it was obvious from the first sight of her. One does not
forget that sort of face, those extraordinary eyes.

Her name was Aimee Semple McPherson, and she was
said to be a prophet.

The tent I stood beneath, waiting for her to speak, had
taken laborers half a day to put up—a new tent,
astonishingly enough, and these days with the whole world
at war there were no new tents of any size.

Tents were not the only scarcity. I stood quite near the
front of a large and still-growing crowd, but as I looked
around I saw only old men, women, and children. I blended
with them, as I meant to—an older woman, to all appearances, gray-haired, not yet out of my prime. Well-dressed,
I liked to think, though not ostentatious. Age and woman-
hood had granted me an automatic aristocracy in such a
crowd, and no one tried to push past me for a better view.

I had never been particularly well-mannered, but I certainly knew how to take advantage of it in others.

It had been a tiring walk all the way to the Philadelphia
countryside on the strength of rumors, nothing more. Sister
Aimee spoke with the voice of God, people said. She
healed with His hands. I, doubting, had come expecting
an evening of lukewarm platitudes. Such was the state of
Christianity—it had been raw, intoxicating wine when I was
young, but now it was milk, suitable for children at their
mothers' knees. I had walked with martyrs in the shadow
of crosses, and I had never learned to love milk.

The buzz of conversation went on around me. A farmer
to my left was worried for his daughter, taken ill with a
fever—not the dreaded and still-raging influenza, he has-

tened to add. He received medicinal advice from a young plump woman and her stick-thin husband. If anyone looked for me to join the conversation, they were kind enough not to demand it; I watched the dais and waited. Sister Aimee sat passive, eyes closed now, while her assistants whispered around her, measuring the crowd with piercing looks, checking the time against a battered pocket watch.

They could not wait much longer, not with safety. The crowd stretched to the limits of the tent, a swelling, murmuring beast with thousands of heads. So many years since the first such crowd I'd been part of. I'd been far to the back, then, and the words had come faint but clear in the silence. Five thousand people, that day, crowded together, and I the least of them. Sometimes I could still hear the sound of his voice, smell the goaty stink of too many people crowded together. Nothing in my life had ever been the same again.

Sister Aimee rose and stepped forward, arms upraised, eyes still tightly shut. The crowd rippled into silence, responding to some electric presence gathering like lightning. I could feel its fire from where I stood. No fraud, this one. No false prophet.

She stood, arms upraised, quivering with tension as if held on an invisible rack, the torture of the Lord's favor. Quiet washed over the crowd. Were they afraid? I began to think I was. My life had become comfortable and routine, and here she was, fire in her eyes, to rip it apart again. It was what I craved, what I feared. A spark of light in a long, familiar darkness.

She wore a plain white dress, severely cut, well-used. Her hair was dark and worn in a conservative bun; she wore no jewelry except for a wedding band. A plain woman, except for her face, that radiant face.

It was blinding, now, as she gave herself to the ecstasy of God.

The effect of her still, silent prayer caused the crowd-beast to whisper prayers of its own. Next to me, an old woman carrying a photograph of her son wept into a ragged handkerchief. She'd come for a blessing on him.

An hour before I would have told her, kindly, that it would be useless. But—

But.

Sister Aimee lowered her arms; her eyes opened and they were the eyes of a savage saint, so full of love they were fatal.

And she began to speak.

I cannot remember what she said, it was not the words, the words have been said before and to little effect. It was the naked terrible beauty of her belief. Her voice was a sword, piercing every person in the tent, sending some to their knees in pain, driving most to tears. She burned so bright, the sun in my eyes, the pulse of her heart like a drum in my ears. As she spoke, she ran with sweat and her white dress clung like a lover's hand, skin pink beneath. She paced the platform like an animal, screaming out her pain, God's pain, her love, God's love.

Likely the trouble had been going on for some time before the ripples of it reached me so far in the front, shaking me from my trance; Sister Aimee had stopped speaking and waited, staring toward the back. The world tasted flat and dusty after the glory I'd seen, the sound of screams and shouts harsh. A wedge of young men—a shock to see so many together—came driving through the crowd, heading for the stage.

Mrs. Dowd, the greengrocer's wife, had warned me of Catholic protesters at the revival meetings, but these young men looked more serious than that. They had the righteous look of men steeling themselves to violence. And they were heading directly toward me. I looked for an exit, but escape seemed very far away; I would force a way through, if I must, anything to avoid being caught in the riot that must surely erupt any moment. The boys were taking their lives in their hands. They had no idea how certain Sister Aimee's control was of her people, or what those people might do to protect her.

A dark-haired, pink-cheeked boy leading them raised his hand and pointed at Sister Aimee, and shouted, "Whore!" The other boys took it up like a battle cry and began to lay about them with makeshift weapons—knobby clubs, homemade blackjacks, boots, fists. The crowd surged back from them, pushing me into the arms of a thin old man with the pinched face of a banker.

Sister Aimee stood like a porcelain statue, illuminated with sweat and the halo of her passion, and watched the violence with unnerving eyes. Few of her audience scattered for the exits; there was a curious sense of *waiting*. Frustrated with their lack of success, one of the boys slammed his club into the ribs of the farmer near me who'd come to pray for his daughter; the old man went down, weeping. I stayed where I was, unwilling to flee but certain that I was watching the destruction of the glory I'd glimpsed. Prophets were fragile things, made and broken in a day.

And then Sister Aimee said, in a cold clear voice that carried to every ear, "Kneel and pray, brothers and sisters. Kneel and pray for our burdens to be lifted."

I remained standing, waiting, watching her face. Next to me, the weeping mother clutched the picture of her son and sank to the hard-packed earth. Behind me I heard rustles of cloth, creaks of protesting joints.

In ripples of obedience, the crowd kneeled. I lowered myself as the last few touched earth, and folded my hands in a position of piety. I turned my head so that I could watch the reaction of the ruffians from the corner of my eye.

They were the only ones left standing, and it clearly unnerved them. They spun in circles, looking for a fight. With a scream of rage, a boy farther off to my right brought his club down on the head of a middle-aged woman. She toppled against an elderly man in expensively cut clothes. The boy smashed him in the face and kicked him, turned on the woman, then on a young girl. No one rose to fight. He screamed his rage, over and over, *cowards, cowards, cowards,* and stopped, panting, in the destruction he'd done.

Sister Aimee closed her eyes and began to dance. I turned to watch her, riveted by surprise. Her hips swayed slowly, her shoulders followed the curve, her arms lifted and carried the motion above into the air. It was breathtakingly, frighteningly sensual, as if her body had given itself over to another power. She began to turn, slowly, deliberately, to the beat of her unheard song.

Her tormentors came to a standstill, staring, weapons forgotten in their hands. We were all her creatures, trapped in the sway of her body, the jut of her hip, the slow circle of her feet. I closed my eyes and still saw her, heard her, felt her as she moved.

For the first time in a hundred years or more, I took a breath. She had touched something within me that was fearfully strong, love and death and desire and pain all bound together, the dark wine of the faith I'd known in my youth when we were slaughtered by the thousands and kissed the knives that killed us.

She had discovered the secret of ecstasy. I had not been so close to the light in so long, felt its heat, heard the echo of his voice inside it. It was painful and glorious and horrifying. I had kept control of myself for so long, and now she offered—no, *demanded*—my surrender.

Someone cried out, and I heard myself crying, too, lost in the bright vision, the knife-edged fear of falling. She was near the piano now, and, still dancing, reached out and struck a thunderous chord, chaotic and intense, a thunderstorm of music like the cries and prayers around me. And she continued beating the piano, punishing it, and we were all dancing now, swaying to the strange wonderful beat of her song. Someone touched my arm, feather-light, and the breath I'd taken in burst out in a rush. I was trembling, near to falling. Close, so close ...

Sister Aimee turned from the piano and stepped down from the stage to dance with us, a silent striving of bodies toward God. Her eyes were dark as wells, promising salvation, promising a reunion with all that I'd lost so long ago, and before I could stop myself I reached out to her.

Our hands met, shock of her hot flesh on my cool. The clamor of her pulse was deafening.

"Dance with me," Sister Aimee whispered. "Oh, sister, dance with God."

My feet moved without me, drifting to the beat of her heart, and the tent spun in a glory of light and shadow, faces and eyes. I felt nothing but her skin pressed against mine and frantic hunger inside me, driving me on.

She had turned me to face the crowd, and as she stepped forward and I back, I felt the smooth cool wood of the podium behind me. She stepped forward again, close, so close, God staring out of her eyes. I had forgotten so much, oh Lord, so much.

She placed her hands palm to palm with mine and pressed my arms back and up, toward the crossbars of an invisible cross. When she released them, they stayed, I could not have moved them if I'd wished. She was too bright to be so close to me, and her heart raced like a deer, mad with ecstasy.

She drew back her right hand and brought it in a wide swinging circle up, fingers clasped around an invisible hammer, and her left hand held an invisible nail to my palm.

I opened my mouth to scream as she brought the hammer down, the pain was blinding and horrifying and ecstatic but there was no pain, only knowledge, only God. The doors had been thrown open, and the light, the light ... I felt her fingers holding another invisible nail to my left palm, and as she drove it home, she transfixed me in the agony of the lamb.

When I was able to scream, I fell forward into her strong, warm arms. She held me while she fought for breath, while her heart raced and then quieted and, passion fading, she eased me to the cold ground. I lay helpless while she folded my hands, one over the other, on my breast.

She turned toward the crowd, but not before I saw the fevered bliss in her eyes.

"Thy busy feet that have walked the world must be nailed to the cross," she said. In the utter silence, one of the Catholic boys fled, then another. The rest followed. Watching their retreat, she said, "Thy heart that has beat for this world must be pierced for me."

I closed my eyes and wept silently, tears streaming away through my gray hair to drip on the hungry ground. Her warmth swept in again, and her fingers touched my tears.

"What's your name, sister?" she asked kindly. I gasped and gasped and finally, like some secret treasure from the depths of a well, brought out my true name.

"Joanna," I whispered. "Joanna, wife of Chuza, servant of Herod."

They kept her long into the night, but finally even the most ardent of her converts slipped away, toward home and bed.

I sat outside on the cool grass, lit by the moon, and waited. Lanterns dimmed inside the tent. Her assistants and rough-dressed tent-pullers started back for town.

One light glowed inside the tent, a spot of emerald on black shadows. It moved toward the huge main opening and became the yellow halo of a lantern. She carried it casually, dangling from her right hand, and it cast a long golden path in front of her.

She turned and looked toward where I sat, though I was a shadow in shadow.

"Sister?" She tried to keep her tone quiet and reassuring, but I heard a tremor buried deep. "I hadn't thought you would wait so long."

"Not so long," I said, rose to my feet and brushed grass from my skirt. "By my standards."

She took a tentative step toward me and raised the lantern. The light flowed over the cool, serene lines of her face, made secrets of her dark eyes. Her lips parted as I stepped into the circle of light.

"I would not harm you," I said. "I would never do that. I only wanted—wondered—"

She was weary. The lamplight had given her a false color, but her arm trembled with the weight of the lantern and her shoulders sagged. Of course she was weary. *He* had been weary in the press of a crowd. So many hungering, needing, demanding.

And here I was, hungering, too.

"If I could heal you," she finished for me. "Take away your thirst and give you peace."

She could not have known, not just looking at me. I was hearing the voice of God.

"No, sister, I'm not the one." Her arm was trembling so much she was forced to lower the lantern and set it beside her feet. "I'm so sorry, Sister Joanna."

I looked down at the light, glowing between us. "I had no hope, really. But I thank you for showing me my faith again."

I turned to walk off into the darkness that was my home. Before I could enter it completely, she called after me, and I turned and met her eyes.

"Joanna, wife of Chuza, servant of Herod." Sister

Aimee's voice broke as she repeated my name. "You knew Him, didn't you?"

I closed my eyes against the radiance of the light.

"Yes," I said. A surge of wind blew the grass in billowing waves, a lapping silver lake in the moonlight. The tent sighed and groaned. "I knew them all."

I had come with the lepers, wrapped in layers of rags and castoffs. The crowd was still great, even at so late an hour, but no man held his place before lepers; we moved through solitude even here, in this sweating throng. Some of the faces knew me, another reason to veil myself. They would know me for a follower of Simon Magus, and stone me.

I saw him for a brief second as the crowd shifted, and his eyes were wonderful and terrible and knowing. The veils, the concealment, all that was useless. He recognized me for what I was.

I fell back, hoping to drift off quietly, but a hand closed around my arm. I turned, shocked that anyone would dare to touch a leper, and saw a stocky, bearded man with a kind face and smile.

"Quiet," he advised me. "I have been sent to bring you."

His name, I learned, was Judas Iscariot, one of the twelve who served. He took me to a small, ill-repaired house with blankets and packs spread out on the rough floor, and told me to sit. He offered food, not knowing how useless it was, and then wine and water. I took a little of the water to allay his suspicion.

"You should not drink after me," I said as he took the bowl back and raised it to his lips. He had an impudent grin.

"You are no leper," he said, and drank the rest.

At the doorway, a shadow, a confusion of movement. The shadow turned and spoke, and the protesting murmurs melted into silence. He ducked through the door and came to sit opposite me as Judas put an oil lamp between us.

For all the strength of his eyes, he was only a man, no taller than most, no more beautiful. He had the smell of the road on him, and the sweat of a hard day's work. No longer young, but not old. Not yet. He had lines of weariness in his face that had not been there when last I'd seen him, when last I'd believed his lovely words.

"Lord," I murmured, and bowed my head to the floor. When I looked up, he was watching with a small, amused smile.

"Humility should come from the heart," he said. Judas came forward to clear a place for him to sit, and he lowered himself into it with a sigh of relief.

"Master, this is the one—" Judas began, but his master lifted a hand to stop him.

"Joanna," he said. "Chuza's wife. I remember you well."

I sat upright, more afraid of him than ever. I had not unveiled, I was as anonymous as a thousand women outside his door. He had seen me before only once, and I'd been different then. So very different.

"I heard that Chuza died," he continued. "I am sorry. He was a good man."

"How—"

"Did I know you would come here? Because I know." The amusement was closer to the surface now, but not cruel—a child's gentle amusement, full of wonder. "Your road has been hard."

"I have not traveled far."

"I did not say you had." His smile faded. "You may take away the disguise now. I am not afraid."

I unwound the scarves to show him my unnatural pallor, my too-red lips, my too-green eyes. I smiled to show my sharp teeth.

"A long road," he said, unmoved. "It will be longer still, Joanna. Have you the strength?"

"I—" I swallowed; begging did not come to me as easily as even mock humility. "Can you help me, master?"

"Did not Simon Magus promise to heal you?" I bowed my head, but he continued, kind and merciless. "My rival took you in when you were dying and promised you everlasting life. Are you happy with your bargain?"

"No." I felt tears welling up, but they were mortal tears, and my body no longer knew them. "No, master, please, help me. I went to Simon Magus because I needed— Master, I asked·you for healing, and you said my time was done."

"It was."

"He said he could—give me—"

He took the plate of figs that I had refused and chewed on one while I sat in silence, ashamed. He sipped from a bowl of wine Judas handed him.

"I only want to die," I said at last. Judas, wide-eyed, sank back on his haunches and shook his head. "I killed a man, master, because I was so thirsty. I can't bear it anymore. Please, give me rest."

His eyes were full of sorrow and pain, knifing through me and leaving ice in their path. I reached out to him and touched his hand. He did not draw it away.

"It is not my place to take your life," he said. "But I can give you rest, of a kind."

He reached into a pack leaning against a cracked wall and found a sturdy sharp knife. He held it out toward our joined hands and, before I knew what he would do, drew it across his own wrist. I cried out, and Judas lunged forward and grabbed for the knife. The master hissed a little with pain and held our joined hands over the empty bowl that had held his wine.

His blood dripped like jewels into the plain clay, fast at first, then slowing. When he turned his wounded wrist upward to show me, there was no cut at all.

"Drink," he said, and let go of my hand. I looked down at the bowl.

He'd only bled a little, but the bowl shimmered with blood, full to the brim. I raised it and sipped, the raw fire of it burning down my throat and into my veins. It tasted of honey and flowers and tears, and I drank until the bowl was empty.

"You will not need to kill," he said. I clutched the bowl to my breast and bowed, no mock humility this time, wishing I could weep for joy. Here was the water of life, in my body, and in my heart I felt the pulse of God. "When you hunger, the bowl will fill again."

"Master, what do you ask of me?" I whispered. Simon Magus had asked, everyone had always asked. There were no gifts, only exchanges.

His hand touched my graying hair, gentle as the wind.

"Walk your road," he said. "Walk to the end, where you will find your healing."

I waited at the train platform in the beating fury of the sun, protected by a hat and heavy clothes and a parasol topped with faded satin flowers. It was early morning, the sunrise an orange cream confection behind the unlovely black hissing box of the train. Passengers scuttled around me, bound here and there, clutching hats against the white steam and cool breeze.

I held a single suitcase in my left hand. The burden was too precious to set down, even for a minute.

Sister Aimee's party emerged from the station, a threadbare gaggle of white dresses and severely dressed, sober-faced men—her roughnecks had passed through earlier, loading baggage and tents. Near the center of the crowd I saw the porcelain curve of her face, a lovely smile. She had her hand on the shoulder of a young girl who walked with her.

I did nothing, said nothing, as the party passed me on the way to the train. Pride had always been my downfall, but I could not beg, not now, not ever. I watched them board, one by one, and no one so much as glanced in my direction.

Then Sister Aimee turned, one foot on the iron steps, and looked directly at me with a smile warmer than the furious sun.

"Sister Joanna," she said, and the sound of her voice silenced those around her. It woke tingles in my back; I fought them off with a straightening of my shoulders. "Come to see us off?"

No begging. Not now, not ever. I met her eyes.

"I come to join you," I said. Her smile faded. Perhaps she was thinking of what I was, what the presence of so much shadow might do in the midst of her light.

"Do you?" she asked. My hand tightened around the grip of my suitcase and I willed it to relax. Her assistants were frankly staring, whispering among themselves. There was doubt in Sister Aimee's eyes, moving like clouds over a clear sky. I was something old and unknown, something dark. I had a second's grave disquiet and thought, *I should not have come. It's too late to go home.*

She held out her hand to me. I moved forward, skirts brushing aside those who stood in my way, and realized as I arrived that I had no free hands to take hers. I must put down the suitcase, or put away the parasol.

I folded the parasol. The sun pressed on me with cruel, unforgiving hands, burning even through the layers of clothes, through the straw hat that shaded my face. I pressed the parasol into the crook of my arm and reached out to take Sister Aimee's hand. Her fingers folded warm around mine.

Only a moment of agony, and then the cool shadow of the train was around me, and Sister Aimee's fingers touched my face. I couldn't see her; even so small an exposure to the sun had turned my vision to grays and blacks. It would be minutes or even hours before I could see clearly again.

"Brave," she commented, a smile in her voice. "Come aboard, Joanna. We have a long way to go."

He had a huge, expansive house outside Jerusalem's walls, surrounded always by knots of people seeking blessings or miracles or just a good look. He also had disciples, rough men, ready with fists and knives. Two of them were on duty outside the door when I arrived in my leper's disguise; one reached down to find a rock to throw. I pulled the veil away and showed my face. The one with the rock grinned and shrugged and tossed the stone over his shoulder. The other just spat near my feet and settled back against the wall more comfortably.

No pauper's hut would have done for Simon Magus. Inside, soft lamplight glimmered on fine cedar tables, delicate pottery, gold lamps and jars. The floor was covered with soft carpets and furs. A doorway at the other end of the room was covered by a black drape that glittered with sewn gold coins; they chimed in the cool evening breeze. The air simmered with costly incense, gifts from rich benefactors.

"Simon?" I called. The coins chimed. Outside, the guards laughed coarsely.

"You used to call me 'master,' " he observed. I whirled to find him standing quite near me in the shadows. As he came into the light, I saw that he wore a new robe, no doubt another gift. The umber and gold of it put sparks in his large dark eyes, made his skin seem gilded. Beautiful Simon. Never a man born so beautiful. "I missed you, Joanna."

His voice sounded sad and fond, and it shamed me. I found myself looking away and knew that weakness would destroy me unless I was careful.

"I went to him," I said. He reached out to touch my cheek and it was like being touched by fire, beautiful and agonizing at once. Before I could recover, he was gone past me to settle himself on a thick tasseled pillow—master greeting servant.

"And how did you find the carpenter?" Simon made the word sound faintly scandalous. "Still working miracles, is he?"

I had the bowl hidden inside my robes. My hand brushed it before I could stop myself, like a woman betraying a disgraceful, ill-gotten child. He saw it, of course; I saw the delight flare in his eyes.

"What miracle did he work for you, my love?" he asked, voice low like a cat's purr. "Did he offer you forgiveness for your sins? Did he heal you? Oh, no, my apologies, I see he did not. Too bad, really. That *would* have been a miracle."

I stood silent, watching him, his beauty like a whip against my skin. Simon made a graceful gesture with his hands and produced from thin air a gilded bowl of wine, from which he drank slow, measured mouthfuls.

"Thirsty?" he asked. I shook my head. "Liar. Joanna, I will forgive these indiscretions of yours with my rival if you will sit and drink with me. Will you do that?"

I had lain there on those same soft pillows, fever burning me to ash, and he'd lifted my head and held a bowl to my lips and said, *Drink, woman, drink and live,* and I had taken bitter mouthfuls, feeling the stain of it in my soul even as I swallowed. If I had been strong, I would have spit it out. Would have refused a second mouthful.

But I had drained the bowl, and now I had to pay the price for that selfishness.

"I believe in him. I am going to join him," I said quietly. "I came to tell you."

Silence. The curtain of coins tinkled like dreams breaking. Simon held his bowl in both hands, mouth curled into a smile, and watched me.

"Then do that," he said, and shrugged. "What do I care? You are nothing, less than nothing. You served Herod, and betrayed him by skipping off to follow your carpenter when he crooked a finger; you turned your back on the carpenter when you sickened, and came to me for miracles. Now that you are well, you betray me. You are a whore of the spirit, Joanna."

It seemed impossible that he could still hurt me so deeply, but the casual chill in his voice, the sharp edges of the words, made me feel sick with grief. I looked down at my clenched hands. When I looked up again, Simon was gone. There was a hollow in the pillows where he'd sat. Outside, the guards laughed. Where had he—?

His hand closed around my throat from behind me, dragged me into the heat of his embrace. He had strong hands, clever hands, and before I could fight he reached beneath my robes and pulled out the bowl.

"This?" He let me go, and I whirled to face him, terrified by the sight of my salvation in his casual grasp. He turned the bowl this way and that, looking at the poor quality of the clay, running his fingers across the uneven surface. "A miracle? Perhaps a miracle that the potter managed to give it away. Here."

He tossed it to me. I clutched it gently, like a newborn. Simon's smile was no longer beautiful, only wide.

"Or is it this one?" He snapped his fingers and another bowl appeared, identical to the one I held. He tossed it toward me; I caught it, fumbling, panicked. "Perhaps this one?"

He produced another bowl, and another. The fourth I could not catch; it fell against the corner of a cedarwood table and smashed. I went to my knees and scraped blindly at the mess.

When I looked up from gathering the fragments, distraught, I saw him looking down on me with rage in his eyes. Perhaps he knew then how completely he'd lost me.

"Put them down," he ordered. "Put them all down."

I tried to keep the bowls, tried desperately, but they

writhed out of my fingers and thumped to the carpet, one after another.

"Simon—" I could not beg, not even now. He raised his foot and brought it down on the first bowl. It shattered into a thousand dusty pieces.

"Come back," he invited, and put his sandaled foot over the second bowl. I shook my head, not knowing whether I was denying him or denying the moment's pain. "Come back to me and I'll forget all this foolishness."

Another bowl smashed into clay dust and shards. One left. I stared at it with fevered eyes.

"You don't belong with him, Joanna. You know that." He raised his foot. In his dark eyes, my reflection flickered and stretched into shadows. "I am doing you a favor, you know."

There was a film of red at the bottom of the last bowl. As I watched, it bubbled up, a magic spring of life. His foot came down toward it.

I leaped forward and knocked him away. He fell against a table and overset a lamp and jug; wine spilled over his robes and the carpets in a purple tide. I scooped up my bowl and drained it in two quick, guilty gulps and backed away, toward the doorway, as Simon turned on me.

He did not scream, he did not curse. He only stared. It was enough.

I lunged out into the darkness, between the two startled guards, and ran, leaving strips of leper's gauze flying on the wind as I ran toward the moonlit walls of Jerusalem.

Someone waited at the side of the road. The moonlight touched his face and his kindly smile.

"He said you'd come this way," Judas said. "It's not safe to walk alone."

I cast a look back at Simon's house. He was standing in the doorway, arms folded, watching me go.

It was a queer change, sitting behind Sister Aimee as she exploded into the fury of her belief; she directed it out, at all those hungry faces, those empty eyes. In the backwash, where I sat, there was only a tingle of power, nothing like the tide I'd been swept away on before. I was grateful, in a way. One should not know God so closely on a daily basis.

I learned quickly that every revival looked the same—another empty field, sometimes dry, sometimes muddy, another town on the horizon. Sometimes the crowd was older, sometimes younger. The routine was grinding. Sister Aimee preached and prayed far into the night, rose with the sun and participated in the camp chores like anyone else. I did one-handed tasks, like fetching water or scrubbing clothes; everywhere I went in the sunlight, I carried my parasol. One acute young lady said that I must have a skin disorder, perhaps leprosy, that made my skin so white. They all thought it was highly appropriate that Sister Aimee should count a leper among her followers, though privately they must have wondered why I hadn't been healed.

I realized, as I knelt beside a lake in Idaho and scrubbed spots of mud from the hem of Sister Yancy's dress, that I had done such work before. I had only misplaced the memories, never forgotten. They loomed so close now that I could smell the dust of Jerusalem, feel the harsh fabric on my skin, see the heat shimmer from the stones of the courtyard where I had gone daily to fetch water. I had been shunned there, too, and had gone at odd hours to avoid the curses and thrown stones of the other women.

I pushed the painful, precious memory aside and scrubbed industriously. A cooling shadow fell over me, and I squinted up to see Sister Aimee dropping down next to me, a load of washing in her arms.

"I thought I might find you here," she said. She had not spoken to me—to anyone—for days now, lost in the routine of preaching, healing, sleeping, working. She was visibly worn, and had a tremble in her hands that had not been present before. "How are you, Joanna?"

"I am well," I said. "You're tired."

She gave a little laugh and lowered her head toward her work, soaking the clothes, wringing them, scrubbing them with soap. The water was very, very cold. Her fingers took on a more pronounced shiver and a bluish tint.

"Perhaps I am," she admitted. "Perhaps that's all it is."

I stopped working and watched her. I had been traveling with her for almost a year, though the time hadn't seemed so long. A year was nothing to me, but for her, burning so bright, a year was an eternity.

"Did you notice, last night?" she continued more slowly. "Something felt wrong. I felt—lost. I called, but he didn't come, it was only me. Only me."

I *had* noticed, and not only last night. Some nights Sister Aimee seemed to be searching for that fire I'd always seen so clearly before, nurturing a spark, not a conflagration. Sometimes she'd fallen into a routine, like a salesman's patter. Perhaps that was to be expected, as weariness gutted her spirit. Even *he* had needed rest.

"I'm afraid," Sister Aimee said. She was staring down at the petticoat she was wringing, and there were tears coursing down her cheeks. "Oh, sister, what if he never comes back? They come looking for miracles, you know. For faith. What if I have nothing to give them?"

I took the petticoat from her and put it aside, dried her chilled hands in the folds of my skirt. She put her head on my shoulder and I rocked her gently, stroking her hair. My poor prophet, burning so bright.

What happens when the candle burns out?

I should have known better than to come here and destroy her faith.

He stepped out of the shadows like fog swirling, a simple trick he often used to impress his followers. I was carrying a jar of water across the courtyard, hurrying to get out of the burning sun, but I came to a breathless stop when I saw him. The sun pressed on me like the hands of a giant, and my arms tightened around the heavy jar. I was going blind, but *he* stood out like a brilliant stain on the dark.

"Fetching water?" Simon Magus asked, and leaned his shoulders negligently against the rough stone wall. He looked the part of a savior—beautiful, wide eyes as gentle as an angel's. "Sweet Joanna, surely our misunderstanding didn't lead you to slavery to a Galileean carpenter? What will people say?"

"Go," I said, not loudly because I did not want the men inside to hear. "Go, please. You have no right to be here."

"I have every right." Simon Magus stood straight and tugged his robes into place. "Come into the shadows, my dear, before you burn yourself beyond repair. Such as you don't belong in the light."

The pain of the sun was intolerable; my arms shook violently, spilling water over the front of my robe. My eyes were fading, but I saw him hold out his hand to me. Beckoning. Commanding.

"No!" The jar slipped from my arms and shattered on the stones with a crash. "Simon, I left you! You have no right!"

"He's left you lost between light and dark," Simon continued. "Come back where you belong, where you are loved. Don't run any longer, Joanna."

I sank to my knees, gray hair a veil over my sweating face, and tried to find my faith. In Simon's presence it curdled and vanished.

And then Judas said, "You, what do you want here?"

I looked up but he was only a vague shape in the sun-blindness. He knew Simon Magus, of course, they all did. I thought he would call for help, but he stepped out into the sunlight. Alone.

"My property," Simon purred; I heard the gloating smile in his voice. "Little man, run and tell your master that I've come to worship at his royal feet."

"He will not come."

"No? Then I'll take what is mine and go." He held his hand out to me again and snapped his fingers. "Up, Joanna."

A man's arms went around me, holding me close. Judas. He was trembling, though not enough that Simon would see; afraid, after all. But willing to risk everything in spite of that fear.

"In the name of God, go!" he shouted. His words brought a stir of movement from the house; I heard sandals scrape on the courtyard stones and knew others were joining us, ready to fight. Which? Peter, perhaps, good-hearted as ever. John, with his chilly, determined eyes, always ready for conflict.

"She must say it," Simon Magus said. His voice was as warm and sad as I remembered, and traitorous. I had believed once, so strongly, and been so vastly betrayed. "Joanna, my dear? Won't you come home?"

Home, I thought with a piercing grief. There was no home now, only Simon's fraudulent smiles or the harsher, more honest love of the Twelve and the One. I could never be one of them, even if I stepped out of shadow entirely.

But I could never go to Simon Magus. Never again.

"Go," I said. It did not sound as strong as I wished. "Leave me."

Judas' arms went around me as my knees buckled; as he picked me up to carry me inside, I sensed that the shadows were empty. Simon was gone, vanished like a nightmare.

My sight was entirely gone now; I knew that he carried me inside only because of the sudden relief on my skin and the babble of voices around us. Peter shouted for order and began telling of Simon Magus; the words drifted into distance as Judas carried me away into the room set aside for stores and my pallet. Someone followed us; I heard the scrape of his footsteps behind us. Judas lowered me to my blankets and smoothed sweaty hair back from my face.

"She is ill," he said over his shoulder toward whoever watched. "Get the master."

"No," I protested, and caught at his hand. "No, give me time, I am well. It's only the sun."

The other man made a disgusted sound deep in his throat, and I did not have to see him to know him; John would be staring with those chilled eyes that saw so much, so far away.

"Leave her," John said. "We must report what she did."

Judas' hand left my forehead as he turned. "What did she do, John, but renounce a false messiah? Don't bring this out again, it's an old argument. Joanna, would you like some water?"

I had spilled the water outside on the cobbles, but he'd forgotten it. I summoned up a smile and shook my head. After the dreadful punishment of the sun, I felt languid and lost.

"Just rest, please," I said. He squeezed my hand gently and stood. "Judas, I—I didn't bring him here. I would never want him to come here."

"I know," he said kindly. "Rest now."

I turned my face to the wall and listened to them go.

Hours passed, filled with the muted buzz of heated conversation outside. My vision lightened from black to gray. Colors returned dusty and bleached. I would be days recovering, but I could see well enough to move around, to straighten up the meager supplies kept in the room with me. While I ordered sealed jars of oil, someone slapped the stone outside my door, asking entrance. I rose to pull the curtain aside and found James standing there, head down, avoiding my eyes. He was a small man, wiry and strong, quick to laugh. I had always liked him, had always believed he liked me, as well as a man could like a widow whose eyes had the taint of poisonous hunger.

"You are wanted," he said, and turned away. I watched him walk quickly away, shoulders hunched, and knew with a sinking heart that my welcome was ended.

It was not a very long walk, of course, only one short hallway, but the silence that greeted my approach made it seem longer. The twelve of them were present, seated in a rough circle. Judas had left a place open beside him and I took it, kneeling decorously on the hard-packed floor.

"Brothers," I said, and bowed my head. It was only the twelve, no sign of the master. I had seen little of him, lately, and when I did, his eyes seemed unfathomably far away. Perhaps he was gone again. I could hardly imagine the Twelve meeting like this without him, but surely he would have come if he could. Surely.

"She is humble," Peter said, and he meant it as praise. "She knows her place. What harm can she do?"

I put my hands flat on my thighs and looked down at them. No pride, not now, Joanna. Pride is your enemy.

"She is causing rifts in our brotherhood," John said. Ah, John, I had known it was you, I had known. But it was not simple jealousy, or even simple fear. John was the protector, and he fought higher battles than that. "You all know what's being said. How can we teach truth when our enemies have such fertile ground for sowing lies? Surely it is true that we keep women in our house—she and Mary Magdalene, women of uncertain virtue at best! How can we stop the lies if we do not eliminate the cause of them?"

"It would be different if she were a wife, or even a sister," Simon Peter offered. He was a big man, scarred from the years he'd spent working the sea, but his voice was strangely smooth and calm. He was not a man I cared to have arguing against me. "But a woman alone, even a widow, can hardly be above suspicion. We must be seen to be righteous. Sometimes truth alone is not enough."

"Are we speaking of Joanna or all women?" James asked, frowning. "Should we forbid the master's mother entrance? Should we turn away believers? He has never said so."

"Joanna is different." John's voice stopped James cold, stopped even the breeze traveling through the room. "We all know that. It is that difference that is at issue. She is not a creature of God. She cannot bear the light of day."

"Many of the sick cannot," Peter said.

"And many are possessed! But we should not lie down with devils, brother! Let us heal them and send them on their way." I felt John's eyes rake over me and suppressed a shiver. "I think her true master came for her today. Will she say differently?"

The silence that fell was deadly. Surely they were all looking to me. I kept my eyes down, kept my voice even as I said, "Simon Magus made me what I am. Do you think I am grateful for that? He is no master of mine. Not ever again."

"So you say now. What if you sicken? What if—"

"Enough, John!" Judas stirred next to me; I looked up to see him staring across at John's rigid face. "You've accused enough. Joanna is not causing a rift here, *you* are. If the master wants her to leave, he will tell her. He will tell us all. Until he does—"

I felt the surge of a presence suddenly, like a strike of lightning behind me. He had not been there before, I knew, and others knew it, too. I saw John's face go feverishly brilliant with worship. The master burned hotter as the days went by, a force of power and love that warmed us even in passing.

And he said, "You are right to be concerned. Joanna must leave us tomorrow."

I cried out, turned, and threw myself full length on the floor at his feet. Such hardened, well-traveled feet, in dusty patched sandals, so different from Simon Magus' pampered, well-cared-for flesh. I laid my cheek on them and wished I could weep, wished I could wash his feet with my tears, wipe them clean with my hair. Instead I could only pray, silently, for mercy.

"It is my wish that you leave us," he said quietly. He sounded so sad, so final. I looked up into his face and saw bottomless sorrow in his eyes, a pain that had no human definition.

"Then I must go," I whispered, and kissed his feet and remained lying there until he reached down to lift me up. I had never been so close to him, face-to-face, near enough to feel God beneath his skin and see heaven in his eyes. Words burst out of me like blood. "Master, I would never betray you!"

It was as if the rest of them had vanished for us, as if he saw only me. I was no longer looking at a man, I knew. I was no longer speaking to a mortal. The light in his eyes reached deep inside me and woke something vast and fragile. Something more than love, more than devotion. Faith. Absolute faith.

"I know," he said, and smiled sadly. "That is why you must go, my faithful Joanna, before it is too late."

I shared a tent with Sister Tabitha, a sweet young girl with a voice like a songbird; she led the hymns before and after Sister Aimee's service. Lately, Sister Tabitha had voiced her doubts to me about Sister Aimee. They were no longer doubts for me, but certainties.

In the two years in Sister Aimee's service I had watched the flame burn lower and lower, and now there were only fading sparks. Sister Aimee no longer paced the stage like a lion, she strode like an actor remembering marks. Her frenzies were carefully crafted, discussed at length with one or two of her close companions; Sister Aimee rarely spoke to me now, except during the service. She had asked me to dance with her once, in Indianapolis, but there had been nothing of God in her eyes, only a desperate hunger like lust. She had wanted me to give back her faith. I had become something to touch in place of God.

I had stepped away from her, grieving, and seen the trust die. I had been wrong to come, so wrong. There was no healing with Sister Aimee, and now I was watching my beloved prophet die, inch by inch, and I was helpless to prevent it.

I had come to a decision; I would leave when we reached the next stop. The decision soothed my grief, if not my conscience. A night's sleep, and then I would be gone. Simple enough.

I woke in agonizing hunger. Not the géntle hunger I was used to, but a painful, ripping hunger, a need for flesh and blood, a need to rend and tear and scream. It took me that way, sometimes—not often, perhaps once in five or ten years. But when it came, it was like dying, mortally terrifying. I lay in my narrow bed and pressed trembling hands to my convulsing stomach and stared up at the tree-shadows waving on the roof of the tent. God, God, Sister Tabitha lay no more than two steps away, sweet young face upturned to the dim moonglow. Her heartbeat ached in my ears, a torment I would give all to stop.

Kill her, a whisper from the shadows said, but it was not Simon Magus, not after all these years. It was only my own darkness, subtle and powerful. I *had* to drink, *must* drink, before the tide of madness sucked me down.

I rose in the dark and found my bag, clawed aside layers of clothing and precious, ancient memories—a Greek Bible, bare scraps of words after all these centuries—a newer Tyndale version, one of the few saved from burning in those dark days in England—a single piece of silver. The tarnished coin rolled unevenly across the dirt floor and tilted to a stop.

I could not stop, not even for the coin, not even for that most precious memory. I found the smooth clay of the bowl and hugged it to my chest, careful, careful. There was some magic in it that had kept it unbroken all these ages, but still, I did not dare trust it too far.

The hunger rose like a living creature inside me, clawing, destroying. I gasped and heard Sister Tabitha move behind me, sitting up perhaps. The rustle of the sheet was as loud as a gunshot. Her heartbeat speeded faster.

"Sister Joanna?" she whispered. "Is everything all right?"

Oh, no, child, no, not all right. I could not do it here, not with her awake. The need to flee took me out of the

tent, out into cold dewy grass, the chilly tingle of moonlight.
I was wearing only my nightdress but I dared not stop for
anything more; Tabitha was rising, calling after me. I forced
myself to pause and turn back toward her.

"It's nothing, child," I whispered. So hard to speak, with
the beast so close. "A call of nature."

She murmured something doubtful, but I turned and
strode away, through the cool chilling grass, scattering dew
like diamonds where I stepped. Up the hill, then, toward
the moon, toward safe solitude. Tabitha had not followed.
I clutched the bowl close and panted as I climbed, not for
the air but to hold off the attack of the beast.

I gained the top of the hill and turned a quick circle—
the camp glimmered below me, one huge waving ocean of
revival tent, the smaller ponds of camp tents where Aimee's
faithful slept. The grass waved silver-green as the wind
stroked it.

I went to my knees and took my bowl in both hands.
Hunger beat at me with clenched, bruising fists and I waited
for the red to collect at the bottom of the bowl, to bubble
up like Moses' desert spring. It was slow, this time, or perhaps that was only my own desperation.

He would not betray me now. Could not.

I closed my eyes and whispered a prayer, first in Hebrew,
then in Greek, then in every language I could call to mind.

Warmth cascaded over my fingers. I gasped and opened
my eyes to see the bowl brimming with life, with light, with
salvation. I could almost see his face, sad and worn, his
hands welling with open wounds.

"Joanna?"

No, oh, no. It could not be, not now.

Sister Aimee came around to face me, face wild and
white, hair loose. The wind teased it out into a veil of
shadow. She was dressed, like me, only in a flickering white
gown, feet bare and pale as marble. Tears tracked silver
down her cheeks.

"Go," I whispered. "Go away."

My arms trembled with the strain of holding the beast
back, the shadows were not whispering now, they screamed,
kill her, kill her, kill her, and I was close, so very close.
Sister Aimee knelt down opposite me, the bowl trembling

between us, but she was not watching the bowl, only my face. Such desperation there. Such hunger.

"I have lost him," she said. More tears, spilling diamond bright. "Oh, sister, help me. Only you can help me find what I've lost. I can't go on, I can't, so many hungry, feeding on me, I have nothing left, nothing, you understand, *I can't feel Him anywhere now.*"

I understood, had spent lonely years tending my few precious sparks of faith but none of that was important now, only the beast was important, only the shadows, the bowl that was my person, precious salvation.

Her eyes flared wide with dark grief, and before I could stop her, she struck the bowl out of my hands. It spun away, spilling a precious red ribbon over the grass, and disappeared into the shadows.

I woke from a nightmare to cry out, and found a man's hand across my lips, sealing in the noise. His skin felt feverhot. I twisted away to sit up against the wall, blanket drawn over me, shivering.

"Shhh," Judas touched a trembling finger to his lips. I understood well enough; if he were discovered here the penalty would be grave. For me, it would be fatal. "You must go."

He turned away to start gathering my pitiful things, wrapping them together with trembling hands. I clasped his wrist to stop him.

"I have until tomorrow. The master said."

"Tonight. You must go tonight." Judas breathed in suddenly, a tormented gasp as though a knife had been driven into his side, and tears sheeted over his eyes. "If he asked you—"

"Judas?"

"If he asked you for your life, would you give it?" he whispered. His voice seemed to echo off the stone, loud as a shout. *"Would you?"*

"Yes."

The tears spilled over, coursing down his face, catching in his beard like stars.

"He asked for my soul."

"Judas—" I reached out for him, but he scrambled up

and bolted away. I hurried after, but the outer room was empty, only the fluttering door curtain witness to his passage. I turned to go back to my pallet, my weary confusion.

The master stood in my way. I had never seen him look so weary, so worn.

"I have asked him for the greatest of gifts," he said, though I did not have the courage to ask. Had I thought Judas suffered? There was all the grief of the world in these eyes. "Of all of them, only he has the strength, the faith, and the love. The others could only do it out of hate."

"Master, please don't send me away," I whispered. Around us lay the sleeping forms of his disciples, but somehow I knew they would not wake, not until he wished it.

"You must go. All roads branch from here. You cannot follow where I am going, none of them can. You have the longest road, and you must be sure of your course. I will not always be with you."

The dazzle of his love broke through, glowed like the sun on my skin, and I knew he was not turning me away, only lighting me to another path. Even so, I tasted ashes at the thought of walking away from him, from all of them.

"You will always be with me," I said, and touched my fingers over my heart. "Here."

He leaned close and kissed me on the forehead, a brief brush of light and love against my cool skin.

I thought about the horror in Judas' eyes, the desolation. Had he also received this kiss of peace?

"I'll go tomorrow," I said. He shook his head, frowning. "Tomorrow. I'll stay for Judas."

He looked at me for a moment, then smiled through the sorrow and said, "Yes. He will need you."

The pain of loss was so extreme that for a moment the world went gray, lifeless, and hunger was shocked into silence. I could only stare at the darkness, where the bowl had fallen.

Sister Aimee grabbed my shoulders and shook me, crying out. I wrapped my hands around her wrists and pressed. When I turned my eyes to her, she saw the beast staring, and fell silent. Her face went the color of cold ash.

"Never do that again," I said, as calmly as I could. "It's not for you to touch. Ever. It is *mine*."

Her wrists pulsed with life under my crushing fingers—red, warm, easy to find. How long had it been since I'd tasted mortal flesh? Long enough that it had been in that expensive, long-lost house outside the Jerusalem walls, among the cedarwood tables and gold lamps.

Simon Magus had stood watching while I'd fed, his smile gentle and protective. He'd loved the beast well. The memory of his beautiful smile sickened me, and I let Sister Aimee go and crawled slowly, painfully, into the shadows where the bowl had fallen.

It had struck a stone, but there was only a small chip on the rim, a raw, rough gouge in the ancient finish. I lifted it in both hands and closed my eyes, heard my beloved master's voice, felt his touch around me.

I lifted the bowl and drank until the beast was drowned in honey and flowers. I drank so much that it spilled red over my lips and down my chin to patter dark on the grass, and even then I could not stop taking it in. So close to him, so close.

This is my blood, which is shed for you. Only for me, this blood. None other.

I was senseless with the ecstasy and hardly felt the brush of Sister Aimee's hands against mine. When I blinked and the world came back in dusty blacks and shadows, she was holding the bowl and backing away from me. Her eyes had a dangerous shine. I tried to reach out, to tell her, but she stepped back and I was too weak to follow. As she cradled the bowl, her face came alight with understanding.

"*His,*" she breathed. "Communion. This is My blood, He said. And it is. It *is*."

She did not understand. Miracles were personal. They could not be traded, like unused tokens at the county fair. That way lay defeat, and madness. That way lay Simon Magus, and the false glitter of easy faith. Her face took on the fever of passion, the hunger of lust, and behind her Simon Magus stepped out of the shadows, as if I'd somehow conjured him, shimmering with beauty and treachery, that sad smile, those angelic eyes.

"Drink," Simon whispered. His voice was the shadows,

the wind, the leaves. "Drink, woman, and live. Live forever."

Impossible. It was not Simon's dark, poisoned bowl, it was *holy,* it was *sacred.* Surely she could take no harm from it.

But damnation, like miracles, was a personal thing, and I was not sure.

The house was cold, the fires all burned to ashes. I sat in the gray dawn and listened to the chaos outside on the street. Running feet, now, and screams in the distance. The house was deadly, deathly silent.

I heard his footsteps outside in the courtyard before he entered—slow, clumsy, stumbling. He pushed aside the curtain to my room, gripping the fabric in one white-knuckled hand as he stared.

"I betrayed him," Judas said hoarsely. "They took him at the garden. I betrayed him."

He sank to his knees there in the doorway, all strength bled away. I took him in my arms and rocked him gently, back and forth. His skin was cold and gray, and he shivered. I put my blanket around him and held him in silence while the noise continued on the street. The followers of Simon Magus would be rejoicing. There might be rioting before the day was out. I could not guess where the rest of the Twelve had gone—fled, most likely, before the devastating betrayal.

"I warned you to go," he said, and he sounded so tired. I rested my cheek against his and felt his tears run hot on my skin. "They will come here. They will kill you if they find you."

"He asked you for this."

"They'll show you no mercy."

"He asked you to betray him," I said again. Against my cold silent flesh, his heartbeat continued, a strong, desperate beat like fists on a wall. "You bear no shame."

"I love him," he answered, and turned his face against my neck and wept like a sick and grieving child. "I have never loved anyone so much."

I kissed his forehead, gentle, as the master had kissed me. I had no tears, only a great hole in my heart where tears would have been. *All roads branch from here,* he had said. But he had not said the roads would be so short, or so bitter.

In the distance, a cock crowed.

"Time," Judas whispered. "Time to go."

I walked with him into the courtyard. He stripped off his robe in silence, folded it carefully, and put it aside. Over his shoulder the sun rose, as glorious as the eye of God.

I knelt there on the hard stones while the sun burned me, and watched as he hanged himself from the tree, with the silver coins scattered at his feet like a gleaming fallen halo. He never spoke, not even a prayer.

I had no prayers left in the ashes of my heart, only a vast, aching silence. I took one of the coins, only one, to remember him.

Oh, Judas, my love.

"She is already doomed," Simon said to me. Was he really there, or only my own doubt and fear given form? Did she see him? Sister Aimee only had eyes for the bowl, the ecstasy she had so loved and lost that glimmered dark in its depths. He only offered what we most wanted, of course. What we most had to have. "If you save her now, there will only be another time, and another. She is no carpenter from Galilee, Joanna. And people cannot bear so much arrogance without smearing mud on it. Eventually, she will fall."

"She is stronger than you know," I whispered. The beast had sapped every ounce of strength and left only the grief, only the pain. "Stronger than I was."

"You only wanted your life," he smiled, and walked a half-circle around her. His sandaled feet left no mark in the dewy grass. "Her pride is much greater. She thinks she can drag the whole world to heaven."

Strange, but I had missed him, missed the casual cruelty of his smile, the graceful contempt in the way he looked at me. One needs enemies, I found, in order to feel alive. And he was my enemy, my last and truest one, closer than any lover, any friend.

Simon's smile turned deadly.

"You choose bad companions," he said. "Men of dishonor and treachery. Men so faithless their names become curses. Tell me, has the world forgiven him yet, your Judas?"

Trust him to strike at my weakest point, at my most precious, most hidden memory. It had not mattered, really, whether the world cursed Judas, or even whether the master had. It was Judas who had been unable to forgive himself.

Sister Aimee raised the bowl toward her lips, and I remembered a thousand things about her, good things, bad things, moments of pridefulness and arrogance, moments of love and kindness. She was strong, but he was subtle. It might destroy her.

All of us, trapped by our own greatest sins. Judas, unable to forgive. Aimee, too proud to admit her faith was incomplete. Me—

Me, too selfish to die. What had the master said, that evening when I'd sat so close to him? *It is not my place to take your life.* No.

I had *stolen* my life. Only I could give it back.

All these years I had looked for healing, believing that I deserved another chance at mortal life. All these years, and I had not learned from my errors.

Now my pride dragged her down. I knew where our healing lay, if only I had the courage.

He knew I did not.

I knew I did not.

"Mine," Simon sighed in satisfaction, as the bowl touched Sister Aimee's lips.

I stumbled to my feet and grabbed the bowl away. She stared at me dull-eyed, mouth dripping red, and I had no time for thought.

I found the rock that had chipped the edge of the bowl, my salvation, my precious miracle.

And I brought the bowl down on it.

The sound of it breaking was lost in Sister Aimee's cry, in my own gasp. Three sharp pieces. The edges slashed my fingers like steel. I smashed them again and again, mixing my own blood with the red clay.

When I was done, there was nothing but rubble left of my dream.

In the silence, Sister Aimee whimpered and dropped to her knees. Behind me, Simon Magus said, "I never thought you would have the courage. Welcome to the end of your road, Joanna."

The world was empty and quiet. Dawn blushed the horizon. I felt an easing in my chest, as if some long-tightened spring had begun to unwind.

"You have not saved her, you know," Simon continued. He sounded very far away, one of the fading shadows. "She cannot last."

"I know," I said. So quiet, the world. My cut hands ran ruby now, a thick continuous stream. My stolen life escaped. "None of us can last, Simon. That is the lesson."

When I looked back, he was gone. As my strength bled away, I curled on my side, where the grass was soft. The dew touched my cheek like teardrops.

For the first time, the sun warmed me without burning.

A hand stroked my cheek, and I opened drowsy eyes to see Judas' face, his kind, sweet smile.

"Time to go home," he said. I sat up and looked at Sister Aimee, lying asleep nearby. "She will be safe. Time to go home."

There was another man standing over me, holding out his hand. Luminous eyes, smiling now, no longer sad.

"Master," I said, and felt his fingers closed over mine. "It's good to be home."

Author's Note:

Aimee Semple McPherson began as a preacher in the early 1900s and quickly progressed to a nationwide phenomenon as she led startling, charismatic tent revivals in cities all across the country. Her mission led to the founding of the Foursquare Baptist Church, which exists to this day.

In 1926, Sister Aimee disappeared for a month and was later found wandering alone. She insisted that she had been kidnapped and held for ransom, and managed to escape her abductors. Rumors claimed that she had run away with a lover, but though several inquiries were staged, nothing was ever proved. However, she was convicted in the court of public opinion, and that was enough.

Though she continued to preach until her death, Sister Aimee never lived down the scandal of that event.

Joanna, wife of Chuza, servant of Herod, is one of the women mentioned in Luke 8:3. Really. Any other heresies are entirely my own.

Roxanne Longstreet is the author of vampire novels *The Undead* and *Cold Kiss* and the thriller *Red Angel*, all published by Zebra. Her latest novels, *Slow Burn* and *Red Rover*, are forthcoming in 1996 from Pinnacle. She resides in Arlington, Texas.

BLACK SOUNDS
by Lawrence Schimel

Blue like an endless sky ... I crumpled the vest in my lap and sat on the edge of the fountain in Plaza Bib-Rambla, wanting desperately to cry. I held back my tears, since men don't cry. But I felt like a tremendous fool; what was I doing here?

A small dog yipped excitedly. I looked up and watched a handful of gypsy children chase after it. Their limbs swung wildly as they tumbled over one another on the stone flags, racing and laughing, full of exuberant life.

I stared down at the brightly colored vest in my lap and wondered how much their carefree spirit was due to youth and how much to their gypsy upbringing. I'd always wanted to be bohemian. It's why I was here in Spain, an ocean away from everything I knew, pretending to learn to dance flamenco.

If you don't try now, I'd told myself, you'll soon be tied down with a job, with family and kids, permanently rooted in the humdrum existence of earning a living and daily mundanity.

My whole life, it seemed, had been pushed by my parents' desires, geared toward my obtaining some tedious job I hated which I worked at for the next forty years, earning piles of money and, Scrooge-like, never enjoying any of it. Was this what I really wanted out of life? Something—perhaps fear of the known, the inevitable future I saw for myself—helped me find the inner strength to defy my family's expectations of me, to throw caution to the wind and come here; a gamble; a risk. Nothing in life happens without vulnerability. I knew that, intellectually, but even knowing it, understanding it, it was hard to live that way.

I'd fallen in love with the idea of the gypsy through

poems and novels. I knew, as I came to Spain, that I would not find them as I had in these stories, that the authors had changed them, made them larger than life. But I knew this was the English-speaking side of my brain, the critical side, which had studied and dissected the poetry at university, written essays about its symbolism and meanings. When I read the poems in Spanish, they existed in a different world, a different level of meaning and understanding. In that world, they were still real. In that world, flamenco was a way of life.

By abandoning anything that was American, thrusting myself wholly and completely into the language until I thought in Spanish, dreamed Spanish, made Spanish the daily substance on which I lived, by so completely losing myself in it, giving myself up to it, I hoped to enter that world of those poems and stories.

It hadn't worked. I'd been here for three months. Tonight the Corpus Christi began, and I still couldn't dance. I knew the proper steps—intellectually. I could demonstrate their sequence. But I didn't feel *duende*.

The word itself had confused me at first. Duende also means "faery," those wee folk of legend: imps and brownies and hobgoblins. But in flamenco it meant something much more complex, the passion that is the energy of the creation itself. But like those fey creatures, who could only be seen out of the corners of your eyes, who, when you turned to stare directly at them, were gone, the duende of flamenco also had to sneak up on you when you least expected it. It was a feeling of contradiction and impossibility: The struggle to find duende is the struggle to stop searching for it, for some external muse to inspire you, and to simply feel the act of expression and experience the feeling of it. It is the creation in process, which is why you can never catch duende. You can achieve duende, perhaps, but it passes through you.

It sounds so simple, neatly expressed in a phrase or two, but it continued to elude me despite knowing the theory of it. And without duende, flamenco means nothing. You must feel the passion burning so fiercely you are consumed with it, and yet the dance is all control, the fire kept just under the surface, ready to explode, waiting to explode, wanting to explode. And you let it, sometimes, a controlled leak in the violent stamp of a foot, the sudden clap of a hand, loud, and powerful in the force of its desire. I've watched dancers achieve duende, and even as spectator it's one of the most exhilarating experiences I have ever felt. In those moments I knew why I had made this rash decision to come all this way on a gamble, with so little assurance of success of any sort.

Tonight the *feria* began, a week of festival and dancing, and I still couldn't feel duende, couldn't break free from my shell to experience life. That was my entire problem; duende *is* the breaking of form, the bursting free of raw idea and emotion. It is the marrow of creation turned outside and exposed to the audience. It's a painful-sounding metaphor, but pain is exactly when duende is most powerful. It will not approach without the possibility of death, for then it's too safe. There's nothing for it to work with. Without the possibility of death, one is already dead.

I threw the vest in the fountain and stood up. No matter how brightly and flamboyantly I tried to dress, I was still dead, inert, living an emotionless life. I thought of my older brother, the model son, who'd so meekly gone to The Great War and never came home. Young as I was when I left, I'd been grateful that I was too young to go, since I knew that I would not have been able to as blindly follow everyone's expectations of me. I guess my entire life I'd been waiting for my chance to rebel. I wondered if I might not have been happier if I'd just followed the path of least resistance and wound up rich and shallow and always too drunk to notice any pain, real or emotional.

No, I just couldn't do it. I thought of getting drunk now, to celebrate my defeat, to be melodramatic like some failed writer who later turned out to have been a genius, someone who drowns his sorrows in some foreign bar when his novels are rejected again and again, too brilliant and advanced for his own time—but I was too much the coward to do it, it wouldn't have made my problems go away, so instead I went back to the room I had rented.

Bleak as my anticipation of the event was, I had to go to the Corpus, much as I tried to talk myself out of it with superstition and dark portents. I knew I would not feel duende, would probably not even dance at all since the few people I'd met weren't going to the feria. But if I didn't go, I would always wonder if maybe I had been wrong.

Why wasn't life simpler? All I wanted was to be spontaneous like the gypsies those authors had written of. A sudden flash of color, an image they threw at you, by itself, alone on the page like a bright red rose against a clean, lime-white wall. I could not even think that way. I sat with my journal and stared at this same city they had written about, but I could not see it the way they did. I tried to write poetry, in Spanish, in English, it made no difference. My mind refused to grab wildly at life, to latch onto the most prominent aspect of what I saw before me and exaggerate it, enlarge its proportion until it became truth.

Truth. Duende. I ached for life to be simpler, to be content with simpler goals.

The fairgrounds had been built just outside the town, a small carnival with games of chance and wild animals in cages. But most of the area was taken up with *casetas,* little canvas houses where people drank and ate food and danced flamenco on wooden platforms that rose between the tables.

Casetas were like speakeasies in a way, places where the liquor flowed like water and you had to know someone in order to be admitted. There were metal gates on most, and guards at the entrances. I knew from overheard gossip that there were some casetas run by the city of Granada, and open to all, but I'd only passed one of those so far, the largest of the tents at the entrance to the fairgrounds, and while people were inside buying food and drinks, no one was dancing. I wanted flamenco, that was what I was here for, and I wandered about the fairgrounds looking between the canvas flaps for glimpses of people dancing. All of the casetas played music, sung and performed by people inside, and I was itching to dance to it. But I was on the outside, uninvited. I didn't know anyone who could get me into one of the casetas where people were dancing, and even if I did, I didn't know any girls to dance with. Hearing music all around me, watching people enjoy themselves, I was not just itching to dance but feeling intensely lonely at the same time.

The only thing to do at the Corpus, it seemed, was eat, drink, and dance. Or feel lonely.

I wandered around the feria for another half hour, an outsider, a stranger, a foreigner, before beginning to walk back to the city, my new boots covered with dust but not danced in.

A young couple sat on a bench outside a caseta and I couldn't help feeling a pang of jealousy as I stared at them, cuddling and laughing together. Everyone had told me I would find a girl at the feria, since men who danced were always in short supply, and the constant repetition had made me believe the thought was my own. I shook my head to put the young couple out of my mind and continue on, but I couldn't. Without giving myself time to think, I bought wine from a vendor and hurried over to the couple, accidentally tripping over their legs and spilling it all over them, dousing their happy young passion in the dark red liquid.

The boy stood up, angrily towering over me as he shouted something in the gypsy language. I couldn't understand him, though I knew his tone of voice and gestures. I turned and ran, losing myself in the crowd.

Why had I done that? I asked myself. They had done nothing to me. And I didn't even feel better having done it; pain and angst still sat heavy in my belly.

There was motion and noise all around me, but I felt safe. The boy would forget me and return to the girl sitting on the bench. I looked around more attentively, wondering where to go to next, and realized suddenly that in my hurry to get away I had accidentally put myself in exactly the position I had wanted to be—inside a caseta. I still didn't know anyone, and wanted desperately for someone to dance with, but for the moment it was thrilling simply to stand among the throngs of people listening to the music and watching the occasional couples dancing Sevillanas in the center of the room.

Everyone was dressed to dance: the women in elaborate *gitana* dresses, frilled and tasseled and ornate, and the men in somber gray suits, a bright swatch of color at their waists

from their cummerbunds. I again felt conscious of how out
of place I must look. I wished I had kept the bright blue
vest, now floating like some alien blue fish in the fountain.
If I weren't more afraid of never again having this opportunity, I would've bolted for home and changed. But no one
questioned my presence, and I stayed. I still felt isolated
and alone, but was determined to stick it out. I glanced
about the room, half-defiantly, daring someone to come
over and tell me to leave. My earlier almost-fight had gotten my adrenaline racing, and I could feel my blood pounding in my ears in a syncopated rhythm that matched the
music.

A beautiful, dark-haired woman across the caseta noticed
me watching her. An odd expression crept over her face,
as if she half-recognized me. As she began walking toward
me, I realized it was that she had recognized me, and
planned to throw me out. I looked elsewhere, at the couples dancing on the wooden platform, feeling my chance at
ever getting there sink rapidly.

She was before me, looking even more striking than from
across the room. Her lips were the same lush color as the
red stripes snaking their way up and down the ruffled white
fabric of her dress. White roses were twined through her
black hair, pulled tightly into a bun, away from her face. I
imagined it loose, spilling over her smooth olive skin, over
me ...

She opened her mouth, as if to speak, and I imagined
the words she would use, telling me to leave. But she did
not say anything, merely smiled, and took my arm. I drifted
after her, unable to believe what was going on. We climbed
onto the platform as one set ended and stood, staring into
one another's eyes, as the music began anew. I did not
think, not about dancing, or the music, or steps. I watched
her, and wanted her, and felt our mutual desire become
movement. Later, I would realize what had happened, how
she had made me forget to strive for duende, so preoccupied instead with desiring her, which allowed duende to
well within me, all those years of repressed emotion exploding through my blood at once. But I was in control; I directed it toward her, in our dance, gestures of power and
wanting and need.

I was almost faint with the heady sensation of potency I felt. We danced, and I was sustained by the dance. If my mind had been capable of rational thought, I would've remembered that to feel duende should exhaust one, since passion is both generated and released. I was swollen with our passion, buoyed by it. I did not question its release. She stepped toward me, her lips full, ignoring the dance to kiss me. Our lips met, and a charge ran through my body as she spun away and continued dancing as if she had never broken step. I did not know whether to expect another kiss as we both stepped toward one another again. We danced, duende coursing through me, changing, but always part of me; it was like that saying that you can never step twice into the same river, for the water that made up the river when you first stepped into it is now gone, replaced by new water, different water that makes up the same river. Even when you stand within it, duende is a different river.

The music was building toward its climax. We danced. She spun. She reached out for me, breaking the form, breaking the duende, kissing my lips, my neck. I felt her lips warm against my flesh. She nipped at my skin, as if desperate for a taste of the duende rushing through my blood.

I must have fainted from the cessation of dancing, I thought, exhausted by the expenditure of passion and energy, by the passing of the duende through me and out of me when the music and our dance ended. I opened my eyes. Men I did not know were helping me sit up. Faces pressed about me, talking in a language I no longer understood. I blinked and tried to stand, to push past them and find her again. I needed her. Where had she gone?

They held me as I fell back again. She was nowhere to be seen. I had one last memory of her, from just before I fell, of her staring into my eyes, her lips full and red like the stripes on her dress, and red roses woven through her hair, which hung in black cascades about her shoulders.

Someone pressed a handkerchief to my throat, and I reached up to touch it. My fingers felt slick. I pulled the handkerchief away and stared down at the dark red splotches, reminding me of that line of poetry about roses startling against a lime-white wall in sunlight.

I wanted to cry out then, my frustration, because of what she had done, because I would never see her again. But of course I could not, and would never be able to do so, to shout with abandon, a wild and exuberant expression of emotion. For I knew she had taken from me my capacity for duende, not just the passion of our dance together, but all the passion that was in my soul, my capacity for creation and expression. I knew I should rail against her cruelty, for taking me to the top of the world and showing me exactly what she was forever taking away, what I had always been hoping for, all of my life. But I was drained, empty, devoid of life, and could not summon the energy for it. I was emotionally inert and knew, deep in my bones, that I would always be this way.

They had moved me to a seat at one of the tables, these strangers, when it was I who was the stranger within their midst. And slowly the world closed around me again, like flesh creeping over to heal a wound, and couples started to dance when the music started up again, but it was all just noise to me, black sounds and darkness.

Author's Note:

Write what you know.
This is perhaps the most-common statement made to young writers (or new writers of any age) rivaled only by "Always enclose an SASE."
Now, at the ripe old age of twenty-three, what is history and memory for many of my readers is instead historical for me, and beyond the scope of my experience and years. While daunting to write from outside one's own experience, this is ever the writer's challenge—to create verisimilitude. Whether one is writing from the opposite gender in the present day, or from an alien point of view in the far future, the writer's task remains the same—to convince the reader that he writes from authority.
I might have felt more comfortable, perhaps, writing of the far-distant past, where my "historical" fiction would not be as subject to the scrutiny of an audience who may, some

of them, remember the times about which I wrote. Perhaps I've skimped on the details of the period, choosing to rely on mood and tone rather than weighting the story down with carefully-researched facts. My slacker generation, Generation X, lost and aimless, trying to find itself, is very like "the lost generation" of the mid-1920s, as chronicled in works such as Hemingway's The Sun Also Rises. *These are feelings universal to the human condition.*

I wrote about what I knew and, since I had myself fallen in love with the idea of the gypsy in literature and studied flamenco in Spain, this story grew out of the details of my experience of dancing, of the duende coursing through one's blood and the desire, watching someone else who'd achieved duende, to taste that feeling.

Lawrence Schimel is co-editor with Martin H. Greenberg of *Tarot Fantastic,* along with other collections, and his own works have appeared in over 75 anthologies, including *Weird Tales from Shakespeare, Phantoms of the Night, Friends of Valdemar,* and *100 Vicious Little Vampire Stories,* among others.

THE GHOST OF ST. MARK'S
by Elaine Bergstrom

Father Brian Stewart sat alone in the chilly vestibule of St. Mark's Church in the town of Dersham, located midway between Norwich and the English Channel. Once the town had been glowingly described in tourist guides and local brochures as the best-preserved example of village life in the time of Shakespeare. That had been before the war and the night of bombings that had reduced the historic south end of Dersham to charred rubble. Only the church had survived.

Brian had been born in Dersham, and had lost much of his family that night. After the war, he had asked to be assigned to a different city, among people he did not know. But recently he'd requested a return to St. Mark's and found its ancient walls comforting.

Not so the memories. Brian usually sat so that, if he looked into the church, he saw the magnificent northern windows instead of the less skillfully crafted windows on the south side of the church. In spite of this, he could not help but think, fleetingly, of the bombing. He was hardly the only one. If he listened after any service, he would hear some older parishioner mention it, and the crowd in front of the church would fall silent for a moment out of respect.

A shaft of light cut through the dimly lit church as the side door opened and shut. He sat in the darkness listening for the familiar shuffle of one of the older parishioners coming to pray, but heard instead a muffled giggle.

"Do you know for certain it's haunted?" a girl whispered.

"It should be. The guidebook said twelve people died here after being rescued from the fire."

Tourists and American from the sound of them. Brian

studied them from the shadows. One wore a white halter top and jeans, the other a sleeveless blouse over skin-tight athletic shorts. The first girl giggled again, as if she were trying to be frightened and not able to manage it on a sunny autumn afternoon.

Brian almost wished he could manage a howl, or a moan—some sounds a ghost might make—and send them running. But if he tried, his ruined lungs would protest. He'd start to cough and reveal himself as nothing more than the frail old priest he was. Besides, laughter in St. Mark's might be just what the place needed. If not, he doubted that God would mind the girls' impiety.

"The guidebook says that the north windows were made by the same family that crafted Notre Dame." A pause, almost respectful, then the girl continued. "It says that St. Mark's was one of the last holdouts of Roman Catholicism in England. There's even supposed to be a hidden priest's hole somewhere near the altar."

"If no one found it, it's probably just some sort of a lure to get us peddling all the way down from Norfolk and too damned tired to peddle back. I'm not spending the night in that buggy-looking hostel we passed, do you hear?"

"Don't be such a pessimist, Nikki. We'll rest until after dinner, then peddle back. Now look at this stone. Do you think this leads to the passage they were talking about?"

"The stone marks the mass grave of seven unclaimed bodies pulled from the rubble after the bombing."

"There's something carved on it."

Father Brian shifted his bulky body forward. The dark vestibule, his cassock and the distance between him and the altar would keep his presence a secret. As he'd expected, the girl was kneeling beside the memorial stone, trying to make out the inscription.

"I can't read it," the girl said.

"Of course you can't," the one called Nikki replied. "It's in Latin, you idiot. I've got a translation here. Do you want me to read it? . . . Anita? Anita, what's wrong?"

"Can you feel the heat?"

"Heat? There's no heat. It's cold as hell in here all of a sudden."

"It's all around me. It's burning. And the noise ... too loud!"

"Anita, the fire was fifty years ago. Now cut it out." This time Nikki sounded genuinely upset. Her companion was probably playing a trick on her but even so, Brian should go and remind them that St. Mark's might be listed in some tour book, but it was also a house of God.

He was pushing himself to his feet when he heard Anita scream.

"Anita?" Nikki said, her voice lower now. Brian saw her backing away from the memorial stone.

"It's so hot. So hot it's burning me!"

The very act of standing so quickly left the priest breathless. He managed to reach the last pew and began moving forward, gripping the side of each pew for support.

Anita shrieked, a sound of terrible agony. Nikki responded with a more normal cry of fear. Panting, the priest looked forward and saw Anita, in the shorts, lunge toward Nikki. The force of Anita's attack made the other girl lose her footing. She fell backward, hit her head on the side of the altar, and lay still.

As the priest watched helplessly, Anita's nails tore at her friend's throat. With a growl of rage at their uselessness, she bit the side of Nikki's neck and began to suck on the wound.

The words for exorcism were rarely used. Once Brian had memorized them purely for the arcane pleasure they gave him, but he had long since forgotten all but a single line. "In the name of the Father and the Son and Holy Spirit, I cast you out," he said, his voice modulated for the breath his lungs allowed was hardly more than a whisper.

Anita looked at him, a strange smile on her lips. "Out of this church? I don't think you have that power," she replied in a voice that bore little semblance to her own.

A wave of searing heat rolled over the priest and he thought the death that would come all too soon for him had decided to take him by surprise. He pitched forward, unconsciousness before he hit the ground. . . .

"Please wake up. Please. Please."

The plea was accompanied by a shaking, a dash of cold

water in his face. When Father Brian came back to consciousness, he saw Anita crouched beside him, blood and water dripping from her hands. Her face was stained with blood as well and her white shirt and shorts were spotted with it. There was a nauseating smell in the church, familiar to the priest though he could not place it. "Thank God!" she exclaimed and helped him to stand. "Something's happened to Nikki."

"I know," he said, wondering if she understood that she was the cause of it. "I'll see to your friend. In the meantime, I want you to go to the rectory. It's the newer brick house over there." He pointed to the south side of the church. "Father Kenneth will know what to do."

As he watched her leave, he saw that the blood was not confined to her hands and face. Her back seemed coated with it as well and her legs were red and blistered as if . . .

He recognized the smell, then. Burning flesh.

He moved toward the victim, stopping at the holy water font. The water had a rusty look to it and there were drops of blood on the marble bowl. Pleased that Anita had the presence of mind to act so logically, he dipped the hem of his cassock in the water then went and knelt beside the victim. Though the wound on her neck was deep, there was still color in her face and the hint of a pulse. Though he did not know her religion, he began the Last Rites.

Brian heard the atonal sounds of the ambulance siren even before Father Kenneth joined him. When both girls were on their way to the hospital and the police had taken Brian's brief statement, Father Kenneth began questioning him, the nature of the questions making one point obvious.

"How many times has this happened before?" Brian asked.

"There have been any number of people who have commented on the heat, and four somewhat serious incidents since the war," Kenneth replied, "but nothing as serious as this. The girl who came to get me even has burns on her back."

"Do you believe in ghosts, Kenneth?"

"I believe in souls. That's enough, I suppose. I'm going to follow the ambulance to the hospital. Do you want to go back to the rectory now?"

"No," Brian said. "I need to sit here a while."

Once alone, he concentrated on everything that had happened. There was something about the possession that he ought to understand. It eluded him for the better part of an hour, then came to him with sudden, perfect clarity.

When Anita had challenged him, it had not been her voice he'd heard, but he'd recognized it.

As quickly as he was able, he made his way to the side door of the church and across the yard to the rectory. Relieved for the chance to be alone when he made the call, Brian phoned Chavez, Portugal.

"AustraGlass," the operator said.

"I need to speak to one of the Austra family," Brian said.

"To whom?"

"It makes no difference. But this is a personal matter," he replied. He gave his name, then added, "Tell them that I was a friend of David Austra."

The priest had expected to be ignored, or treated with the smooth sympathetic tact most people reserved for the obviously unbalanced. Instead, the charming woman he spoke to was as concerned as himself and promised immediate assistance.

Stephen Austra arrived promptly the following afternoon. He asked no questions but instead stood beside the memorial stone, eyes shut, as if waiting to be possessed as the girl had been the day before.

Brian sat in the front pew and watched him. He'd expected the family to send someone older, someone more capable, someone who would not be a constant reminder of David. This man and David had nearly the same face—more beautiful than handsome, the same strange dark eyes, the same black curly hair, the same hands with their long fingers. Artist's hands. Musician's hands. Lover's hands. He recalled them too well. Their almost delicate indecision as they hovered over the chessboard while David contemplated his next move. Their strength as he worked with Dersham residents shoring up the houses damaged in the occasional random bombings. Their bleeding wounds, their blackened skin as he reached for Brian, and his eyes. . . .

No, he would not remember that. Far better to recall the dreams he'd sometimes had before the bombings had begun. In them, David came into his room, the delicate hands brushing the side of his face, their touch seeming to push Brian into a deeper sleep in which only the echo of his presence remained. And in the moment when David, dying, reached for him the passion the dreams had roused in him had somehow surfaced, bringing its own horror.

"Do you think he had any control over his need?" Austra asked.

"What do you mean?" Brian responded. Though an answer had immediately formed in his mind, he could not understand how the man had known to ask the question unless he had been reading Brian's thoughts.

"And if he had no control, what made you think you would be able to resist your own passion," Austra persisted.

"I have no idea what you're talking about," Brian said indignantly.

"David did not have a strong mind. If you try, you can remember." The man moved toward him. His hands gripped Brian's shoulders, squeezing lightly, though the emphasis was not needed. The touch was enough. It astonished Brian how, after fifty-plus years of hearing confession, he still had the capacity to blush. He tried to look away. Something in the man's eyes made it impossible, and it seemed as if the final command were being repeated in his mind in the man's strangely accented tone.

Remember. Remember.

The last thing Brian recalled before the past came crashing into the present was deciding that this man was not young, nor even a man at all, and that David had been much like him.

Remember.

Brian began his story. "David arrived in Dersham in the spring of 1942, a volunteer from London coming to assist us in warning of imminent bombings. At the time we had no radar to warn of incoming planes and had to rely on our eyes and ears. The younger men and women would go to the high point just east of the town and spend the days

with their binoculars, and their nights in silence—blind
and listening.

"At the time nearly all of the residents had visitors in
their houses. There were children sent by relatives from
London who wanted to protect them from the bombings
or the adult relations themselves when their houses had
been destroyed. There were old men and women who could
not fight or tend the victims. And of course, there were the
recovering wounded.

"But even if there had been room elsewhere, David
would have stayed in the rectory. I knew his family name,
of course, just as I knew his profession from the windows
his family had crafted for us centuries before. And he admitted that staying in the rectory close to the church his
family had helped construct would remind him of home.
He seemed to have a need for that."

Brian pointed at the south side church windows. The
glass was flat, the work hastily done, but at least it filled
the empty spaces, kept out the rain and cold and shed the
same soft light inside the church. "He preferred the night
watches and though he had a room in the rectory, he would
lie along these pews and sleep in the morning. Above him
was a marvelous scene—Christ walking on the water
toward the apostles in their little boat. The glass would
color David's arms and face. It was the only time I saw
him at peace."

"You were not at peace either, yes?"

Brian shook his head. "I was the only son of a family
that with the exception of me was far from devout. I had
been expected to marry and pass on the family name. After
my vows, the bishop sent me here because he thought it
would do me good to begin the priesthood among my own,
but the family despised me for what they saw as weakness.
I never tried to explain that to have done their wishes
would have condemned me and some poor woman to a
web of lies and a life of quiet pain."

He had said too much, intimated more than he had ever
revealed to another soul even in the confessional. "I have
kept my vows," he added.

"Of course you have," Austra replied mechanically, and

Brian sensed that the man understood just how easy it was in the years after David died. "You cared for David, yes?"

"I cared, yes," Brian, the man not the priest, replied. "I cared for his mind, his understanding. I valued his company, as he did mine. At the time he came here the pastor was absent, working in the battle zones, ministering to the wounded and the dying. Managing a parish alone was a heavy responsibility for me. I needed to unburden myself on someone I could trust."

"Or an outsider."

Brian nodded and went on. "I said that David came to help us with our defense. He went with the others to the cliffs just once, but found the presence of the volunteers distracting. He began keeping watch in the St. Mark's belltower. The spire rises over a hundred feet. We had thought of posting watchers there, but we needed earlier warnings. However, David seemed to know when the Germans were coming well before the men standing watch some miles to the east.

"I never understood how he knew where the Germans were going to attack, but he would sound the bell—one toll for London, two for Norfolk—and I would radio the cities with the news. At first I did so to humor him. Later, I realized that he was always right.

"One evening, the bell sounded with a series of high harsh peals, obviously an alarm. I walked toward the tower to find out what was going on and saw him running out the door at the base even as the last peal was droning on above us.

"It's Dersham this time," he cried, and as I turned to rush back to the rectory to call our police, the first bombs hit.

"They landed to the west of the church. The explosion deafened me. The fire started moments later, lighting the sky, marking the Germans' target.

"The church was the strongest building in town with stone walls four feet deep, and a steeply pitched thick slate roof we thought might deflect any bombs that hit. Beneath the slab marble floor of the church was a stone basement we could retreat to if need be. The initial bombing lasted an hour. Even before it ended, the first of the wounded began trickling in. Some walked on their own, dazed or in shock from loss of blood or burns. Others were carried in by relations. Mothers cried. Children screamed. And David ..." He hesitated. How could he explain the young man's anguish, the dreadful fear in his dark eyes.

"David shared their pain," Stephen said.

"So it seemed, yet though it appeared to cause him an almost physical anguish, he stayed.

"The south windows had begun to glow, making it appear that the water Christ walked on also moved. At any other time it would have been beautiful, but David like the others was watching it with growing horror. 'It will be all right,' I whispered to him. 'The boulevard will hold back the fire.'

" 'No!' he replied and looked at me. 'The planes are coming back. Take the wounded downstairs.'

"He'd always been right about the bombs. I did not question him, but began directing the others. We had gotten nearly everyone into the lower level when a second bomb hit just to the south of the church blowing the windows inward.

"I don't know how to explain, but David seemed to cross the church ahead of the blast. I was not so lucky. Shards from the windows were embedded in the exposed skin on my hands and face, and though in the shock of the moment, I did not realize it, some of the larger pieces had also ripped through my cassock and shirt and cut open my back.

"David looked at me. His features were taut, as if he were poised to attack or flee. I had not expected to see such fear in him, but then this was the first time our little town had been heavily bombed. 'Come below with me,' I said and held out my hand.

"He took it and let me lead him forward, but at the top of the dark stairs, he halted. People were moaning in the crowded space below us, and the children, even those who had escaped the bombing unharmed, were screaming.

" 'I cannot go down there,' David said, pulled free of my grasp, and bolted for the north door.

" 'No!' I called and stumbled after him. I could not have moved fast enough to catch him, but he paused and bowed his head. In that moment I heard a sound come from him—

half shriek, half sob, unlike any sound I ever heard a man make.

" 'David?' I called. He did not answer though the anguished sounds grew softer.

"I went toward him. He turned. His face was dimly lit by the fire burning outside. His eyes had always seemed too large for his face, but now they appeared immense, totally black, glowing faintly as he looked toward the fire. He said someone's name but I don't recall it."

"Mark," Austra replied. "London was also bombed that night. His brother died there. David felt it happen."

"How could he?"

"The entire family felt it. It is a part of what we are," Austra said simply and for a moment Father Brian saw the same unnatural glow in the man's eyes, an emotion he could scarcely fathom.

"Aren't you afraid to be so candid with me?" the priest asked.

Austra shook his head and Brian remembered something the man had said early in their conversation. David's mind had not been strong enough to wipe his memory clean. This man—this creature—could do it easily.

Remember. The word pealed on in his mind like the bell that David had once tolled.

"This was David, a person I knew and had come to love. I went to him, and laid a hand on his shoulder. 'We can go to the basement of the school, if you must,' I said.

"He shut his eyes, seemed to consider the matter, then nodded.

"It was only a hundred yards or so from the side door of the church to the school, but on the way the wounds I had ignored made me stumble. David helped me until we heard a sound we both knew all too well—the whistling of another bomb falling above us.

"Everything happened quickly, but I recall it all. I fell and hugged the ground. David stood, his face to the sky as the bomb hit the roof of the church. It was a simple incendiary sort, a hundred pounder. As I had hoped, the thick roof held, and the missile slid sideways down the polished slate, breaking apart rather than exploding when it hit the ground, spreading a pool of noxious-smelling fuel across the schoolyard.

"David dragged me to my feet and we ran toward the shelter of the school. David seemed to fly across the space, forcing open the locked doors with only the strength of his hands and arms. As I rushed toward the safety of the building, I paused. Though I don't know how I could have perceived the sound, I distinctly heard the soft whimpers of a terrified child.

" 'There,' David said pointing across the yard to a small, pale figure huddled just inside the brick gates.

" 'I'll go,' I said.

"He shook his head. Once more my sense of reality shifted, for he fell to his hands and feet. His form seemed to stretch, and keeping low to the ground he bounded across the yard as gracefully as a large cat. The fire in the town had grown, the moving shadows making it hard to see David even though he was no more than a hundred feet from me until I saw him running toward me with the child on his back, her white nightshirt waving behind her.

"I knew the girl well. Her mother lived near the church and since the war had begun had been helping some of the nuns manage a nursery to watch over the small children while their mothers went to work in Norfolk. The fact that Emma had come here alone could only mean her mother had been killed and she had made her way to the one place she associated with shelter.

"Though I'm sure it only took moments for David to cross the schoolyard, I recall everything that happened next so distinctly, it seemed as if time itself had been stretched.

"I heard a deep boom, and saw a shower of sparks climbing into the southern sky. The sparks seemed to hover in the air, then fell, catching the flammable liquid on the ground. The entire schoolyard went up in a burst of light and heat.

"David had sprinted across the puddle to get the child. Now he was caught halfway back. As the flames rose around him, Emma lost her grip. He turned and pulled her into his arms just as the gas tank of the truck we had been using to transport the wounded to the church exploded from the sudden heat.

"Mercifully, the girl seemed to die instantly. David was not so lucky. Carrying the girl, he rushed from the fire. He rolled on the bare ground with her still in his arms, putting out the flames, then lay still with the girl beneath him."

"Fire would not have killed him," Austra said.

"So I discovered. As I walked toward what I was certain were a pair of corpses, I saw David's hands move. He raised his head. Though his face and hair were burnt, and his skin black from the oily fire, his eyes were bright. I started to run toward him, then saw the pieces of metal embedded in his chest and neck. One was the width of my hand, the others were smaller, but from their location and the way the blood spurted around them, I knew there was no way he could still live. Yet he moved. He opened his mouth as if to speak to me, though he said nothing.

"I froze. His eyes seemed to draw me forward, and I had to fight the pull. He rolled sideways and pulled the child from beneath him. He ripped at the girl's neck then began to ... to ..."

"To feed on the dead," Austra whispered, "as he would have fed on you."

So many questions had been answered during that terrible night—from David's reclusive habits, to his strange nocturnal disappearances, to his incredible empathy. "He would not have harmed me," Brian said.

"No? Then why didn't you go to him?"

"I wanted to, but I was afraid."

Austra moved toward him, the same seductiveness Brian had seen in David was evident in the stranger. Austra leaned over him, hiding nothing as he asked. "Of what? Of these fangs? These eyes? The hunger you sensed in him?"

"I was afraid for my soul, for giving into ..." Brian halted, looked away.

"And for that you let him die," Austra said bitterly.

"You have to understand. The entire night was nothing more than a prelude for what I saw in that churchyard," Brian said. "Do you think I didn't condemn myself for what I failed to do?"

Brian paused to catch his breath, then went on. "I backed away from David, and when I had put some distance between us, I turned and ran back to the church and the company of the others from the town. I spent the night surrounded by misery, certain I deserved the guilt I felt.

"The bombing stopped by midnight. We remained in our little shelter until morning, then went out to find half our town a mass of rubble and glowing cinders. The burning was so complete that we only rescued a handful of survivors from the wreckage. And though we knew over three hundred had died, we only found four bodies in the wreckage. But of all the tragic scenes, the one the survivors encountered in the churchyard aroused the most sympathy. David had been a stranger, a foreigner, but invaluable to us. Seeing his blackened arms still wrapped around that tiny girl's body gave everyone a focus for grief that all could share equally. They did not understand why he gripped her so tightly, and I hardly felt the need to enlighten them. Instead, as soon as we emerged from our shelter, I had rushed to the churchyard and made certain that any traces of what he had done were disguised as a wound from the bombing, and that his eyes and mouth were shut.

"Days later, we buried the few bodies together in a memorial grave.

"There was already a cellar beneath the altar, a place that had once hidden priests from the king's soldiers. It was an easy matter to open it up, to lay the carefully wrapped bodies inside. We had a memorial Mass. The survivors came, and we laid the marble stone over them. The names are engraved there. You'll see David's among the rest."

"You said the body had been burned. I read your note. You used the word destroyed," Austra said bitterly.

"We needed him here—in death as we had in life."

"You condemned his soul to an earthly purgatory," Austra retorted.

"We needed him here. We needed to remember the stranger who died trying to save one of our own."

"And now someone has nearly died because of it. All you would have had to do was write and tell us the truth."

"The truth. The truth is that he is dead."

"Is he?"

Brian shuddered. After what he had seen and heard the day before, he really was not sure.

*   *   *

Austra had the tools assembled by evening. He'd barely begun chipping away at the concrete anchoring the memorial slab when Father Kenneth returned from his day of trying to explain what had happened in St. Mark's—first to the authorities, then to the girls' families, and last to his bewildered bishop. The sight of a stranger in his church about to violate what had become the town shrine did not sit well with his already overtaxed nerves.

He rushed up the aisle, intending no doubt to eject the sacrilegious stranger, his voice rising as he demanded to know what was going on.

Austra introduced himself politely, and held out his hand. Kenneth took it. As he did, Austra began to speak to him in a soothing voice that began to take on a mesmerizing cadence. A quarter hour later, Kenneth left, looking bewildered and oddly calm.

"He'll leave us alone tonight," Austra said and resumed the work. Brian knew he should be in bed, getting the extra rest his doctor had prescribed. He felt light-headed, and his vision seemed blurred. The doctors had told him that he should be inhaling oxygen through the day and after every attack, but that would only prolong his dying. Besides, growing used to being close to some cumbersome machine would only take away what little independence he had left.

He made his way from the front pew to the altar and sat on one of the wide, carpeted steps, resting his head on the step above. Stretched out, with his head raised, he watched Austra work.

The man's hands moved competently and quickly, cracking the mortar and pulling it away. Within an hour he'd freed the stone and began to slide it sideways.

Brian shivered with a sudden, terrible cold. The presence he had sensed here the day before had returned. He could feel it, struggling weakly, trying to possess him, to communicate.

Austra had sensed it, too. His dark eyes were fixed on Brian's. "So weak. I can hardly touch him," he whispered and went on with his work, prying the carved oak top off the single coffin, exposing the bodies.

After fifty years, Brian had expected to see nothing more than a few bones and some scraps of the blankets in which the bodies had been wrapped. He saw that for the others, but after Austra had pulled David's body out of the grave, Brian saw that it had changed little from the day it had been placed there.

There were the same long fingers, still burned but seeming less damaged than years before. There was the same face, but somehow the eyes had opened since the body had been interred. Their huge dark pupils stared at nothing. David could hardly be alive, but if the body had sat up and pointed an accusing finger at him, Brian would not have been any more surprised.

"We didn't inter the bodies for three days after the fire," he said. "There was no sign of life, but if so, why does he look this way?"

"Had he lived, he would look no different now than he did when you knew him, or as he had looked a century before that. And when he died, his body refused to submit to death. It held his soul and refused to give it up."

"What will you do now?"

"That's up to your ghost, yes?" Austra knelt beside the grave and touched David's face. He shut the eyes, then called David's name as if he expected the blackened mouth to open, the dessicated lungs to draw in breath and answer.

The chill Brian had perceived increased. He shivered and automatically tried to draw a deep, calming breath. His lungs refused to allow it. He fought the spasm, knowing the coughing was useless and tiring. Austra called the name again.

"Do not try to raise me," Brian said, his voice barely audible.

Austra whirled and stared at Brian. For the first time since he'd come here, he seemed surprised. "Say it as you would to the Old One," he commanded.

The response was in a language Brian did not know. The guttural consonants, the strange inflection set him to coughing. Tears were running down his face when he finally was able to calm himself enough to begin to breathe shallowly again.

"Are you certain?" Austra asked.

Brian nodded. "For half a century they've called to me from both sides of the gulf. It's too late for life, Stephen.

Release me from this world," he said, speaking for the soul he felt inside him.

Austra nodded and Brian felt his grief, profound and oddly angry. He understood. Unlike men, their deaths were not inevitable. And what did he, a mortal man, fight for now? Not years, certainly. Not even months. He felt weary at the thought of going on, and troubled by the lack of faith his struggle implied.

Austra cradled David's head in his lap, bending low over the blackened face, whispering something in his own language. Brian found himself nodding, and Austra gripped the back of David's neck, squeezing hard. The snap was audible and a moment later, the body began to decompose, the flesh to fall from the bones. The lips pulled back from the mouth revealing the long canine teeth once more.

"I will take his body back to Chavez and burn it," Austra said.

"Tske!" Brian replied, the alien denial forced from his throat. "Lay me back where I was."

The words were strong as was the presence which ordered them, but no sooner had Brian spoken them than he felt David's spirit fading. "Wait!" he cried. "Wait, you've been alone so long. Wait a bit and take me with you."

The loud cry took more effort than Brian normally expended. He began to cough, to struggle as always. As he did, he looked up and in the center of the soft-toned light of the church, he saw a figure form. Human in shape, yet not human. Moving, yet not alive. He looked to Stephen Austra and saw that his eyes were open, staring not at the vision but at Brian.

Ghost? Vision planted in his mind by the creature beside him?

No matter, he surrendered to death. His heart pounded as if it were going to break free of his chest, then with a hot burst of pain, stopped.

Such a beautiful place to die, they thought, and Brian felt the delicate fingers of David's kin close his eyes.

When it was over, Stephen Austra moved to his cousin's body and lovingly held the long thin hands, then squeezed them seemingly without effort into a pulverized mass of tiny bones. He looked at the face, then paused, unable to continue except to do what had to be done. A quick, deft motion and the long pointed fangs that had been hidden behind the canines rested in his palm. There would still be differences in the shape of the eye sockets, the hinge of the jaw, the length of the leg, but nothing that should arouse suspicion in a casual observer when the grave was opened again.

And it would be. After the wake and the Mass the town would say for Brian Stewart, the young pastor would rise and remind everyone that the old priest had been the one who had rallied the town on that terrible night, and that his last wish had been to be buried with those who had died in the bombing.

The words had already been planted in Father Kenneth's mind, just as his memory of meeting Stephen in the church had been erased.

Stephen would return for the service. As one of David's relations come to pay his respects to his uncle's old friend, his presence would arouse no suspicion. And if it did, or if someone noticed that the concrete sealing the stone seemed to have been recently applied, he could handle the matter as easily as he'd handled this one.

In his centuries of life, he had come to understand the human race and its predictability. It was his own that so often surprised him.

But David's last wish would be granted. He would rest beside the man who had failed him once, then redeemed himself in the last hours of his life.

Author's Note:

"The Ghost of St. Mark's" was inspired first off by my need to tie up loose ends in my story. In this case, a brief mention in Shattered Glass *that "Mark and David died during the bombing of London." The source for many of the details was a chance meeting with a German who owns a bicycle shop here in Milwaukee. He kept me enthralled for nearly two hours with tales of growing up near Hamburg*

during WWII, including how the locals would empty the contents of unexploded incendiary bombs to use as fuel.

Elaine Bergstrom, a graduate of Marquette University in Milwaukee, is the acclaimed author of several novels featuring the Austra clan of vampires, including *Shattered Glass* and *Daughter of the Night*. She has also written several dark fantasy novels for TSR Inc., and under the pseudonym of Marie Kiraly continues the Dracula story in her chilling sequel, *Mina*.

WALKING TOUR
by *Jean Graham*

Singing bugs indeed. London's blithering over them, and I think it's outright peculiar, because the species in question most certainly does not "sing." I know, because the beetle happens to be one of my favorite shapes: one that I kept for three-quarters of a century, albeit accidentally.

By hell's measure, 76 mortal years is a trifling catnap. Inclined as he is to whim, the Master might easily have arranged my sleep to last a millennium. So I've decided to be grateful.

At least I rested in my element. Given the choice, however, I might have wished for a less ignoble departure from the London I knew.

My London of 1888—a great, stinking, glorious place—brimmed with sweat and soot, with horse dung and pungent sewers, and with every variety of unwashed mortal.

The perfect killing ground.

I'd fed well and often, and my notoriety had spread far beyond the squalid little slums of Whitechapel. Six ladies of the night I took that dusky autumn, soul-harvested, blood-drained and carved to culinary perfection. The mortals even gave me a name, and shivered when they spoke it. I delighted in that, and fed upon their fear; it sustained me almost as well as the flesh of my conquests. My fame was already propagating across three continents when the sleep fell. Apparently, the Master found my exploits rather less impressive than the mortals and I did.

On the night I left my sixth blood feast, someone followed. When five twists through the puissant filth of Whitechapel's midnight streets failed to dissuade him, I turned into a closed-end mews that I knew concealed, beneath mounds of refuse, a wrought-iron sewer grating. I paused only a moment to appreciate the alley's aromatic fetor before plunging into the muck, startling a wailing tom-cat from his dead-rat dinner. My human form melted into dung beetle shape, slithered through the fragrant garbage and between the grate's rusted bars, plopping into the sewer below.

By the time my pursuer's footsteps crunched and clattered overhead, I was happily lost in my element, scuttling through those remarkable tunnels built to carry plagues of cholera away from the Thames.

Unfortunately, I was fresh from the kill and inattentively euphoric. How else could I not have seen or heard a ton of rock, brick and sludge hurtling down from that chute above? Careless of me. Utterly stupid.

A near century had passed before I woke to the shriek of machinery chewing away at the walls of my tomb. When shafts of horrid sunlight stabbed through, my beetle form stirred, sought an opening back into the blessed dark, and at long last bolted free—to emerge anew, once night had fallen, into the year of our Adversary nineteen hundred and sixty-four.

Famished, I harvested the first human soul I encountered: that of a bricklayer repairing the sewer walls farther down the passageway. He left an acrid aftertaste, being some years short of ripened, but desperation is an onerous taskmaster. I took his form and his wallet, carried him still further into the fetid brick maze of the sewer, and left him in an alcove. I moved that very night into his run-down flat in Bayswater, and have spent the six nights since rediscovering my London.

What a queer place she's become!

Black tar and gray slate have covered her once-muddy bricks and cobblestones. Soot belches not from her chimneys (still here, though little used) but from motored carriages that dominate the streets in bleating herds, absurdly warring for twentieth-century preeminence on narrow twelfth-century roads. Though the carriages do emit a superb stink all their own, I must say I rather miss the basic, fragrant stench of horse dung. My kind prefers the simpler things.

And the mortals here! A fumaceous cacophony of noise

and blatant colors, jabbering some incomprehensible mockery of the Queen's English. In varying states of undress, they gyrate in "go-go clubs" to obscenely bizarre rituals which they call "frug," "monkey" and "watusi." (My dear old Victorians would perish from apoplexy at the very sight.) And everywhere there is delirious gabbling about these supposedly musical insects. I really must learn more about that. Perhaps they are some sort of sideshow, akin to those ridiculous flea circus fiascos that were once the rage of Europe.

For the moment, however, I have a more pressing interest. I found it yesterday in the lobby of a seedy hotel on Queensway, jammed with its fellows into a rack full of gaily colored brochures. "TOUR JACK THE RIPPER'S LONDON!" it screams in flaming red block type. "See where the mutilated corpses of his victims were found! Walk the dark streets he stalked! Feel the terror! Take our expert guided tour of Whitechapel. Learn the TRUE FACTS about London's most notorious murderer. £2 10/6—with this coupon; £2. Do not detach."

Well, naturally it captured my attention. It's most flattering to know I'm still remembered, though just how accurately will remain to be seen. I certainly hope it's more reliable than this culture's view of my kind. They seem to have acquired an outright obsession with the *wampyr,* thanks to a wonderment called the cinema and to some turn-of-the-century dime novelist named Stoker. But they have it entirely, excruciatingly wrong. Even the ancients knew better. The true *wampyr* is no dashing romantic figure content merely to skulk through graveyards and slake its thirst on the blood of breathless, cleavage-enhanced femme fatales.

The true *wampyr* steals the *soul.*

I peruse the brochure's promising text yet again as I stride toward Paddington Station. "Meet at Whitechapel Underground Entrance, 7 p.m.," it commands. Absorbed in its adulating rhetoric, I scarcely glance at Bayswater Road's street vendors, busy packing in their trinkets and black velvet 'art' for the night. I revel instead in the aroma of rotting leaves and standing water wafting from the park; in the acrid green lichen coating the stone wall; in rusted ironwork, gutter sludge, street litter and pigeon droppings all tantalizing my nose as I hurry along. With the sun's last light expiring behind Kensington Palace, I turn onto Westbourne Terrace and again onto Craven Hill Road, passing white-washed row houses that were crumbling even in my day. At last, the steel-girdered canopy of Paddington hoves into view; I descend with the black tar pavement into its maw and into the midst of thronging, trampling humanity.

Here I find twice the din of London above ground: a polyglot garble of chattering voices, bawling children, the screech and hiss of brakes, and over it all the unintelligible squawking of some disembodied entity apparently endeavoring to proclaim the arrival and departure of trains. The mortal gaggle appears not to hear it at all, but bustles on about its mysterious business, running over the heels of any who dare dawdle in its inexorable path. The air smells of damp tar and machine oil, of leather baggage and frantic anxiety.

I cannot resist the temptation to mingle, just for a taste or two. So I sidle into their midst and touch one here and there, an "accidental" meeting of feet, shoulders, arms.

My sampling of souls.

Here's one old and nicely desiccated, ripe for taking soon. Another—oh-so-seductively packaged in that skin tight crotch-length skirt and long red hair—is a budding young hedonist in the making. I'll give her forty or fifty more years to hone the art. This one, middle-aged and balding, reeks of cheap suit and cheaper aftershave, and his soul is—

Phaugh!

Millions to choose from and I have the foul luck to sample one of the two per cent committed to the Opposition. Damn! Must clear the palate, quickly. She'll do—the haughty female with the platinum hair that smells of glue. Ah, yes. A healthy lust for power, money, possessions, men. Much better.

Time to follow the red and blue symbols deeper underground. Trains below trains. I pay my fare at the turnstile, already delighting in a new set of sounds and smells as I ride the moving stairs down and down again. Old dust and grease cake the wooden slats; frenzied travelers too hurried to wait push past on the left and tromp down each step on their own. Stand on the right if you don't care to be trampled. The stairs creak and groan their way to the bottom, where they are devoured by the floor, and their passengers scatter in several directions. I pause to consider the multiveined map on the wall, where the route to Whitechapel is drawn in bright purple, and follow the arrow toward METROPOLITAN LINE.

Arriving on the crowded platform, I wend my way through mortal clumps puffing odoriferous tobacco clouds, and stroll to the far east end, where emblazoned yellow warnings demand that I proceed no further. Something tastes of fear nearby. I am not sure what it is, until I touch the dirty, chipped tiles of the rounded walls and drink in lingering terrors more than twenty years gone. It is horror left behind by thousands who once huddled here not to board trains, but to escape the rain of death wreaking havoc aboveground. What a time *that* must have been!

A growling rumble vibrates through the tunnel, and with the stirring of stale air currents, the Metropolitan Line train screams into view. Burnished metal doors hiss open, and immediately, a human stampede surges out, momentarily pushing back the herd attempting to board. Above the din, another disembodied voice repeatedly bleats, "MIND THE GAP!" but no one pays it any heed.

I slip inside just as the doors slam shut and find myself instantly engulfed—squashed would more accurately describe it—in a tight press of bodies, swaying in tandem with the train's sudden motion. Here, another wood-slat floor traps the schmutz of a thousand shoes, and my nostrils are assailed by the salty aroma of human sweat ill-masked by soap, perfume and underarm lotion.

I steal little tastes of soul after soul as we hurtle through the dark. The herd shifts and repacks itself at Edgeware, Marylebone, and again at Baker Street. (Who on Earth is that meant to be—that silhouette with the pipe and silly hat etched into the tiles at Baker Station?)

The mob has thinned by the time we reach Liverpool Street; I claim a threadbare seat on the partitioned bench and watch the remaining riders study the overhead advertisements, their feet, the decking—anything but each other.

Only the tourists and two bead-bedecked teen-aged females converse (loudly), whilst seasoned Londoners practice the delusion of solitude behind their newspapers. Something stinks of flowers—the adolescent females have apparently mistaken cologne for bath water. And while I'm fairly sure they're speaking English, much of the dialect confounds me. "Oh, sheez, cumoffit, Ellie luv, you know Paul's gotta be just the most totally fab, I mean how can you even *think* John's groovier, and just never mind George or Ringo, well I mean they're all fab, you know, but Paul's the most *totally* fab, so boss, so, oh you know, so teddy bear *gorgeous* I could just scream my insides out. If I can't pinch a lock of his hair somehow, I'll just die, that's all, I'll just keel over and totally *die*."

Wait a moment—I've heard those appellations some-where before. Those singing insect sideshow performers again. It seems the bugs have names. And if I interpret anything correctly amidst the gibberish, this is a resound-ingly favorable review. Curious. The descriptions I've heard from a number of more mature Londoners have been rather more akin to "shocking," "outrageous," "buffoon-ery," and "that hair!" I try to eavesdrop on more of the adolescents' chatter, but they bundle up their schoolbooks and disembark at Aldgate East. Perhaps another time ...

When at last we jerk to a stop at Whitechapel, I alight alone. At least it seems so at first, but now three other figures have emerged from other cars and immediately hus-tle off into the tiled maze. No one boards.

I stride toward the WAY OUT sign; behind me, the train rumbles back into its shadowy labyrinth, stirring more warm, musty air in its wake. In these walls, too, the fear-scent from long ago tarries. I drink from that font, one finger raking the porcelain tiles as I stroll. Up gray stone steps and moving stairs, through the clattery turnstile (EXIT ONLY), past a bored and dozing ticket-taker and at last out into the night's cool breeze. And greeted by a comforting sight. The red brick battlements of London Hospital loom across the way, unchanged from the facade I remember. Whitechapel itself has changed little. I know these houses, these streets, and for some reason there's a comfort in the knowing.

As for my tour ... Two likely candidates loiter near the newspaper vendor's kiosk (where headlines declare some-one named Khrushchev deposed by Brezhnev). One is an American, judging by his baseball cap (I've seen a great many of his ilk since my "arrival"). He is perhaps forty, paunchy, and exudes the salty aroma of stale sweat. The other is female, and far more attractively packaged: youth-ful, blonde and daintily lilac-perfumed. She notices my scru-tiny and smiles coyly. Not afraid of me, then. Good. That may prove useful later on.

Here are two more customers: a middle-aged couple tot-ing brown box cameras and paper satchels (the name "Har-rods" stamped prominently on the sides). Both are chomping something made of mint from a crinkly little bag, and converse with their mouths full.

Still another prospect hanging about is one of those mod creatures—male, at a guess, with hair sprouting to the col-lar of an outlandish orange-and-purple shirt. He smells dis-tinctly of pine cone incense, the sort used by Hindus, though he does not appear to be one. The small black box he carries is presently squalling over and over again that it wishes to hold my hand. Daunting prospect.

"All right, everyone for the Ripper tour, gather round!"

Our Guide has materialized from the underground. He's tall, thin, and bespectacled, with a head of close-cropped blond curls. Looks positively cherubic. One nibble at his soul says otherwise: It tastes enticingly of corruption.

"I'll need two pounds ten and six each," he announces, every inch of him crisp-voiced authority. "And your names for the rota."

Out come his pen and writing board, and the little group clusters round him like chicks to a hen. Mr. Sweat hands over two one-pound notes crumpled together with a bro-chure identical to mine. "Got a coupon," he grunts, and tugs at the baseball cap's brim. "Name's Lenz, Walt Lenz. L-E-N-Z."

Guide nods, but fails to entirely hide a smirk as he re-cords the information and simultaneously pockets the money.

Miss Lilacs proffers a náme card with her cash and a coupon as well, but Guide thrusts it all rudely back at her and snarls, "That coupon's no good. It's detached. It's no good if it's detached."

"Oh."

Miss Lilacs looks about to cry, so Mrs. Mint puts a matronly arm round her shoulders and coos, "That's all right, dear. I have an extra one that's *not* detached. You're welcome to it. Here."

Fearless Leader Guide, however, will have none of it. "That's no good either," he huffs.

"Whyever not?"

"Well, I saw you give it to her just then, didn't I? Look, it's two pounds ten and six, sweetheart. Are you going on this tour or aren't you?"

Over protests all around, he collects the full fee from Miss Lilacs. Her erstwhile protector and husband give up their coupons and cash; Guide scribbles down the names they give him. Mr. Incense pays the full fee as well, mumbles a name, and the pen scritches. It poises above the next line while Guide's blue eyes glare at me over the spectacle rims.

"Name?" he demands.

I present my brochure and pound notes, smiling because I have decided to use my favorite nickname.

"Slash," I tell him, and revel in the mildly startled response this evokes.

He scowls, but jots the answer down anyway. What does it matter? As long as my money is good.

"Right then, let's begin." Guide snaps the pen's cap into place, tucks it into a pocket and launches into a recitation. "In the summer of 1888—"

"Autumn," I interrupt politely. "Er, it was in the autumn, actually."

Guide glowers, clears his throat, pushes up his spectacles. "In 1888," he resumes as though I hadn't spoken, "six women were brutally murdered here in Whitechapel. Their gruesome murders have never been definitively solved. Until now." He proceeds to delineate each of my six ladies of the evening and how they were killed (in glorious gory detail), all in a rapid-fire, soft-spoken voice that forces his already-captivated listeners to press closer, straining to hear.

"It was here, in fact, just across this very street, to London Hospital, where Jack once mailed a package containing the bloody dissected liver of one of his victims."

"It was a kidney." I cannot resist correcting the error. How can they have got it so wrong? "Half a kidney, actually."

This time Guide ignores me altogether, though the suitably shocked tourists gasp in tandem. "This way, then. Follow me, and stay together." He sets off down the street so rapidly that the others must scurry to keep up. By the time I arrive, the lecture has already resumed at some new point of alleged interest. Camera shutters are clicking at the whitewashed doorway where the corpse of one of my ladies was discovered. Guide makes skirting mention of the "Jewes" message which I scrawled here, but before anyone can ask what it might mean, he hurries off again. Flash bulbs pop furiously, lighting up the empty doorway in the vain hope that some remnant of the horror might linger. It is here, but not for their lenses to reveal.

When they rush on, I trail behind to savor more of Whitechapel. Gray paving bricks shift and tilt beneath my feet as I navigate through the strewn garbage left by the day's street market. Brown wilted lettuce leaves and rotting strawberries squelch appealingly. I inhale their miasma, and know contentment.

A derelict, deep in his cups, slouches in one of the filthy doorways and peers out at me with suspicion. I look back into empty eyes that reflect an equally barren soul, ripe but tasteless. I much prefer a hunt with more challenge to it, and more attractive prey. Miss Lilacs, for example.

I have caught them up again. Still barely above a whisper, Guide is pontificating now on the pubs I supposedly frequented (well, one of my borrowed human forms *was* rather fond of drink), on my Masonic connections (still another incarnation, that, but both were Jack), and upon the absurd if rather flattering theory that I might have been related to the royals. Sheer drivel, that last, but I find it amusing. Queen Vickie, of course, would not have done.

"Excuse me." Miss Lilacs is waving a hand. "Could you speak up, please? We can't hear you."

"You'll just have to stand closer," Guide snips in reply,

though before they can do so he dashes off again. His long skinny legs run them a merry chase, but he pauses a few blocks farther on, this time to discuss my medical prowess and my obvious qualifications as a surgeon. (The third persona of Jack's career was the surgeon, though all my human forms know the art of carving flesh.)

This time it is Mr. and Mrs. Mint who interrupt the spiel to complain. "Must you walk so terribly fast?" they pant. "We can't keep up!"

"You'll just have to try harder," he says, and resumes his lecture without missing a beat.

When two curious passersby pause to listen in, Guide angrily waves them away. "This is a *paid* tour!" he barks, and no one has any trouble hearing him this time. "It can't be joined in progress!"

After the chastened interlopers slink away, he leads us back three blocks to the front of London Hospital, there to deliver his summation. This is a brilliant contrivance of fictitious "facts" reaching the improbable conclusion that Jack was a royal who, with two accomplices, slew six prostitutes who knew first hand of his dalliances and harbored intentions to blackmail the Crown.

"And that," Guide finishes primly, "concludes our tour."

"What?" the Mints object. "That's it?"

Mr. Sweat emits a snort of bovine derision and stalks away. Miss Lilacs, shrugging, heads for the underground. Guide peers over his spectacles to watch her retreat, and there's an air of the licentious in his look. Incense plants himself on a cinder-block wall, lights a most peculiar smelling cigarette, and induces his black box to caterwaul again, some nonsense or other about Lady Godiva and long blonde hair. Mrs. Mint, still unsatisfied, corners Guide against the hospital fence. "About that royal theory," she starts to say.

But Guide's attention is still riveted on the ample attributes of Miss Lilacs, disappearing down the underground stairs. I savor the lust roiling in his soul. (I might also savor Miss Lilacs.) He taps his wrist watch, cuts Mrs. Mint off in mid-sentence, "Yes, yes, thank you," and leaves her sputtering on the sidewalk while he hares off across the road as fast as his scrawny legs can carry him.

Mrs. Mint goes right on complaining, but I am no more interested than was her previous sounding board. I make my own way across the street, dodging scores of hurtling chariots with lamps that blind the night. Oh, I really do miss coaches and coachmen, horses and horse dung: It just isn't London without them.

Safely back inside the tile-walled tunnels, I trail a trace of Guide's pheromones back down into the depths. The sharp, spiked odor of new fear hangs here at the Shadwell/Shoreditch juncture. It leads into the Shadwell half, then shortly turns off the path and down a stair marked NO ENTRY. That takes me around two bends, past a feeble barricade, and—abruptly—into darkness. Gravel crunches underfoot. My human eyes can just discern the steel-ribbed walls and curve of track, but it is my nose that tells me of something more interesting nearby.

Blood.

I follow that trail into the blackness, around the bend of wood and metal wall, and find . . .

Limned in the yellow light of a maintenance lamp farther on, Guide stands poised above an indistinct shape that I know, from its scent, is Miss Lilacs. Or what is left of her. Has he no concept of properly carving, draining, harvesting? Not one of us, obviously. A rank amateur.

He's noticed me at last. Fear, apprehension, and fury all stream from him at once. For a moment, he freezes. Indecision. Should he attack or flee? The light flickers behind him. An electric sizzle and snap runs down the railing and the tunnel begins to vibrate. He doesn't move, so I do, drinking in his terror, his blood-lust and his loathing of all things female as I near. Deliberately, he waits for my approach. When he lunges, I grasp his bony arm and twist. Something metal and stinking of blood clanks onto the gravel. His bellow of rage is all but lost in the train's sudden shriek. I feast on his terror, and so distracted, allow him a momentary advantage. He uses it to clench my shoulders and hurl me away from him.

With a flash and crackle of live current, I land on the track scant seconds in front of the oncoming train.

Time enough.

Twitching man shape dissolves, leaves only singed clothing behind, and recongeals itself into a smaller, more compact form that huddles and waits for the howling behemoth to pass overhead. Four clawed feet clutch the shale. A keener nose draws in burnt fabric, electrical discharge, the blood-scent of Guide's nearby kill, and lastly Guide himself, receding now.

Making good his escape.

With brakes keening, the train halts just beyond our bend of tunnel, and idles briefly before rushing on.

Rat shape nimbly vaults the rail. I scamper after Guide's scent, across pebbles now become boulders, to the passageway. He is running. His big flat shoes slap the gray slate like whiplashes. I take the steps one bound apiece and re-emerge into the tile maze, too bright, too clean, and cluttered with a half dozen passengers leaving the train. Unseen, I nestle on the moving stairs and ride them to ground level, where my nose finds the spoor of blood and grease that Guide has left behind. This I trail out into the night and down a lightless street.

Perfect.

Here he is. Confident again, no longer in a hurry, striding smugly along on his way to ...

I grimace a rat smile. On his way to hell.

On silent pads I race until I catch him up. He has no inkling I am there—until I scurry up the gaping black cavern of his trouser leg. Now he knows. Too late.

These teeth were designed to rend meat. Such as the soft, fleshy calf of a human leg.

I am too strong to be dislodged by Guide's flailing and swatting, and because he fears discovery, he dares not scream. Not that it would help him. By the time I am blood-sated, he has ceased his struggle.

I crawl out, resume man shape. His shape.

A pity I have no tools to carve him with. But there is still the harvest.

I pull it, black, wet and writhing, through the nostrils. A soul ripe with its own depravity—that essence is my banquet while I clutch it, palpitating, to my breast. When it has squirmed its last, the soul shrivels and pales to insubstantial gray. I release it. Ashes crumble to the ground.

The freed spirit leaps outward—only to be jerked violently down again. It is dragged, shrieking, to the pavement and sieved, a slow and exquisite torture, between the bricks—into the Master's realm.

No less than you earned, Ripper Guide. I hope you have a pleasant walking tour of *my* world.

That will be two pounds ten and six.

Now as to the remains ... I kneel and resculpt the face to resemble no one in particular, then remember to alter those bothersome patterns on the fingertips. An ingenious new police method, fingerprints. I read of them only a few days ago, and went at once back to my sewer workman's hiding place to change those patterns as well. It would never do to have my identity challenged by a dead identical twin.

And I mustn't forget to relieve the corpse of its credentials. They're the beginning of my new life and new job, which I dare say I will perform far better than he did. I rather look forward to that.

I turn and head back toward the station. Perhaps it is not too late to harvest Miss Lilacs' soul. And then, who's to say? The night and the century are both young yet.

I may even have time to learn more about those hirsute singing bugs. . . .

Jean Graham is a Southern California writer, editor, small press publisher and part time office manager who resides (by night, primarily) in San Diego with her husband Chuck, 5000 books, 600 video tapes and 7 1/2 cats. "Walking Tour" is based on an actual incident during her first visit to London.

NIGHT OF THE
VAMPIRE SCARE
by Julie Barrett

It all started when Fred got the Oral Roberts haircut. Looking back, it was probably the first real outward manifestation of the trouble that had been brewing all along. No one recognized—or cared to acknowledge—the signals poor Fred had been giving off before his trip to Earl's Barbershop.

Most people say it really started with the cross. Since Fred was a churchgoing man, no one thought twice when he took to wearing a small cross on his lapel, especially since Reverend Walters had asked for the town to wear them as a show of support for the Weems family after the Army sent home the remains of Bobby, who had been missing in action in Vietnam for three years. While everyone else put theirs away after a respectable period (although they still wore them on Sundays and religious holidays) Fred kept wearing his. There was talk around town that he even wore a cross on his pajamas, and that his wife Irma said it put her right out of any romantic moods she might have harbored at bedtime.

About that same time Fred started asking Irma to cook with more garlic. He'd read a report in some medical journal by several doctors with a lot of letters after their names saying that garlic was good for you. Fred always felt you could never get too much of a good thing, which really got him in trouble the time he read of the healing powers of mud baths. Later on he got the idea that strings of garlic in the kitchen would make a good decoration. Naturally, Irma didn't take too kindly to that suggestion. "You go take care of your garage," she told him in no uncertain terms. "The kitchen is *my* domain." Sometimes Irma would come home and find a string of garlic cloves hanging in the kitchen. Without a word to Fred, she would take it down and bury it in the bottom of the trash can. After a few weeks of this nonsense she got to realizing she was seeing the *same* string of garlic over and over. From then on she took garbage duty.

Then came the day when Fred strolled out of Earl's Barbershop, his hair all slicked back except for a little pompadour at the crown. Someone remarked at how he looked like the TV preacher. Of course, *that* may have been the catalyst rather than the haircut, but suffice it to say that Fred somehow took the image of the preacher to heart, although his message was not taken from the Gospels as we know it.

"The scourge has come," Fred said to no one in particular as he waited in line fill up his Buick one April afternoon. Everyone laughed, thinking he was just making a joke at the expense of his hair style. "It's true," he whispered, pulling Billie Mae Threkeld aside with a jerk that almost gave the poor woman whiplash. "We are being visited by vampires."

Most people would have thought Billie Mae was the wrong person to talk to about such nonsense, but looking back, it was probably all part of Fred's plan. All Billie Mae had to do was to tell the rest of her bridge club, and in no time the word had spread: Fred had gone off the deep end.

After that Fred told everyone who would listen, and by the end of the week that number was about three. He passed out religious tracts in the streets and slipped them under the windshield wipers of parked cars. After yet another week had passed, someone finally had the good sense to ask the obvious question: "How do you know, Fred?" On second thought, that act may have been totally senseless, but often people do strange things out of the sincere notion of trying to do some good. Suffice it to say that the five-year-old girl who asked that question has been forgiven.

"Come tonight, 8:00," Fred said, as he pressed a tract into her clammy hand. Folded inside the tract was a leaflet announcing a lecture that very evening at the VFW Hall.

By 6:00 the word about Fred's lecture had pretty well spread around town. By 6:30 everyone knew that Irma had packed her bags and moved into Hank and Velma Robertson's spare room. By 7:00 a line had formed outside of the VFW Hall that stretched clear down the block to Dot's all-night café and truck stop. Needless to say, no one in line cared about the vampires. They all wanted to know what happened between Fred and Irma, and the best place to get the dirt is from the source, as Billie Mae Threkeld would say. And she would know. She runs Billie's House of Beauty. Billie herself silently prayed that Farley Wills would get the heck down and open the doors to the hall, because her platform shoes were killing her. By the time 8:00 rolled around, nearly every adult in town and more than a few children had squeezed into the folding chairs. By now the topic of conversation had turned to the subject of the lecture, and everyone was pretty well agreed that vampires only existed on the north screen at the drive-in. There was some brief conversation about Martha Freewell's ex-husband, but it was pretty well agreed that an ogre and a vampire were not the same kind of creature. Someone offered that her best friend had a hickey, but that was about the extent of vampiristic behavior that anyone could remember.

Fred may have been strange, but one thing you could say about him was that he was prompt. At precisely 8:00 he walked to the podium and softly cleared his throat. The murmur in the room softened to a low buzz as Fred cast an eye over his audience. Dressed in his shiny Sunday suit and carrying a book, he looked every bit the part of the TV preacher. The image was further solidified by the first words to come from his mouth: "Let us pray." After everyone had bowed their heads, he beseeched God for strength, deliverance for the town, and for his wife to be healed. Not surprisingly, the final request brought a fresh ripple of low conversation through the group, which Fred ignored.

"I come to you tonight," he bellowed, "to warn you. We are being visited by vampires." A screech of feedback followed the final word, and Fred jumped back, startled.

"It's one of those vampire bats," came a teenage voice

from the back of the room. A few people sniggered as Fred
regained his composure and continued with his speech.

"Doubtless you've heard about the deaths of a number
of cows in the area," he continued. Yet another screech
followed this pronouncement, but when Fred moved away
from the podium, the sound increased in volume, changing
in tone to an inhuman wail. A second cry joined the first
as Farley abruptly rose and ran from the room.

"It's Farley," someone shouted. "Farley's the vampire!"
Peals of laughter rang out. Everyone knew that Farley had
been decorated for valor in the second World War, so the
sight of blood was not unfamiliar to him. Still, he had once
passed out after his daughter cut her toe on a piece of
glass. The town was not about to let him forget it.

"No," cried another. "It's the boiler! Everyone out!"

Farley managed to get the beast under control, and swore
to everyone he had checked it just a couple of hours before
it began to whistle from the build-up of pressure. Hank
Robinson confirmed his tale and added that only a week
before the heating and air conditioning company had been
in for the semi-annual cleaning and inspection. Velma had
sent Hank out to see what Fred was up to, with the idea
that if Irma was going to file for divorce, she'd need all the
ammunition she could get.

It didn't take long for the rumor to spread around town
that Fred had sabotaged the boiler. Farley pointed out that
Fred couldn't even change a flat on his Buick, much less
figure out how to work a boiler. Besides, why would he
want to undermine his own campaign?

In the meantime a few locals had convinced themselves
that the boiler trouble was connected to Fred's speech, and
that perhaps he did know something after all. At his behest
they assembled a host of garden tools and marched to the
graveyard. It didn't matter that this so-called vampire had
yet to be identified. And even if there was a vampire (as
Reverend Walters tried to point out as they filed past the
church), how were they to know that he (or she?) was
local? Of course the pastor did his best to convince the
small assemblage that they were on a wild goose chase.
What proof did they have, after all, but the ravings of
one man?

The group, which by now had grown to a small crowd of mostly onlookers, had become quiet. They next turned on Fred, whom they pressed against a tree. Reverend Edwards tried to talk some sense into the crowd, but the scene began to turn ugly as taunts of "lunatic" and "Fred, the Vampire Killer" filled the still spring night air.

As for myself, I had been content to let Fred put himself into the stew, as I had known the man a fair number of years and watched him get in and out of one absurd scheme after another. Until now they had been mostly harmless, and I had hoped that Fred's current fascination would have had a far different outcome. I am an old man, and mostly content to sit and observe, but Fred didn't deserve the fate that was about to be handed to him. I had no choice.

"Hold on," I cried, though my voice had trouble carrying over the racket. "How many other strange things has this man gotten into over the years? You should know by now that they just blow over. Instead, you contribute further to his problems." The group turned to face me, and grew quiet. Fred slid down the tree to rest uncomfortably on the ground. "He's harmless. And you *know* there are no vampires," I finished, looking each one in the eye to prove my point.

A low murmur ran through the group as the majority cast their eyes to the ground. A few men patted Fred on the back and offered apologies and help in the future as the others picked up their implements and filed slowly off.

I saw Fred home and told him not to worry. Things would get better, and that I even suspected Irma would come back to him.

And so the vampire hysteria passed as quickly as it began which was just fine with me. I may be an old man, but I prefer to be an old man in which no one believes.

Author's Note:

The idea for this story came from small town life in Texas and Maryland, and someone I once knew who had a life-changing bad hair day. Admittedly, this person's life was changed in a far different manner, but to this day people swap stories about how one fateful trip to the stylist spawned a complete change in personality. This, then, is a bow to two strong influences in my life: Texas storytellers and really bad hair days.

Julie Barrett Lives in Plano, Texas (which was originally named after Millard Filmore, but therein lies another tall Texas tale). Her book, *Quantum Leap A-Z,* is available from Berkley Boulevard. In between fiction projects she makes her living writing ad copy, which many consider to be simply another form of fiction.

TOOTHLESS VAMPIRES CAN STILL GIVE HICKEYS
by James E. Schutte

Nicholas Johnson pulled back from the microscope, spun 180 degrees on his swivel stool, and began typing into the computer. He stared intently at the monitor as his pale, spidery fingers recorded his observations. He heard the door behind him open, but didn't look away from the screen.

A familiar female voice said, "It's 5:15, Dr. J. Sunrise is at 6:37. Wouldn't want you getting caught out in this neighborhood after it gets light."

The jocular warmth of her voice made the back of his neck prickle. "Thank you, Samantha," he said dryly. "I'll finish in another ten minutes or so. Do shut that door on your way out."

Oblivious of the hint, the voice continued. "This month's issue of *Clinical Hematology* just arrived. It has your article on quality control in blood banks."

"Well, that's certainly the first pleasant news I've heard in some time," he replied, still not looking up. "Toss it in my briefcase *on your way out*. I'll read it this morning before bed."

He heard the thunk of the magazine landing in his briefcase. But the footfalls, instead of moving toward the door, approached him until a broad-framed figure dressed in white loomed at the far corner of his vision. He still didn't look away from the monitor. If the relentlessly cheerful voice didn't identify the intruder, there could be no mistaking the fog of cheap perfume thick enough to overpower the aroma of a rotting camel.

"Is that a musk version of Ben-Gay you're wearing?"

"Now don't start on me, Dr. J. My children gave it to me for Mother's Day, and I'm proud to wear it."

Besides being a dedicated, capable, and intelligent assistant, Samantha was a selfless mother and an all-around generous and compassionate human being. All the more reason to despise her.

She didn't move.

"Do you want something or did you just drop by to asphyxiate me?"

"Well, actually, Dr. J., I came to tell you that you've got a visitor." Her voice showed an uncharacteristic hesitation.

"If it's that damned exterminator again, you sit on him while I puree the cockroaches we found last night and feed them to him through a nasogastric tube."

"No, nothing like that. It's a woman. A woman with an accent. She says she has to meet with you in person—alone."

Dr. Johnson put one elbow on the counter beside the keyboard and leaned his head into the outstretched hand. "Not Immigration again! Those fools still can't locate my naturalization papers?"

"No, not that, either. I . . . I'm not sure what she wants." Samantha recovered her stride. "Of course, if you don't want to meet with her, I'll just tell her that you're in here filming a Monty Python skit and can't be disturbed."

The bane of Nicholas Johnson's existence was his uncanny resemblance to comic actor John Cleese. Tall, thin, and with receding black hair, Dr. Johnson even spoke with an upper-middle class British accent he'd acquired while attending medical school at the University of London. The similarity was so striking that the simple act of taking a walk in public mandated running a gauntlet of autograph-seekers. Even a T-shirt with large letters announcing, "I'm not who you think I am, so shove off!" failed to discourage them.

Exasperated, Dr. Johnson smashed his forehead into the keyboard, scattering ampersands, asterisks, and dollar signs throughout the data field. "Better yet," he growled, "tell her that I'm throttling my assistant and am not to be disturbed until she stops breathing."

"Sure, you talk that way. But who would do everything that I do around here without demanding twice the pay?"

"The name Godzilla comes to mind." Dr. Johnson raised his head and stared back at the monitor. "Is this mystery visitor by any chance smiling, happy, and cheerful?"

"No. In fact, she seems quite nervous and upset."

"That's a relief. I always need a good cheering-down after a night around you. Send her in."

"By your command," she said in the metallic, nasal monotone she used to impress on him that he was being a rude, overbearing asshole. He liked it when she talked in that voice. It meant that finally he'd gotten something through to her.

He heard her leave the room. Then the door opened and closed again. He didn't look to see who'd come in. What did it matter? He'd long ago decided that the only good thing about visitors was that, by definition, they eventually had to leave.

A husky female voice rose from just inside the door.

"Nicolai Pyotr Ionescu!"

Instantly recognizing the accent of his native Romania, he buried his face in both hands. "Spare me," he whined to no one in particular. "Not another Bucharest boat bimbo."

"Nicolai Pyotr Ionescu," the voice rasped again.

Instinctively, Dr. Johnson stood up, pulled out his money clip and peeled a bill off, then offered it with an extended arm. "Look, here's a twenty. That's all I can afford. I mean, I've given too much to you people already. And still you keep coming at me like some malignant swarm of post-Marxist lemmings. At least real lemmings have the common decency to drown before they wash up on somebody else's shores to muck up the lives of total strangers. And while I'd like to welcome you to America, I'm afraid we've got entirely too many peasants here already. Further, if you insist on communicating with me, it will have to be in English. I haven't spoken Romanian in decades."

The woman was of medium height, thin, and still pretty despite the crows-feet lining her deep-set hazel eyes and the streaks of gray in her shoulder-length chestnut hair. She appeared to be about forty. She wore a clean but oversized

pink and gray floral dress and carried an overloaded shopping bag in one hand.

She didn't move, so Dr. Johnson stepped around the desk and proffered the bill at arm's length. "Look, this is all I'm giving you. Do you want it or not?"

The woman didn't move, but fixed him with a morbidly intense glare. "You are Nicolai Pyotr Ionescu!"

"Well, once upon a time. But I changed it to Nicholas Johnson back when—"

"You are a wampyre!"

"I beg your pardon? Wam-peer? What in heaven's name is a wam—?"

"Vampire!" she exploded, stamping her foot in frustration. "You are a vampire!"

"Oh. *Vampire*," he said, forcing a slight smile intended to convince her that he was indeed being cooperative so that just maybe she'd leave sooner. "Now I understand. Carry on."

She spoke slowly and deliberately out of apparent concern that Dr. Johnson was overlooking a rather important point here. "You, Nicolai Pyotr Ionescu, are . . . a . . . vampire!"

Dr. Johnson nodded patiently. "And . . . ?"

"You are a *vampire*!" she repeated emphatically, voice rising in obvious frustration.

"Yes, yes, I do believe we've established that," he replied calmly, trying to reassure her that he was, in fact, following the conversation. "I am a vampire. And . . . ?" He gestured for her to get on with it.

"*You are a vampire!*" she screamed, bobbing up and down as if physically jumping on the statement might somehow drive it home.

Dr. Johnson sighed, looked down, and rubbed his forehead with one hand. His voice reflected irritation and confusion. "Do forgive me, but I'm afraid I don't quite follow your line of reasoning here. I am a vampire. We all agree on that point. Right? Right. I am a vampire, and . . . *what?*"

The woman took a halting step toward Dr. Johnson, intruding herself on the outer boundary of his very broad personal space. "You are *evil!*"

Dr. Johnson gasped, taking a step backward and jamming

the bill into a pocket in his lab coat. "Evil? *I'm* evil?" He snorted, then turned away in disgust and walked back to his desk. "Well, stone the crows and starve the lizards! You people finally crawl out from under forty years of Communism, and what do you do? Do you work at putting your pathetic little lives in order and try to elevate yourselves to some semblance of human dignity? Do you try to rebuild your shabby little archeological ruin of a country into something capable of turning out more than badly made shoes that never bloody fit? Nooo! First thing you do is hop on a boat, all cock-a-hoop to cross the Atlantic. I can just hear you now. 'Come, Igor, let's ignore our own misery and go to America where we can torture some poor, hard-working hematologist trying to support himself with a night job at a blood bank.' And all because you superstitious hooligans have somehow convinced yourselves that a man's craving for an occasional corpuscle makes him EEEEvuhl!"

He slammed his briefcase shut angrily. "You know, Ceaucescu was too good to you people! How I miss the poor chap! At least *he* had the decency to keep you shut away from the civilized world."

He turned back to the woman to continue his vendetta when she reached into her shopping bag and jerked out a braided rope of garlic bulbs. Thrusting it toward him with an outstretched arm, she took a step forward.

He wrinkled his nose with revulsion. "No, thank you. I wouldn't dream of cooking with those after you've grubbed over them." He turned back to his desk, scanning it to make sure he hadn't forgotten anything before leaving. "Besides," he continued, half to himself, "you probably need them to mask your body odor."

He turned back to the woman. "Now if you'll kindly excuse me, it's late and I need to—"

The woman dropped the garlic, then reached back in her bag and yanked out a tarnished but ornate metal cross. She held it at Dr. Johnson's eye level with an outstretched arm, and took another step toward him. He leaned back and looked at the cross in surprise. She took another step toward him, until the cross hovered barely a foot from his face.

Eyes narrowing, he reached up and grasped the cross with one hand. The woman tried to jerk it back.

"Well, let me see it!" he hissed impatiently, wrenching it from her.

He studied the filigreed relic intently, turning it over several times. "Not bad," he said approvingly. "Not bad at all. The workmanship isn't exactly stellar, but certainly competent. Central European, mid-eighteenth century, I'd say." He examined the hallmark. "Badly tarnished, but sterling nonetheless. Should polish up very nicely. Tell you what. I'll give you $1,500 for it."

He looked up at the woman. She'd backed away, and now stood plastered against the door, staring at him in bug-eyed terror.

He sighed in disgust. "Oh, spare me the histrionics! It's a good price and you know it."

The woman didn't move.

"Oh, all right! $1,750. And that's very generous. It's hardly a masterpiece, you know."

No response.

"$2,000?"

The woman still didn't move. Her breath now came in loud, ragged gasps.

Dr. Johnson threw up his hands in resignation. "All right, have it your way! I don't have time to bargain. $2,500. But that is absolutely my final offer." He reopened his briefcase, took out his checkbook and scribbled in it. He then extended the signed check in one hand and the cross in the other. "Make up your mind. Take one or the other. Do hurry!"

With one hand, the woman hesitantly reached toward the cross. Then she stopped halfway, took a deep breath, and instead pulled the check from his hand.

"My God, you people drive hard bargains!" he muttered, walking back to the desk and dropping the cross in his briefcase. "And then you have the gall to complain that the gypsies are thieves." He turned back to the woman. "Now if you'll kindly excuse me, I really do need to leave."

"You're ... you're not going to suck my neck?"

"What? After all you've put me through already, you now expect me to give you ... a ... hickey?"

"No, I mean, you don't bite people's necks . . . and drink their blood?"

"Are you out of your mind? With all the diseases going around today you can't just . . . you . . . can't . . ." An old longing overtook him. He stepped toward her. She remained spread-eagled against the door as if fastened there by some deranged interior decorator. Dr. Johnson pushed the hair back from her neck with one hand. It was a long, pretty neck. Very appealing, at least in a culinary sense. And thin enough to reach the jugular without creating one of those sticky messes that always seemed to agitate the cleaning crew. It *had* been a long time since he'd drunk straight from the tap. He felt his gums throb, his long-disused fangs beginning to swell from their sockets.

"Well, I suppose I . . . when was the last time you had a bath?"

"This morning," she whispered, voice fraught with confusion. "I took a shower."

"Hmmm. We'll still have to sterilize the area, of course. I have some alcohol swabs, but the isopropyl leaves a terrible aftertaste. Then again, there's some cognac in my desk. I imagine that, if we douse the skin thoroughly, we could . . ."

He jerked away, shaking his head violently. "What am I saying? I must be losing my mind. I mean, God knows where you've been! I'm sorry, Madam, but if you want the blood sucked from your neck, I'd suggest you invest in a supply of razor blades and a shop vac. Now, if you don't mind, you're blocking the door."

"You mean . . . you mean I just walk out of here?"

He nearly doubled over in exasperation. "Well, you surely don't expect me to *drive* you home, do you?"

She still didn't move. He jerked the twenty from his lab coat and thrust it at her. "Here! This will pay your cab fare. Take it and go!"

As she took the money, she dropped her bag. A large mallet and three wooden stakes clattered out.

"What on earth are you building?" he asked as the woman bent over and hurriedly scooped the materials back into her bag. "I don't suppose it's a boat big enough to float you back across the Atlantic? No, I guess that would be asking too much, wouldn't it? Now, I really must be

going. It's been a fascinating encounter. We should get together like this much less frequently."

He took advantage of her distraction to open the door,
then used it to pry her out of the way. The woman righted
herself and looked back at him in obvious bewilderment.

"Do you mind?" Dr. Johnson said curtly, pointing the
way out.

She hesitated.

Dr. Johnson's felt the right side of his face twitch invol-
untarily as his final reserves of self control slipped away.
"Ciao ... Adieu ... Auf Wiedersehen ... *Via con diablos!*
... *GO AWAY!*"

The woman edged out the door, never once taking her
eyes off him. She backed several paces down the hall, then
turned and scurried away. Her baggy clothing and awkward
gait gave the appearance of a rag doll being dragged down
a bumpy road.

"Worst of all, my shrink will probably accuse me of making this up," he grumbled as he hung up his lab coat and
walked out the door. "I can just hear the crazy bugger
now," he continued, switching to a mocking falsetto.
" 'These things wouldn't happen to us, Dr. Johnson, if we'd
just remember to take our medication on time.' If that idiot
woman wants to hunt down blood-sucking vermin, why
doesn't she go after him?"

Two minutes later, the elevator delivered Dr. Johnson to
the parking garage. As he strode to his Jaguar, he checked
his watch: 5:28. If he hurried, he just might make the 5:45
mass and still be home before sunrise.

Author's Note:

*"Common knowledge" is often common ignorance. That's
certainly the case with vampires. Just ask Dr. Nicholas Johnson. He's been a vampire since ... well, for a very long
time. And he's utterly mystified by some of the ridiculous
superstitions we harbor about his kind. That is, he would be
if he had either the time or the patience to listen to us babble
on about them.*

It's not that Dr. Johnson doesn't like people—although he doesn't. It's just that he's a very busy man. Besides, he'd probably have to clean up after us when we finally left, and the smell of Pine-Sol makes him ... we digress.

Rather than waste any more of Dr. Johnson's time, just read the story and absorb as much information as you can without asking a lot of silly questions. Then kindly leave as unobtrusively as possible.

And do shut the door behind you on your way out.

James E. Schutte is a former research scientist who became a writer because his short attention span precluded a successful academic career. His eclectic writings include a novel, *The Bunyip Archives* (Baskerville, 1992), a textbook for physicians, *Preventing Medical Malpractice* (Hogrefe & Huber, 1995), and magazine credits ranging from *Playboy* to *Urologist's Sportslife*. He lives in Fort Worth with three of his four sons, but hopes to have moved to Taos by the time you read this.